This book is due for return on or before the last date shown below.

1 2 JUL 2022

2 8 JUL 2022   1 0 NOV 2023

4/8/22

1 2 OCT 2022

1 7 NOV 2022

- 7 SEP 2023

1 5 NOV 2024

Cwmbran Library / Llyfrgell Cwmbrân
01633 647676
www.torfaen.gov.uk/libraries

Book No.1747707

For Charlotte, Dan & Anthony,
You never let my head drop.

AN EXTRACT FROM 'LIFE ON THE BEAT: MEMOIRS OF A THIRTY YEAR POLICE OFFICER.' BY PAUL FLETCHER.

I was never a massive believer in the five stages of grief. It always felt a little distasteful for someone to write out a set path for another to follow.
A blueprint for coping.
As somebody who has worked a lot of murder cases throughout his long career and broken his fair share of bad news to those who have lost loved ones, I can safely say that I still don't believe in it.
The Kubler-Ross model, its original title, is generally considered to be spot on. To accept or to recognise this cycle of grief means you will be well on the road to recovery. As a police officer, the more deaths you investigate, the more you can see the logic. It still breaks my heart when I think of the breakdowns unsuspecting mothers have had after I've informed them that their son had been executed in a gang-related incident. Or the sheer, almost statue-like stillness that comes over husbands when I notify them of an accident and their wife had been killed.
The denial that people show in times of great loss demands to be seen. However, is it really a denial? Or is it more of an acceptance of what society and the findings of others have put forward as a coping mechanism? I don't know, I'm not a psychologist.
All I know is, when I lost my dear Susan to the cold, relentless

grasp of cancer six years ago, all I felt was numbness. I didn't cry nor did I deny what had happened. I was simply numb. My wife had been a teacher for as long as I had been an officer of the law, teaching geography at the local university. She was a tremendous woman, full of life and quick wit and the kind of beauty that people used to write poetry for. A life lived with nothing but love for the world, for our two beautiful daughters, our impending grandchildren and for me. Effortlessly and completely, she loved me every day for thirty-nine amazing years.

When I decided to retire after thirty years as a police officer and detective for the Metropolitan Police, Susan described it as the first day of the rest of our lives. Little did we know that only five months later, that would be a life I would face alone. We took a few of the trips we had spoken about, a wonderful week in Beijing was certainly a highlight, but eventually, as her health deteriorated, so did the future we had worked toward.

Numbness. That's all I felt then and to some extent, all I feel now.

I didn't deny any of it was happening - I had seen too many deaths in my years of service to know what was coming. I think it was that cold, black and white look of things that drove both Annabelle and Christine, my estranged daughters, away from me when their mother finally left us.

I didn't get angry, although my dependency for sitting up in the evenings and nursing a few whiskeys has led to a few outbursts from time to time. Bargaining? Depression? Acceptance? I couldn't follow the rules of the model, it just wouldn't work. I was numb.

To the world.

To my daughters.

To the inevitable.

I will never forget my Susan, nor will I ever relinquish the wonderful memories that we built together. But I skipped all the stages and accepted it from the very beginning. What more could I have done?

That question was asked so many times throughout my career, by the desperate family members of the recently departed - a question that was always followed by the tried and trusted 'There was nothing you or anyone could have done.' That was the stock answer. That was what many officers had sworn by for years, as it showed compassion yet it meant not having to get further involved.

That all changed when Lucas Cole decided to deal with his grief in the way he saw fit. The ripples of those two weeks are still shaking the Metropolitan Police Service and the city of London itself. When I look back on that tragic period I always wonder about the part I played in it all. Could I have stopped it from happening?

I doubt it.

And whilst I sit here, allowing the archives of my memory to pour out from my fingers, I doubt Lucas would have wanted me to. His grief manifested into something that shook everyone to the core. Lucas asked the question; 'what could I have done?' and then set out to answer it.

I remember the pain in his eyes when he looked at me.

I remember the anger in his voice when he spoke.

And I remember the purpose radiating from him as he set off to bury his grief.

There was no five stages. No Kubler-Ross model. No denial, no anger, no bargaining, depression or acceptance.

There was only violence.

And thinking about it now, I am happy that when tragedy struck my family, I remained numb.

CHAPTER ONE

The alarm clock went off at five a.m. and as soon as the first note rang out, Lucas Cole immediately hit the off button. He had been lying awake for the past twenty minutes, his eyes gazing upon Helen. As he watched her peacefully sleep, he couldn't help but be moved by how lucky he was, the feeling of effortless happiness just being next to her.

He slid out of the bed, making a special effort not to wake her. He glanced out of the window as he pulled a t-shirt over his muscular physique followed by a zip up hoody, the sun not yet breaking the horizon line to say hello. He finished getting dressed and hoisted his gym bag onto Helen's dressing table. He had already pre-packed, but ever the perfectionist he checked again.

He glanced into the large vanity mirror on the dressing table, surrounded by different moisturisers and make-ups and smiled. The centrepiece of the dressing table was the jewellery box Helen had clung on to since childhood, its tacky plastic outer shell housing a small, cheaply painted ballerina who pirouetted to a tuneful chime. His wife lay asleep, a smile indicating a pleasant dream. The same smile she had given him the moment she'd walked into that interview room. The same smile she had shared with him for the last eight years of marriage.

Lucas zipped up his gym bag and threw it over his shoulder. Without the sun shining, it was hard to predict the outside world, however the recent cold showers that the sky had enforced on the town led him to pulling a woollen beanie hat over his short, messy brown hair. He took another look in the mirror, deciding he could probably get away with one more day of not shaving before Helen called him on it. 'Like kissing a cactus' she usually joked.

He walked over to the bed quietly and leant down to the love of his life. He reached out and brushed the blonde fringe that strayed playfully across her gorgeous face and kissed her gently on the temple. She stirred warmly and he muttered he loved her and then headed for the door, ensuring every step was silent so as not to disturb her sleep.

A light haze of rain greeted Lucas as he left the house, another sign that the weather wasn't quite ready to give up its current run of unpredictability. He walked to the end of the garden path, pulling his hood up over his hat. He turned and looked back at the quaint little house he shared with his wife. The garden, usually maintained to the highest standard had perished over winter and even as they entered April, the weather had played such devilish games they hadn't been able to restore it to its former glory.

Lucas turned and began to jog up the street. The milkman drove past, his small white float gliding through the empty roads and he waved a good morning at Lucas who responded in kind. As he continued his jog, the small town of Brinscall was still on the cusp of waking up. The village existed behind the glamour and the business of big city living, a true community where everyone knew everyone. As he continued his jog towards Abbey Village, he passed the resident's homes, all steeped in individuality and character, set back from the large roads, hidden behind their well-kept gardens.

Lucas loved the town; it had allowed him to escape from the harshness of London and the pain-stricken years before he'd met Helen. The quietness of the mornings and the sheer tranquillity of the surroundings had enabled him to move on, start afresh and put those darker moments in a faraway place.

He put his head down and picked up the pace.

———

Alex Thornley reversed his car into his reserved parking space outside of Abbey Village Sports Centre and lifted the handbrake. The drive had been a pleasant one, albeit only fifteen minutes. He let out a deep sigh and checked his reflection in the rear view mirror, the lack of sleep evident on his face. He couldn't complain though - his beautiful, yet heavily pregnant, wife Dianne, was having an uncomfortable evening and it was an honour for him to lie awake with her, discussing the possibilities of their rapidly approaching foray into parenthood.

He wondered about what kind of father he would be; having lost his at the tender age of five he'd never had a role model. It was the untimely death of his father which caused him to embrace his Mother's Thai roots, who had moved to England to marry his dad before he was born. He didn't exactly look like a 'Thornley', but Dianne said it gave him a unique look. His skin was slightly tanned and his straight, black hair was swept to one side. He always thought he looked a little odd, but if Dianne liked it then that was enough.

He yawned and then pushed open his car door. A slight chill filtered through the breeze, making him shudder slightly. The wind carried a moistness that wasn't quite rain but it was enough for him to pull his hood up. As he closed his car door, a voice startled him.

"Morning!"

He spun round immediately and saw Lucas smiling back at him.

"Jesus, Lucas!" he said, frustrated. "You nearly gave me a flipping heart attack!"

"I thought you were, as you say, always prepared."

"Not at five thirty in the morning I'm not." He took a calming breath. "And I don't say that anyway. Makes me sound like a boy scout."

He opened the boot of his car, pulling out a large gym bag which he slung over his shoulder. Lucas took off his wool hat, his hair flattened from the pressure. Alex reached in and pulled out a few thick, blue shin guards and handed them to Lucas, who helpfully took them.

"We are going to work on your kicks this morning."

"Fine by me." Lucas replied.

"God, I'm shattered."

"Long night?"

"Dianne's back was giving her all kinds of grief. I'll tell you what, people always say you should be as helpful as possible during the first few months of parenthood. They don't tell you how helpless you feel in the nine months leading up to it."

"I'm sorry to hear that."

"It's okay," Alex shut the car boot gently, adjusting his bag as he turned to face Lucas. "Just want to feel useful again."

"I couldn't imagine it myself. If I knew Helen was in pain and there was nothing I could do about it, I'd probably go crazy."

"Yeah, let's not go down that path." Alex smiled at him, the rain starting to come down a little heavier. "Ready?"

"Sir, yes sir!" Lucas exclaimed, accompanied by the Scout salute.

"That's the army." Alex rolled his eyes. "Idiot."

The two friends broke into laughter and walked briskly towards the building entrance.

Inside the Sports Centre, Alex and Lucas walked through the main doors to the right of the large oak desk in reception. They continued down a long, pale green corridor, lined with framed pictures of sporting events that the venue had held, a tool used to encourage children to participate in the variety of activities the centre offered. They turned right and headed down another corridor, this time lined with Muay Thai themed décor. Silhouettes of traditional Muay Thai stances and attacks were painted onto the walls, surrounded by uplifting words of encouragement. At the end of the walkway a trophy cabinet stood proudly to the right of the door, a substantial oak cabinet fronted by thick glass.

Inside, championship trophies were displayed, along with photos of Alex in the middle of some hard-fought victories. They stopped in front of it as Alex rooted in his pocket for the keys. Lucas gazed upon the trophies, letting his gym bag slide from his shoulder so it hung down by his side.

"That could so easily be you, Lucas." Alex said, as he slid the key into the lock.

"Never competitively. "He smiled back, walking past Alex as he opened the door to the dojo. Alex followed in behind him, muttering to himself.

"I know. I know."

With the flick of a switch, the lights burst on one after another, illuminating the dojo in stages. The red and black mats that occupied half of the floor were first to explode out of the darkness, well-worn and beaten from years of training. The heavy black punch bags hanging almost from ceiling to ground were next, some of them wrapped in masking tape to add extra thickness and increase the weight. The long weight rack was next to jump into visibility, with its assortment of weights, all organised in order of heaviness, shimmering like the freshly polished steel that they were. Then the traditional Muay Thai ring in the far right corner was suddenly hauled out of the darkness as the final light flickered on. The red ropes hung low, connected to the padded, black beams in all four corners. Lucas smiled as he saw it, reminiscing about the many sparring sessions he and his best friend had had in there.

To the left of the dojo was a small door that Alex had already unlocked and ventured through. The light flicked on and Lucas knew that Alex was booting up the computer in his office. Classes didn't begin until ten thirty, however Lucas knew Alex liked to get his own workout in after their morning session. He dropped his bag to the side and unzipped his hoody. He peeled off his tracksuit bottoms to reveal his traditional Muay Thai shorts, black and white in colour, and then sat on the short, white wooden bench running the length of the wall up to the office door. As he was putting on his ankle supports, Alex walked out, already in his training gear, carrying a large black body pad. It had two latches on the back for the holder's arms and was thick enough to withstand the most vicious of kicks.

He walked over to Lucas, past two large posters positioned side by side on all four of the dojo's walls. They were canvases that Alex had commissioned professionally. They were neither elaborate nor fancy. A faded red background, adorned with a few Muay Thai symbols painted in black in the bottom right corner. In the middle of them, they had a single word painted on each:

Discipline.
Control.

This was a message that Alex conveyed at every single

training session he held, the potential fighters lapping up every word of it. Alex had spent twenty three years practising Muay Thai, something that Lucas admired and respected. Alex had honed his craft, dedicated himself to its practice and become one of the best. His trophies and accolades in the cabinet outside rang true to that. Lucas wished he had spent twenty years studying the sport, not just the seven he had been. He was good, very good according to Alex, but he wouldn't compete.

He *couldn't* compete.

As his mind wandered to the reasons why, and what his life had been prior to Helen, prior to Alex and Muay Thai, his best friend snapped him out of his reverie as he approached.

'Oh, did I tell you about Jeremy?' Alex asked casually, putting the fighting gear to one side. Lucas pulled on his last ankle support and immediately started wrapping the boxing tape around his wrist, crossing it across his palm and around his thumb. He looked up with interest, shaking his head.

"Well, he was this guy, no more than twenty years-old. Big guy, built like a brick shithouse. Not the kind of guy you want to mess with." Alex began his own wrist taping, speeding through with the experience of a man who had done it every day of his life for the past twenty or so years. "Anyway he walks in here, tells me he wants to fight. Not learn Muay Thai. Fight. So I tell him, there is more to fighting than being big. More to fighting than being strong. He gives all the talk in front of the group, telling me he could knock anyone in the room out."

"Sounds like a nice guy." Lucas said through a wry smile.

"I know, right? Anyway, I told him to glove up and to meet me in the ring. I know I shouldn't have risen to it, but I think it's a good idea every now and then to show my pupils why I'm their trainer." He raised his eyebrows and smiled. "So Jeremy gets in the ring with me, he's got his gloves on, he's got his gum shield in and he is bouncing, right. Like this."

Alex began bouncing on the spot, letting his arms flop around like they were numb. Lucas chuckled at how ridiculous his friend looked. Alex stopped bouncing and turned to Lucas.

"Do you know how many punches he landed?' Lucas looked at Alex blankly. "None. Do you know how many I landed?"

Again, blank.

"None."

Lucas finished taping his wrists and pushed himself up off the bench and began stretching, spreading his legs and reaching for the floor. Alex continued.

"Do you know how many kicks it took to take him down?" Before Lucas could answer, Alex did it for him. "Just one."

"I'd have loved to have seen that." Lucas stood up, placed his hands on his hips and started to rotate them as if spinning an imaginary hoola-hoop.

"Do you know why I'm telling you this story?" Alex asked, the first time in this entire exchange that he sounded serious.

"Because we are about to focus on kicks and you want me to realise how vital they are?" Lucas offered.

"True, but it's more than that." Alex came in close, as if to keep it a secret despite them being the only two men in the room. "I didn't win that fight because my technique was superior or because he was cocky. It was because of strategy. He came into the fight thinking all he needed was his strength and his brawn, two things he easily outmatched me on. That's not a strategy. That is playing to your strengths. A strategy is what can lead you to winning against the odds, to overcoming obstacles or winning battles that running blindly into won't."

He reached out and gently slapped Lucas in the stomach, just below the arch of the rib cage. "The diaphragm is one of the most important muscles in the body. So, instead of going for a barrage of punches, trying to pummel him into the ground, I struck quickly, I struck brutally and I struck effectively. It's the key to winning any fight. Lucas, I know you don't compete, but as my star pupil I see it in you most. If you find the most devastating avenue of attack before the fight has started, then it's already over."

Alex's face suddenly contorted into almost confusion and he slapped Lucas in the same spot again.

"Whoa, what happened to the diet?"

"What?" Lucas was pretty shocked, his body almost perfect, his abs hard and his muscles rounded. "I've been stricter than ever."

"Yeah, yeah fat boy." Alex said smiling. He pointed to the mat on the ground. 'A hundred sit-ups. Now!'

One thing Lucas could never accuse Alex of was going easy on him. On the contrary, he felt Alex pushed him harder than he would another pupil because they were best friends. Lucas had always kept himself in shape in the years before he'd met Helen, which in turn led him to meeting Alex.

Exercise was one of the few pastimes he'd had to break the monotony of those long, empty days. But since he'd started training in Muay Thai, his appreciation of the idea of dedicating oneself to a practice, be it martial art or ballet or dance or whatever, skyrocketed. Helen was certainly appreciative of his physique, she had let him know that a number of times, but the vanity factor never came into it for Lucas. It was about the discipline and control that came with it, the structured regimen that kept his mind straight. He worked on his body, ensured his body-fat was low, his muscles rock solid. So he could improve.

His fitness levels had never been so high, a tribute to his five sessions a week with Alex and the few miles he jogged to and from the Centre in the mornings to attend them. That, along with the strict diet he adhered to, it was no wonder Alex called him a machine.

Lucas accomplished the hundred sit-ups with minimal fuss and immediately rolled over to his front. He placed his hands flat at shoulders length apart and with a perfect firmness, lifted himself up. Alex was barking encouragement as Lucas pushed himself up and down with the fluidity of a calm sea and after his fiftieth press up, returned to lying on his back.

Alex handed him a gym ball. Lucas stretched his arms as far above his head as he could, his legs completely straight. Then in synchronised fashion, he brought his legs and his hands up to meet each other at the same time. As they connected he secured the gym ball between his shins, stretched himself out again, pulling his stomach to its very limit. He repeated the exercise fifty times, then hopped up to his feet and jumped up in the air, bringing his knees into his chest. Straightening before landing, he immediately squatted down, planted both hands on the floor and flicked his legs back as far as he could. Lucas hated doing burpees, they were his least favourite exercise but he did agree they were effective.

Alex was almost tyrannical in his classes when it came to burpees. It was his go to punishment when someone spoke out of turn, disrespected or didn't listen. Five minutes of burpees for the entire class and the second he saw someone struggling he added on an extra minute. Alex expected beyond perfection and pushed everyone towards it.

Lucas finished his five minutes of burpees and Alex

handed him a towel and a bottle of water. Lucas was equally grateful for both, smiling as he dabbed his now sweaty forehead, before taking a huge swig of the mineral water.

'Right, set one out of the way.' Alex slapped him on the shoulder encouragingly. 'Four more to go.'

Lucas said nothing, but his eyes conveyed how much he hated Alex at that moment, especially as he was antagonising him with a foolish grin.

Lucas dropped to the mat again and began another hundred sit ups.

Alex extended a hand and pulled Lucas up from the floor, as the fifth and final round of burpees came to an end. He patted him on the back as a well done and allowed Lucas a few minutes to catch his breath and get his intake of vital fluids. Whilst Lucas rehydrated, Alex moved a weight bench into position, adjusting the back and bringing it to a diagonal angle.

Lucas sat down, took a deep breath as Alex handed him the heavy dumbbells from the bench and began doing his incline presses. With his friend spotting him, Lucas performed five sets perfectly, straining on the last few as his chest muscles were almost ripped from his frame. They immediately dropped the bench flat and Lucas performed another five sets, this time upping the weight but lowering the number of repetitions, Alex counting them out and reminding Lucas to breathe through them.

Alex had already laid out three more sets of dumbbells in a row, heaviest at the front and then dropping down a few weights each time. With a silent focus, Lucas hopped in front of the heaviest weight and performed ten dumbbell curls on each arm. Alex was barking encouragement as Lucas dropped them and then picked up the next set, performing eight reps, his arms straining and shaking as he curled the metal to his chest. After those, he moved on to the next set and although lighter, he struggled through six more reps, dropping them and letting out a roar of anguish, his biceps screaming as they pushed against his skin. Alex applauded, patted Lucas on the back and then demanded he start again as he had two more rounds to complete.

Lucas's favourite part of his training was the punch bags and he afforded himself a wry smile as he slid his hands into his gloves, pulling the ties across with his teeth so they stuck to the Velcro pads. Alex stood to the side, barking out striking combinations which Lucas then introduced to the thick, padded target. His stance was nigh on perfect and he hammered the bag with such a fury it rocked on its chain. Ten minutes passed in what felt like seconds with Lucas not missing a beat, every punch, kick and knee sending a hard thudding echo around the dojo.

Alex called time and Lucas took a few moments to swig his drink and take deep, helpful breaths. The beads of sweat trickled from the back of his short hair and down under his t-shirt, which was darkened almost entirely by perspiration. Alex worked him damn hard that was for sure. Alex threw the large pad he had brought in earlier into the ring and then crouched in front of Lucas, fitting the padded guards onto his shins for him. Lucas had tried to do it once before whilst wearing his gloves and that ended with him on his back and Alex in a fit of laughter.

Lucas hopped in through the ropes and bounced on the spot, getting a feel for the canvas under his feet as Alex fitted his arms into the holders on the back of the large protection pad. It ran from shoulder height down to his knee and he turned his body and leaned into it slightly, ensuring both of his feet were well planted on the mat. Lucas stretched out his legs, his eyes closed as he got his mind ready.

'I want you to kick it all out Lucas. I want you to reach

inside of you, beyond the barriers you have put up and I want you to bring out the bad stuff.' Alex instructed, Lucas deep in thought, taking in his words.

'I want you to bring it, channel it and then let it explode out through your shins. I want you to knock me over!'

Lucas finally opened his eyes and took up his stance, ensuring his back foot had plenty of scope to turn but was also locked, balance being one of the biggest factors in the success of a perfect kick.

Possibly the greatest weapon in Muay Thai is the shin kick. Generated with enough power and combined with a competent technique, it can be a real game changer. Many traditional practices have required pupils to condition their shins, which involved striking the bare shin against a solid surface with enough force to strengthen it. It is a gruelling and painful experience, one which Alex had made Lucas go through once a week. Although Alex's conditioning pole did have a thin mat taped around it, an apparent attempt at generosity which Lucas constantly poked fun at.

Alex took his stance and goaded Lucas to strike. Lucas pulled his leg back, channelling the anger and fury, the darkness of his pre-Helen days...those thoughts...

Those thoughts...

THWACK!

Alex shuffled back slightly as Lucas connected with the pad, his shin colliding against it with a furious velocity. The power was all generated from the turn of the hips, the balance of the standing foot ensuring the solidity of the swivel. Alex barked out a command for more, as Lucas took a few steps, staying in front of Alex who was also moving slightly. Another solid kick followed by another. Alex demanded Lucas kick higher. Lucas took a small step and then hammered the pad into Alex's ribs, knocking him a few steps to the right.

'Come on Lucas, kick me! I didn't ask for a game of footsie did I?'

Lucas, his eyes locked on the pad like a lion on its prey, made a split decision to mix it up. A 'teep kick' in Muay Thai is a great setup move, a thrust forward with the bottom of your foot into the opponent's mid-section that pushes them back, potentially knocks some wind out of them and also causes openings to emerge as they adjust for balance. Lucas took a step and in one fluid movement, connected with a teep kick to the centre of the pad, knocking Alex back slightly and just a mere fraction off balance. The surprise kick called for Alex to put more pressure to his left side to steady himself and in doing so left himself exposed for the follow up shin kick to the side that Lucas delivered instantly with pin point accuracy. With Alex's body already leaning left, the hasty arrival of Lucas's shin pushed him over, his foot gave out and Alex crashed to the mat.

Lucas lowered his guard and smiled at his fallen friend.

"You sneaky bastard!" Alex chuckled, looking up at him. He pushed himself up, as Lucas shrugged. Alex adjusted himself, planting his feet firmly in place and then leant into the pad. Lucas took up his fighting stance again, as Alex shouted out.

"Again!"

Lucas moved forward in his fighting stance, lifted his leg and obliged.

After the sparring finished, Alex stuffed the large pad and the shin guards into a store cupboard while Lucas slowly walked over to the short bench where his bag was. His body ached, his abdominal muscles straining against the skin trying to re-enact their own version of the film Alien. His chest muscles were slowly stitching themselves back together with each burning second. He lazily dropped his gloves by his bag, turned and slumped onto the bench. He draped a towel over the back of his neck, absorbing the constant stream of sweat falling from his hair line.

He loved every second of it. It had taken him a long time in his life, down some dark and horrible roads but he now had things that he cared for.

His wife.

His friends.

His Muay Thai.

Lucas sipped his drink, smiling slightly as his gaze took him off into the distance. Alex snapped him out of it as he squatted down in front of his thoroughly worked pupil.

"Why do we do this Lucas?" His voice soft but lined with purpose.

"Discipline and control."

Alex wrapped his hand around the back of Lucas's head and pulled him in so their foreheads touched.

"Again!"

"Discipline and control."

"Louder!"

"Discipline and control!" Lucas shouted.

Alex pushed his head in harder as a sign of solidarity and then released his hold. He got up and placed his hands firmly on his hips.

'Right, you have a job to go to and I have to make it look like I'm busy.'

Lucas got to his feet, taking a moment to honour and thank his best friend for the session with a bow. Alex reciprocated and walked over towards the weights that needed clearing before the gym and dojo opened to the public. Lucas quickly pulled his tracksuit on over his sweaty body, hooked his gym bag to his back and stopped as he approached the door.

"Same time tomorrow?"

"You bet'cha," Alex responded warmly, carrying the

heavy weights back to the stand. "Although next time, try to actually hit me, yeah?"

Lucas nodded in sarcastic agreement and walked out, back into the long corridor. He admired the trophy cabinet for a few seconds and then made his way through the building. As he opened the front door, his hood immediately went up. He began his jog home, head down and into the onslaught of rain that had begun to fall.

The water rushed over him with a cooling feel and Lucas tipped his head forward. He said a silent thank you to Helen for insisting on buying a power shower when they'd revamped their bathroom two years ago. She was always good at making decisions like that and Lucas loved how insistent she was. He certainly wasn't going to complain as he pressed his hands against the wall, his head facing down as the water ran through his brown hair, down his stubbly cheek and dripping onto the shower floor.

He stood like that for nearly four minutes, letting the water beat down against his muscular frame, now bulging from the intensity of his morning workout. The pressure of the incoming droplets was like a mini massage and Lucas reminded himself.

Discipline and control.

That's why you do it, Lucas.

Discipline and control.

He ensured that the barriers leading to the earlier days of his life remained fully intact, sending his current thoughts to Helen's conversation the night before about booking a holiday for the summer. He felt a smile creep across his face, loving the reminder that she was almost as organised and meticulous as he was.

He loved her.

So much.

He reached out and turned off the shower and the last flow of water crashed against the floor as Lucas stepped out onto the white bath mat. He instantly grabbed his towel, running it over his body and head, drying himself swiftly. He checked the clock. It was ten to eight, time to make breakfast. He wrapped the towel around his waist and strolled out of the bathroom, turning past the guest room and walked towards the door to their bedroom.

Helen was already awake, her short blonde hair pulled back into an adorable pony tail. She was wearing a very short and very thin dressing gown and she had a frown on her face. Lucas looked at her smooth legs before returning her glare with a fake one of his own.

"Can I help you, Miss?" he said, the sternness in his voice obviously playful.

"I honestly thought, that after eight years of marriage, you would know me by now!" She looked angrily in his direction and Lucas began to wonder what he could have done wrong. She stormed towards him, her large, beautiful blue eyes locked on his.

"You know what time I have my shower in the morning." She grabbed the top of his towel and pulled him towards her. She kissed him firmly, her hands running up the defined muscle lines in his back. She slowly brought her mouth round to his ear and whispered.

"And you know that I like some company." She flashed a devilish grin at Lucas and then walked towards the bathroom. Lucas's gaze followed her as she walked, admiring her figure as she approached the bathroom door. Before she went in, she pulled open her dressing gown and dropped it on the floor, giving her husband a quick glimpse of her stunning naked body before disappearing through the door frame.

Lucas took a deep breath, thought about the things he

had to do before leaving for work and then immediately disregarded them. He walked back to the bathroom, dropped his towel and joined his wife in the shower cubicle, much to her delight.

Lucas thought of that moment as he waited in front of the grubby, grease stained sink for the water to flow from the rusty tap. He thought about how happy he was, how making love to his wife in the morning, their two bodies interlocking in the hot stream from the shower above was what dreams were made of.

The water struggled but eventually drizzled out from the old metal, an orange tinge to it. He sighed and held his hands under it.

He thought back to that morning almost three weeks ago.

He thought of Helen.

He thought of her kiss.

It made him clench his fist in anger, as he began to wash the blood from his hands.

CHAPTER TWO

Their house had never felt the same after Susan had died. Thirty nine years of marriage, a family, laughter and tears had all blessed the house. Now, as Paul Fletcher finished his morning cup of coffee, it felt empty. It had been nearly six years since cancer had taken her from him and in the time since he had felt his world shrink smaller and smaller by the day. His daughters, Annabelle and Christine had less and less contact with him and he barely saw his grandchildren.

The only thing getting him up in the mornings was his job for the Metropolitan Police, volunteering in the admin offices. It was monotonous work, however the only thing he had loved as much as his wife and kids for the last thirty nine years was his career as a police officer for the Met.

He was good at it too, earning several commendations for bravery and forging a respected reputation as an officer of the law. His last ten years had been spent as a detective, his life becoming an endless sea of evidence and puzzle-solving.

He lived for it.
He loved it.

When the time came, they had both retired together so that they could spend their twilight years doting on their grandchildren and seeing the world. *Life has a funny way of paying you back for being a good person* thought Fletcher, as he looked at yet another empty bottle of Jack Daniels sitting on the kitchen counter. His hangover headache pressed sharply against his skull and he took a deep breath and finished his coffee. He put the empty mug in the sink, next to the whiskey-stained glass from last night's drinking session, making a note to wash them when he got home.

He walked out of the kitchen and through the hallway, glancing at the photos hanging from their hinges, faces of a family that he used to be the lynchpin of.

He turned into the front room, his desk full of papers scattered untidily around his laptop. He had begun to write a memoir of his time in the police service but he was struggling to keep to anything resembling a writing schedule. He lifted his jacket from the leather recliner that was his usual destination most nights. An ashtray lay on the oak coffee table, a pyramid of cigarette butts jutting out over the edge of it. Next to it was another empty bottle of whiskey, alongside a police radio that he kept for company.

It was hard letting Susan go.

He couldn't lose the police as well.

He slid his arms into his jacket, the weather outside once again infuriating the nation with its unpredictability. The light rain that had drummed gently against his bedroom window as he awoke that morning had turned into a full-on downpour.

He stood in the hall way and looked at the picture of Susan that hung with pride over the small, oak side table. A tinge of sadness bolted through his body.

"I miss you, darling."

He forced a smile at the photo: the one returned by his wife was constant and beautiful.

He zipped up his jacket, opened the door and disappeared into the rain.

Lucas pulled into the gravel car park outside the front of 'Minute Motors', parking his car with precision in the space between the others. Lucas enjoyed his job as a mechanic. A chance to fix things, solve problems and make things better had appealed to him and he was a valued asset to his manager, John Bracken.

John had been a mechanic for over thirty years and had opened his own body shop six years ago. Although he still got involved with the day to day work, John was spending more time inside the office overlooking the work area, pushing the company towards a better future. He waved to Lucas as he got out of the car, his large belly pushing against the shirt and blazer of his suit.

"Morning Lucas," he smiled. "We thought you were going to be late today."

"Really? How come?"

Nick Partridge, the young apprentice was also standing in front of the shutters, a cigarette in his hands and the pale face of a man who had had a heavy night. Although at times he could be lazy and unprofessional, Lucas enjoyed having him around and was regularly in fits of laughter due to the young man. Nick spoke up.

"You're usually the first one here. Like, every day." He took a long pull on his cigarette. "Do you have the shutter key?"

Lucas shook his head, the hood of his jumper pulled up to block off the rain. He joined the other two men under the protruding arch of the building, Nick making a conscious effort to blow his smoke away from Lucas.

"I told you, Nick. I don't mind," Lucas offered.

"Yeah right. You're the world's healthiest man. I would blow the smoke in your face however you would probably batter me, so I think I'll let it slide."

John and Lucas both laughed, and before Lucas could ask where Den was, Den Harvey pulled up in his van. He had a sheepish look on his world-weary face and he quickly scuttled out of the driver's door. Den was in his mid-forties and he suffered from what he called a 'chronic appetite'. His large frame was covered by a thick coat, his thinning black hair already wet and stuck to his scalp. He jogged over to the rest of them, a set of keys jingling in his hands.

"Sorry guys." His embarrassment was obvious in his voice. He immediately crouched down to the padlock of the shutter, scrambling the correct key from the chain.

"No worries." Nick said sarcastically through a plume of smoke. "I wasn't too attached to my bollocks so it's okay that they've frozen off."

"Last night didn't go well then?" Lucas enquired.

"Don't even get me started."

"Of course it didn't," John said chuckling, the metal shutter rising slowly as Den turned the correct key in the mechanism. "Nick's an ugly fucker."

"Excuse me!" Nick said, faking offence. The cigarette in his hand dropped a clump of ash to the wet pavement. "I think you'll find she was up for it. I just decided not to."

"Is that because she looked a little bit like Stephen Fry?" Den asked, standing up now the shutter had fully retracted. Lucas immediately turned to Nick with an 'is that true?' expression on his face and Nick's stuttered silence was all the confirmation that was needed.

"Oh, Nick..." Lucas shook his head.

"Right, someone get the kettle on!" John barked as he turned on the lights to the workshop.

The long, halogen bulbs flickered and then burst into life, a low humming sound resonating from the ceiling.

Three work bays were lined along the garage on the right, two with cars in mid-repair. One was situated in the sheeted-off spraying area, a speciality of Den's although the job had been delayed due to a mix up with a paint order.

Den scurried past them all to the small kitchen in the break room at the far right of the building, clicking on the kettle and pulling four mugs from tiny white cupboard above the counter. Lucas approached his work station. The Ford KA had seen better days. The red car belonged to a young lady named Joanna, who had panicked behind the wheel no more than five weeks after receiving her licence. The head-on collision with the lamp post had left her with moderate whiplash and the entire front of her car in a 'v' shape. As he stared at the wreck of a day's work he had in front of him, Nick threw a white hand-towel at him, breaking his trance and garnering his attention.

"Look out, Lucas," He nodded to the open shutter. "Missus alert!"

Lucas turned to the shutter to see Helen's black Honda Civic pull in to the gravel car park. Surprised, he walked to the shutter entrance as his smartly dressed wife climbed out of the driver's seat, a smile on her face.

"Hello, honey." Lucas said as he walked out to meet her, the rain immediately hitting his face. Helen sneered at the weather, shielding her immaculate blonde hair with the box she was carrying.

"Hello, you!" She kissed him, who sheepishly smiled, fully aware that his colleagues were all watching from the dry doorway.

"What are you doing here?"

"Well I didn't lovingly prepare lunch for you, for you to then leave it on the kitchen counter." She playfully pushed the lunch box into his chest.

"Whoa hold up!" Nick interjected. "Are you telling me

that 'Mr Everything to the last detail' forgot something? Jesus!"

"Well, Nicholas," Helen said, her arms wrapped around her embarrassed husband's neck. "Lucas may have been a little distracted this morning."

She winked at Lucas's colleagues and he buried his head in her shoulder.

"Anyway, I have a patient at nine, baby, so you have a good day." She kissed him gently, but through it he felt how much she loved him. She then reached up and with her index finger pushed the tip of his nose up, oinking at him. He immediately felt the warmness of love; the 'pig nose' as Helen called it had been something she had done for years, their little show of affection. She then kissed him again and then turned to the onlookers.

"Goodbye boys. Don't get him into any trouble."

"We won't Helen," John said, taking charge. "Lovely to see you!"

She waved to them all as she got into her vehicle, and pulled out, her tyres crackling over the wet stones. Lucas watched his wife leave, the rain falling on his lunch box he clasped in his soon-to-be oil-stained hand. He turned, the entire workforce looking at him with over the top expressions of love on their face.

"That was...tender," Nick said as Lucas walked past them, trying not to laugh.

"Shut up!"

Lucas walked through towards his work station, putting his recently arrived lunch next to his tool box. John barked orders for everyone to get to work as the wheels of the morning routine began to turn and the work day started, while rain continued to fall.

Helen turned right out of the garage car park, and followed the main road down towards the dual carriage way that would take her to Preston. Her office was situated in one of the large buildings just to the south of the town.

She watched the wet road disappear and then quickly reappear through her windscreen wipers. She thought of how much fun it was to potentially embarrass her husband in front of his work colleagues and was almost intrigued to see how he would get her back.

Lucas always had a creative yet wicked sense of humour.

It was one of the first reasons she'd fallen in love with him all those years ago. Yes, it helped that he was very handsome and had that fractured past that draws women in, but it was the dry humour, the way he spoke about his situation that made her fall and fall hard.

Their love had blossomed so fast. As she looked at her hand that was gripping the steering wheel she swelled with pride to be wearing the wedding ring he'd given her.

He loved her.

She loved him.

Her family may have taken a while to come around to the idea. Her father instantly dismissed Lucas as a mistake and still hadn't really warmed to him. Although recently he had admitted he was happy that his daughter was with somebody that would keep her safe. Her mother always showed her support, coming into more than one argument with her husband over their daughter's relationship with Lucas. Her younger sister Kelly was the one who really made Lucas feel welcome, so much so that she asked Helen and Lucas to be Godparents to their nephew, Alfie.

She brushed her fringe that had danced across her face to the side and looked at her ring again. Her heart tightened with happiness, vanquishing any frustration she would usually feel as she meandered slowly to a stop in the rain-soaked traffic on the long road to work.

She thought of Lucas at work, getting teased about earlier this morning and then getting on with the job that he was exceptionally good at. Another trait she loved about her husband: his meticulous attention to detail. Her heart pounded.

Lucas was a good man.

She had seen it from the very first moment and had loved him ever since. Their life together had been so wonderful and she thought about this coming Saturday, her conference in London that Lucas was attending with her and she shook with excitement. His interest in psychology was healthy - all things considered - and she appreciated a husband who showed interest in her line of work. It was another reason to love him.

After this Saturday, after her trip to London, she knew her life would change forever. And she couldn't wait to share it with Lucas.

The love of her life.

Her husband.

A good man.

"Scalpel."

Lucas opened his left hand, his right hand holding the nut in place. The car was lifted off the ground, securely locked in the frame as he stood underneath it. Nick was standing nearby, chewing his gum loudly and handed a wrench to Lucas with an oil-stained hand. Lucas accepted, and began turning.

"So I checked on my phone and I was right." Nick seemed a little agitated. "She was at his house. After she told me there was nothing going on with him. Fucking unbelievable!"

"Hold on," Lucas finished tightening the bolt and stepped away from it slightly, casting an expert eye over his handiwork. "That should hold. Sorry, Nick, she was with him?"

"Yeah. The whole evening. Lying bitch!"

"So what, did you call her?"

"No I used 'Phone Finder'."

Lucas looked blankly at Nick, oblivious to the knowledge Nick assumed he knew. Nick rolled his eyes and pulled his mobile phone from the pocket of his dirty overalls, attacking the touch screen with grubby fingers.

"It's an app you can download for free." Nick started up the application on his phone. "So, take yourself for example. If Helen's phone is connected to Wi-Fi or she has her phone internet switched on, this app will allow you to trace the location of the phone."

Lucas stared at Nick, almost in disbelief.

"You can trace a phone through your phone?"

"Yeah. And she was at his house. It's disgusting."

"It's stalkerish, is what it is," Lucas said, almost a twinge of disappointment in his voice.

"Welcome to the world of technology my friend," Nick said sarcastically. "Where everything you do, think or say is accessible at the click of a button."

"Hmmm." Lucas didn't seem too impressed and turned to inspect the underside of the car. The job had been a long one and didn't show any signs of ending soon.

"So... do you think I should confront her?" Nick suggested.

"About what?"

"About being with this guy.'

'No I don't think you should confront her," Lucas shook his head.

"Maybe I should kick his arse?" Nick smirked. "Or maybe you could? You're like a fighting machine, can you do me a favour?"

Lucas stared at Nick, trying not to smile. Nick held up his hands in apology, shrugging his shoulders. "What do you think I should do?"

"Honestly?"

"Honestly." Nick stood, hands on his hips. Lucas wiped his hands on a towel, making zero progress on removing oil stains.

"She is your ex, right?" Nick nodded. "As in not with her anymore? Maybe you should just leave her be, forget it and move on. Seems to me like she has."

"So what you're saying is I should give her space?" Nick asked, and Lucas sighed.

"No. What I'm saying is, if she wants to be with this guy and you seem to care this much about her, then maybe you should do what would make her happy? Just leave her to it."

Nick looked at Lucas with a shocked look on his face. Lucas raised his eyebrows, suggesting he had no other answers for him.

"See, this is what I was saying to you the other day Lucas. It's your wife's words coming from your mouth. All of this psychic nonsense."

"For the last time, my wife is a psychotherapist. Not a psychic." Lucas shook his head, picking up his cup of tea from atop a tool box. It had cooled down a little too much and he shuddered slightly as he sipped the coldness.

"Still, she has got you good and proper up here." Nick poked his own temple a few times. "That's why she knows you so well. She has you brainwashed."

"She hasn't brainwashed me." Lucas said, chuckling at yet another of Nick's wild rants about relationships.

"Well she has you being all sensitive, she makes you

lunch, she knows you inside out. And she has you saying things like 'do what's best for her' et cetera." Nick counted off the list on his fingers, much to Lucas's amusement. Somewhere on the other side of the shop, Den dropped a metal tool and the clang echoed around the garage.

"Everything okay, Den?" Lucas yelled across.

"Yup," Den could be heard but not seen. "Just got cow's tits for fingers."

Lucas grinned at the comment, and then looked across the garage to John's office. The blinds on the window were open and John was sitting back in his chair, the phone planted between his cheek and shoulder as he shuffled with papers on his desk. Lucas turned back to a rather stern looking Nick, who obviously hadn't finished.

"So if it's not brainwashed, Lucas, then what is it?"

Lucas took another sip of his cold tea, grimacing slightly. He paused to think and then looked at the young, unlucky in love apprentice.

"Marriage."

Nick nodded as if he agreed and then began chuckling. A smile glided across Lucas's face as he picked up the wrench and wandered back underneath the vehicle. John strode out of his office, his blazer left behind and he seemed excited. He marched towards the two of them, his tie flapping wildly. Both of them turned in interest.

"Lucas, can I have a word?"

"Sure." Lucas turned from the car and picked up the cloth, wiping his hands again.

"In my office." He smiled a warm, reassuring smile at his mechanic before turning and heading back to the door. Lucas looked at Nick who shrugged. Lucas tossed the cloth at Nick.

"Finish tightening them up for me, will you?"

"See, there you go again, using brainwashing techniques." Lucas laughed as Nick picked up the wrench. "It's like I'm working with Helen, it really is."

Lucas shook his head as he laughed, heading to the office. Nick blew a bubble with his chewing gum and meandered under the vehicle, as another clang could be heard from the other side of the garage followed by a string of curse words from Den.

The rain was falling at a rapid rate all over the country and it was no different in Romford, Essex. Through the downpour, pockets of sunshine were struggling to break through and PC Oliver Starling was actually impressed with how nice a day it was going to be. His shift began at midday, however he had taken the morning to drive out of London to the Romford Hills Retirement Home to visit his father.

Starling knew his dad was proud of him, proud that he had made something of his life. An honest man with little education, Starling's father had worked his fingers almost to the bone on construction sites to give his son the opportunities he himself never had. And Starling made good on them.

He excelled at school, getting straight A's in both his GCSE and A Level exams. He graduated from university with a first class degree in Law. His father, of sounder mind back then, had pushed for him to be a lawyer. But Starling had always known what he wanted to be. It was that intelligence and commitment that had led him to ace his police exams and finish with one of the highest test and training scores the Hendon Police Training Facility had ever seen.

Now twenty-six years-old, Starling was considered one of the Met Police's finest officers, with important people high up in specialised units keeping an eye on his progress.

It made him proud.

And he knew it made his father proud. Especially as that morning he had decided to wear his uniform, his father showing him off to all of the other residents who ventured into the lounge area where they had their tea and catch up. His father even tried to pair him off with one of the care workers, Kimberly, a pretty blonde who had built quite a rapport with his ageing father.

The years after Starling's mother had passed away in a traffic collision had been hard for his father, he knew that. Having spent thirty-five years with one person, nothing can prepare you for the void it creates when they are gone. After a few years of trying to fight through it, his father fell victim to a stroke. Although he made a wonderful recovery, Starling was more than aware that his father hadn't completely returned. Now he sat in the retirement home, where he received the best care and tried to set his son up with every woman who came into their vicinity on his visits.

Of course, Starling respectfully declined the notion, instead informing his father of his new girlfriend, a geeky, computer whiz who was also drop-dead gorgeous. He showed his dad pictures and beamed as his dad told him 'You done well there, son.' That would stay with him.

Life was turning out quite well it seemed. And even though it made him sad to leave his dad, he stepped out into the rain, admiring the beautiful flowers that were beginning to reveal their spring bloom. A few rays of sun cut through the trees at the far end of the car park, and Starling smiled to himself.

Great career.

Great girlfriend.

Great flat.

You done well there, son.

Another year on the beat and he would be ready to

move on, take his detective exams and begin to delve deeper into cases.

His police boots clomped along the wet tarmac, his uniform getting damp. His short, blond hair began to stick to his head and the rain splashed against his handsome, clean-shaven face. One of the doctors exited their car and shared a respectful nod at a fellow public servant.

Starling thought about the day ahead. The few stops he had to make on his rounds to follow up on a few crimes he'd been working on. Thursday involved a trip to the local court house to testify against a man who had been arrested and charged with breaking and entering. Starling had been first on scene and knew, like always, his testimony would be clear, concise and on the mark. His sergeant had already told him he had the gift of gab. He was able to charm the court room but in a way that made him seem like one of the Met's elite, and not, as his superior so eloquently put it; 'a slimy wanker.'

It was a skill that he knew would make him a great detective when the time came, the ability to not only communicate with people but to draw information, gain trust and illustrate important points that were going to be invaluable.

He got to his car and removed his helmet, ducking in from the rain. He tossed it onto the back seat, next to his stab-proof Met vest. He reached up and pulled his seat belt across and let his mind dream of a time when he would be driving at full speed to catch a murderer or any other overly dramatic cliché they spin out in detective shows.

He longed for the excitement, the chance to build on what was already a great career. To see the pride in his father's eyes when he told him he had caught the bad guys.

"You done well there, son," he said to himself with a smile, as he turned the key. He reversed out of the car park and headed off for another good day in the city of London.

Starling dreamt of excitement.

He pulled out onto the main road and drove off into the rain.

CHAPTER THREE

John held the door to the office open, welcoming Lucas in and ushering him into the chair opposite the desk. The manager's office at 'Minute Motors' used to be a staff room so size-wise it wasn't anything grand. However John had made the most of the space, his small oak desk pushed against the far wall and and sticking out almost cutting the room in half. In the corner over Lucas's left shoulder was a grey filing cabinet, every folder and file organised to the finest detail, which Lucas admired.

Above John's seat, on the wall behind, was a thick shelving unit with three shelves, all of which were occupied with folders and books.

Lucas looked up at the framed certificates of safety in the workplace, workshop of the year and other accolades that John was so rightly proud of, which hung to one side of the shelves..

John poured himself a cup of 'posh' coffee from his cafetière, offering one to Lucas who respectfully declined.

"Oh yeah, I forgot," John said as he poured a generous spoon of sugar into his steaming cup. "No coffee for you."

Lucas smiled warmly as John walked to his leather

chair behind the desk and dropped into it, almost in relief, crushing the blazer that hung over the back of it. Lucas went to rest his hands on the arms of his own chair but decided not to upon seeing how filthy the sleeves of his overalls were.

"Right then!" John always perked up after a few sips of coffee. He stacked a few sheets of paper in front of him and propped them on top of the closed laptop situated to his left, next to his phone. "How are you Lucas?"

"Me? Same as ever, boss. Can't complain." Lucas responded. He realised how nice John's office smelt and concluded it was the bowl of pot-pourri on his desk. It made a big difference, especially compared to the amalgamation of paint, exhaust and oil fumes that made up the atmosphere of the workshop.

"You never do. I'm beginning to think it's all this healthy living nonsense." Lucas let out a sharp laugh, his fitness regime had long been a source of ridicule for John, especially as John was a bit on the heavy side. "Although I will say, if you get any bigger, you can pay for your own bloody overalls."

Lucas looked down and he had to admit John had a point. The sleeves of his overalls were tightened around the bugle of his biceps, and the rest of them clung tightly to his well-built physique.

"Well if you paid me a decent wage..." Lucas cheekily replied.

"It's probably not that bad for business. Think of the lonely housewives who will probably total their cars just to watch you rolling around underneath them. I could charge for tickets."

"Are you flirting with me, John?" Lucas asked, almost provoking a response.

"Oh god no. You've seen my wife, right? I prefer a much rounder figure, evidently," John replied, looking at the framed picture of him and his wife in Portugal that he had on his desk. "Besides, you could probably get a much better guy than me if you wanted."

"Thanks?" Lucas shrugged.

"I fear we may have gone a little off topic," John suggested, taking another sip of his quality caffeine boost.

"Yeah, I was going to say something," Lucas smirked. "How are you?"

"Busy," John said through a sigh.

"That's a good thing, though. Right?"

John nodded his head and then finished the last pf the coffee, placing the empty mug to the side. He pulled out a piece of paper from the previously moved stack and laid it in front of him. Lucas watched with admiration, John had always carried himself with an air of authority during the years he'd worked for him. Even on his very first day.

———

"So, you want a job, huh?"

John was slightly slimmer seven years ago, his hair thicker and fuller, swept to the side with a hard parting. A scrawnier, younger Lucas stood with his hands tucked into the pockets of his jeans and nodded his head.

"A lot of kids come walking in here telling me they can fix cars. Turns out they are all cock and no bollocks. Ain't that right, Den?"

"You're always talking about cocks," Den piped up from his work station, his hair a healthier colour but his belly still pushing unflatteringly against his overalls. "Or bollocks."

"Look, Sir," Lucas interjected. "I can fix cars. You show me how to do the things in this garage you need doing and I will get them done. I'm not going to lie and tell you I know it all. I don't. But I know enough. And I know that I can learn."

John wiped his mucky hands on his overalls, knowing he was coming to the end of his time as one of the UK's leading panel beat-

ers. He looked Lucas over one more time with a curious eye. Lucas held his gaze, kept his back straight and radiated someone who could back up his claims.

The garage was slightly less PC back then, the work stations all being papered with calendars of naked women straddling car equipment, filthy jokes written on paper and John's 'How to have a perfect shit' chart covering part of it. How time shad changed.

Eventually, John nodded at him.

"Well we have been thinking of taking on an apprentice." He smiled at Lucas, who returned in kind. "Be here at eight on Monday and we'll give it a shot."

"Thank you, Sir. You won't regret it."

"Make sure I don't. Oh, and Lucas." Lucas turned back as he headed for the open shutter.

"Yeah?"

"Don't call me sir."

———

"Yes, you're right, it's great. Business is booming." Something about John's tone didn't convince Lucas, who leant forward in his chair, his hands resting between his legs.

"So what's up?"

John picked up a paperweight from his desk and stared intently at it as he slowly turned it in his fingers.

"Lucas, have you ever given any thought as to why Nick and Den listen and react to everything you say? You know, apart from the fact that you are built like a brick shithouse and could karate them to death within seconds."

"Well I'm not too sure about that, John" Lucas said, politely chuckling. "And I don't do karate, I practice Muay Thai."

"Either way, you can hand somebody a pasting if need be, right?'

'Never competitive, you know that," Lucas hunched his

shoulders a little, the uncomfortable feeling of talking about his fighting evident.

"But I'm right. They both listen to you the second you start talking and they both ask for your opinion on either the work they're doing or need to do. Ideas. Suggestions. They always come to you." John put down the paper weight and sat up straight, resting his arms on the table and interlocking his fingers, his gaze firmly on Lucas. "Nick is understandable, that idiot still has a lot to learn. But Den, he was doing his job when you were starting school. Yet he still comes to you on near enough everything. Why?"

Lucas blew air out of his mouth and shrugged, too modest to say what John was about to.

"It's because you set an example, Lucas. I mean, you're never late, you're never hungover. You never come in first thing with a face like a wet Wednesday and bore us all with your personal problems. And even if you did, I would bet this whole business that you wouldn't let it interfere with your work. You're dedicated Lucas, you don't believe in the no-win situation. You see a problem and you stand and you face it. Head on. It's admirable."

"Thank you, I suppose..." Lucas looked openly shocked at the compliment and John nodded in appreciation.

"I'm not kissing your arse for no reason Lucas, but it does need to be said. The fact that you complete every job, no matter how much of an arseache it is, has helped solidify this garage's reputation as having the most thorough but also fairest mechanics in this county. I know if something happens, or something fucks up, you will do everything you can to put it right. And for that, I am truly grateful."

"You sure you're not flirting with me?" Lucas smiled, trying to break the awkwardness of being praised.

"I'm just being honest, mate. The best decision I ever made for my business was giving you a shot. I mean that." The sincerity in John's voice was surprising and Lucas sat up straight.

"You're welcome, John. I take a lot of pride in my work and how far this business has come. So thank you."

"Don't thank me," John flashed a cheeky grin before tapping the piece of paper he had set in front of him. "Not yet anyway."

"Eh?" Lucas raised an eyebrow, suspicious of what his now excited boss was up to.

"Like I said, I didn't call you in here so we can hold hands, kiss each other's arses and sing kum-bay-ya. I mentioned that our reputation has grown, didn't I?" Lucas nodded, interested. "Well I have been on the phone a *lot* this week, speaking to a gentleman named Steve Draper."

He looked at Lucas, gesturing with his hand that Lucas should know the name. Lucas shrugged.

"Well, Steve Draper is the head of Premier Ride, the biggest independent luxury hire car service in the entire North West of England. Beamers, Mercs, Astons, you know the score. Well, I've just secured us a deal, based on a trial period, where we get to service all of their cars exclusively."

"John, that's incredible!" Lucas smiled at his boss who looked thoroughly pleased with himself, evidence that hard work does pay off.

"It *is* incredible. It's great news and not just for me. With this deal and the work that needs to go in around it, I am going to have to take a seat further back from the workshop. I know I don't put the overalls on any more, my back won't allow it, but it does mean with the increase in business, I am going to have to hire a Body shop Manager."

"That makes sense. I mean, we get a lot done but having someone in to keep it all ticking over isn't the worst idea you've had." Lucas said, nodding in agreement at the idea. The smell of pot-pourri was beginning to get too sweet and he found it odd that he wanted to get back out to the garage.

'Interested?' John held his hands up, as if offering the job physically. Lucas sat back in his chair.

"Me? Really?"

"I just spent the last ten minutes feeding your ego, I didn't do it for my health!" John smiled and Lucas looked completely overwhelmed. "It's a lot more pay for a bit more responsibility."

Lucas leant forward again, taking a deep breath. He loved his job, perfecting his craft over years of hard work and broken vehicles. This would mean actual progression, responsibility and having to make decisions, not suggestions. He knew it wasn't important to Helen, but he wanted to be able to bring home more money, treat her to nicer things and pay for expensive holidays.

He looked up at John and smiled.

"Yeah. Go on then."

John clapped his hands in celebration and pushed himself up off the chair, his belly wobbling gently. He extended his hand as he walked around the desk. Lucas stood, wiping his hand against his trouser leg with the faint hope of removing some of the oil. John obviously didn't care, as he grasped it and shook it powerfully.

"Brilliant! I'm excited!" He beamed in Lucas's direction. "Steve is dropping off five cars this Saturday that need a going over. I told him you were the best and he has personally asked for you. I'll get Den to give you a hand."

John then reached into his pocket and suddenly a look of panic took over his round, pale face. His hands quickly went to the other pocket, then in a blur to his back pocket. He marched back to his blazer, and let out a 'thank god' sigh as he fished a set of keys to the garage from the inside pocket. He tossed them across the desk and Lucas plucked them out of the air with one hand.

"Saturday. Eight o'clock."

Lucas nodded and grinned, stuffing the keys into his overall pocket.

"No problem. Thank you, John. For everything."

"Easiest decision I ever made."

Lucas opened the door to be hit by a toxic wave of smells. The radio was playing a mindless dance song but was immediately drowned out by the loud echo of a tool dropping and Den once again turning the air blue. Lucas walked towards a frustrated looking Nick who was staring at his phone and with a spring in his step, went back to work.

Helen sat across from Kurt Chalmer, her legs crossed and her face attentive. Her pad lay on her lap, the pages open and covered in scribbled words. Her patient, lying on the comfy leather sofa, continued to talk.

"I just don't understand why it seems to always be my fault. I try and I try to do the right thing, but it never seems to happen."

Helen scribbled a note before responding.

"Sometimes people look for something to blame to justify a situation. More often than not, the easiest solution is to turn that blame upon themselves."

Kurt sat up, his chubby face turned to his therapist. His blue eyes were stained red from tears and his receding brown hair aged him beyond his current forty seven years. Despite his constant strain of self-hatred, Helen knew he was a decent man and had strived to help him over the past few years.

Kurt wiped his eye and took a breath.

"Do you blame yourself for things, Helen?"

She smiled, appreciating the use of her first name as it helped to create a friendlier environment and relaxed patients who looked at her profession with scepticism.

"Sometimes," she said calmly. "But only when I am truly at fault."

"I am always at fault." Kurt's reply was crestfallen, his head falling sadly.

Helen sympathised with the man. He had caught his wife sleeping with another man and she had used his fragile state of mind to not only make him shoulder the blame, but also convinced him of other misdeeds. He agreed to them and she had laughed all the way to the bank with her divorce settlement.

"Kurt, we can only be at fault for the things we have control over."

"I should have paid more attention to her needs."

Helen reached across the small, glass coffee table and retrieved the box of tissues. She softly offered them to him and he accepted, weeping tears into a handful.

"Kurt, we have already spoken about this. You did everything you could. Sometimes, bad people do bad things."

He sniffed a few times, composing himself.

"I don't think she is a bad person, though."

"Maybe not," Helen said, calmly but with an undercurrent of authority. "However, everyone does bad things in their lives. *Everyone*. You, me, my husband, even the Queen. It's what people do when they do these bad things that define them."

"What do you mean?"

"Well you can either try to put things right, or you can try to twist it to your advantage." Helen glanced up at the clock on her wall. She was five minutes over Kurt's allotted time. She closed her pad and stood up, her patient looking slightly disappointed.

"What should I do then?" His words were empty, full only of false hope. Helen smiled at him as he stood up.

"Go away for the weekend and think about it. Think about how you reacted and what you could do to stop it from happening again." She walked over to the office door, her heels clattering against the wooden floor. "Then next week, we can discuss how we can put that in to practice."

She smiled her warm smile again, her blue eyes locked on him as she opened the door. He shuffled over slowly, wiping his eyes with the now soaked tissue.

"Thank you, Helen."

"No worries, Kurt." He walked through the door. "Speak to Sarah on the way out and she will book you in next week. Enjoy your weekend."

He nodded weakly and then slowly meandered towards the receptionist's desk, which overlooked the waiting area. Four low, black sofas lined the wall, an array of magazines sprayed out over a long, oak coffee table. A few patients sat on opposite sides of the room, showing little interest in anyone else. With Dianne on maternity leave, Helen had taken on her patients which led to back-to-back days like today. She had told her best friend that it wasn't a problem, but she was beginning to regret not hiring in another therapist to cover.

"I'll be with you in a minute, Janine."

Helen smiled at the teenage girl who sat furthest from her office, her eyes thick with eye shadow behind her jet black hair. She grunted a response as Helen closed her door and walked slowly back to her desk. As she rifled through the folders to find the young girl's past visit reports, she thought of how cruel Kurt Chalmer's wife had been to him.

How could someone claim to love someone but treat them so badly?

She shook her head and then looked at the photo of Lucas on her desk. It was the two of them together, sitting on a plane and making the most horrendous face they could into the camera.

It made her realise how much she had to be grateful for and how she was glad she had never given up on him. She checked her phone and saw a text message from him and shrieked in delight as it described his promotion. She replied instantly, her words of pride accompanied with a promise of organising a celebratory dinner. She put her phone back in her bag and then did her utmost to remove the beaming smile that adorned her beautiful face.

Her finger pressed down on the intercom.

"Sarah, could you send in Janine, please?"

She straightened her suit jacket as the door opened, as she promised herself to hide her happiness until the work day was done.

———

"To Lucas!"

Alex lifted his glass of water, proudly looking at his friend. Lucas smiled sheepishly as Helen and Dianne, Alex's wife, all held up their glasses and clinked them in unison.

"It's unlucky to cheers with water." Lucas stated, getting a playful shove from his wife. Helen looked as beautiful as Lucas had ever seen her, wearing a classy red dress. She had insisted they dressed smartly to celebrate his promotion, leaving Lucas feeling a little uncomfortable in the blazer and fitted shirt he usually reserved for christenings and weddings.

"The man has a point. I want a beer." Alex said, turning around in his chair, looking to signal a waiter. He too was wearing a blazer but had also matched it with a stylish bow tie which Lucas was sure Dianne had picked out for him. Dianne and Helen had studied together at university, where they'd become best friends and now worked together as psychotherapists in town. Dianne was a small woman, no more than five foot two, which made it more obvious that she was almost eight months pregnant. Despite his playful charm and faked disregard for parenthood, Lucas knew that Alex was excited for the arrival of his first child. Despite the large swelling of her stomach, housing the child seemed to be working for Dianne, her face having a beautiful glow beneath her long, flowing brown hair. She gently rubbed her husband's back as he caught the waiter's attention.

Helen leaned over, sliding her hand over Lucas's thigh and squeezing it gently. He looked into her ocean blue eyes.

"I'm proud of you, honey."

She leaned over and kissed him gently, a wave of physical attraction washed over him. Every kiss from her since their first had that effect on him. Alex turned just as they kissed and scrunched his face in disapproval.

'No, stop that. We know what kissing leads to.' He gently patted Dianne's stomach, getting a playful slap on the arm. He blew a kiss at his wife and then turned to Lucas.

"So now that you are a manager man, I guess that means any hopes I ever had of getting you to fight competitively are gone?"

"Alex, I've already told you..." Helen interjected immediately, her voice tinged with firmness.

"I know, I know…" Alex held up his hands protectively. "You don't want Lucas fighting in case it messes up his beautiful face. It's the same reason Dianne doesn't let me compete anymore."

They all laughed at the comment and Helen leaned into Lucas who smiled at her reassuringly.

"Not that your face isn't beautiful, honey. But that's not what I'm worried about."

"I know." Lucas looked down at his hand resting on the white table cloth, ashamed to look at his wife.

"You are a good man."

Lucas sat back, pulling his lips into a thin line to hide his discomfort. She rubbed his arm lovingly and when he did turn to look at her, she looked at him with so much love in the swirling blue lakes that were her eyes, Lucas couldn't help but return the smile.

"You make me good."

He reached out and held her hand, feeling her squeeze it immediately. He ran his finger over the modest wedding ring on her finger as the waiter approached the table. It was the symbol of their love binding them together.

"Sorry for the wait," the waiter said apologetically, fumbling with the pages of his notebook. "Are you ready to order some drinks?"

"Yes, I think we are." Lucas looked at the two women around the table. "Ladies?"

Dianne gently rubbed her bulging stomach and smiled at the young waiter, who could have been no older than eighteen. Probably just a student trying to make a little extra cash in his spare time.

"Can I just have an orange juice please?" Dianne gave him her best smile, which he returned as he scrawled it down.

"Me too. Show of support," Helen raised her fist in the air. "Girl power!"

Lucas and Alex both looked at her, their faces

conveying how unimpressed they were. She shrugged and Lucas turned to the young man.

"I'll just have a mineral water, please." Lucas said softly, nodding as the waiter noted it down. Alex shook his head.

"Wow! You guys really know how to celebrate, huh?" He turned to the waiter. "Sorry about them, I'll have a beer. Thanks buddy."

The waiter thanked them and scurried away to action their request.

"Unbelievable. I'm the only one drinking…" Alex said, faking disappointment.

"No alcohol during the week for me." Lucas said, looking at his friend across the table. "I have this real pain in the arse Muay Thai instructor that would cut my balls off if I turned up hungover.'

"Is that so?" Alex goaded.

"Yup. Massive pain in the arse!" Lucas returned in kind.

"He sounds like a very handsome man," Alex replied, posing like a model with his hand on his chin and pouting. Both of them started laughing and Dianne, not for the first time in their marriage, rolled her eyes. She turned to Helen.

"To think, I am having his child."

"And therefore providing evidence of why you are the luckiest woman in the world."

Alex flashed his loving wife a grin, proving his wonderful talent for having an answer for everything. Lucas admired Alex's confidence, his quick wit often making him the life and soul of the party. It was very easy to like him. Alex turned to Lucas.

"I take it you will be having a few drinks on Saturday night, then?"

"Maybe."

"You would've earned them, mate."

"This Saturday?" Helen questioned, her eyebrows raised. The reaction of realisation that covered Lucas was immediate.

"It's your conference, isn't it? Oh shit, I'm so sorry. I told John that I would do the trial work on the new cars. That Draper guy is dropping them round at eight in the morning."

"Lucas, its fine." She reached out and squeezed his hand.

"I mean, I could work through lunch and then drive straight down afterwards. I'll probably get their a bit late but we can always grab a late dinner?"

"Lucas," Helen turned and looked directly at him, something she always did when she was being firm. "It is fine."

"Really?"

"Of course. Don't be silly. This is such a great opportunity for you and I know you're really not too keen on going back to London anyway."

Lucas shuffled in his seat. She was right about that.

"Besides, the conference is going to be very boring," Dianne interjected, supporting her friend.

"At least you have a good excuse for not being there."

"You're welcome." Alex stated as he patted his wife's stomach, and received a playful slap in return. Helen grinned and then turned to Lucas, whose eyes were screaming a thousand apologies.

"I'll give Mary a call. She was excited that I was going to be in London for the weekend so I will see if she wants to have a catch up.

"Are you sure?"

Helen leaned across and gave Lucas another heart fluttering kiss.

"Positive."

She flashed her perfect smile at him one more time and eventually he squeezed her hand. He turned back to Alex, who had been patiently watching his best friend.

"Well to answer your question, yes. I may very well have a beer on Saturday."

"Whoa! Calm down!" Alex's sarcasm was never hard to detect. "There's a big night of Ultimate Fighting on pay-per-view. I figured it would be pretty good to watch. There's this new fighter, Ryan Turrock. I think he'll be worth watching."

As the two fighting enthusiasts began to discuss the upcoming event and the possible fighting styles, the waiter approached the table carrying a small, circular tray. He carefully lifted each drink individually and placed the beverage in front of the corresponding person. He smiled politely and left them to their conversations. Dianne shuffled her seat around the table a little and leaned in to speak to Helen, lowering her voice to just above a whisper.

"That orange juice," She pointed at Helen's glass as she took a sip from her own. "It's not really a show of support is it?"

Helen looked anxiously at Lucas, who was deep in a discussion about the benefits of connecting with an elbow to the back of someone's head. She then smiled at Dianne, a buzz of excitement radiating off of her.

"No."

"Oh my god!" Dianne had mastered the low volume shriek. "How far are you?"

"Only seven weeks. Dianne, I am so excited."

"I'm so happy for you. Have you told..." She nodded in the direction of the still oblivious Lucas.

"Not yet. I was going to save it for London this weekend, give him a nice memory of the city for once. But I think I'll surprise him with it when I get back."

She looked at her husband, who was laughing at something Alex had said and was slightly overwhelmed by how much she loved him.

"I'll tell him I've got him a surprise and then bam! I'll hit him with it. Do you think he'll be happy?"

"Oh without a shadow of a doubt."

Helen clenched her fists and shook a little in excitement and then lifted her glass and took a sip of her juice. No more alcohol for her. Not now that she was with child. She knew Lucas doubted the man he was, but she could see it. She could see that all he ever wanted was to love someone, to have someone to put first. And the idea that she could put a second person on that list, a person created by the unconditional love that they felt for each other made her place her hand over her stomach and close her eyes.

A warmth spread through her body and it took every ounce of her strength not to cry at the realisation of what true happiness was. She was snapped back to reality by Dianne.

"This is so exciting!" She grabbed Helen's hands and squeezed them.

"What's so exciting?"

The two ladies turned at the sound of Alex's voice and realised that their husbands were staring at them with curious eyes. Dianne released Helen's hands and sat back, flattening the dress over her protruding mid-section.

"Oh... erm... there's talk that they are making another *Sex and the City* movie," Helen lied, although she lied with a measure of calm.

"Oh wow! That *is* exciting!" Lucas's sarcasm was a lot more blatant than Alex's. "I can't wait."

Helen stuck her tongue out at her husband. Before Lucas could retort, the waiter once again approached the table, this time carrying four menus.

'To be continued.' Lucas warned, an air of playfulness wrapped around his words. The waiter warmly re-entered their evening, which continued on down a path well-worn by good friends enjoying their lives together.

———

Lucas pulled up outside the house and came to a slow and steady stop. He looked out at the small, quaint house he shared with his wife and felt that feeling of relief to be home. It had been a very long day. Helen stroked his hand which was still on the handbrake.

"Come on. Let's go in."

He nodded and pulled the key from the ignition and pushed open the car door. As he turned to close it, he noticed that Alex had left his wallet on the back seat. He had driven the Thornleys home *en-route* and wasn't prepared to make another trip back. He reached back in over his chair and scooped it up, the leather cold in his hands. He would give it to Alex at tomorrow's session, which he knew was going to be a more exercise based morning due to the amount Alex had drunk.

He closed the car door quietly, noticing the coldness of the night was being chauffeured by the faint drizzle falling from the moonlit sky. Helen had already scarpered to the front door and turned the key in the lock, opening the door and stepping into the warm hallway. Lucas jogged up the path, past the unkempt garden and jumped through the doorway. He closed the door, shutting out the coldness of the night and the sleeping world surrounded by it.

"Hello house!" Helen said adorably, flicking on the lamp on the hallway table. She immediately picked up a white paper carrier bag resting next to it and handed it to a confused Lucas. The bag was folded over and its contents were pushing against the sides.

"What's this?" Lucas looked at his wife with a suspicious eye.

"I didn't have time to wrap it when I got in."

She looked on nervously as he unfolded the bag and reached his hand in. He immediately felt the quality of the leather on his palm and his fingers brushed against the small, metal teeth of a zip. He pulled his arm out and unfolded a black, leather bomber jacket. He looked at it in disbelief and then back at Helen who was standing cautiously to the side, the nerves of whether he would like it had made her wrap her arms around her body and she gently bobbed on the spot.

Lucas was speechless.

Three months ago, they had been out for a walk through some of the neighbouring countryside, stopping for a Sunday lunch in a local pub and enjoying their time together. As they'd walked through the cobbled streets of a sleepy village, Lucas had stopped in front of a small, privately owned leather shop. He saw the jackets hanging in the window, the lights of the shop were out and the sign said closed. But he and Helen cast their eyes over the potential jackets, the calibre of the leather reflected in the hefty price tags. He had wanted to return at some point and buy one and here he was, holding one in his hands, a gift from the best gift the world had ever given him.

"Thank you. So much!" His voice was soft and conveyed how moved he was by the gesture. He twirled the coat around and slid his arms through the sleeves, pulling the front collar forward, the jacket wrapping comfortably around his imposing frame. Helen walked up to him and flung her arms around his neck, her face arched up towards his.

"I'm proud of you, Mr Manager Man."

She kissed him softly, which grew in intensity and passion for a few moments. Lucas pulled back, a gentle smile on his face.

"I love you, Helen."

"How much?" She cheekily swung from side to side, her arms still draped around her husband's broad shoulders.

"Oh. Too much." Lucas said, adding a stern head nod to underline the point. She kissed him again.

"More than muay Thai?"

"More than anything." She kissed him again, slower, her tongue gently sliding over his. She leaned back again.

"More than the potential new *Sex and the City* movie?"

"Hmmm," Lucas frowned. "That's a thinker."

She laughed and gave him a gentle punch in his solid arm. She then looked up at him, almost giddy. She raised her hand and stroked the stubble on the side of his face. He closed his eyes and enjoyed her soothing touch. Her hand glided across and with her index finger, she pushed up the front of his nose and oinked at him. He smiled at her; her cheeky grin was inviting.

"I actually feel like a pig. I'm stuffed."

"Well then." She stood on her tip toes and kissed him. "Let's go burn some of it off, shall we?"

She grabbed his hand and turned to the stairs, leading him up to their bedroom. Their clothes were off before they even made it to the bed and they made love as passionately as they did eight years ago.

Lucas lay next to Helen afterwards, his arm wrapped over her stomach as she pushed her back into him. He felt her stomach move up and down as she breathed, sleeping peacefully in the arms of the man she loved.

He felt blessed.

CHAPTER FOUR

"Christ, Helen."

Dressed in a smart black blazer, white shirt and a thin, black pencil skirt, Helen smiled at her husband as he reached into the boot of his car. He wrapped his fingers around the handle of the suitcase.

"I thought you were only going away for one night?"

"Oh ha ha ha!" She pulled a face at him, as he hauled the large suitcase out of the back of the car, overacting that it was too heavy. He was right though, although she would never admit it. She had packed her largest suitcase even though she was only staying in London for the one night. Lucas closed the boot of the car and Helen looked towards Preston Train Station.

As one of the central points for commuter trains to and from London, it sat in the heart of Lancashire. Usually the main car park directly out of the front of the station was at a standstill, with too many cars trying to park in too few spaces. The foot traffic was usually even worse, the lines for the ticket machines stretching across the concourse and to the entrance doors. However, at six o'clock in the morning on a Saturday, Helen appreciated the calm and the quiet.

She pulled her black coat, her 'smart jacket' as Lucas called it, over her shoulders, the early morning wind delivering a body shaking chill like an unwanted mailman. Lucas locked the car, and began following her towards the entrance of the large station ahead. She looked back, smiling at how handsome he looked in his new leather jacket, his broad shoulders pulling the jacket tight around his upper body.

Lucas trundled towards the entrance where his wife walked in from the cold, the drag-along suitcase jittering over the uneven ground, wobbling in his hand. The doors automatically opened revealing an almost empty platform. The usual sea of commuters, standing around armed with coffees and newspapers, were nowhere to be seen. Instead, a few early risers were looking up at the large screens, scanning for information about their trains.

A few cleaners were sharing a joke to the side of one of the platform gates. A large man was buying a coffee and a breakfast baguette from the only one of the numerous food outlets that was open, hoping to make a little extra from the first few travellers. Helen gave Lucas a kiss on the cheek as he came to a stop and she quickly walked over to the self-service ticket machine, her booking confirmation printed and firmly in her grasp.

Lucas watched her walk for a few moments, revelling in her beauty and reminding himself how lucky he was, before turning his attention to the screens like the few others littered along the main platform.

He located Helen's train; she still had ten minutes before boarding. He turned, surprised to see her already returning with the tickets in her hand. He had never used the self-service machines and had no desire to. As Nick always said at work, he was medieval when it came to modern day technology, a statement he himself confirmed during a rather embarrassing trip with Nick to the local supermarket. After that incident, he refused to ever use a 'self-service' machine again.

Well, that's what happens when you spend eight years of your life.....

Helen broke Lucas's train of thought by kissing him on the cheek again, her blonde hair straight and her make-up spot on. She looked really good. Too good for him, Lucas told himself.

"Right. Got my tickets, got my phone…" Helen was thinking out loud.

"You've got half your wardrobe, too," Lucas added and Helen gave him a playful look that told him he may be in trouble when she got home.

"I have everything." She let out a sigh of relief. "Good."

"Do you want a coffee or anything?" Lucas offered, nodding in the direction of the only open outlet. Suddenly, the smell of coffee and bacon wafting on the air became very strong and Lucas made a note that he needed to eat as soon as Helen got on her train. Helen shook her head.

"No thanks. I'll get one on the train."

She reached out and rubbed his arm, silently pleased that he was wearing the jacket she'd got him. He had worn it every day since she had given it to him earlier in the week and it pleased her that after eight years of marriage she could still surprise him. Lucas leaned over and gave her a kiss on the side of her head. She smiled warmly, leaning into her husband's solid chest and nuzzled into him. He arched his neck down and kissed the top of her head.

"I'm sorry I can't come."

"Don't be. I'm so proud of you. You'll knock it out of the park today." She gave him a reassuring smile, her pearly white teeth twinkling in the bright lights of the station. A few more people carrying suitcases made their way towards platform ten.

"I'll give you a call after the conference. Let you know how it went."

"Oh please do. I'm upset that I can't spend the weekend with you, but the fact I have to miss a conference about the advances in psychotherapy is unbearable."

Lucas grinned waggishly at his offended wife, who shoved him back. He reached out, gripping her elbows and pulled her towards him. Their lips locked and Helen tiptoed to push more love into the kiss.

"Don't you get lippy with me mister just because I'm going away for the night."

Lucas pushed his tongue out between his teeth, goading Helen into another push. He looked up at the screens, the words 'Boarding' were flashing next to Helen's train. Helen held Lucas's hand and followed his gaze.

"Say hello to Mary for me, yeah?" Lucas smiled.

"I will. But only if you go and make us both proud today."

"Deal."

She reached up and stroked the thin, brown stubble along Lucas's jawline and then pushed her mouth into his. Lucas may not have been a fan of public displays of affection, but they were the envy of any passer-by who happened to look up from their tired state.

She kissed him as hard as she could.

He returned in kind.

After a few moments, Helen pulled back and then wrapped her arms around him. He once again kissed the top of her head.

"I love you, Lucas." She relinquished her hold and took a step back, her suitcase standing next to her. It was the blue and white polka dot suit case that Lucas had bought her for their last holiday.

"I love you too."

Lucas stuffed his hands into his pockets as she turned

on her heels, pulled up the handle from her suitcase and marched over to the gates. She turned back, watching him standing and waiting. She blew him a kiss, drawing that handsome smile of his into the open. She passed through the ticket barriers, politely smiling at the attendant and then followed the few other travellers as they wandered down the side of the train to find their coach.

Lucas watched her walk into the distance, checked his watch and then followed the strong smell of bacon pulling him towards his breakfast.

———

The rain had decided to take the day off which Fletcher appreciated. It had been too wet recently, drenching the fine city of London and dampening the mood of its inhabitants. But the rainclouds had cleared just in time for Saturday, with rays of sun threatening to burst through at any moment. Still, despite the chill that flowed through the breeze, it had turned into a pleasant spring day.

Fletcher checked his mirrors and then turned right off the main road, heading down a street with thin houses cramped too close together. Susan used to say London was overpopulated with houses too expensive to buy, filled with people who had too much money to spend.

He himself had never given it much thought. He had always been happy and comfortable on the solid wage he received from the Metropolitan Police and was living comfortably off the pension he had spent years earning.

It's hard to struggle when he only had to pay for himself, a fact that he wished he could change every minute of every day.

He took the next right, his new model Ford Fiesta taking the corner smoothly as well as the speed bump just after the turn. Years of driving a 'panda car' at high speeds had meant leisurely drives were a cakewalk, however he was always very diligent on the roads, having seen too many dead children who hadn't looked both ways.

He stopped at the lights and could see the corner fence of Regent's Park ahead. Suddenly, a nervous hand gripped around his entire body and he swallowed hard.

It had been so long.

Almost five years.

The light changed to green, but Fletcher didn't move. He stared ahead, trapped in a battle of pushing on to the park or turning around and letting things stay as they were.

BEEP! BEEP!

The impatient honking of the horn from the car behind jolted Fletcher like he had just been struck by lightning and auto pilot kicked in. Accelerator, clutch, second, third. Before he could make a conscious decision to stop, he was approaching the parking spaces outside the west entrance to the park. He rolled slowly down the long stretch of pavement against the park fence, eventually finding a space between a Jeep and a Clio. In one fluid motion he popped the car into reverse and swung it expertly between the neighbouring vehicles. He shut off the ignition, the car purring its way to gradual silence. He sat.

Ten minutes passed.

Fletcher focused on the dashboard, his eyes glued to the hazard button but his mind a million miles away. It had been too long, this was a bad idea. Thoughts kept running through his head, his own consciousness trying to convince him of the mistake he was making. But somebody had to make the first step and he felt it should be him.

"Right then," he muttered, exiting the car, and locking it with the electronic fob while walking towards the gates. He stuffed his hands in his pockets and spent the next few minutes battling with notion of just turning around. When he snapped back to reality he was standing at a crossroads a good thirty feet inside the park gates. He took a left turn, walking past large fields which were filled with groups of friends playing football and other groups lounging on blankets on the grass, enjoying each other's company.

He longed to have Susan back with him, holding his hand as they ambled, her delicate fingers locked between his own. If that was the case, then none of this would have been necessary.

It had been five years since Susan had lost her battle to cancer and people would say that by now he should have moved on, made his peace with it. It wasn't as easy as that. Susan was not just his wife, she was his everything. She was his first vision in the morning, his last at night. She was his voice of reason, the one who questioned how and why. And she was the rock of the family. As much as it hurt, he could admit to himself that he wasn't the father he had set out to be.

He walked down the pathway cutting through the fields, the bordering trees lightly frosted with blossom. He loved his daughters – that fact was never in question. However the awkward shifts he'd worked for years and the ugly side of the world he'd walked through had caused him to be distant. He saw the world for what it was and while he never showered Annabelle and Christine with love, he fiercely protected them. Now, grown up and with families of their own, they didn't need protecting.

And it made him feel redundant. He had nothing else to offer them.

Suddenly, Fletcher stopped in his tracks. Further up the path he could see the entrance to the adventure playground, metal constructs with childlike blurs scattered all over them. The joyful sound of innocent laughter filled the air. Just outside the entrance gate, sat Annabelle. Her unmistakeable auburn hair pulled back in a ponytail. She was wrapped up in a fleeced hoodie, a book open on her lap, resting upon the four months-worth of pregnancy. Fletcher suddenly felt sick, swallowing the lump growing in his throat and fighting back the tears forming in the corners of his eyes.

Now or never, Fletch.

Someone had to make the first step.

He did, followed closely by another, until he was no more than a few feet from his daughter. Her beautiful face that resembled the mother that he had - and still - worshipped. It had been five years since he'd seen her, five long years since he'd wrapped his arms around his eldest daughter.

"Annabelle?"

The words came out, cracked and broken. Annabelle looked up from the pages of her book, the optimism immediately flooding from her face, replaced by shock. And pain.

The silence said more than any words could and Fletcher immediately began regretting having made the journey. He shuffled his foot awkwardly, his hands stuffed in his pockets. Annabelle composed herself, stuffing her book into her handbag as she pushed herself off the bench.

"You look well." Fletcher offered with deep sincerity.

Annabelle sighed.

"You can't do this, Dad," she somehow mustered, her words struggling to breathe.

"I just thought, I mean, it's been so long…" Fletcher struggled to get the words, looking down at the floor. Annabelle looked on, hands on her hips, heartbroken to see the strong man she'd depended on for so many years in such a fragile state.

"I'm sorry, Dad," She shook her head. "But you can't

just turn up to try and build bridges out of the blue. You just can't."

"I know. It's just been years since we spoke. Since we were family. I haven't even met Laura."

"And whose fault is that?" Fletcher tried to hide inside himself as Annabelle continued. "You can't just become 'granddad of the year' after so many years of absence. When Chris and I needed you, after mum died, you checked out. Not us."

"I know and for what it's worth, my dear, I am so sorry."

Annabelle's eyes began to water and she looked up to the sky, shaking her head. Clouds had begun to form overhead, the weather once again deciding to revel in its own unpredictability.

"I know when Mum left us, it hit you hard. I understand that. I really do. Because it hit us too."

There was silence between them, the home truth resonating in the air that was beginning to bring with it an element of cold. The origins of a storm.

"I can't do this, Dad, not now." She looked at her father, a tear gliding over her cheek. Fletcher wanted to reach out, wipe it away and let her know her dad was there. "Maybe one day, but not right now."

"Anna..."

"I have to go."

Annabelle turned from her father, taking with her any hope Fletcher had of reconciliation. He watched as she strode towards the gates of the adventure playground, her hand moving up to her face. He knew it was to wipe away tears.

Tears because of him.

Unable to move, he saw the gate to the playground open and through it ran a vision that, had his heart not been completely obliterated already, would have shattered it immediately. Into Annabelle's arms ran Laura, the granddaughter he had never met. Her blonde hair covered with a pink woolly hat and a thick, red coat protecting her body from the cold. She was the epitome of beauty. He could see them talking, the little girl curious as to why her mum was crying.

All he could see was his beloved Susan, knelt down in front of a crying Annabelle all those years ago.

The tears slowly slid from his eyes and down his wrinkled, weary face, as the realisation of the family he had isolated walked away from him.

The tears were soon washed away by the unsurprising downpour from the sky above.

―――――

By the time the final car had been rolled into the bay, Lucas was filthy. His overalls, originally blue, were almost completely black from oil. His face was stained, his hair damp from the sweat of a hard day's labour. He rested his hands on his hips and looked out of the shutter of the garage. He shook his head as hailstones decided to join the rain on its invasion of the planet.

"This weather is fucking ridiculous!" Den broke the silence, approaching Lucas and handing him a cup of tea, the steam slowly rising and disappearing.

"It's only rain," Lucas smiled, taking a sip from the mug and then silently cursing himself as he knew it would be too hot. "At least it pisses everyone off without prejudice."

"That's not much of a silver lining," Den joked, turning with Lucas back to the final car. They had completely checked and repaired four of Steve Harper's luxury cars. Three Mercedes and a BMW 5 series had been serviced and were all parked in a row in the gravel-based car park out front. Lucas was excited about the final car, an Aston Martin that he couldn't wait to get his hands on.

"Right, shall we get this done and get out of here?" Den suggested, obviously tired from what had been a full-on day. Lucas gave him a disappointed look, but in truth, had really appreciated Den being there to help him. He had put in a lot of effort, which he knew would sit well with John. He'd got the job done.

Lucas smiled and nodded, putting down his cup of tea. He thought of the night he had planned ahead of him with Alex.

He thought of Helen and how he would miss her, even though she was only gone for one evening. He never slept well when Helen wasn't next to him.

Still, she had only gone for one evening.

As Helen stood in the queue at the reception desk of the Euston Hilton in the centre of London, she couldn't help but feel it was flashy for the sake of being flashy. A glass table sat in the centre of the foyer, a substantial, obviously fake, plant in a stylish bowl sitting as the centrepiece. The concierge was busy checking in a family of American tourists, all of whom had too many questions.

The conference had been worthwhile she thought and Dr Steve Wilson's lecture on the ripple effects of depression had been fascinating. She still had her note book under her arm, crammed with comments and contact details of the peers she had met during the networking lunch that Lucas mocked so frequently. She had made sure she'd removed the 'Hello, my name is: Helen' sticker from her blazer.

The young receptionist seemed to be making progress

with the American family and Helen made a mental note of where she had placed her booking confirmation sheet she'd printed off the night before. Now that day one of the conference was over, the realisation that Lucas couldn't join her set in and she sighed. It would have been so lovely to spend a night out in London together. It had been a long time since that had happened. They could have gone to the restaurant they'd gone to on their first date, a little Italian place just off Charlotte Street. She would have walked him to 'their' statue, the place where they'd solidified their love with their first kiss.

She would have told him that he was going to be a father.

That would have definitely provided her husband with better memories of this city, although she understood his disdain for the place. She smiled, the thought of Lucas play fighting with a miniature version of himself, filled her with a love she had never felt before.

"Sorry for the wait, ma'am." Helen was pulled from her thoughts, greeted by a wide smile from the young lady behind the desk. "Welcome to the Hilton."

Helen strode up the desk to check in. She handed over her booking confirmation, who immediately began hammering the keys of her computer. Helen quickly checked her phone.

She had a missed call from Mary, whom she had arranged to meet in a few hours. She'd also had a text from Lucas, a message that simply read:

'I love you. Xxx'

A grin spread across her face, she felt so giddy.

She turned her attention to the desk, to complete her check in.

"So it went well then?"

Helen held the phone between her shoulder and her cheek as she used her free hands to straighten the hair framing the other side of her face. Her make-up was already done and she had finally decided on an outfit of a fitted, black shirt, jeans and pair of heeled shoes. She sat at the large dressing table in the far corner of her hotel room. A king-size bed sat in the middle, a flat screen TV attached to the wall facing it. The bathroom was situated near the door, a cupboard for her clothes opposite.

"Yeah, I think so." Lucas was walking from the bus stop a few streets away from Alex's house, the carrier bag containing some alcohol and peanuts swinging casually beside him as he strolled. "We got all the cars done, so we shall see."

"Baby, I am so proud of you!"

"Thank you. You always believe in me and it means a lot."

"Well of course I do!" Helen replied merrily. "So what are you doing with your night off? Behaving yourself I hope?"

"The usual - Alex and I will probably hit a few strip clubs, do an awful lot of drugs and it'll probably end up with some sort of inexplicably X-rated orgy involving animals."

"So the usual then?" Helen giggled. She loved Lucas's dry sense of humour although he never realised quite how funny he was.

"Alex has bought the Ultimate Fighting pay-per-view, so we are going to have a few beers and watch people beat other people up for money."

"Is that why you're not driving tonight?"

Helen shifted the phone to the other shoulder, running the straighteners through the other side of her hair, her eyes locked on the mirror of the dressing table she was sat at to avoid messing it up.

"Well I haven't had a beer for a few months," Lucas looked down at the carrier bag swinging in his left hand, the bottles clinking gently. The wind swept through, a moistness in the air hitting his face as it passed. "I fear I am being wildly optimistic by buying four bottles."

"Whoa! Calm down!"

"I think I have a problem," Lucas said sternly, eliciting a laugh from his wife. He turned onto Alex's road, the drizzle turning into more solid drops of rain indicating it was set to dominate another night. He pulled the collar up on his jacket, his beloved gift from his wife.

"I wish you were here tonight," Helen said dejectedly, turning off the straighteners and admiring her hair in the mirror.

"I know, me too," Lucas agreed..

"Well I do have some good news for you. Just you wait until I see you tomorrow!" The excitement in Helen's voice drew a smile from Lucas, as he reached the gate to Alex's front garden. The garden was immaculate, despite the recent weather, and Lucas was a little envious.

"What is it?"

"You'll just have to wait until tomorrow, won't you?" Helen sniggered over the phone.

"Oh god! Mary isn't making you get a tattoo is she?"

"No!" Helen laughed again, the cute chuckle that Lucas adored. "I just have a surprise for you, Okay?

"I'm excited now."

"Well I'm sure you can wait until tomorrow." Helen pulled her arms through the sleeves of her jacket, ready to leave. "Right my love, I have to go otherwise I'll be late meeting Mary."

"Yeah, I'm at Alex's now too. I'd better go inside,

before Dianne sees some creepy guy hanging around outside. Have a lovely time and say hi to Mary for me."

Helen grinned.

"I will. You have fun with your four beers." Lucas rolled his eyes, as he opened the gate to Alex's front garden. "I love you, Lucas."

Lucas went quiet, hearing her say those words always made him stop in his tracks.

"I love you too."

Both of them smiled and then Helen hung up the phone and headed out of her hotel room. Lucas pressed the doorbell on Alex's front door, hearing movement from the other side to suggest he wouldn't be waiting long.

CHAPTER FIVE

The spring night had a crisp chill hanging in the air however the threat of rain was minimal. Tommy Drayton sat in the driver's seat of his black cab feeling indifferent about working that evening. He sat up straight, stretching out the ache in his back.

Although he sat behind the wheel, Tommy was a cage fighter, shown by the hulking physique that he possessed. He twisted his body to the left, hearing the crack of his bones and he immediately felt better.

The cab rank he was parked near already had a number of cabs queuing up for business and London seemed awfully quiet for a Saturday night. He checked the clock, realising it was only half past eight and saw the reason why.

He sighed.

This was going to be a long night, but he was under strict orders to pick up his passenger by Russell Square station. His boss could be a real arsehole sometimes.

It had crossed his mind many times how easy it would be to just knock him out but Tommy knew the way the world worked. He understood the need for leadership and for a hierarchy.

Besides, would he want to be running things?

Having to deal with all the complaining, whining people who felt this world owed them more?

No. He told himself that it was just an evening and so he sat back and waited. It may be a few hours, but he only had to do this gig every few months.

He thought about the next fight he had planned and the preceding training he had to undertake. He swept a concrete-like hand through his short, black hair, sweeping it to one side. He glanced around the street, the underground station just a few feet away. Across the road adjacent were a few shops, a supermarket and a coffee chain and that was it. The road directly behind him tailed off towards Euston but to the right was the large Russell Square Park, gated off and dwindling in its population as the night began to seep in.

Tommy leaned back in his chair and waited for his job to begin.

———

"You ever heard of an umbrella, Fletch?"

Fletcher had left his car at Regent's Park, the emotional devastation he'd suffered that afternoon had necessitated a long walk in the rain. So by the time he had arrived at Holborn High Road Police station, he was soaked through, much to the dismay of Grace, the receptionist.

"Yeah. I just felt like walking is all."

Grace raised her eyebrow and Fletcher didn't know if it was due to confusion or disbelief.

"Well I think there are some towels in the cupboard near the locker room. Help yourself."

She gave him a warm smile which he returned in kind

before making his way down the corridor. He walked past a few administration offices and one of the supply cupboards, before needing to remove his ID card to swipe himself through the security door. He passed through easily and continued towards the locker room. Sure enough, in the cupboard were fresh towels and he pulled one out and began dabbing his thinning, white hair.

"Been raining, Fletch?"

Fletcher pulled the towel away from his face, to see Officer Starling standing opposite him, already in his uniform. He smiled warmly at the old detective, raising his mug of what looked like black coffee and took a sip.

"Just a tad."

"What a fucking surprise," Starling rolled his eyes, taking another sip. "What are you doing here anyway? It's Saturday night. Haven't you got a rave to get to?"

Fletcher laughed. He liked Officer Starling. He reminded him of himself at that age, his warm and friendly personality matching his top notch police skills. The boy would have a stellar career in the Met, Fletcher was sure of it.

"I'm a little too old for raves nowadays," Fletcher smiled back, running the towel over his hair one more time before opening the locker room door and dropping it in the towel bin just inside.

"Maybe so, but you're retired Fletch. You shouldn't be volunteering here during the weeks, let alone on a Saturday night." Starling seemed genuinely upset that Fletcher didn't seem to have a life outside of the police. It was something that upset Fletcher himself, but he hid that well behind the drinking.

"Well I love working here. The archives have needed to be organised since before you were even a twinkle in your father's eye," Fletcher went on, trying to change the subject. "Besides, I enjoy it."

"You enjoy it?" Starling didn't sound convinced as he took the final swig from his mug.

"Well what am I supposed to enjoy?"

Starling looked at him, a smirk filled his face.

"Your retirement."

Fletcher chuckled. Starling checked his watch.

"What time does your shift start?" Fletcher asked as he eased himself out of his wet coat, his administration badge hanging around his neck and swinging with his tie.

"Ten," Starling sighed and patted Fletcher strongly on the arm. "I'd better get going anyway, told the missus I'd give her a call before I started. Have a good one Fletch."

"You too, son."

They politely smiled and nodded, then Starling stalked off down the corridor, hammering his phone screen with his thumb. Fletcher felt better, happy to see that the job he'd dedicated his life to was having the same fulfilling effect on the next generation.

He went through the nearby double doors and made his way across the busy office to his file-covered desk in the corner.

Lucas and Alex sat forward on the sofa, intently watching the TV, as one of the competitors was knocked to the ground. Lucas took a sip of beer, his third of the night and reached forward for a handful of peanuts. Alex angrily gestured towards the screen.

"You see that? Crap defence! I told you he was weak on that side."

Dianne had walked into the room behind them, a dressing gown over her large baby bump and damp hair. She had just enjoyed a long, relaxing bath.

"Oh calm down, dear. It's just a game."

"It's not a game, Dianne. It's a fight." He looked at Lucas, shaking his head.

"Well whatever, you are not involved, so there is no need for you to get your pants in a bunch."

"Well it's a good job I'm not wearing any pants today, isn't it?"

Lucas almost spat his beer out and Alex looked at him smugly. Dianne slapped him round the back of the head with a rolled up newspaper. She giggled and strode off to the kitchen. Alex rubbed the back of his head, looking at Lucas who was checking his phone. It was almost half past ten and he hadn't heard from Helen.

"Still no word?"

"No, none yet." Lucas tried to disguise his worry. "She's probably yapping away with Mary. You know what they're like."

"Yeah, definitely." Alex looked at the TV, the closing credits of the pay-per-view flowing across the screen in a waterfall of words. "Cards?"

"Cards." Lucas agreed, nodding and pushing himself up off the couch. Alex wandered to the dining table with him, grabbing a deck of cards from the side shelf on the way through. The two friends sat in two of the four chairs around the oak dining table at the back of Alex's living room and the host shuffled the deck.

———

"Thank you for a wonderful night!"

Helen hugged Mary Reid at the doorway to her house, the entrance lit up by a small, glass lamp hanging from the side of the wall, illuminating the neatly arranged flowers hanging in the basket just below.

"Oh it's been my pleasure. It's been so good to see you. And I cannot wait for the baby to come!"

Mary shook her hands excitedly, baring her teeth with a big smile. She was slightly rounder than Helen but the same height. She had long, brown hair that bunched out from her head in awesome curls, and had a small dimple in her cheek.

"I know," Helen rubbed a loving hand gently over her stomach. "I can't wait to tell Lucas. To see his face."

She let her words drift and her mind followed close behind. She thought about the look on her husband's face when the realisation of parenthood hit him. The inevitable tears, the soft soul he kept hidden under the rough, manly exterior.

All she wanted to do was climb into bed next to him and hug him till she slept.

"Are you sure you don't want me to call you a cab?" Mary snapped Helen back into the conversation.

"Oh, god no. I'll be fine. It's just twenty minutes down that way anyway, isn't it?"

'Yeah, if you walk up that road there and then take a left you head down towards Russell Square. Once you're through the other side of the park, it's like five minutes to the Hilton."

"Simples!" Helen said in a Russian voice, mimicking the meerkat from the TV adverts. Mary laughed.

"Are you sure? It's pretty late." Mary leant against the wall of her hallway, as Helen finished buttoning up her coat.

"I quite fancy the walk. Besides, I'll just pester Lucas." She beamed at her friend.

"He's so lucky," Mary said with obvious sarcasm.

"He knows. I remind him all the time."

The two friends giggled and embraced once again, Mary wrapping her arms around her friend and making sure not to squeeze her too hard.

"Let me know when you get back, okay?"

"Will do. Bye!"

Helen trotted down the few thick, concrete steps and out through the small, metal gate. She turned back and waved to her friend standing in the doorway and then headed off in the direction of Russell Square. The air was cold and Helen pulled her collar up but she was grateful it wasn't raining. Her steps echoed, the heel of her shoes clomping against damp, uneven pavement. There was no traffic leaving the roads empty: however she could hear a bus a few streets away. She pulled her phone out of her pocket.

The time was just after eleven p.m.

She flicked through her contacts and selected Lucas and then lifted the phone up to the side of her small, beautiful face.

Nothing happened.

She frowned, pulling the phone from her ear and then tutting with disappointment. The screen was black, with an image of an empty battery flashing in the centre.

"Useless!" Helen cursed, keeping the phone in her hand as she continued walking. Eventually she came to the gates of the park. The trees lining the pathways hanging over the pavement covering it in complete darkness. If she continued on the road, she could walk around the park but it would add another ten minutes to her journey. Suddenly, an angry gust of wind flew by, sweeping up leaves and chilling Helen to the bone. A few drops of rain began to spit from the sky. She nervously looked at her phone, still no signal.

It would only take five minutes.

Five minutes and she would be out by Russell Square station.

Then she would head straight to the hotel.

With his head resting against the driver's door window, Tommy had dozed off. Still in the exact spot that he'd been parked in for the last few hours, he was snoring softly, his neck arched at a horrible angle that would undoubtedly stiffen the next day.

Suddenly, his phone vibrated on the dashboard and the text message tone chimed out loudly.

Tommy awoke with a snarl, taking a few moments to familiarise himself with the surroundings, remind himself where he was and why. He looked at the clock buried within the dashboard, under the fare counter.

11:15pm.

He blinked the remaining sleep from his vision and gently slapped the side of his face, encouraging himself to wake up. He stretched the top of his back and snatched up the phone. He pressed the button, the screen illuminating his face and the car around it.

"Five minutes. Look alive."

The message was clear and concise and Tommy turned the key in the ignition. His headlights came on as the engine roared into life. He pulled his seat belt across, indicated and then pulled out onto the main road.

―――

It had only been two weeks, but Starling was thrilled to be working with Officer Henry Boulder. The man was hilarious. Starling had to breathe through the laughs before turning to his colleague.

"Do it again!" he demanded through broken chuckles.

"Okay, last time." Boulder's voice was deeper than you would expect, his small frame and messy hair hardly making him an imposing figure. Especially in comparison to Starling, who had more than a few admirers from the women within his team.

"I AM THE LAW!" Boulder belted, his impression of Sylvester Stallone nigh-on perfect. Starling laughed instantly, hunching over and holding his stomach. "DROP YOUR WEAPONS!"

"Okay, please. Please stop!" Starling again tried to breathe through.

He leant forward, resting his forearms on the steering wheel of the police car they were sitting in. Boulder was in the passenger seat, allowing Starling, who was one of the top drivers in the whole of the Met, to take the wheel. They were stationed just under the rail bridge near Waterloo station.

The nightlife was picking up and the two of them watched from the warmth of their car as the inebriated and the drug using denizens of the night went about their business. In the distance, between the station and the Southbank Centre, Starling spotted the London Eye, the giant wheel turning slowly and lit up with dazzling effect, watching over the capital.

The shift was only an hour or so in, yet Starling secretly wished for something to happen. Something that involved more than calling someone an idiot, confiscating their illegal substances, and sending them on their way.

He wished something exciting would explode his shift into life.

———

In a well maintained, spacious three bedroom house in Abbey Village, Lucas sat across from his best friend at the dining table, their eyes locked as he laid down his cards.

"Twenty One!" Lucas said, confidently.

"Fuck!" Alex slapped his cards down angrily, pushing the chips into the middle. "I thought house always won?"

"They do…" Lucas said, smirking. "Usually."

Lucas picked up his phone. It was just past eleven fifteen. Still no word from Helen. He clicked her name, hit the phone button and raised it to his ear.

"*It has not been possible to connect your call.*"

He hung up before the message played out and dropped it on the table in frustration. He picked up his final beer and took a sip.

"Voice mail, huh?" Alex asked, dealing the cards out again.

"Yeah," Lucas sighed, gathering in his cards. "She's probably just had too much wine at Mary's or they're putting the world to rights. You know what Helen's like."

Alex chuckled as he put the deck to one side and held up his cards.

"Yes I do." He took a look at his cards and smiled.

"Fold," Lucas threw his cards in.

"Goddamn it!" Alex threw his in as well. "Anyway man, I'm sure she's fine and you'll hear from her in a bit."

"Oh absolutely!" Lucas said, taking the deck and shuffling the cards. "I've no doubt she's safe and sound."

———

Another freezing blast of the evening's ferocious breeze, alongside the now rapidly occurring droplets of rain, made Helen's mind up. She stuffed her phone and hands into her pockets, hunched her shoulders so her mouth was covered by her coat and took a deep breath.

She then strode purposefully through the park's metal gates and disappeared into its shadows.

The noise of the traffic from the main road abruptly disappeared, blocked out by the surrounding nothingness and silence. The narrow, concrete path felt coarse beneath her, the emptiness of the surrounding grass stretching beyond the trees intensifying the feeling of isolation.

It was so dark. She could barely see the benches that lined the pathway, and felt closed in by the overhanging branches of the tall, pillar-like trees.

Her footsteps echoed.

The rustling of the trees shimmering behind, above, and in front of her. She focused her mind, just a few minutes and she would be out the other side. She looked ahead, the small square of orange in the vast stretch of black was the entrance to the park, a small gate slicing the row of hedges in two.

Suddenly, about twenty feet ahead of her, a figure of a man walked from one side of the darkness to the other. It was a brief moment, the outline of a man cutting across the orange square of safety.

She stopped in her tracks, taking a deep breath. She thought about going back, it had been safe for the few minutes and the several feet she'd walked already.

She turned around to retrace her steps and looked back to the gate she'd entered through.

A hooded figure stood in the middle of the path.

Helen shook, her knees felt like jelly and she started walking backwards, deeper into the dark clutches of the park and away from the figure who was about ten feet from her. As she slowly walked backward, she collided with something.

"Hello princess."

She felt warm breath on her ear and screamed, the arms of a stranger ran around her waist, trying to restrain her. She struggled, flailing her arms about, before striking her sharp, pointed elbow back and catching the attacker just under the ribs. She felt the air fly from his lungs and he released her. She fell to one knee, her handbag hitting the floor and spilling everywhere.

She looked up and saw the other figure striding

towards her, coming from the direction she'd walked alone just moments before.

She left her bag, turning on her high heels and then began to run, flicking her shoes off into the dark to aid her cause. She could hear the footsteps gaining on her, two unknown men, men she had never met in her life, chasing her with nothing but ill-intent.

Every step began to feel heavy, the concrete below acting like quicksand and Helen was struggling to lift her feet to run. The orange square of freedom began to shrink from her view, she could feel the darkness ebbing its way closer to her with its dark, spindly fingers.

"Gotcha!" one of the men yelled as he leapt forward, wrapping his arms around her shoulders. Helen struggled, and managed to fling a fist behind her, catching the hooded man in the groin. The attacker stumbled back, howling in pain as the other chaser stopped to help him.

Suddenly, Helen felt lighter, her pace picked up and the exit began to expand. Freedom in just a matter of seconds.

The first figure stepped out once again, just in front of the exit. His hood was up and his head was down, a black outline of a man. A shadow.

Helen began to slow down, screaming for help, hoping to be heard through the darkness and over the traffic and the London nightlife.

Footsteps grew in volume behind her, so she ran straight towards the exit and then quickly turned left at the last second, evading the man's grasp and running up the side path just inside the park.

"Run all you like, bitch!" the man shouted. "We'll find you."

Helen felt the tears racing down her cheeks, her heart pounding at her rib cage. She was on the verge of a panic attack.

She wanted Lucas. Lucas would keep her safe.

If only he was here.

She stopped as she ran past the end of the bush and looked up at the dark night sky. She only just realised it had been raining the entire time and she was soaked through.

"Thank you!" she uttered to the darkness.

She turned and ran out through a side gate and into the street, waving down the first cab she could find.

———

Tommy Drayton turned right off the main road, down the small residential street running alongside the west side of Russell Square Park. He watched the road appear in front of him through systematic sweeps of his windscreen wipers, the rain unforgiving and unrelenting.

"What the fuck?" Tommy exclaimed as a petite blond woman ran from the entrance of the park, drenched from head to bare toes. She was waving frantically, her arms like propellers slicing through the rain.

Tommy braked immediately and the blonde woman ran to the car. She flung open the door and dived in as quickly as she could.

"Is everything okay?" he asked, as she slammed the door, her tears mixed with the rain on her face. She slumped into the chair, sobbing.

"Please just drive," she pleaded, looking back through the droplet-covered rear windscreen to see if her attackers were still chasing. Tommy drove on slowly, looking at the poor, young woman in his rear-view mirror. She was shivering and her right knee was bleeding.

"What's your name?" he asked, trying to bring her back from whatever had happened to her.

"Helen," she answered, her mascara leaking down her face like black veins.

"I'm Tommy," he told her reassuringly, smiling into the mirror. "Don't worry darling, we'll get you home."

"I'm staying at the Hilton."

"The one by Euston?" he asked softly, his eyes looking at her in the mirror.

Helen nodded and searched for her phone, remembering that it was lying on the pathway in the park where she'd been attacked.

She wanted to call Lucas. Hear his voice.

She began crying again. Tommy pulled up at a red light, braked and then turned in his seat, sliding the plastic partition to the side.

"Hey, Helen." She continued to cry. He handed her a packet of tissues. "Would you like me to take you to the police?"

"No thanks," Helen mustered. She took the tissues and dabbed her eyes, shaking her head at the amount of makeup staining the soft paper. Tommy offered her an apologetic smile.

"What happened, if you don't mind me asking?"

Tommy started up again as the light turned green, turning right onto the next street. "I mean, if the police ask me what happened, I kind of need to know, right?"

"I was chased by some guys." Helen had managed to compose herself a little, showing that strength that Lucas always told her was beautiful. "I think there were three. I think they wanted to rape me."

"Fuck me!" Tommy exclaimed, his eyes widening with horror. "They didn't hurt you did they?"

"No, not at all." Helen took a tissue and wiped the blood from a small cut on her knee, the rain washing the blood down her shins towards her bare foot.

"The hospital is just up that road there," Tommy pointed ahead.

"Please, can you just take me to the Hilton? I need to call my husband." Helen steeled herself not to cry again.

"Absolutely," Tommy smiled.

Helen sat back in the seat, tilting her head back to look at the ceiling. She could feel tears forming at the sides of her eyes as the relief of surviving the horrible attack came flooding in. She thought of Lucas, how he would be in the car straight away to come and collect her.

She wanted to hear him on the phone.

Lucas would protect her from anything.

"I hate this town, I really do," Tommy interrupted her thoughts. "There are so many fucked up people out there, you know? You can't be too careful."

Suddenly, Tommy slammed on the brakes. Helen lurched forward from her seat, colliding with the panel separating the front from the back section. She pulled herself up angrily, but before she could say anything the door to her left opened.

The three hooded men poured in from the cold, wet outdoors, two of them grabbing her by the arms and hoisting her up onto the row of seats. The other closed the door and while Helen wriggled to free herself, she realised that Tommy had just been circling around the park. They were back at the side gate she'd burst free from minutes ago.

Helen struggled and screamed, pushing as hard as she could to get to the door. The two hooded men sat either side of her were trying hard to restrain her, but Helen was a fighter. She elbowed and clawed, screaming for help at the top of her lungs.

"For fuck's sake, can someone shut her up?" Tommy yelled back through the partition while driving towards the red light ahead.

The struggle continued and the hulking driver

slammed on the brakes. In one fluid motion, he slid the plastic panel to the side again and leant in.

With one hammer-like fist, he struck Helen straight on the side of the jaw.

Her world went black

CHAPTER SIX

Helen would never recall the drive, as she was still unconscious when they'd arrived. The three men left the back of the cab as soon as it came to a halt and Helen woozily came to as they moved. She tried to struggle, but found her arms tied up behind her back, and her feet tied together at the ankle.

Her jaw ached from the blow she'd received earlier, but nevertheless, she tried to scream. She was gagged, the cloth tied too tightly for any sound to come out apart from a deep muffle.

Panic began to spread through her, her muscles shaking in fear. The driver's door slammed shut and she could hear the crunch of Tommy's shoes on gravel. Tommy appeared in the doorway, holding up his hands to try and instil a measure of calm.

Helen tried to scream again, thrashing her body about as he reached in and hoisted her up over his well-rounded shoulder. She was tiny in comparison, his arms almost bulging out of the black jumper he wore over his solid body. He hauled her from the car and marched across the gravel to an empty, rundown garage. Helen wildly looked from side to side, trying to find anything she could recognise.

She was completely lost.

She began to cry, pleading with a higher power she never had faith in to send someone to save her. She begged for Lucas, heartbroken as the realisation set in of what was about to happen.

If only Lucas had been there.

If only.

Tommy pushed open the side door and walked into the dusty room. Some objects were covered by a sheet in the far corner. A lone light hung from the ceiling, the bulb just bright enough to cast a small pale circle over the room. The only object the light reached was a relatively new-looking sofa, a dark leather three-seater.

Tommy dropped Helen on the out of place sofa.

"I'm sorry."

He couldn't look her in the eyes. He turned and disappeared into the darkness. She heard his footsteps heading away from her and she lay on the sofa, terrified and alone.

She heard the door slam shut.

She began to cry.

―――――

Tommy let out a deep sigh as he closed the door. He rested his hands against it, dropping his head just to clear his thoughts. That poor woman. She had a life. She had told him she had a husband.

This was the way things were. He had made his peace with it a long time ago.

He walked across the gravel to his black cab, his three younger brothers standing around it. Matt, the oldest of them, sat in the driver's seat, his hood still up and a furious expression on his face. For years he had been at loggerheads with Tommy, voicing his disagreement with his and the rest of their brothers' actions. Tommy knew Matt felt out of place in the family due to having a different mother which was evident as he was mixed race, his complexion much darker than the rest of the Drayton boys. Standing by the boot of the car, Harry was hunched over, sniffing a small pile of cocaine from a metal scoop he'd retrieved from his pocket. He was gangly with greasy black hair, almost the complete opposite to Tommy. If Tommy had had his way, Harry would have been removed years ago. He was nothing but a junkie. But Curtis had said Harry was the youngest, he needed the most looking after.

Tommy believed all he needed was a bullet through his skull.

On the bonnet sat Lewis, the runt of the group and the youngest after Harry. Lewis was thin, with almost see-through hair that floated around his head like black mist. His face was thin and gaunt, his teeth broken and jagged.

He looked like a rat and Tommy didn't believe that was far off from an accurate account of Lewis's character. Tommy approached all three of them, stuffing his hands into his trouser pockets.

"All three of you did well tonight."

Before any response had been voiced, the sound of tyres crackling over the gravel grew louder and a shiny, black Bentley pulled up alongside the four Drayton brothers. The engine died, the door flew open, and dressed in a custom-tailored suit, out stepped Curtis Drayton. The eldest of the brothers, Curtis was only beaten in size by Tommy, who he treated with equal respect and disdain. A silence fell over the family as Curtis stepped across the gravel towards Tommy.

"Well?" His voice was husky, the wind carrying it. Curtis was in his forties, a few wrinkles beginning to appear on his permanently angry face. His hair had thinned and was cut short to hide the fact. His eyes were the darkest brown, like simmering coals of fury.

"She's in there," Tommy pointed with his head and Curtis smiled, showing his immaculate teeth. He patted his brother on the shoulder and strode across the car park, disappearing into darkness as he approached the door. He entered the building and slammed the door shut behind him.

Tommy ran a hand over his face, shaking his head slightly. He folded his arms, turned and slumped against the side of the black cab.

"He'll appreciate what you boys have done tonight," Tommy said, like a football coach addressing his team. "He always does."

"If it keeps him happy then it means life is easier for us," Harry said, before bending down and sniffing another line of cocaine up his nostril.

"Can you not fucking give that shit a rest for one fucking hour?" Tommy angrily chastised Harry. The youngest brother immediately batted it all off the back of the cab, rubbing the remnants of the drug under his nose, sniffing deeply.

"Fuck this shit!" Matt said, pushing himself out of the driver's seat.

He pulled a cigarette out from his pocket, lit it with a zippo and then blew out smoke into the air. He nodded at them all and began walking in the direction opposite to the way the cars were facing. Tommy didn't look up, he stayed, arms folded.

"Where do you think you're going?"

Matt stopped in his tracks and turned back, catching his older brother's stare and returning it with venom.

"Me?" Matt showed no fear of Tommy, despite being half his size. 'I'm going home. I've done what I've been asked to do and it's all bullshit. I'm not going to stand out here to shake that sick bastard's hand and congratulate him on raping that woman. Fuck that. And fuck you, Tommy!"

Tommy pushed himself gently off the car and stood face to face with his brother. They were the same height, but Tommy had at least eighty pounds of muscle on Matt and they both knew it would be over in seconds.

"Why don't you think before opening that trap of yours, hmm? It might get you in trouble."

"I couldn't give a fuck anymore." Matt flicked his cigarette into Tommy's chest and shrugged. He began to walk away. "You can tell Curtis if he's got a problem with me leaving, he knows where he can find me."

"We'll be having a chat about this soon, son. Trust me." Tommy yelled out after Matt, who faded into the shadows. Matt threw up his hand with a raised middle finger, before disappearing from view. Tommy, his face distorted in an ugly scowl stood with his hands on his hips. He spat on the ground, on the verge of losing his temper.

Lewis slid off the boot of the car.

"Let him go, Tommy. You know what Matt's like." Lewis's voice was high-pitched and croaky. "He doesn't like having to answer to you or to Curtis."

"Lewis, the next time you ever tell me what to do, I will break a bone for every fucking word you use." Tommy turned, his eyes piercing through Lewis like razor blades. "Is that understood?"

Lewis nodded in agreement when the door burst open again. The footsteps were heard first, along with the clicking of a zippo. Smoke filtered through the air, the smell of the cigar thick and heavy. Curtis emerged through the smoke and the shadow, adjusting his belt. He looked flushed, tired.

"Get rid of her."

Tommy nodded and Curtis took a big puff on his cigar

and blew it out as he watched his brother faithfully walk over to the doorway to oblige him.

"In the stomach," Curtis demanded, his eyes flickering with twisted delight.

"Curtis. Come on. Hasn't she suffered enough?" Tommy asked, his voice trying desperately to hide its disgust.

"It's not a request."

Tommy stared at his brother, who took another puff on his cigar, his face disappearing behind a cloud of thick, grey smoke. Tommy sighed and walked to the shutter, his head shaking. Curtis smirked, watching his brother obey his order before heading to his car.

He walked past both Lewis and Harry, barely acknowledging their existences, and got into the back seat of his Bentley. The window rolled down and a puff of smoke filtered out.

Tommy could hear the crying before he could see her. He always hated this part, the walk through the darkness to see what his brother had left behind. He knew it was wrong, but his loyalty to his brother was unbreakable. Curtis was a disturbed man, Tommy would never deny that. But whatever it was that happened, Curtis protected Tommy and his siblings from it. Tommy knew their dad was a bad man, one of the worst criminals London had seen. Curtis took the brunt of their old man's twisted actions and maybe that contributed in some way?

Tommy didn't know.

And he never asked.

———

Helen heard the door open again, followed by the echo of footsteps approaching. She would have cried out, but she was emotionally, physically and mentally exhausted. The second man had hauled her off the chair by her hair, before punching her twice, once in the face and once in the ribs. There was a trickle of blood from her mouth to the floor that had expanded to a puddle.

Her top was ripped, her breasts exposed and pressed against the cold, dusty floor.

Somewhere in the room were her jeans and underwear, which he had thrown in whatever direction as he ripped them off her.

The footsteps drew closer and with the last ounces of energy she had, Helen tilted her head to look through her quickly swelling eyes.

Tommy.

He lowered himself down, squatting near to Helen with a genuine look of sorrow on his face. He knew this woman was innocent in all of this. She had a life that he and his brothers had just completely shattered. He reached round to the back of his trousers and from the band he pulled out a very large, very sharp hunting knife.

Helen's eyes widened as much as they could against the bruising and she tried to muster words. Tommy put a hand over her mouth.

"Don't. It won't make it any easier, trust me." He gripped the knife with his hand, and lowered his arm towards her body. Helen was crying, trying her hardest to beg for mercy. Tommy looked at her, his eyes cold.

"I'm sorry, Helen. It's nothing personal."

Helen felt the searing pain burning through her as the knife was rammed forcefully into her stomach. Tommy held it there, staring her dead in the eyes as she felt the striking agony course through. She could feel the warm flow of blood as it oozed out from the wound and once Tommy pulled his hand back out, it came gushing forth.

Tommy stood up and took a step back away from the rapidly expanding pool of blood. He pulled out a handkerchief and wiped the blade and the blood from his hand, before turning and walking purposefully back to the door.

Helen lay in silence, feeling her strength and life ebbing away from her. The room's darkness moved, ghostly black shadows reaching out to take her to the afterlife.

Her eyes felt heavy.

She thought of Lucas. How he looked. How he smelt. How he kissed her. How he held her.

How he loved her.

How she loved him.

In the distance she thought she could hear the high-pitched wailing of a siren.

Helen closed her eyes as consciousness left her.

———

Officer Starling pulled the collar of his police-issue coat up and willed his body to warm itself. The rain was hitting the earth as hard as it could, the cold spreading with every drop that fell. He blew into his hands and rubbed them together, thinking about maybe climbing into a warm bed with his girlfriend for the hour between his shift ending and her having to leave for work.

That was the one thing he most hated about the night-shift. The bitterness of darkness.

He let out a sigh and turned and walked back down the path through Russell Square Park, looking around for any further clues. Officer Boulder was taking a statement from a young couple, huddled under an umbrella and dressed as if their night was just beginning, not ending.

"So you didn't see anyone?" Boulder asked, not looking up from the notepad that he was trying to cover with his hand.

"No, Officer," The young man answered politely. "I

tripped over the shoe there and then found the handbag over there... seemed a little peculiar, y'know?"

Boulder nodded, scribbling down. Starling watched approvingly, knowing he was working with a like-minded man of the law.

II mean, you'd notice if you'd forgotten your handbag. I know I would." The lady added, her face telling Starling she feared the worst.

"Also, her purse and phone are in there. The phone is smashed the pieces," the young man added.

"So you moved the bag and its contents"' Boulder asked, careful not sound accusatory.

"I'm afraid so," the young man didn't take offence. "I thought maybe we could find her phone and be able to contact a friend or something?"

The young man shrugged and he and his girlfriend both looked on helplessly. Starling took a few steps forward, aware that he must have seemed like the more intimidating of the two. The rain slapped against him as he approached.

"You did the right thing calling us," he reassured them with a warm smile. "We have her driver's license and we ensure that these items are returned to her."

"Oh good," the girl seemed relieved, holding onto her boyfriend's arm. "You hear so many stories that my mind just leaps to the worst-case scenario."

"Well, you've been a tremendous help," Boulder said warmly, scribbling the final notes before flipping the note book closed. "If we need any further information, we will be in touch."

"No problem, officer," the young man replied.

"Have a lovely evening," Starling said, indicating they could leave. The two of them smiled and left, heading towards the exit of the park to re-join the London nightlife.

"What do you think?" Boulder asked, bending down to

collect the scattered items. Starling didn't turn to his colleague, instead he stared out into the darkness beyond the trees. He closed his eyes, allowing the wetness of the night to crash against his face.

"I think we need to find this woman."

Suddenly, Boulder's radio began to crackle into life. Attached to the breastplate of his Met vest, he struggled slightly turning the volume dial with a wet, gloved hand.

"Any available units, we have a grade one call, immediate response. Anonymous call. Reports of a serious sexual assault on a female. Vale Park Industrial Estate, Bermondsey. Any available units."

The two officers looked at each other instantly and Starling gestured at all of the possessions spread out across the wet, stone path.

"Bag them and take them. Quickly!" He turned and walked briskly towards the exit, back to their car, and detaching his own radio from his chest in one fluid motion. "Officers three-three-four and four-two-nine attending. ETA fifteen minutes."

Starling turned back to Boulder, who had collected the evidence and was rapidly catching up. He took a deep breath, the night changing in a matter of seconds. They exited through the gate, Starling jogging around the front of the car and sliding into the driver's seat. Boulder hopped into the passenger side, clicking his seat belt and firing up the siren.

"Is a member of SOIT en-route?" Starling said into the radio, as he turned the ignition, the motor of the car roaring awake from its cold, wet slumber.

A faint cackle from the radio.

"They are aware. The Sexual Offence Investigation Team will meet you on scene."

"Received!" Starling barked. Boulder looked at him as he whipped the car into reverse, the blare of the siren causing the traffic behind them to stop. With his hand firmly on the wheel, Starling yanked it downwards, the car spinning around, cutting through the main road. He shifted from reverse up to fourth in a matter of seconds and accelerated up Holborn High Road, slashing through the army of rain drops.

"You don't think it's her do you?" Boulder asked, a sense of dread dripping from every word. Starling kept his eyes on the road, weaving in and out of the cars and buses that had haphazardly moved to the side of the road to clear a path for the wailing blue light.

"'I don't know, Henry," Starling said coldly. "I just pray we get there in time."

The white police car turned the corner, whipping around the static traffic and disappeared into the rain in a whirlwind of noise and flashing lights.

Fletcher was hunched over one of the metal filing cabinets at the back of the office, finishing off the implementation of a basic yet efficient colour coded sticker system. It may not have been crime fighting, but it was a job he took seriously and was proud as he stepped back and admired the organised rainbow. Working a double-shift that ate into his lonely Saturday was just the tonic he needed, the thoughts of the afternoon's earlier heartbreak were being repelled, held back by more pressing matters.

"Lovely stuff!" He afforded himself a smile and trudged back to his messy desk, paperwork and files he had pulled from the cabinet piled everywhere. He briefly scanned the desk, finding his mug of coffee and he took a sip. He grimaced - it had gone cold, but he still sunk the rest of it in a few gulps allowing the caffeine to shoot through his old body.

"Fletcher."

He turned to see Officer Patrick McCarthy approaching his desk, holding what seemed to be an ID card in his hand. McCarthy was a small, plump man with pasty white skin, fluffy ginger hair, and a thick Irish accent. He was also a fine police officer, resigned to desk duties for a few months after injuring his knee in pursuit of a carjacker. He limped all the way to Fletcher's desk, casting a disapproving eye over the mounds of paper.

"Don't worry, Pat," Fletcher reassured him. "It's all going back in the cabinet."

Before he could proudly explain the order he had brought to the cabinet, McCarthy raised his hand to cut him off. The expression across his chubby face told Fletcher that something had happened.

"What is it?"

"It's not good, Fletch." McCarthy shook his head, looking at the desk.

"What?"

McCarthy went to speak, struggled for the words and then let out a sigh accompanied with another shake of the head.

"Pat, what the hell is going on?" Fletcher looked over his colleague's shoulder, watching as a few uniformed officers jogged towards the exit of the station, fastening their met vests and checking the equipment on their belts.

"We received an anonymous phone call about a young woman being attacked." McCarthy shook his head, having always hated having to say it out loud. "She was raped, Fletch."

"Oh god!" Fletcher put his coffee mug on top of the nearby shelving unit and held onto it, steadying himself as the horrifying news set in.

"She was abducted in Russell Square Park. Two of our officers were called in as her possessions were recovered.

They responded to the anonymous call but it was too late. Whoever had done it was long gone, but…" McCarthy scowled, his mouth pulled into a thin line of anger. Fletcher waited for merely a few seconds.

"But what?"

"They fucking stabbed her." McCarthy's pale face illuminated, red flushing through his round cheeks. "They raped her and stabbed her! Sick bastards!"

Fletcher raised a hand to his mouth, his thoughts immediately with the poor girl and her family. He thought of Annabelle and was instantly thankful that it wasn't her. McCarthy handed him the ID card he'd almost crushed in anger, his other hand balled up into a fist.

"Starling sent this back, he's at the scene. It's her driving licence." He reached into the pocket of his trousers and pulled out a brand new smart phone. "This is her phone. We need you to contact her local police, get them to find her husband."

Fletcher nodded, obligingly taking the items and finding some space to lay them on his desk.

"We charged her phone as the battery was dead. It hasn't got much juice but it has enough. Going through the texts he is spending tonight at a friend's house. Alex, is the friend's name I think. It's in the text messages."

"Sure," Fletcher said with conviction, wanting to do what he could for this woman. "What was her name?"

McCarthy smiled at Fletcher, appreciating that this old, retired policeman genuinely wanted to know.

"Helen. Her name is Helen Cole."

"Okay. Well let's make sure we do everything we can for her."

"Aye," McCarthy agreed, patting Fletcher on the arm and awkwardly turning away, doing his utmost to avoid putting pressure on his bad knee. Fletcher looked at the woman's driver's licence, the piercing blue eyes staring back at him. She was a gorgeous woman, her face a symmetry of beauty that exuded happiness. Judging from her address, she was a long way from home. A long way from her safety.

Yet something was gnawing at Fletcher, something banging at the side of his mind like a woodpecker. He felt like he knew her, that he could remember meeting this woman before.

Helen Cole.

He looked up from the licence as McCarthy made it to the doorway.

"Hey Pat!" he called out, causing McCarthy to turn around, wincing slightly at the pain. "What did you say her husband's name was?"

Fletcher drew a breath, making a silent prayer that the name to come out of McCarthy's mouth was not the one he thought it might be.

"Lucas. Her husband's name is Lucas."

Fletcher froze.

His prayer had gone unanswered.

―――

Lucas feared the worst when he and Alex heard the knock on the front door. His bemused best friend got up quickly, scurrying across the living room to answer it.

Lucas hadn't heard from Helen, which was unlike her. She may have been out drinking with Mary and he was aware it had been a while since she'd seen her old friend.

But Helen would always let him know she was okay.

Always.

When he heard the soft, well-spoken voice of Officer Chamberlain apologise to Alex for calling so late, he felt his stomach flip, like someone had put his insides into a washing machine and set it to maximum spin. He tried to push himself up off his seat, his hands pressing on the table but he felt no strength in them.

A dark dread spread across him.

When Alex informed the officers that Lucas was right inside, Lucas could feel the build-up of vomit begin hurtling up his windpipe, only to fall back at the last minute as he swallowed. He pushed himself up, steadying himself on the table.

Dianne had wandered down the stairs in her dressing gown and switched from sleepy to concerned the second she saw the uniform of the police officer.

He offered a sympathetic smile.

It was all he could do.

The officer began to speak to Lucas but he couldn't focus. The room began to blur around the edges, objects began to merge with their surroundings. The words turned into a humming sound buzzing around Lucas but didn't register.

Alex held his hands up to his mouth in shock. His hands dissolved into his face. Dianne fell to the floor crying, her wailing disintegrating into the low, deep humming surrounding Lucas. The fluorescent blur extended an arm out, a comforting hand on Lucas.

He batted it away, feeling dizzy as he stumbled against the table, glass bottles falling and smashing, cards tipping onto the floor.

He heard a crash and felt shorter.

He had dropped to his knees, but as he looked down he couldn't see them.

An image of Helen flashed into his mind.

He hunched over and vomited, an unstoppable current of sick pouring from his throat. He was sure it was Alex who placed a hand on his back in a vain attempt at provided him with comfort.

Everything registered as nothing more than a blur. A horrible mixture of fading images and incoherent sounds.

An emptiness crawled through Lucas, burrowing through his body like a swarm of insects.

Alex maybe offered some words of comfort. He couldn't tell.

That loud, far off sound could have been Dianne crying.

Perhaps Officer Chamberlain was giving him information.

None of it registered. Only one thing was swirling through Lucas's mind, engulfing his vision as the world around him began to matter less.

Helen.

Lucas stared blankly at the floor, he couldn't see the large pile of vomit fanning out around his knees.

Helen.

The vision of her began to flicker, like an old VCR cassette when the tape became entangled.

She flickered.

He reached out a hand, trying to touch her.

Helen.

She began to fade.

CHAPTER SEVEN

The flashing lights of the ambulance illuminated the rain drops. The wind was harsh, ripping through the crime scene which had been set up around Vale Park Industrial Estate. A lone police officer was unravelling thick, yellow police tape to cordon off the area. Another few were taking statements from potential witnesses, although none of the information seemed to be of any use. Officer Claire Mills of the Sexual Offence Investigation Team was standing by the doors to the ambulance as the busy paramedics carefully dragged the gurney across the wet gravel, an unresponsive Helen positioned on top. One of the paramedics held a pack of blood aloft, the tube connecting from the base to the unconscious victim.

Starling stood a few feet away, his body trembling. He didn't feel the wet of the night or the sharpness of the wind.

All he felt was anger.

This poor woman, despite the large swelling on her face was the same woman whose ID they'd found in the park. He had sent Boulder back to the station with her possessions, making it a personal obligation to stay with poor Helen until she either pulled through or....

He gritted his teeth.

By now, efforts would have been made to contact her husband up in Lincolnshire. This innocent woman was so far from her day to day life, it sickened Starling to think how alone she must have felt. How helpless.

He cursed himself for not getting there sooner, fully aware that he couldn't have driven any faster had he tried. There was nothing he could have done.

This woman was taken from her evening, ripped out of her life and placed into a nightmare.

She'd been beaten.

She'd been raped.

And now, more than likely, she was going to die.

"Excellent work tonight, Starling."

His thoughts evaporated into the rain at the voice's intrusion. Officer Mills smiled at him. She was in her mid-forties with copper hair pulled back into a ponytail. Her sharp facial features actually made her look younger than she was. Behind her, the ambulance roared into life, the piercing howl of the siren shooting through the cold air as it departed the scene as quickly as possible.

"'t wasn't enough," Starling shook his head and turned to walk away.

"We can never do enough, Ollie," she called after him. He stopped in his tracks, refusing to turn. Refusing to let her see his eyes watering. "I've been doing this for nearly twenty years. I've seen things happen to women, men and kids that would haunt the worst of dreams."

Starling turned, his lips pulled tightly together in fury. Mills' heart sank as she saw his red, blurry eyes.

"Then why do you do it then?" he asked, searching for something on a night where only death hung in the air.

"Because we are some people's only chance."

Her words echoed through the night, dodging the onslaught from the sky and finding their way to Officer Starling. He nodded, not entirely in agreement and looked at the ground. Wet stones were scattered around his feet, all climbing over each other. *The way the people in this city do at times*, he thought. Mills took a few steps towards him, her heels crunching the gravel. Her copper hair was pushed wetly against her head.

"You were her only chance, Ollie," she reached out and gently stroked his arm. "You did everything you could for her."

Ollie retracted his arm, the fluorescent jacket flicking droplets into the sky.

"It wasn't enough though."

He nodded a thank you to Mills, who could only half force an attractive smile. He turned away from the crime scene, walking with purpose to his car.

Someone had left that poor girl to die.

His fists clenched, water trailing down and dripping off his knuckles, turning white through pressure.

His boots crunched over the stones and he threw open his car door. Without even bothering to put on his seatbelt, he flicked on the siren and swung the car around, stones shooting upwards from the spin of the tyres.

He would not abandon this girl.

He sped off in pursuit of the ambulance, his car ripping through the wet night.

———

It took Alex less than three minutes to snap Lucas out of the trance he had been sent into, calmly telling his best friend to get his coat and wait by the car. Lucas silently obliged, an urgency in every single movement.

Officer Chamberlain had been nothing but respectful

and it had looked like breaking the news to the unsuspecting husband would give him endless sleepless nights. Whilst Alex had been helping his best friend, trying to get him to breathe, Officer Chamberlain had managed to calm Dianne down. She was still weeping uncontrollably by the time she lowered herself gently into the driver's seat of the car. Her hands were gripping the steering wheel but her arms were shaking.

Alex couldn't drive, he had had too much to drink but if he had to, he would have carried Lucas on his back all the way to London.

He climbed in next to his wife, who was sobbing, thoughts of her best friend suffering relentlessly beating against her mind.

"Just take your time, my love," Alex said softly, ensuring the heartbreak in his voice wasn't evident. The last thing Dianne or Lucas, who sat quietly in the back seat, needed was for him to be swallowed by the sadness as well. "Everything is going to be okay."

He smiled warmly at his wife, who dabbed at her eyes with a tissue. She had put on a thick coat over her dressing gown and in light of what had just fractured their lives, Alex had never loved her more.

"Okay," she repeated a number of times, composing herself while she adjusted the mirrors. Alex looked in the rear-view mirror as she turned it, observing Lucas.

He said nothing.

He sat in the seat behind Dianne, his body twisted at a slight angle, his forehead pressed against the raindrop-coated window. His eyes were empty, staring off into an unfathomable distance.

"Don't worry, Lucas," Alex said, turning to look at the shell of his friend. "We'll get there soon. I promise."

There was no response.

Alex smiled in Lucas's direction, but the man sat motionlessly, his gaze transfixed on the outside world. His eyes, a dark pink colour, had no tears left. He sat, lost in a sea of thoughts, trying to hold onto a small glimmer of hope that he would see his wife again. That he would bring her home.

Alex turned away, gently resting a hand on Dianne's thigh, comforting her as she sniffed through heavy breaths, a continuous stream of tears falling slowly from her eyes.

He loved her so much and couldn't imagine what was going through Lucas's mind.

He thought of Helen then, feeling his own tears forming, knowing his dear friend had been assaulted. He held them back.

He couldn't cry. Not yet.

He had to keep Dianne calm and they had to take Lucas back to the one place he had never wanted to go, to face a situation no one would ever want to be in.

As Dianne pulled onto the motorway, she turned her full beams on to burn a hole through the darkness.

Alex reassured her with soothing words, putting her at ease.

The rain crashed against the windscreen before being swept away by the wipers.

Lucas remained still, staring out into nothingness.

There was nobody in the men's toilets on the third floor when Fletcher entered. He called out, seeing if anyone was in any of the cubicles and was answered with silence. He crouched down, peering under the doors but saw no feet. His back ached, a sign of age that he tried his best to ignore as he straightened up.

He strode to the sink, staring at the tired, wrinkled face he barely recognised any more. Sadness built inside him and he turned on the tap, a stream of warm water gushing out. He held his hands under it, cupping the water and then, despite the pain, bent down and splashed it across his face.

It did nothing to assuage the misery, but the nausea subsided.

He thought about that horrible feeling when the doctors had told him that Susan wasn't going to make it.

The harsh, hollow emptiness of the world that he had had to embrace since the day she'd left him.

He thought about Helen.

Beautiful Helen, one of the sweetest girls he had ever met, as intelligent as she was attractive, and blessed with a heart that was overflowing with kindness. Wonderful Helen, the woman who had done so much to fix Lucas.

He thought of Lucas.

He thought of the pain he must be going through. His mind then raced to the horrific ordeal that Helen had faced, on her own.

He knew Lucas would never forgive himself.

He thought of their world collapsing.

Fletcher walked to a cubicle, his shoes slapping against the tiled floor, echoing off the tiled walls. Closing the door behind him, he jolted the rickety lock into place, and sat down on the closed lid of the toilet.

Fletcher began to cry.

———

Immediately the ambulance pulled into the bay outside The Royal London Hospital, a swarm of nurses rushed to the back doors. The driver killed the ignition, hopped out

out and raced to the rear, ignoring the rain. The paramedic who was with Helen hurled open the doors and barked orders to the nurses as they quickly lifted the gurney to the wet pavement.

A crowd had begun to form.

Starling could see it as he pulled up, his lights still spinning like a Christmas tree inside a tornado and the siren wailing anguished screams into the night. He shut them off, not even bothering to park the car properly and leapt out.

One of the paramedics and the nurses wheeled Helen in through the hospital's automatic entrance, the other paramedic following close behind. His overalls and hands were red with the blood of innocence. Starling approached him.

"How is she?" he asked, looking beyond and in through the glass front door. A doctor had joined the group of medics buzzing around Helen, conferring with the paramedic who had his hands pressed solidly over Helen's midsection. Starling could see the blood from where he stood.

"Not good, I'm afraid," Starling was told. The medic looked to be in his early thirties with a strong jaw covered by a two-day stubble. He looked shattered. "She's lost a lot of blood."

"Will she make it?" Starling asked, watching Helen being wheeled round a corner and out of sight. Droplets of cold water ran from his hair and into his eyes.

The paramedic offered his best, positive smile but Starling saw through it. The man had seen enough in his time to know the score.

Starling was still learning.

Helen wasn't going to make it.

He trudged into the main hospital slowly, asking where

the operating theatre was. A flash of the badge and he was led there by a young orderly, whose efforts to strike up a conversation fell on deaf ears. Starling walked down the corridor, bright white walls lit up by bright white lights. It stung his eyes and made him realise how tired he was. He sat down with a squelch on a seat in the waiting room, the only person there.

Not many people require emergency lifesaving surgery at this time, he mused tiredly.

He thought of poor Helen, knowing full well that any chance she had was minimal.

He cursed himself for his earlier wish for excitement.

He cursed the world for the cruelty it generously handed out to undeserving people.

Sitting in a small green plastic chair, Starling waited, feeling the walls close in. Rain dripped off his clothes, off his skin and off his hair. He trembled, exhaustion and the chill of the night forming a formidable alliance.

Time passed.

At what rate, Starling couldn't tell. But he was snapped awake, as Helen's husband stormed into the waiting room.

———

"Where is she?"

Lucas had returned to reality when Alex had told him they'd arrived. He blinked a few times, the hospital appearing behind the car's rain-speckled window He didn't say a word instead throwing open the door and storming out through the unrelenting elements and straight into the hospital. Dianne agreed to remain in the car while Alex chased after his best friend.

Lucas strode straight to the reception desk and it seemed like the nurses already knew who he was, sending him to the fourth floor. Alex caught up with him while he waited for the lift, trying to calm him down. Lucas stared at the metal doors, waiting for them to part in silence. Stepping into the lift, Lucas pressed the button to begin the ascent to the operating theatre.

They stood in silence; Alex couldn't even look at his friend.

Lucas stared ahead and barged out through the doors as soon as they opened, banging his shoulder on the metal as it slid back. He followed the arrow signs, the familiar hospital smell hitting the back of his throat. He ignored it, striding down the bright corridor. He passed a few nurses, their overalls thick with blood. He pushed open the double doors as hard as he could, making a beeline straight for the surgeon who was standing outside the archway to the waiting room, down the corridor from the operating theatre. His green scrubs were dark, heavy and stained red. He pulled his mask down as Lucas approached, ignoring the young police officer sat at the far end of the small waiting room.

"Where is she?" Lucas repeated, stopping just a few feet from the surgeon, looking over his shoulder at the door.

"Are you Lucas?" Dr Amrit Singh was a tall, thin man. His nose seemed slightly too big for his face and his eyes displayed nothing but sorrow. His voice however, was calm.

"That's me.," Lucas again peered over the doctor's shoulder at the door, his voice breaking under the emotional strain. "I'm her husband."

"I need to tell you what's happened."

"I know what's happened. Can I see her?"

"Mr Cole, your wife has been subjected to a very violent sexual assault. And…"

"She was raped!" Lucas said coldly through gritted teeth, his eyes leaking, tears dropping from his cheeks to the white plastic-tiled floor below. Singh went to respond but couldn't.

"Can I see her?" Lucas suddenly felt weaker.

"Mr Cole, the stab wound your wife received did considerable damage to her insides. She's lost a lot of blood."

A visible pain struck Lucas, and he hunched over at the thought of his wife in so much agony. Alex, who stood quietly to the side, slowly placed a hand on his friend's back for comfort. Starling looked down at the ground from his chair.

"And I'm afraid she's lost the baby."

Lucas looked up at Dr Singh immediately in confusion and when Alex turned with surprise, the doctor realised that this wasn't common knowledge. Lucas tried to say the word, but couldn't muster the ability to.

Helen was pregnant.

Had been.

Lucas felt very light headed, stumbling a few feet to the side and colliding shoulder-first against the wall. Alex and Dr Singh tried to help him and Starling leapt from his chair.

"Don't touch me!" Lucas yelled, resting the side of his face and shoulder against the plaster wall. Tears fell from his eyes rapidly. All three men watched him feeling completely useless.

"Lucas, I'm afraid the damage that was done to Helen was extensive and...."

"What?" Lucas looked at the doctor, who had tried everything to save his wife. The man looked defeated.

"I'm afraid there is nothing more we can do."

The doctor's voice was covered in resignation and Lucas pushed himself from the wall. He stared beyond the doctor, at the thick, brown door to the theatre at the end of the corridor. Alex turned away, the events of the evening finally overwhelming him and he began crying. Starling angrily punched the wall.

"How long has she got?" Lucas mustered a whisper.

"Not long…" Shah said sorrowfully.

Lucas blinked away tears and took a few deep breaths. The leather jacket she'd bought him was soaked through. He slid it off and dropped it on a nearby chair. He rubbed his eyes with the palms of his hands, hoping to remove the evidence of sadness. He then slowly walked past the surgeon and towards the door.

He drew a lungful of air to steady himself, knowing the only thing that awaited him on the other side of the door was what he feared most.

He pushed open the door and entered.

The constant beep of the life-support machine was the only sound in the room, reverberating off the dark walls. Only a few lights were on, directly above the operating table. The sides of the room were smudged with deep, lightless shadows, but Lucas could make out the outline of cupboards and apparatus.

Beep! Beep!

The sterility of the room hung in the air and nearly knocked Lucas to the ground as he inhaled. He refused to look to the centre of the room. He knew Helen was lying on top of the table, illuminated by lights like a grand prize on a game show.

Only this was not a prize Lucas wanted to win.

He slowly approached her, looking in all directions but ahead. He noticed splatters of blood on the cold, tiled floor. Incongruous patches of red amongst the bland white environment which had been scrubbed ferociously but had only slightly faded.

Beep! Beep!

Finally he halted, light engulfing him as he stepped up

to the steel rectangular table. He closed his eyes, his mouth curling up in a scowl. Tears fell down his cheeks.

He looked at Helen.

Instantly his world collapsed the moment he saw her. Lying on her back, her eyes were closed, hidden behind swellings that even now were turning from purple to black. A tube ran from her mouth to a respirator, which was hissing air as the bag inflated and deflated rhythmically. Her lips were swollen, cut and bloodied from what Lucas instantly recognised was a right hook.

He clenched his fists.

More tears rolled down his face.

Beep! Beep!

Helen looked so much smaller, laid out on the table like a china doll. She was motionless, her thin arms resting weightlessly against her petite frame. She was covered by a white cloth but Lucas could see blood stains beginning to soak through.

He trudged around to the side of the bed opposite the life-support machine, adjacent to the blood transfer and breathing apparatus.

All of this just to keep her alive, to keep her safe.

Something he hadn't been able to do.

He ran a hand over the top of her head, his fingers weaving gently through her messy, blonde hair which was now tainted by a few splatters of blood.

He swallowed hard and then very gently scooped up her hand, running his finger over her wedding ring - the symbol of their love binding them together.

"Hello my angel," he whispered quietly, his words feebly dropping into the room. Helen's fingers lightly squeezed Lucas's hand. He looked at her hopefully, a tear dropping onto the table.

Beep! Beep!

"I'm so sorry, Helen. I should have been here. I should

have. When we got married, my love, I made a promise to you. I promised that I would love you every day and I have. God I have!

"But I also promised you that I would look after you. That I would never let anything or anyone hurt you. That I would protect you. I failed you, Helen. I failed.'

Lucas looked at his motionless wife, his heart breaking.

"And I am so, so sorry."

Lucas lowered himself to the side of the bed, his knees resting on the hard, cold floor. He still held Helen's hand, but he bowed his head, sobbing. Resigning himself to going home alone.

A wave of fear washed over him and he was suddenly aware of everything that Helen had done for him. How she had saved him all those years ago and how, throughout the years of their marriage, she had never given up on him.

He felt the first wave crash against the walls she had helped him to build.

"I need you, Helen. I *need* you. I can't control.....I mean, I don't know how to....please don't leave me."

Beep! Beep!

"Please!"

Lucas pushed his head into Helen's chest, his tears immediately absorbed by the sheet. He rested for a moment and cried bitter tears. Helen again, gently squeezed his hand. Lucas pushed himself up, rubbing away the wetness of his eyes with the back of his other arm. He looked at his wife, an avalanche of love falling upon him.

"I need you so much, Helen," he said, meaning every word with every fibre of his being. "I love you so much!"

Abruptly, Helen's swollen eyes flickered and she let the sharp brightness of the lights above her in. Nothing made sense. Her surroundings were unfamiliar, the smell of the room was peculiar. She heard the sound of a machine, and a hissing sound every few seconds. A high-pitched beep, like an alarm from a digital watch, kept piercing her ear drums every few seconds.

The only thing she recognised was Lucas.

She attempted a smile, but pain and something plastic hindered her.

Beep! Beep!

She slid her hand from Lucas's grasp, she was sure she used to be able to do this with minimal fuss. Flashes of her life began to filter through, the moment her and Kelly, her younger sister, had put on a dance show for their parents. When her mum had brought home Buster, the Labrador she would love for thirteen years. The day she'd graduated from university, her dad crying tears of joy at her receiving her degree in psychotherapy.

The moment she'd met Lucas.

Their first kiss.

Walking down the aisle towards him.

Beep! Beep!

Her vision of Lucas was beginning to blur and he looked at her, the bright lights reflecting off his eyes. His strong, handsome face was locked onto hers. She raised her arm, using every inch of effort that she could muster to reach a hand towards his face.

A vision of Lucas surprising her at work with flowers entered her mind and left just as quickly.

She reached beyond his mouth and then with a weak index finger, she pushed the end of his nose up. Lucas broke, the 'pig-nose' causing tears to pour forth and down onto his jumper.

Helen didn't say a word.

A vision of Lucas lying next to her in bed, leaning on his elbows, filtered through bit by bit. The vision was grainy, the colour fading from it. Lucas told her he loved her. The colours all evaporated.

Helen's hand dropped to the table.

Her swollen eyes closed.

The breathing apparatus didn't inflate.

A long, constant beep from the life-support machine.

Helen was gone.

CHAPTER EIGHT

Time became a measurement that would never register with Lucas again. How long he'd remained beside Helen's lifeless body, he would never know nor care. He knelt, his watery eyes fixed on her motionless face. The swollen lids of the beautiful eyes he would never see again. He controlled his breathing, short, sharp exhales as the impending darkness of his lonely future took shape in his mind.

No more surprise presents.

No more security of holding a hand that wanted its fingers interlocked with his.

No more Helen.

A final tear formed in the corner of his eyes; he blinked a few times, his eyes sore. He pushed himself up to his feet, using his free hand to grasp the side of the table to support himself. He took a deep breath, looking down on the body of the woman he loved more than anything.

The one person who had seen the man he truly was.

Who had never given up on him.

Who had pulled him from the abyss.

He gently soothed the back of her hand, his fingers

sliding over her delicate, lifeless skin. Her nails had been painted the pale shade of purple he loved so much. He looked at her for what felt like an eternity, everything around her fading to darkness. He didn't even register the table, just his wife's face. The final tear rolled from his eye lid and took an eternity to roll down his face.

He had no idea how long he'd been standing there for.

He gently slid his hand around her finger, his fingers clamping onto her wedding ring, the humble symbol of their love. It wasn't worth much financially, but that didn't matter. Lucas had never held anything that had meant more to him.

Apart from Helen.

Who he would never hold again.

He gradually eased the ring from her finger and clenched his fist, squeezing so tightly that it left an imprint on his palm. He carefully put his hand into his pocket, releasing the ring so it stayed safely next to his wallet. He gently lowered her hand to the table, letting her fingers slide from his hand as he withdrew it. He took a few more sharp breaths, his heartbeat slowly returning to normal. He placed a hand softly onto her head, running it through her hair. Her face didn't move. No warm smile to accompany the show of affection.

"I love you, Helen."

He quietly whispered it as he leant forward, kissing her warm forehead as softly as he could, like he'd done every morning. He didn't want to wake her.

She was now sleeping peacefully.

He stood up straight and took one last hard breath.

The final tear fell from his jaw.

The splash it caused on the table sent an echo coursing through Lucas. He felt a strange measure of calm.

His fists clenched.

He looked at his wife one final time and then walked away.

It had never been clearer in his mind of what he had to do.

Helen didn't say anything as he left the room.

The moment Lucas had walked through the door to say goodbye to his wife, Starling moved quickly to console Alex. Realising how close this man was to Lucas, and his soon to be departed love, Starling felt so much guilt for not getting to Helen soon enough.

Of course, logically he knew it wasn't his fault. Officer Mills had been right when she'd he had done all he could. But all that resulted in was an overwhelming sense of failure.

He had failed this man who was crying for his fallen friend.

He had failed Lucas, who was having to say his hard goodbye to the love and life he had cherished.

He had failed Helen and her unborn child, both of them eradicated from a world where they would have been surrounded by love.

"It's just so fucking messed up!"

Alex was speaking whispered words between sobs, struggling to get them out over the rapid breaths he was taking. Starling couldn't help but be impressed by the physical peak Alex was in, having been informed that Alex was a Muay Thai instructor when he was told that Helen's husband had been located. Lucas was also a physical specimen and Starling felt a little inadequate that he wasn't in the same shape. He looked after himself, he boxed regularly and competed in long distance running. But he wasn't as obviously capable as these two heartbroken men, whose world had been obliterated by his failure.

No, not his failure.

"We never know why these things happen," Starling said softly, his police training shining through. "There was nothing anyone could have done."

Alex almost chuckled to himself, wiping his eyes with the sleeve of his jacket. Both of them sat on small green chairs, the, white walls illuminated by the loud bulbs. Alex composed himself and turned to the young police officer.

"You try telling that to him."

Alex nodded in the direction of the door, which was closing slowly behind a surprisingly calm-looking Lucas. Colour had begun to return to his cheeks, however his eyes were red and bore the marks of soreness. He didn't wear the mask of someone experiencing heartbreak. Nor did he have the look of a man on the edge.

He exuded calm.

A worrying, almost threatening calm.

Starling immediately stood up, straightening his tie which had long been pulled to the side, and adjusted his damp shirt which had long since been untucked. The strain of the night was visibly showing by his appearance.

Lucas seemed even more imposing, his jumper damp and clinging to his muscular frame. He strode purposefully past the nurses and doctor who rushed into the operating theatre in the vain hope of reviving a woman who had long since left this earth.

Lucas walked straight to Starling.

"Who did this?"

His stare pierced through Starling, who made an instinctive movement of his hand to the police baton on his belt. The words were cold, purposeful.

"Lucas, I understand that this is a difficult time for you and you are emotional...."

"Who did this?"

Starling had to move into a position where he was in control.

"Mr Cole, I advise you to leave this to the Metropolitan Police." He straightened his back, knowing he was not posing any threat to the grieving Lucas. "Go home, rest and begin to think about funeral arrangements."

Lucas shook his head angrily and stared at the ground, pulling his lips tight to stop himself from saying something he would regret. Starling did that for him.

"We will do the best we can."

Lucas looked up at the young officer, his dark eyes betraying any hope he had of trying to show he was calm.

"The best you can?" He looked at the closed door to the theatre, knowing that beyond, nurses would be covering his wife's body with a sheet whilst Dr. Singh announced her time of death. He looked back at Starling, who tried sheepishly to not make eye contact.

"The best you can do has left me without a wife and a child, so don't you tell me...."

"Okay, come on Lucas," Alex pulled an arm around his angry friend, ushering him away from the young officer, who was beginning to get agitated by Lucas's manner.

Alex was fully aware of where Lucas was heading.

"Sir, take him home," Starling valiantly tried to wrestle back his authority in the situation. Alex politely nodded, but before he could apologise, Lucas pushed his arm off and stalked aggressively towards the exit.

His world had been clinging to life by a thread.

A thread that had long since snapped.

Alex stopped himself from chasing after him, allowing Lucas the freedom of his anger and thoughts. Lucas raged down the bright, white corridor, passing a few faces showing their sorrow for the newly widowed. As he slammed open the next set of doors, Helen watched him.

He walked straight past her, not looking back. She was wearing a white gown, which was slightly flowing in non-existent wind, the edges not defined and ending in a blur of white. Her hair was swaying slightly atop of her now fully healed face, her piercing blue eyes filling with tears.

None of her edges were defined. She seemed to smudge around the outline, as if someone had coloured her in with felt tips but hadn't stayed within the guidelines. Her words hung in the air as she did.

"Don't lose control!"

Lucas continued down the corridor.

"Don't let this happen, Lucas."

She called out, her voice resonating through his body like a single shout in an auditorium. It echoed through every tunnel of his body and he stopped in place.

Helen was gone.

He reminded himself a few more times.

Helen was gone.

She didn't move: he wasn't even sure if her feet were there. He turned his head slightly to the side, taking a few moments to decide whether to respond to this incomplete projection of his wife.

"It already has."

Lucas resumed his march to the exit, into the long forever of loneliness and a life of constant absence. He turned right before the lift, hurling open the door to the stairs and disappeared through the doorway.

The vision of Helen had disappeared long before that.

———

The journey back up to Brinscall was shrouded in a heavy silence. Alex had sobered up sufficiently, the emotional weight of the evening plus a few bottles of water had enabling him to take the wheel.

The endless dark of the road, interspersed by oncoming headlights seemed to last an eternity. The rain still fell down, but even that didn't register to any of the passengers as a problem anymore.

The emotional avalanche had taken its toll on Dianne, and she lay asleep on the back seat under Alex's coat, her hands protectively over her stomach. Inside, her growing baby was sound asleep.

Lucas stared straight ahead through the windscreen, worrying Alex with his lack of anything. No words. No movements. A statue of a man with nothing other than fury in his eyes.

Alex wanted to reach out to him, say words that would somehow soften a blow that could never be repaired. He felt inadequate, knowing full well that a few feet behind them slept his entire family whilst only a few hours ago, his best friend had lost his in its entirety.

On they drove.

Away from the nightmare.

And into a new one.

Starling turned the keys in his front door, the metal jingling against solid wood. It opened with a soft creak and he flicked on the light switch with a lazy hand.

His flat instantly brightened, revealing a modest-sized living room with store-bought furniture that needed a woman's touch. He kicked out behind him after he'd entered, the door slamming shut and possibly waking a neighbour or two. He didn't care, dropping his keys and his coat where he stood.

He didn't allow himself the luxury of crying, this was part of the job. He had to take the failures with the successes.

He walked slowly through the front room, past the leather sofa and the coffee table, dropping his personal effects on its oaken top. They hit the wood with a clatter, yet he carried on walking, past the kitchen and into the small, clean bathroom. He pulled the cord to summon the light and stared at himself in the mirror.

He felt like he'd aged a decade in a single night, the bags under his eyes prominent, as if he'd been punched with all of somebody's might.

He thought of Helen.

He bent over, turned on the cold tap and splashed water on his face and on his short, blonde hair in an attempt to cool down. His hands clenched the rim of the sink, tightening with anger as his knuckles turned white.

He had failed.

He looked up into the mirror again, making a sworn promise to himself that he would not let her, or this case, disappear like so many others had done. That he would make sure those responsible would pay with interest.

He left the room abruptly, plunging it into darkness as he exited. He turned left, through the next door and without even turning on the light, collapsed onto his double bed.

He hit the mattress and felt the trials of the day lift from him like dust from an old cushion. He hadn't realised how tired he was until he'd lazily kicked off his heavy boots and gave up undressing himself.

He thought of Annette, how he should introduce her to his father.

His father who was so proud.

'You done well there, son.'

Not tonight, Dad. Not tonight.

Starling slipped into a dreamless sleep.

———

The car came to a slow stop at the end of Lucas's gate, the house appearing much larger now that only one person was returning to it. The rain wasn't as heavy, caressing the vehicle with a gentle, wet rapping.

As soon as Alex cut the ignition, Lucas unclipped his seat belt and reached for the door handle.

"Hey Lucas..." Lucas turned to Alex, appreciating the gesture as his best friend searched for any words of comfort. Alex smiled at him, admitting defeat. "If there's anything we can do...."

"Thanks, Alex," Lucas nodded. He turned and looked at Dianne, still sleeping off the pain.

Alex tried but again gave up on saying anything and Lucas got out, closing the door quietly. Alex watched as the man approached the gate, apprehensive to reach out and open it. He finally did so, hesitantly, before stepping up to the front door.

Lucas refused to look at the front garden, knowing that only a few days ago he'd made a mental schedule for how he and his wife were going to recreate it. Make it a garden they would be proud of.

Their home.

It was now only his.

He held the key in his hand and took a deep breath. He heard Alex's car start, the engine purring before vanishing into the night with the headlights big and bright.

He unlocked the door and pushed it open. Nothing but empty darkness.

It was a feeling Lucas was becoming familiar with.

———

The next five days passed as they normally did, however Lucas didn't know when one day slipped into the next. He was neither awake nor asleep, seamlessly drifting from one room to the next without a memory of how he'd arrived there.

The phone rang constantly, names he'd forgotten offering condolences which failed to register.

He had visitors at the house, friendly faces that he couldn't place, offering genuine affection that he would never remember.

Life had become one long trance, as if he was floating through a horrible, never-ending dream. No one had questioned his decision to not go into work. John, at least Lucas thought it was John, had told him to take as much time as he needed. He had a vague recollection that he had a morning routine, but he never even tried to remember.

It was five days of not quite being there, days in which Lucas never left the house. The only thing he focused on was planning the funeral alongside Helen's parents, although they spoke very little.

Words had lost weight and meaning.

Everything had become a tedious exercise in existing.

Even tying the knot in his black tie felt superfluous, his hands on autopilot. He looked around the bedroom he used to share with his beloved, all of her possessions exactly how she'd left them.

All, except the jewellery box that she kept on her dressing table. It now sat proudly on the bedside table, Lucas opening the lid and listening to the clunky tune chiming fragilely as the ballerina pirouetted. It helped him drift off on the rare occasions he did sleep. Treasured by his now deceased wife, she had kept it throughout her childhood, using it to store all of her keepsakes in, the majority from her husband.

He missed her terribly.

He pulled the blazer over his broad shoulders, fastening it then making his way outside, as ready as he would ever be, to bury his wife.

The drive was a long, lonely venture, but it gave Fletcher time to rehearse what he would say. Knowing what it was like to lose the person you relied on as a link to the world, he felt for Lucas. He wanted to wrap an arm around him and offer him words of encouragement to fight off the inevitable cage of isolation.

It was never going to happen.

He knew the man Lucas had been. He knew how much Helen had done for him, and as he drove to the cemetery, he thought of what that might mean for the future.

It had been a long time ago, nearly eighteen years since he'd sat opposite Lucas in a police interrogation cell, a scrawny fourteen year-old with hate in his eyes. Ten years since Fletcher had last gone to visit him.

He knew that he would stand across from him again, only now he would be bigger. Stronger.

More dangerous.

Helen had done so much for the man.

But he could guarantee that the hate in his eyes would still be there.

As he pulled off the motorway and the wind whipped mercilessly against the side of his car, he knew he wouldn't have long to wait before he found out.

Lucas couldn't watch as Helen's coffin was ready to be lowered into the immaculate grounds of the cemetery. The bitterness of the wind rattled through his body and he felt an overwhelming sense of oblivion. Life as he had known it was now officially over.

The cemetery was, despite its overtones of death and

loss, a very beautiful place. The grass was well maintained, and the small fields of grave stones were lined by flower beds, with colours bursting through in the spring showers. Large trees overhung the pathways used to navigate the grounds, family members being covered by branches as they approached their loved ones.

Helen's spot was a wonderful one, at the top of a slight verge overlooking the woodlands to the south of the cemetery. Her parents had chosen the spot, knowing their frequent visits in their daughter's memory would bring them here often.

Lucas looked around at the attendees, lines of people who had loved his wife and those who had been touched by her at some point.

He saw his work colleagues standing a few rows back on the other side of Helen's final resting place, John wrapping an arm around his wife who sobbed into her handkerchief.

The priest was intoning his sermon as Helen was committed to the bosom of the earth, his words floating on the wind and barely reaching Lucas. He looked over the rows of black-clad mourners, smart suits and respectful dresses betokening the sadness and heartbreak of the day.

His mother-in-law stood next to him, crying heavily while whispering a sweet goodbye to her daughter. Her husband, a doting father, held her hand as silent tears fell from him, both staring forlornly at the ground.

Alex and Dianne stood behind Lucas, Alex resting a reassuring hand on his shoulder when the magnitude of the day threatened to encompass him.

Behind his work colleagues, situated in the back row, was an old man who appeared familiar. A face from a past that Lucas had tried hard remove.

He couldn't place him.

"And so we commit Helen's body to the ground."

The priest was entering the final phase of his duty and Lucas forced himself to watch as Helen was finally lowered, the grave digger waiting patiently beyond the trees to the right.

Everybody said their goodbyes to Helen, the majority through sobs, but others in the silence of their thoughts. The group began to disperse, all heading back to the house he'd shared with Helen to celebrate her memory. Lucas stood for a few moments on his own with his hands stuffed in his pockets, looking down at the varnished box. The flower emblem on the front was striking. On the other side of the wood lay his wife.

She had been taken from him too soon.

He clenched his fists inside the pockets, his fingers wrapping around the wedding ring he'd given her all those years ago.

They took her from me.

"Lucas."

He turned, the voice opening a memory he'd long since locked away. The voice belonged to a friendly face which was lined with sadness. Wrinkles had changed it and the hair atop was thinner and lacking in colour.

"I am so sorry," Fletcher offered.

"Thank you," Lucas forced an appreciative smile. "It would have meant a lot to Helen that you were here."

"You remember me?"

"Of course I do, Officer."

"Oh I haven't been an officer for a while," Fletcher chuckled. He seemed friendly, but Lucas could sense there was more to his being here.

"Apologies," Lucas nodded, making a few movements to suggest he was looking to leave.

"She was an amazing woman. She did so much for a lot of people."

Lucas forced out his tried and trusted smile again and

took a few steps away from Fletcher, heading over to the car park.

"She did a lot for you."

Lucas stopped in his tracks. He knew why Fletcher was here. The old man from the past took a few steps towards the recently widowed. The wind blew hard, sweeping up both of their ties, Lucas's fringe flickering as it blew through. Leaves danced down the pathway.

"I know what it's like, Lucas. It's never easy to bury a loved one."

"But I'm not, am I?' Lucas turned, his question rhetorical. "I'm not just burying one."

"I know, son. It's not easy, I know."

"You know, do you? Someone took away my wife and my unborn child. You know what that's like, do you?"

Fletcher couldn't answer. He stood silently, the anger rising in Lucas.

"I am so sorry, Lucas."

"Everyone is sorry. I understand." Lucas clenched his fist around the wedding ring again, trying his hardest to hold onto his calm. "But whoever did this to her is not. And they are still out there."

'I know, and I wanted to be here today to offer my respects to your remarkable wife, to offer my sincerest condolences and to also assure you that the police are doing everything they can."

Lucas shook his head, almost chuckling.

"It's been five days. Five long days and I haven't had a single phone call to tell me what's going on. Not one arrest has been made. Not one avenue has been found. I was told in the aftermath that they suspected it was more than one person, but since then, I've heard nothing. And you want me to put my faith in that?'

Fletcher felt small.

"We're doing the best we can."

The words failed to register with Lucas. He just looked at Fletcher, remembering the conversation they'd had all those years ago. How he felt, out of all of the people in his life at that point, Fletcher was the only one he could trust. And here he was, all these years later, at the worst moment of Lucas's life, feeding him the same line the young officer did at the hospital.

It needed to be more than that.

Lucas turned and walked off, wanting to end this day once and for all. Fletcher could only stand and watch, as the angry form of Lucas grew smaller and smaller, taking steps to an anarchy that Fletcher feared might happen.

Lucas received all of the more intimate condolences, everyone wanting to see how he was and tell him that, if he needed anything, he could call. He politely went through the motions, thanking people for coming and telling them how much it meant.

In reality, Lucas wanted the house empty.

He wanted to be alone with his grief, not so he could beat it, but so he could embrace it. He wanted to cry for Helen, but since that final tear had dropped on her death bed he hadn't been able to.

He couldn't recall much of what had happened since that night; he didn't even know how he'd returned from the funeral. His mind was focused on one thing and one thing only and he wanted to be left alone with that thought.

Fletcher had headed home from the cemetery and Lucas had felt bad for how their reunion had gone. Fletcher was one of the few people he knew he could trust in a world that was increasingly turning its back on him. The old detective had left a contact card with Alex, along with a promise that if Lucas needed anything he would do his best.

Lucas would see him soon anyway.

Without remembering how, Lucas found himself sitting on the edge of his bed in the room that once shook with love but now felt empty and hollow. He leaned back, flicking on the bedside lamp and picking up Helen's treasured jewellery box.

He held it in his hand for a few moments, feeling the weight of it and thinking of his wife's beautiful hands reaching into it. He opened it up and instantly, the poorly painted, plastic ballerina danced her never-ending twirl.

The shrill chimes played an undistinguished tune.

Lucas sat and watched.

He listened and he grieved.

"I can't believe she still had that."

Lucas looked up, locking eyes with Kelly. Helen's younger sister stood in the doorway, a look of understanding across her beautiful face. In many ways she looked like Helen: she had the same piercing blue eyes, however her hair was longer and was a dirtier blonde. She was slightly taller than her older sister and she carried herself well when she walked. Like a model.

Dressed in black, she looked at her brother-in-law warmly, who seemed almost embarrassed to be caught. He slowly closed the box, placing it on the bed covers and pushed himself to his feet.

'How are you?' Kelly asked as she took a few steps into the room.

Lucas gave her a nod, not wanting to speak. He opened up the wardrobe, the smell of Helen radiating off her clothes still hanging there. The smell reminded him of home.

Of happiness.

Kelly sat down on the edge of the bed, running her

hands over the jewellery box, smiling as it filled her with thoughts of her sister.

"Growing up, Helen always looked after me. I mean, it was silly, she was only a year and a half older, but she seemed so grown up. I always looked up to her. She always made sure she was there for me. Looking out for me.

"That's just the person she was I guess. Always putting people first. But not with you Lucas. With you, she put herself first because you were what she wanted. And she was so happy with you."

Lucas had pulled a sports bag down from the top shelf of the wardrobe, but he let his arms fall to the side upon hearing that final sentence. He took a deep breath and wanted to thank her for reaffirming Helen's belief in their relationship. Kelly opened the box.

The shrill chimes returned.

Kelly continued.

"I know I'm going to miss her. I feel bad that I don't right now but it's because it hasn't sunk in. But when it does, I know I'm going to want her above all other people. My big sister. The one person who kept me calm during moments of anger and the one who always held me tightly through the moments of pain."

Lucas was slowly stuffing a few t-shirts into his bag, along with pairs of socks and boxer shorts. Kelly closed the lid slowly, the chimes quieting before being shut out from the world. She stood up, wiping away a tear that had tried to clamber down her cheek. Lucas turned to face her. She sniffed back a few tears before speaking.

"Please don't let everything she did to help you become the man you are unravel."

She held out the jewellery box, the final link to Helen Lucas could hold on to. The unravelling had already begun and he looked beyond Kelly to the doorway.

Helen was standing there, her incomplete form

haunting the hall way. She looked longingly at her husband, whose eyes were transfixed on her.

"Take it, Lucas," her voice echoed, "Please take it."

Kelly looked up at her brother-in-law, his eyes looking beyond her and into the vast distance of a life alone. She loved Lucas, he was a wonderful man and had treated her sister so well. She knew he blamed himself and she wanted to wrap her arms around him and tell him he wasn't alone in his grief.

That he still had a family.

The spectre of Helen spoke, but only to Lucas.

"Please don't go, Lucas."

Lucas snapped back into the room, Kelly refocused in his vision and he could see the tears falling down her cheeks. He gently reached out a hand and placed it on the jewellery box. Very softly he pushed it back towards Kelly.

"You keep that. Your sister would have wanted you to have it."

Kelly sniffed, nodding in agreement. Lucas's words were soft and loving.

"I'll keep it safe for you."

"I won't be coming back."

Lucas looked to the doorway, seeing nothing but an empty staircase. Kelly looked down at the jewellery box, running her fingers over its carved pattern.

"What are you going to do?" she asked, looking up at Lucas. He was a different man. His face was blank as if he'd reset any visible signs of pain. His words were cold and to the point.

"Helen was left to die alone, scared and in a hell of a lot of pain."

Lucas picked up his leather jacket, the last loving gift Helen had given him. He slid his muscular arms in, a sense of purpose radiating off him. He looked at her sister.

"And they're all going to go the same way."

Kelly sobbed gently, knowing this was their goodbye. Lucas picked up his packed bag and approached Kelly. He wiped away one of her tears, granted her one final smile and then turned and left her clutching her sister's precious possession.

She heard the front door open and close behind him.

AN EXTRACT FROM 'LIFE ON THE BEAT: MEMOIRS OF A THIRTY-YEAR POLICE OFFICER.' BY PAUL FLETCHER.

I always find it rather phony, or rather clichéd, when that moment happens in films. You know the one, when the hero has that moment which causes him to change. When he realises what his mission is. When a new purposes breaks out of his chest like an unwanted alien.

I always thought it was a ridiculous notion.

Until I'd seen Lucas.

It had been so long, I'd almost forgotten how innocent his eyes were. I'm not that way inclined, however you can't help but realise he was a handsome man. He and Helen were stunning together.

What a child they would have had.

It was the innocence in his eyes that led me to believe him, all those years ago, when he'd sat across from me. Fourteen years-old, and already a lifetime of horrors and bad memories. A world trapped within a bubble of anger. But his eyes never relinquished that pain.

His eyes called for help.

Help is what I sought for him. The skipper at the time, Sergeant Horlock, he just wanted to throw the book at him. Book him and send him off to juvie, where he would end up another statistic further down the road and spend a life that would never have compared to the one he'd with Helen.

She'd been so good for him.

So good.

I will never forget that horrible day when she was taken from this world. When someone as good and as pure as she'd been could be wrenched from a life she'd built with her true love and to be thrown away like yesterday's newspaper.

And when I'd witnessed the earth swallow her up, her body confined to an eternity inside a small, wooden box, it had broken my heart. It had reminded me of my own daughters, how a few days before that, my eldest, Annabelle, had told me I wasn't good enough. How I couldn't be a part of her family until I realised what it meant.

Looking at Lucas that day, how could I not understand anymore?

He'd stared at that hole in the ground, his one and everything being lowered slowly to a place he would never get to. He'd stood calmly, even as the wind had rattled through the cemetery and as the members of his family and faces of his life had drowned the air with their cries of sorrow.

He'd stared in silence.

And that was the moment. That clichéd moment.

Lucas wasn't the same man he'd been when he'd put on that tie. He'd radiated a purpose, as if he had something he needed to do or somewhere he needed to be.

I look back on it now and I know I should have done more to convince him to believe in the boys in blue. But how can you stop a force of nature, driven by such sorrow and grief?

The answer is you can't.

Did I help him? No I didn't.

Did I stop him? Again, no.

Did I know what was coming?

Truth be told, I did. However, I never believed it would come on such a scale, that a reaction could be so brutal and so forward.

That moment, when Lucas had watched Helen get stored away within the confines of this planet, he changed.

And there had been nothing ridiculous about it.

CHAPTER NINE

Officer Starling slammed his locker door shut with a loud clang and rested against it. The week since Helen had died had been the longest of his life. Constant briefings about plans of action and fruitless follow-ups on witness accounts had led nowhere. He exhaled wearily, the air rushing out of him as his nightshift came to an end.

Annette would be waiting at home - she was on nights as well this week which meant he got to spend more time with her. It was the only thing getting him through. Despite the warnings of his closest friends, he was happy to give her a key to his flat just four months into their relationship.

He already knew he loved her.

Dressed in casual clothes, he wandered out of the locker room and through the busy station, picturing running his hands over her smooth, bronzed skin. He passed the briefing room, where he noticed a few officers taking seats, a few others conversing at the back of the room about last night's football.

Officer Boulder was at the back of the room, pouring coffee from a canteen into a plastic cup. Starling ducked into the conference room, nodding politely at a few of his comrades before approaching his usually chirpy partner.

"Hey Henry!" he smiled.

"Hey Ollie!" returned in kind. "How you been?"

"I'm good, man. I'm good. Yourself?"

"Same old. No sleep. No sex."

"The joys of parenthood, eh?"

Boulder chuckled, taking a sip of his piping hot coffee and struggling with the burn. His eyes were dark, the sleepless nights evident. Starling missed working with him, but the events of a week ago and the new born baby meant Boulder had requested day shifts.

It made sense.

Starling looked around the room, which was now almost full with officers about to begin their day. At the front of the room was a lectern, positioned in front of a whiteboard. Information and instructions were plastered all over it, the ink suggesting the wrong marker had been used. The smell of coffee filled the air and Starling realised how tired he was. The clock on the far wall was at almost half past eight.

Annette would be home any minute now. He turned to Boulder, who was struggling with another boiling gulp.

"What's the briefing?"

"Fuck that's hot!" Boulder held a hand to his mouth and Starling chuckled. He could always count on him to make him smile. "Oh, Bailey is on his way in."

"Sergeant Bailey?"

"No, the Old Bailey. Of course Sergeant Bailey!"

Before Starling could ask why, Sergeant Robert Bailey strode into the room, immediately commanding attention. Bailey was a towering man, his broad shoulders sitting beneath a powerful jawline. Age had caught up with him, but he still had much of the large, heavyset physique that had made him so feared when he was on the beat. His hair, whilst still thick and well parted to the side, was a fine shade of grey. Some officers made the odd comment that he'd gone soft, that the last six years spent behind the desk had whittled his fear factor away.

The intensity in his bespectacled eyes told Starling something different.

"Right people." His voice boomed as he marched to the front of the room. He forcefully slammed his helmet on the lectern, all heads turning to the front.

The room fell silent.

"It's been a week. And... Starling, what are you doing here?"

"I was on my way out, sir."

"You're welcome to stay. You'll hear this later anyway, but it may be of interest to you."

Starling nodded, hiding a smile that that threatened to form due to the fact that Bailey knew him instantly despite limited time working together. Bailey addressed the room, powerful hands on powerful hips.

"It's been a week. A goddamned week! And we have nothing, not one sniff of a fucking lead and that, people, is not good enough.'

A few murmurs flew around the room, worried whispers that Starling couldn't place. He looked to his right and was surprised to see Fletcher standing in the doorway. The old man was leaning against the doorframe, his clothes neatly ironed as always. He was wearing a smart tie and a warm smile. He sent it in Starling's direction.

"I don't need to tell you how it works around here, do I? The powers above have sent word down that unless we can find something on the Cole case quick, and I mean fucking lightning, then resources will be pulled and it will most likely get benched.

"Let's get one thing straight here. I don't want what happened to this poor woman to be forgotten. We've all got families. Loved ones. Most of you probably have a gorgeous wife or girlfriend to go home to. Or a fella, I don't give a shit. But all of us have what was taken from this woman. A life."

The words resonated around the assembled officers, all taking the words to heart. A few uncomfortable shuffles as they thought about losing the person they loved the most. Bailey didn't move, his power stance appearing to cast a shadow over the entire squad before him.

"We will *not* let this fall off the map!" His words were hard and Starling knew he meant every one of them. "So if anyone here has anything they'd like to suggest, or has an idea they'd like to throw out, then now is the time."

He cast his piercing brown eyes over the sea of faces, pupils burning like coal behind his glasses. Several of the officers looked around, expecting someone else to show bravery. Starling looked to Fletcher, whose caring, experienced gaze fell upon the room. Bailey was looking less compassionate.

"For fuck's sake, this poor girl was brutally murdered!"

"What about the Draytons?"

The entire room fell deathly silent, the walls absorbing the remnants of Bailey's voice so only Starling's hung in the air. Every face and set of eyes in the room swivelled and fell on Starling, who immediately began to feel the room closing in. Boulder directed a few gazes at the man, motioning with a flick of his head that he himself didn't suggest such a thing.

Bailey loosened his arms at his side and brought one of them up, running his large, powerful fingers over the bridge of his nose. He massaged under his glasses and sighed. Starling nervously swallowed. The rest of the room watched the Sergeant with anticipation.

"Starling. Let's not go there, shall we?"

The room fell silent, all eyes back on Starling.

"But sir, like you said, we need options otherwise this will just get blown away."

"I'm very aware of what I said, Officer."

'Then why are we not considering the Drayton's?'

Starling suddenly became aware of the raised volume of his voice and the furious expression on Bailey's face which told him he had overstepped his mark. Boulder looked sheepishly at the floor. Fletcher had moved, no longer attending the meeting.

Starling felt completely alone. A lone voice in a vast sea of emptiness.

"Seeing as how Officer Starling wants to know so badly, why don't I tell him, and all of you, while we're here?" Bailey straightened up, immediately restoring the authority that the young officer had challenged.

"We are all aware of the Draytons, what they've done in the past and what many claim they still do. However, it is always easy to pin crimes on them because you know they'll go away. And I will NOT allow that to happen with this case, despite how much Starling may want it."

"Sir, with all due respect, that was not my intention." Starling told himself to be quiet, but he didn't listen.

"With all due respect Starling, I was out on the streets dealing with the Draytons while you were sucking milk out of your mum's tit, so I will tell *you* what we are going to do.

"We are *not* going to try and implicate the Draytons in this attack. I know for a fact that we have people in different places looking into them. The last thing they want is one of you lot sticking your nose in, and the last thing I want is the fucking headache that will bring."

Starling stood silently, looking around at the room of people who had retreated into their shells.

No one stood alongside him.

It was a tough lesson. One he would learn again in the week to come.

Bailey had calmed, the veins in his large, triangular neck no longer throbbing. His face had returned to a normal colour. He still commanded respect.

"The Draytons is a cage we do not want to rattle."

Starling nodded, holding back his tongue. Bailey stared at him, his curiosity piqued by the scrappy, young officer. Starling turned and stormed out of the room, pushing past Boulder, who had done nothing to back his partner up. Bailey raised his eyebrows, almost in admiration that one person in the room had the stones to stand up to him. He turned back to the weakened herd in the room.

"So, if any of you have anything you want to chase up or look into, today is the day to do it." He picked up a small manila folder on the lectern and slid out a sheet. He pinned it to the whiteboard and all eyes drew their attention toward it.

It was a photo of Helen. She was smiling.

The smile was for her husband, who was on the other side of the camera.

"I don't want people to forget that this girl was brutally murdered." Bailey looked at the photo, a twinge of compassion jolting him like a cattle prod. "Dismissed!"

Fletcher lowered himself slowly into a leather seat, the pain stabbing his back like a dagger. Age was catching up and since Helen had died he'd hardly been at his house.

He thought back to the pain in Lucas's eyes, the realisation that his entire world had been decimated. His future, once decorated with the fruitful hopes of a family life and the wondrous chuckles of children was replaced with a barren wasteland of isolation.

He needed to work for the distraction.

Poor Helen.

He raised his hands to his eyes, rubbing away the sleep that was trying its best to wrestle control. As his eyes readjusted to the light of the room, he saw an angry Starling storming through the doors and out into whatever his day held for him.

Fletcher liked Starling. He was going to make a fine detective one day, however he didn't want to witness Bailey rip him a new one in front of the other officers. It appeared that was exactly what had happened.

Fletcher let out a sigh and flopped open the plastic binder on his desk and flicking a few pages. He picked up his red pen and immediately began highlighting the areas that needed his attention.

It was coming near to the end of the month and a lot of budget cuts had been ordered from above. Fletcher was looking through the last six months of expense reports, highlighting trends and potential places to save money.

Sadly, he found himself enjoying it.

Hours passed, coffees were drunk and lunch was consumed in spite of its tastelessness. Fletcher was down to the final few pages, knowing full well he had another two folders to get through by the end of the week. He pushed his glasses up his nose and concentrated, the figures not quite adding up. He clicked the back of the red pen in preparation.

A dusty folder dropped onto his desk.

The noise startled him and he sat upright in his chair. Dust lifted gracefully off the file and settled down like snowflakes over the papers on his desk. He looked up, into the warm, freckled and overweight smile of Officer McCarthy.

"Thanks," Fletcher pretended to cough and splutter, fanning away the dust cloud with his hand.

"Don't mention it!" McCarthy's strong, Irish accent was happier today than the last time they'd spoken.

"What is it, can I ask?"

"I don't know. Some pretty young lass from Archives brought it to me. She'd confused me for you, the cheeky mare. I'm twenty years younger than you, I told her."

"It's because you look wise beyond your years, Pat."

"The hell I do. It's because I'm a fat, overweight bastard and they think I look like a volunteer."

Fletcher laughed out loud, a few heads in the office turning to see why. McCarthy was well known for his sense of humour.

"Thank you for bringing it over."

"No problem. I only got a dodgy knee an' all, but don't you worry." McCarthy began to limp away, overacting the difficulty his injury caused him.

"I owe you a beer for this."

"Oh I know, Fletch," he smiled back over his shoulder while hobbling away. "I'm keeping tabs."

Fletcher grinned at his friend, who limped his way to the door and disappeared into the corridor. Suddenly, a sense of guilt fell over him as he placed a hand on the yellow folder, a thin layer of brown dust coating it.

He thought of failing people, those who had depended on him but whose faith had never been justified.

He thought of Susan, her beautiful smile even to her dying day. How she'd never let go of his hand, even in death.

He thought of the past. How people could bury pain and trauma so far into it, behind so many walls and locks that they believed it would never return.

He ran a hand across the folder, wiping away the dust to reveal the writing.

He took a deep breath as his eyes fell on it.

London Institute of Mental Health – *Classified*

Cole, Lucas Joseph (No: 33875)

The National Express coach ground to a halt just outside Marble Arch Underground Station. The door flapped open with a loud hiss, the passengers all flocking out onto the walkway below. For a Sunday morning, Oxford Street was relatively quiet, although Lucas was more than familiar with this being the less busy end of the famous road. He casually exited the coach, not needing to wait around for the driver to pull the huge luggage bags from the storage compartment, an impatient mob forming around him.

He swung the sports bag over his shoulder and pulled the collar of his beloved leather jacket up with his free hand. The air was calm, one of the finer days that spring had offered so far. He looked around, taking a deep breath as he slowly stepped onto London concrete. Besides the horror at The Royal London hospital a week ago, it was the first time he'd voluntarily ventured to the capital in eight years.

The traffic sounded the same; buses hurtling down the main road, black cabs ducking in and out of small pockets of space between the traffic. A large group of German tourists, kids mainly, trundled by, excitedly taking pictures of buildings that were identical to ones anywhere else in the city.

The journey down had been relatively smooth, a few minor build ups of traffic but it was expected on a Sunday. Lucas had not slept properly since the night before he'd buried his wife and suddenly that tiredness began to constrict him like an anaconda.

He checked the envelope inside his jacket, thick and rectangular. The conversation with the bank manager on the previous Friday had been awkward, almost intrusive, but Lucas had somehow channelled Alex's power of speech and talked his way through. He had taken a large chunk from the savings account he'd had with Helen, almost eight thousand pound.

That would be enough.

That would see him through.

He couldn't remember much about Saturday, only the image of the coffin being lowered into the ground, his wife's body being stored away like unwanted furniture.

A shot of pain jolted Lucas back to life. He marched up Oxford Street, weaving in and out of slow-moving shoppers and map wielding tourists.

He passed Selfridge's and Bond Street Station, continuing up the long stretch of concrete jungle. The smells of the inner city filtered through and memories of feeling trapped and imprisoned came back. Lucas longed for the open fields of green surrounding his village.

As he got to Tottenham Court Road, he turned right, heading down to Leicester Square. A lot of theatre-goers were already waiting to see the latest shows, which had added lunchtime matinee showings at weekends to the bill. Through the waves of faceless people, Lucas eventually made his way to Soho Square. He walked through the gates and into the well-maintained park. On the small, trimmed fields, a few dogs ran off the lead, their elderly owners struggling to catch up with them. On the far field, some students were tossing a frisbee back and forth. The sun threatened to peek its head over the clouds and share itself with the world.

Lucas continued down the pathway cutting through the grounds, spotting at a large white pavilion sitting proudly to the right of the square.

Throughout the park were a number of sculptures, designed to bring a sense of culture and beauty to these already calming grounds. Lucas had always loved this place; this was where he and Helen had always come when they were allowed time outside.

He continued onwards until he rounded a small corner leading to the far exit. There, in the middle of a clearing, stood Kind Charles II, proudly carved in stone and displayed to the world.

Lucas ambled up to the royal figure, circling until he came face to face with it. Memories flooded back, the dam breaking as they came flowing through. Feeling weak, Lucas stumbled over to the damp, wooden bench opposite, his bag dropping to the ground between his feet.

His hand slithered into his pocket, the fingers gliding over the gold wedding ring.

He tilted his head back, closed his eyes and thought of Helen.

The sounds of the world faded out.

He didn't even feel the hours pass while he slept.

―――

Starling lay awake in his bed, naked and still sweaty. Annette had met him as soon as he'd walked in, her mood also soured by a long, night shift. Their combined frustrations exploded into rather aggressive intercourse which had knocked the life right out of them.

Starling had woken earlier than he'd intended. He didn't need to be back at the station for another few hours. He turned onto his side, staring at the smooth curves of Annette's back, her blonde hair lying carelessly across her shoulders.

He ran a finger lovingly down her spine and she moaned slightly, shifting between the sheets. Starling smiled.

He was falling in love.

The events of the morning still resonated with him, his anger at the lack of justice and bravery was gnawing at him like a termite. He tried, unsuccessfully, to get back to sleep.

Fletcher drove lazily back from the station, the day having shifted seamlessly into night without him noticing. Sergeant Bailey had almost forced him out of the door.

"You have to go home at some point, Fletch."

He was right, but since Annabelle's damnation and Helen's death, Fletcher had felt nothing but coldness in the real world. Behind his desk he had a place, where he was contributing.

Outside the station and away from his desk, he felt as if he was just taking up space.

He turned off Southampton Row and headed up to Euston. He had fifteen minutes until he would be parking outside the empty house, to spend another evening accompanied by cigarette smoke and Jack Daniel's.

The dusty folder sat, amongst many others, on the passenger seat.

He wanted to smoke, but he'd promised Susan years ago he would not smoke in the car and as foolish as it might seem, he'd decided to keep his word.

Under the glow of street lamps, Fletcher guided his car home without incident, pulling into the space allocated to his house within the small housing estate where he resided.

He juggled the forms in his arms, his hand fiddling with his jingling keys until he pressed the button to remote lock his vehicle. The wind had grown, a wild gust funnelling through the narrow streets, sending a few papers shooting from the sheets he was clutching.

"Shit!"

He struggled to bend down, the aches of age sending a painful reminder. As he scrambled a few of them from the ground, one blew across the street slightly, until a hand reached down and lifted it from the cold, wet concrete. Fletcher saw shoes behind it and his gaze followed up, past the leather jacket, to the unshaven face of Lucas Cole.

He stood in stunned silence. In the distance he could hear traffic, submerged under a faint whistle of wind.

Lucas offered a smile.

"Need a hand?"

Fletcher couldn't find any words, shaking panic from his head. Lucas gently reached out and took the large pile of forms from him, the papers almost weightless in his powerful arms. Fletcher looked around quickly, the street was empty.

"Thank you, Lucas." He nodded towards the door. "Come on in."

Lucas smiled his thanks, the wind blowing his hair chaotically. Fletcher unlocked the front door and ushered his unexpected guest into the warmth of the house that he found so cold.

As Lucas disappeared into his home, Fletcher took one last careful scan of the street, assessing the situation, and then shut the world behind him.

CHAPTER TEN

"Look at you; you're pathetic."

Curtis Drayton was only eleven years old when he'd seen his father's dark side for the first time. George Drayton was nothing more than hired help for the local crime lord, Billy Mulgrave. Although George didn't have much of an education, he had a lot of muscle and a short fuse. That night, George had faced the wrath of Mulgrave over being too light on those who owed him money.

Mulgrave had humiliated him in front of everyone.

When George returned home to their small rundown house just outside of East Ham, it only took him ten minutes to strike Curtis's mother. The dinner was modest, the healthiest meal a mother could string together on a shoestring budget. It wasn't good enough in his rage-filled eyes and he thanked her with a right hook. She packed her bags and left her children behind with their violent, brute of a father.

Curtis never saw her again.

He'd wished death upon her every day until he heard of her passing.

George wasn't finished, his rage taking over. Curtis put Tommy and Ashley in their bedrooms, each one shared with the younger Lewis or Harry. Curtis returned to the dinner table where George was waiting.

'What the fuck are you looking at, you little prick?'

George was already halfway through his fourth beer, a small speckle of white powder clinging from his nose hair.

"Nothing."

"Nothing what?" George thumped the wooden table, the cutlery and plates leaping off it.

"Nothing, sir."

"That's right! Some respect, at fucking last!" He finished his beer, crushed the can in one mighty hand and threw it at Curtis. It struck him just under the eye, drawing blood and leaving Curtis with a permanent reminder.

"Don't you dare fucking cry!" George pointed at his son, who was holding a blood-covered hand to his cheek. "I will not have a fucking pussy for a son, do you hear me?"

Curtis nodded, holding back the pain. George retrieved another beer from the fridge, leaning against the kitchen side. He sneered at his son, who was taking deep breaths.

"Eat your dinner."

Curtis looked at his plate over his hand, the chicken and vegetable serving suddenly looking very unappetising.

"I'm not hungry."

"Excuse me?" George pushed himself off the wall, taking another large swig of his beer. Curtis tried not to cower.

"I'm not hungry. I don't feel well."

"That's because a growing boy needs his vegetables."

George scooped a handful of vegetables off the plate and slapped Curtis across the jaw with them. Curtis crashed off his seat and onto the floor amongst vegetables and blood, the cold concrete floor colliding hard with his wrist. He refused to cry.

"Eat your fucking vegetables!" His father screamed, saliva shooting out between his violent words. George's eyes were manic and Curtis knew his dad had gone to that place, somewhere he wouldn't come back from until morning. He lay on the floor, the pain emanating from his wrist.

"EAT!"

Ever so slowly, Curtis reached out with the hand that wasn't throbbing and slowly picked up a green bean. It was squashed and covered with dust from the unswept floor.

His father looked on, a twisted smile below his burning stare.

"Come on you little faggot. Eat your vegetables."

Curtis placed it in his mouth, his teeth sinking in and making him shudder. He refused to cry. He heard the sound of another beer can being opened and his father dragging a chair across the kitchen. He sat down opposite his son, now a bleeding mess. He took a sip of his beer, satisfied with himself.

"You are not getting off that floor until it is fucking spotless. Are you?"

Curtis lay very still, trying hard to swallow the bean and not let his dad see any weakness in him. His shirt was covered in blood. His wrist had swollen.

"Are you?" George repeated, louder and angrier.

"No," Curtis managed.

"No, what?"

"No, sir."

Curtis felt the birth of an uncontrollable rage build as he scooped up the next part of his dinner. His father sat back in his chair, a sadistic grin revealing broken teeth. He lit a cigarette and made himself comfortable.

As Curtis sank his teeth in, he heard his father chuckle.

"Look at you. You're pathetic!"

Curtis put the empty glass down on his desk, the brandy washing the back of his throat. He hated thinking of his father. The only satisfying memory he had of that old bastard was when he'd watched him die. He still had the knife he'd used, the blade still stained with his father's blood.

His desk, a large mahogany semi-circle, stood at the far

end of his office and looked at home amongst all the other expensive furnishings. The leather sofa running along the wall adjacent to the door was a faded cream colour, matching the cream bookshelf. Stacked neatly along the shelves were account books, filled to the brim with betting slips from the last six years.

All above board.

All legitimate.

Curtis, wearing a tailor-made suit, pushed himself up and wriggled into his blazer. He checked his thinning hair and his tie in the mirror on the far wall, above the hand-carved globe doubling as a drinks cabinet.

He needed to look his best when handling business.

He marched across an expensive rug and out of the door, descending the stairs to the shop floor.

Curtis owned 'Odds On', a private betting shop just off Brixton High Street. It was an efficiently-run and well-established betting shop catering only for high stakes betting. Curtis was, in the eyes of the HRMC, a tax-paying citizen. Knowing full well the police would never interfere with his or his family's business, Curtis used the gambling industry to filter through the money his brothers pulled in through the other 'legitimate' businesses he had granted them.

He knew they looked up to him.

London belonged to him.

"Not so pathetic now, am I, Dad?"

He marched across the shop, four tall tables standing symmetrically in the room on long, metal legs. Bucket stools accompanied them, four to a table, all facing an array of flat screen monitors hanging neatly from the walls. At the back of the room was a betting counter, usually filled with the money from the day's betting.

Curtis had cashed up for the evening and appreciated the silence of the shop, the only sound the click his Italian leather shoes made as he walked across the hardwood floor.

That and the metallic snap as he cocked his 9mm Beretta pistol.

Pushing open the door in the far corner, his hand pressed just under the 'Staff Only' sign. The door creaked on its hinges, irritating Curtis. Before him were a few narrow wooden steps which made way to a larger staircase leading to a grand, open basement. Fully illuminated with long, halogen bulbs, the private gym was dank with the sweat of ferocious training and bloodthirsty competition. His steps reverberated as he descended into its depths, finally stepping onto smooth, wood panel flooring. A few resistance machines sat to the right hand side, along with a bench surrounded by dumbbells which had just recently stretched muscles to breaking point. The hard crash of a body hitting the matted floor of a cage rang out and Curtis whistled with approval. He threw his blazer back, resting his hands on his hips, the gun loose in his hand.

"Not bad, Tommy. Not bad."

In the centre of the vast, private gym, stood a full-size octagon cage, its black mesh sides all erected and nailed from floor to ceiling. Inside, Tommy Drayton spat out his gum shield as one of his trainers handed him a bottle of water. The other trainer was trying to push himself up off the floor, severely winded from his last putdown. Tommy nodded at his brother, his shirtless body rippling with muscles and prominent veins. The man was a specimen and towered over both of his trainers.

"Where the fuck is he then?" Curtis asked, rolling back his sleeve to check his gold Rolex watch.

One of the trainers yelled at a storage cupboard and the doors suddenly shot open. Two burly henchmen, both wearing identical black suits, dragged out a small, round man, his clothes a little bloodstained. Dilip Parmer was forty-seven years old and was already making peace with the fact he wouldn't see his two young boys again. His nose had been broken by a hard fist thrown by one of the men dragging him, although fear had gripped him so much that their faces had become blurred. All except the one he was dropped in front of.

Curtis Drayton.

He tried to stand up, but one of the henchmen pushed him back to his knees, Curtis standing before him. He had his hands behind his back and he shook his head.

"Mr. Parmer. What are we going to do with you?"

Dilip felt cold sweat dripping from the back of his hairline and down his spine. His hands were shaking and he slowly looked up at the rather inconvenienced look on Curtis's face. Somewhere behind him, he heard somebody getting thrown into the mesh metal fence.

"Don't answer that, okay? It was a rhetorical question." Curtis smirked down at Dilip, who was struggling to control his breathing.

"Look, Curtis, I am…"

Curtis swung out an arm and caught Dilip across the face with the back of his hand. The clap echoed through the gym, the sound making Tommy turn to watch.

"Mr. Drayton to you, you brown piece of shit."

Dilip held back from expressing the pain of both the strike and the racist comment. Curtis returned his hand to behind him, standing almost to attention.

"It would appear, Mr. Parmer, that you have an issue with dates. Like, for instance, we agreed that you would pay back the first instalment of the loan you received by the end of the month. Now we have moved into the next month and I have yet to receive any type of payment."

"I know and believe me, I've been meaning to contact you. We had a break-in at my showroom and I haven't been able to open for the last two weeks."

Curtis held his hand up, cutting Dilip off. The gun still hung from the hand resting against his spine.

"Excuses, Mr Parmer. Excuses."

"I swear, on my kid's lives, I will have it for you next week."

'This is next week, Mr. Parmer.' Curtis squatted down, coming to eye-level with his cowering customer. He slowly drew his arm from behind him, the gun shining in the bright lights. Dilip's breathing immediately escalated as Curtis held the gun to the bottom of his jaw.

"And your kid's lives mean absolutely nothing to me."

"Please!" Dilip begged, his voice cracking as the realisation of his own mortality took over. Tears began falling down while a smile formed on Curtis's face. He stood up sharply, his arm extended and the barrel of the gun stopping a few inches from the top of Dilip's head.

"For fuck's sake, Curtis. Not in here."

Curtis looked up at Tommy, resting against the inside of the cage, his arms up above his head and his fingers interlocked with the black metal. Curtis drew his lips into a tight line and sighed. The two henchmen stood to the side, watching with amusement. All that could be heard were the pleading sobs of the man on the floor.

"I don't know. It may be the only thing that gets through this thick fucking skull of his."

Before Tommy could respond, the sound of the door creaking filtered through, followed by the loud, sharp echoes of high heels on the wooden stairs. All the men in the room turned to the stairs and Curtis disappointingly exhaled.

"Christ, Ashley. I am in the middle of something."

"Obviously."

Ashley Drayton stepped onto the hardwood floor, her shoes clacking as she strode languidly across, her black pencil skirt and white shirt hugging her well-toned body.

Her beautiful, tanned face was framed by her blonde hair, pulled back into a smart ponytail.

She approached her eldest brother, looking at him, the gun and then at Dilip Parmer, the quivering wreck on the floor. She shrugged, having seen this a hundred times before.

"Don't you look grown-up?"

"Well Curtis, surprisingly, I *am* a grown-up. Besides we still have a week more of graveyards until we completely migrate the servers over to the new cloud system."

"Computer shite to me, my dear." Curtis gave her a sarcastic smile, unable to mask his lack of interest in her job. "You should work for me, like your brothers do.'

"No thanks. I've already done my work for you."

"And she was terrific, by the way."

Ashley grimaced, the thought of her brother raping that poor woman made her stomach turn. She hated every aspect of it.

"I didn't mean that."

"Ah, so you spoke to him. What did he say?"

Tommy took a swig from his bottle of water and listened intently. Ashley smiled at him before turning to Curtis, who still held the gun directly at Dilip.

"Basically the police are coming to the end of their search. They pretty much know it was you but they are refusing to come anywhere near to ask questions."

"And why is that?" Curtis asked, pride streaming from his words.

"Because they are scared of you."

"No. It's because they're fucking terrified of me. They know that nothing will happen, or can happen, because this is my fucking city. They associate the name Drayton with death and rightfully so. Isn't that right, Mr. Parmer?"

"Oh god, please don't kill me!" Dilip begged, reaching out for Curtis's trouser leg and receiving a kick in face from the finest of Italian leather. Ashley shook her head and turned.

"Whatever, Curtis. I have a job and a life to get back to."

"Speaking of which, I still haven't met your boyfriend, Ashley."

"I know. I'm fully aware of that."

"That needs to be remedied."

Ashley didn't answer, her high heels slapping against the wood as she stormed up the stairs. Curtis watched her leave, suppressing the rage that built up every time she defied him. Suddenly, the sounds of Dilip's sobs pulled him back to the room and he looked down at the feeble man and smiled.

"Look at you. You're pathetic."

Dilip closed his eyes, pushing a few more tears that he was sure would be his last. He took a deep breath and thought of his two sons and his wife. He thought of how much he loved them.

"I'm not going to kill you, Mr. Parmer." He pushed the barrel of his Beretta down so it parted Dilip's hair and pressed against his skull. "You're not worth my bullet.

Curtis pulled the gun away and Dilip gasped for air, a relief washing over his sweaty, shaking body. Curtis re-engaged the safety on the gun and handed it to one of the henchmen as they came over. They roughly hauled Dilip to his feet, a look of panic still etched across his tear- and blood-stained face.

'Give him five minutes with Tommy.'

Curtis gave the order and stood on the spot, hands on hips and an evil glint in his eye. Dilip struggled, but the henchmen easily overpowered him, dragging him to the cage entrance. The two trainers left and they shoved him through, his feet slipping and he hit the mats hard. He coughed air back into his lung before shakily pushing himself onto to his feet. His body ached and his knees trembled. Fear shot through him, as the hulking Tommy Drayton finished pulling the Velcro straps of his boxing gloves down. He towered over Dilip, his strength and power obvious.

His voice was tinged in pity.

"You really should have kept to the deadline."

The world became a blurry cocktail of anguish and pain as Tommy connected with an uppercut to the midsection, before obliterating the broken nose with a high knee to Dilip's face. As he crashed to the mat, Curtis smiled and urged his brother on.

The lights in the hallway flashed on as soon as Fletcher flicked the switch to the left of the front door. He shuffled in quickly, followed by Lucas who was carrying the folders with ease. Lucas scanned the hallway, seeing the small unit by the wall. Above it hung a photo of a woman, her smile full of love.

Fletcher opened the door just beyond and slipped into the darkness, the light coming on as he flicked the switch. Lucas followed.

The room smelled of old smoke, the ashtray on the coffee table overflowing with cigarette butts. The desk by the window was covered in paper, with a laptop sitting in in its centre, the screen dark. He put the files down on the edge of the desk and picked up a sheet of paper covered with messy scribbles.

"Ah, those are my memoirs," Fletcher said taking his coat off and dropping it over the edge of the sofa. "Well, the beginning of them."

Lucas gave a polite smile and returned them to the desk. He slowly circled the room, stopping at the mantelpiece. There proudly sat a photo of Fletcher at his police graduation, the snapshot of history even more beautiful in its black and white glory. Next to that sat another photo of the woman from the hallway, leaning against a tree trunk in an exotic location. Lucas could feel her absence from the house.

"Is this your wife?" Lucas asked, his eyes still fixed on the photo.

"That's my Susan," Fletcher said, proud to show her off.

"She's very beautiful."

"She was." Lucas looked at him, realising that the absence was stronger than ever.

"I'm sorry."

"Thank you." Fletcher took a breath, remembering Susan for a moment. He then turned to his guest, who stood, arms folded. He hadn't taken his leather jacket off and Fletcher knew this wasn't going to be a social catch-up.

"Can I get you a drink?"

He opened up a drinks cabinet, selecting a half empty bottle of Jack Daniels from a number of bottles inside. He pulled out two glasses, filling one of them.

"No thank you."

Fletcher pulled the glass up to his lips, swallowing the whole drink in one swig. Lucas looked at a photo of Fletcher standing proudly next to a young woman, probably his daughter, at her graduation. Next to that sat a police radio. He looked at Fletcher puzzled.

"Oh that," Fletcher appeared embarrassed. "I like to know what's going on. Sad, I know."

"Each to their own." Lucas continued circling, until he made it back to Fletcher's desk. He looked at the dusty folder on top of the stack he'd brought in, seeing his name hidden by dust.

"Are you sure I can't get you a drink?

"I didn't come here for a drink."

The words were firm, each one retrieved from a place full of anger. Fletcher poured another Jack into the glass, knocked it back and then poured another. He left the lid off the bottle as he turned to Lucas. He immediately felt smaller.

"I figured as much." Fletcher rummaged through the coat on the back of the sofa, pulling out a box of cigarettes. He offered one to Lucas who held up a hand of rejection. Fletcher lit a cigarette and sat on the arm of the sofa. Six feet away from him stood the living embodiment of rage.

"Lucas, I implore you. Please don't go down the route I know you want to go down. These are people you do not want to mess with."

A cloud of cigarette smoke floated around the room.

"Who are they? The police seem to know, Fletcher, but they aren't doing a fucking thing about it. Why?"

"Because Lucas, every now and then you come across people who are above the law." The look on Lucas's face told Fletcher it wasn't the right answer. "You want me to say it, Lucas? Fine. We're scared to go after them."

Lucas shook his head and pushed himself away from the desk and to the middle of the room. Fletcher took a long pull on his cigarette.

"Why?" Lucas asked, crossing his arms.

"Because, Lucas, they're too strong. I hate to admit it, god knows I do, but they're beyond the grasp of the Met. They have their hooks so deep into the criminal underworld of this city that they've become untouchable. The few times we've had them up in court, the families of the police officers involved or the witnesses, even the damn judges, have been attacked. This one time, one of the officers who'd arrested them came home to find his wife and daughters hanging from the stairs in his house. He never came back after that. I can't say I blame him."

Lucas closed his eyes, imagining the things these people had done. His hand found its way to his pocket and he clenched his fingers tightly around the wedding ring. Fletcher took a sip of his whisky and lit another cigarette before continuing.

"The thing is, these attacks are carried out by people so far removed from the Draytons it can't be traced back to them. People swear loyalty to them, out of fear. They kill for them just to stay on their good side."

"The Draytons?" Lucas enquired, his interest piqued.

"Lucas, don't. Because with them it will not be a case of your anger outweighs theirs. They'll kill you as soon as they find you."

"Well, we'll have at least one thing in common then, won't we?"

"It'll be a war, Lucas."

"No. Not a war." Lucas's eyes were burning with pure fury. "It'll be a massacre. Where can I find them?"

Fletcher took a long draw from the cigarette and let the smoke blow out as he shook his head.

"I can't tell you that."

"Fletcher, look at me."

Another puff of smoke plumed out of Fletcher's mouth and he looked up, meeting Lucas's eye. His eyes were red; angry tears forming in their corners. His stubble-covered jaw was quivering slightly.

"These men abducted my Helen, Fletcher. They took her from the street and they snatched her from her world."

"I know, Lucas. But…"

"They raped my wife. They raped her and then left her to die alone and in the dark - her and my unborn child. And I was so far away there was nothing I could do. I could have protected her, Fletcher, and that much I failed her on.

"But these people are literally going to get away with murder. And I owe it to her, the love of my life, to make sure that doesn't happen."

Lucas stood powerfully in the centre of the room, his eyes fixed on Fletcher through the tears. The old man sat, struggling with what was being asked of him. Fletcher could feel the sadness flowering, he felt the pain emanating from the recently widowed.

He thought of Susan.

He thought of Helen.

"She did so much good for you, Lucas. I'm so sorry she's gone."

"Don't be sorry. Be helpful. Give me a first name."

"I can't."

'Give me a name, or I'll burn this city to the ground 'til I find them."

"I can't, Lucas. I can't." Fletcher's voice broke, tears trying their best to choke him. "I know what you're capable of, remember?"

"You have no idea what I'm capable of." Lucas squatted down to Fletcher's eye-level, his voice taking on a softer tone. "Give me one name, look the other way and you'll never see me again."

Fletcher pulled the last cigarette out of the box, crushing it in his hand and throwing it on the table. It clattered against the ashtray, the overflow of butts spilling across the oak. He clicked the zippo, and once more smoke choked the air in the room. Fletcher took a moment, a tear rolling down his cheek.

"I remember when I came to visit you in the hospital. You were so young then and you were so excited." A smile formed on his face. "You kept telling me about Helen, how in love you were falling. You told me about your first date, that magical first kiss you guys shared in front of your statue."

Lucas stood up straight, his nostrils flaring in anger as he thought back to a memory with someone consigned to history. Fletcher took another puff, allowing the smoke to billow from his nostrils.

"It was at that moment, Lucas, that I thought you may have a future after all."

Silence filled the room, both men allowing themselves a few moments to grieve. Fletcher sighed.

"If I give you this name, you can never come back here, you understand? Everything that happens after this moment is going to be beyond anything you could imagine."

"I'm fully aware of where I'm heading. I'm just going to make sure I bring them with me."

Fletcher nodded, almost reasoning with himself.

"What do you plan to do?" he asked, the words wreathed in smoke.

"I'm going to show them why it's called a pain threshold."

Fletcher almost chuckled, knowing none of these threats were empty. One name is all it would take to set off a chain of events that would shake the city to its foundation.

"Lewis Drayton." Lucas's eyes flashed with interest. "He runs the 'Golf in Class' driving range in Sudbury."

Fletcher stood up as Lucas extended his hand. He took it, shaking it firmly. A purpose took hold of Lucas and Fletcher could see the fury driving him.

"Thank you, Fletcher."

Lucas turned and headed to the door. Fletcher took a few steps after him, his body cutting through the smoke hanging in the air.

"Be careful Lucas. This family is powerful in I've never

seen before. They'll come for you with everything they have. It's how it's been for years."

Lucas pulled open the front door. The rain had decided to return to London, it's hard, cold beads shooting down from the night sky. The air felt fresh. Fletcher emerged into the hallway.

"These people have nothing to fear."

Lucas took a few steps down the driveway, heading off on his mission. He stopped and turned, the rain crashing against his face, three more words before he disappeared into the night.

"They do now."

CHAPTER ELEVEN

Fletcher managed to walk through the door to the station at a minute to nine, and relief set in. The drive had been straightforward, but the weather was continuing its mischievous game with the world by beaming bright sunrays from a blue sky. The traffic was almost non-existent.

It was the hangover that was the problem.

That, plus the overwhelming sense of regret of what had happened the night before and his recklessness in sending Lucas in the right direction. The potential danger he'd put Lucas and the Draytons in. The prison sentence he would surely face for mentioning the Draytons to the grieving husband.

The certainty that something had happened.

However, Fletcher found the office to be quiet, almost peaceful, especially for a Monday morning. A few officers were situated on the reception desk, booking in a young offender caught in possession of a knife. Some of the administrators were typing away, sending out communications with great precision. McCarthy was leaning back in his chair, a half-complete crossword puzzle in his hands and a frown on his usually welcoming face.

Nothing had happened.

Fletcher got to his desk and lowered himself into his chair, the ache in his back flaring up with small stabs to the base of his spine. After Lucas had left, Fletcher had continued to empty the bottle of Jack Daniels and had woken up on the sofa with an empty glass on his lap.

His mouth still felt dry; a whole night spent chain-smoking had made his mouth feel like a desert.

He could smell the alcohol on his warm breath, could feel the cigarette smoke clinging to his creased work shirt.

"Christ, Fletch. You look like you fell out of bed this morning."

Fletcher looked up from his desk to see the hulking figure of Sgt. Bailey standing over him, his beefy arms folded across his broad chest. Fletcher raised his eyebrows and smiled, pushing his glasses up his nose.

"Sorry. Rough night."

"You're too old for rough nights," Bailey smiled.

"I'm too old for a lot of things."

"Not retirement apparently."

Fletcher politely smiled again, wishing to be left alone to deal with the throbbing pain in his forehead, and the feeling that the alcohol had shrunk his skull by a third of its size.

"I need to speak to you."

Bailey's voice carried serious overtones and suddenly Fletcher felt a sharp twinge of panic, his old heart beginning to beat faster. That overwhelming feeling of being accountable for whatever Lucas had promised trickled into his mind. Coherent thoughts and strong excuses all deserted him. He coughed a little, nervously clearing his throat.

"You okay, Fletch?" Bailey's concern seemed genuine.

"Sorry. I'm feeling a little unwell."

"Maybe you should head home?"

"But you needed to speak to me?" Fletcher looked up at Bailey, trying to maintain an honest eye contact. The man was impossible to read and reaffirmed to Fletcher why he was a great Sergeant. His conscience was screaming through, piercing the hangover, and impaling itself through his brain.

"Tell him! Tell him what you've done."

"Well, that can wait," Bailey said, taking an authoritative stance by Fletcher's desk. "I was just going to ask you to explain that goddamned filing system you put in. I can't find a goddamn thing."

Fletcher exhaled, relief surfing on the air filtering out of his lungs. He felt his heartbeat rectifying itself, beating over the ever-growing screams of his guilt.

"Come on, go home," Bailey ordered. "I don't want to deal with the death of an OAP first thing Monday morning."

"Thank you, I think," Fletcher said, not even bothering to turn on the computer as he eased himself up, visibly wincing with pain.

"And go and see a doctor about your back, for Christ's sake."

Fletcher nodded and Bailey strode away purposefully out of the office, his subordinates parting like the Red Sea to let him by.

"TELL HIM! Tell him you sent Lucas after the Draytons. Tell him what's coming."

"Sir?" Fletcher called out as he pulled his thin, summer jacket over his untidy outfit. Bailey stopped and turned around. Fletcher swallowed and took a deep breath. This was the moment, a glittering career and a twilight within the force that had garnered him so much respect, about to be ripped apart by his own stupidity.

Lucas did deserve his retribution.

Fletcher deserved to face the law for his actions.

"What is it, Fletcher?"

Bailey stood impatiently, shrugging his large, rounded shoulders to hurry the old man along. Just as Fletcher was about to admit his crime, he glanced at his desk. A photo of Laura, his estranged granddaughter, stared back at him. The beautiful blue eyes watching as he was about to bury any chance he had of holding her in his arms.

Annabelle would never bring her to visit him. He would die in prison alone.

"Thank you sir. I'll be back in tomorrow."

"Just get better." Bailey's compassion was not always gentle. He continued his march, disappearing round the corner and into the day ahead. Fletcher gathered his things, battling the increasingly powerful voice within.

"He'll find out. You started this. You're responsible. Tell him what's coming."

What was coming not even Fletcher was prepared for.

———

'Golf in Class' was set back from the main road, the gravel path cutting through the green hill lining the dual carriageway. Five minutes down the road was Northwick Park hospital, the building having seen better days, which sat on the outskirts of Harrow. Surrounding the substantial golfing establishment were vast swathes of green fields, a few farm yard animals patrolling them.

The sports facility itself had undergone major surgery since Curtis Drayton had bought it, the once run-down driving range had boomed again since the cash injection. The main building was brand new, the entire front of it being made up of large sheets of glass, allowing the oncoming customers to see the plush interior. The 'Golf in

Class' logo stood proudly above the door in big, white letters, underlined by a cartoon golf club.

To the right of the main facility was its unique selling point. A sizeable mesh dome had been built down a sloped pathway housing eight separate batting areas opposite ball-pitching machines. Customers were lined up, all eager to get in and practice their baseball swings.

Inside, the reception area was spacious and airy, a large comfy seating area with small tables taking up the majority, with potted plants dotted between them. A long marble counter ran along the near wall, the sales assistants' backs to the glass frontage. To the left was the club shop and the offices of the two pro-trainers who gave private lessons at extortionate rates.

To the right was the Sports Café, a themed restaurant, all oak with maroon cushions. The bar was well stocked, with beer pumps of the most popular brands poking up from the counter like metal fingers. The staff were young, mainly students from the nearby Westminster University campus.

Opposite the main door was the entrance to the driving range: segregated areas where golf enthusiasts filed out to hit balls as far as they could onto an immaculate range, sign posted to measure distance. A net fence sat around it to protect the surrounding grounds from wayward shots.

The range was particularly busy, the Bank Holiday Monday combined with the pleasant weather summoning plenty of customers.

A number of them were treading the short stone-paved route to the right of the main building near the recently refurbished cages, customers carrying protective helmets that gleamed in the sun and dragging metal baseball bats which clunked against the stone.

The batting cage was a particular favourite, with

groups of students lining up to prove to their peers that they could hit a small ball furthest. The eight cages separated the main structure like a perfectly sliced pizza, each one encasing the batter with mesh metal walls. The floors were padded and marked out so that unfortunate collisions with speeding balls could be avoided. Each batting area tailed off into a slope which funnelled the balls into the centre, each one rolling into a tray so that they could be fed into the automatic pitchers.

Everything ran like clockwork.

The sun beat down from a surprisingly cloudless sky and the only sound was that of metal bats colliding with rock solid balls.

Lewis Drayton loved days like these.

He smiled, taking in a deep lungful of the cool, fresh air into his tiny frame. He wore his usual blue 'Golf in Class' polo shirt, which fitted loosely over his wiry frame. He ran a bony hand through his greasy, thinning black hair as he looked up into the clear blue above.

He could smell the money he was making from a day like this, knowing it would impress Curtis to see that he could run a business. Although his older brother always treated him with disdain, he knew Curtis wanted him to make something of himself. When Lewis ran distribution on the shipments of cocaine Curtis brought in, Lewis made sure to do him proud. Curtis had even seemed impressed when Lewis had killed Martin Stokes, the wannabe gangster who'd attempted to hijack a delivery. Lewis felt the pride from Curtis, and to some extent, from that brute Tommy, when he'd put a bullet between Martin's eyes.

He took a final pull on his cigarette, the smoke disappearing in the sun's glare and he reacquainted his helmet with the top of his head.

"So let me show you how this works then."

Lewis's rasping voice befitted his rat-like appearance.

His excitement was evident as he booted up the new 'Pin Point Pitch' system he'd just had installed. The top-of-the-line technology was the latest in a new range of equipment to train baseball players and was all the rage in Major League in America. The well-paying customer had requested to use the system, a request that was eagerly accepted by Lewis personally.

The machine itself stood out from the other ball pitchers in the centre of the batting area, the metal slicker and shinier, giving off a more futuristic look. The cannon itself made less noise when loading the next hit and was attached to a mechanical sphere which allowed full motion. On the top of the barrel sat a laser scope which sent a thick red dot to the padding tied to the back of the cage behind the customer.

"Now, if you look, with these directional arrows I can move the projection of the ball to whatever angle I want," Lewis explained, fully confident in his knowledge. "So if you wanted a dipping ball I would aim it here."

He adjusted the angle, the light moving upwards across the mat as the customer watched, his muscular arms in front of him and his hands resting on the handle of the bat standing upright.

"And then to give it the dip I adjust the speed to make it slightly slower."

Lewis turned a dial slightly. A small screen on the panel showed a coloured bar, which decreased in size. Lewis smiled.

"Never turn it to full. Comes at you like a rocket."

His customer smiled and nodded casually, hoisting up the bat over his broad shoulders. Lewis couldn't help but admire him. The man was good-looking, dark hair brushed to the side and his stubble neatly trimmed, clinging to his strong jaw. He was intrigued to see how hard the man could strike, the physique he possessed was very impressive. Rippling muscles that he knew he would never have, not on his slight, delicate skeleton. Lewis imagined the type of women that must throw themselves at the man and how they were probably a lot classier and prettier than the trashy, drug-addled women he had to pay for.

This man's life must be perfect, he thought.

He smiled as the man adopted a solid stance and nodded for the shot. Lewis pressed the release button and the machine hummed into life.

———

The warm beams of the sun beat against the back of Lucas's neck and he was grateful that the weather had granted them a nice day. The helmet's visor cast a shadow over his eyes and nose, blocking the sharp brightness of the sun. He gripped the metal bat in his hands, his biceps flexing and bulging under his t-shirt.

How easy it would be to swing right now and take Lewis's head off.

Lucas refrained, looking at the runt of a man who was eagerly playing with his new toy. Lewis was completely oblivious as to who was standing a mere five feet away from him.

He imagined the man grabbing Helen, his dirty, spider-like hands on her.

The cannon shunted, and with a release of pleasure it shot a ball up into the air, spinning as it dipped towards Lucas. He steadied his feet and in one fluid motion swung the bat. The clonk of metal on metal was satisfying and the ball sailed over the machinery and crashed against the metal on the other side of the cage.

It felt good.

Lewis applauded. He had no idea who his customer was.

That would change soon enough.

The evening brought with it a cool breeze, the gentle wind softly ushering in the darkness. The street lights had only recently been activated, the bulbs humming as they started their night's work.

The Bentley turned off the main road, engine purring with quality.

Tommy Drayton clicked off the indicator, one hand resting on the wheel while smoothly navigating through a small amount of traffic. A muscular arm rested on his knee, a stiff, bruised hand lying on top of the gear stick.

His knuckles were slightly purple and felt sore, each blow to Dilip Parmer's defenceless face contributing to the pain.

In the back seat sat Curtis Drayton, his crisp, tailor-made suit fitting him well. He sat with his leg casually resting over the other and looked out of the window, watching his hunting ground flash past the window. He could sense the fear within the city, how the passers-by would quiver if they knew who was sitting in the back of the car as it sped by. Dilip was in hospital, a fractured jaw and cheekbone the most visible of the damage that Tommy had inflicted. The brutal repetition of the body shots had also left the poor man with severe internal bleeding. It could have been much worse and that was the reason why Curtis never let Tommy too far off his leash.

It was also the reason why he was slightly weary of his younger brother at times. He knew Tommy didn't always approve of his behaviour, but he knew his place in the hierarchy. Curtis trusted him and he knew Tommy appreciated all Curtis had done to keep their dad away from him. But the size of his brother and the talent he possessed with violence always made Curtis slightly nervous.

As the car glided up the street, Tommy stared at the car ahead. He imagined Helen sitting in the passenger seat, the husband she had mentioned driving, while they discussed holiday plans. Maybe a child or two in the back, a family who loved each other and shared a life together.

Not anymore.

Because of Tommy and his family.

"Something bothering you, Thomas?"

Tommy snapped back into the present to see Curtis observing him in the rear-view mirror with those piercing black eyes burning a hole through his own. Tommy looked away, ahead to the road before him.

"I'm fine."

"Don't give me that. What's the matter?"

Curtis adjusted his position on the comfortable leather chairs, his stare still locked on his hulking brother.

"I've just been thinking, Curtis."

"People do that from time to time."

"Yeah, well, I've been thinking about things. About the things we've done and the things we do."

Tommy looked into the rear-view mirror, his brother shifting in his seat. His voice sounded as agitated as he looked.

"Please, Thomas. Enlighten me."

"I suppose, Curtis, I just feel bad about what happened to Helen."

"Helen?"

"Yes, Helen!" Tommy felt sick, his brother not even registering that poor woman whose life he'd ended. "The woman from a few weeks back.'

"Oh her," Curtis said disinterestedly. "She was good - didn't cry as much as the others."

"Yeah, well sometimes I just think that you needlessly go too far, you know?"

"No, I don't know. Are you worried about something?"

'Not at all. I just think we have enough now. We have all the money we could need, businesses all over the city, property all over the country. I mean, hell, you have the police shitting their pants the second your name is mentioned. Isn't that enough?"

Curtis shook his head, arching forward and looking into his lap. Tommy felt better for speaking out, the worry of a reaction diminishing. The lights ahead turned to red and Tommy rolled the Bentley to an effortless stop.

Curtis instantly leant forward, planting his hand on Tommy's shoulder and pulling him hard against the leather seat. Before Tommy could react, Curtis pulled his pristine 9mm Beretta up, the barrel pressing hard against Tommy's temple. The lights from the outside street lights reflected off the metal barrel, illuminating Curtis's face which was twisted into a furious scowl.

"What the fuck has got into you?"

"Get that gun off me. Now!"

"Do you know how we keep all of those things, Tommy? Do you? Or how I acquired them in the first place? And how I have given you the fucking life that you have?"

Curtis leaned in, his breath hot against Tommy's face. The younger brother sat stiffly, the opening of the gun pressing into his skin. Curtis leaned in, his immaculate teeth gritted around his words.

"Fear, Thomas. Fear."

"I am not scared of you, Curtis."

"You fucking should be."

"Why? Are you going to kill me? Go ahead."

Curtis chuckled, disengaging the safety of the gun with

a click that seemed to echo in the caverns of their tension. Tommy braced himself, his face a blank canvas.

No indications of fear.

"If I wanted you dead, Thomas, you would be. But I would never do it myself. You are my brother and you know that nothing means more to me than family. I don't like Lewis or Harry and Ashley and Matt piss me off from time to time. But I love them. Like I love you."

"Then why have you got a gun against me head?"

"To make my point clear. You can have all the money and all the things it can buy. You can have love and respect, Thomas. But fear is the greatest power a man can have."

Curtis slowly pulled the gun away, the barrel leaving an indentation in Tommy's skin. The big man turned slowly and looked his demonic older brother in his dark, evil eyes. Curtis smiled.

"When you are feared Thomas, you become a different entity entirely."

Tommy held his brother's stare but refused to share his grin. Curtis slowly leant back into his seat, slipping the Beretta into the inside of his blazer. He adjusted his cufflinks, thinking about how Lewis should be locking up soon and would undoubtedly want to stop by to boast about the day's intake.

The Bentley cruised through the humid streets of London. Tommy kept his eyes on the road and Curtis prepared himself for an inevitable appearance from Lewis later that evening.

———

It had been a busy day.

Lewis had sent a few of the young Sales Assistants home early, even Nancy, who had rebuked his advances a week ago. They had all worked hard but he wanted to be alone to count the takings.

The numbers looked good.

He placed the money into secure ziplock bags, before locking them in the safe. He imagined how good the scotch would taste in Curtis's office later, his elder brother finally showing him some respect and acceptance.

He shut down the computer, flicked off the lights and closed the office door.

He casually strolled across the open plan shop, the tills all clear of papers and clutter and of the clubs and bats standing proudly in their display cases.

He whistled a tune he couldn't place, his feet echoing around the empty space as he approached the door. The keys spinning in his hand jingled out of tune.

He turned off the lights, pulled open the entrance door, and stepped out into a warm spring night. He breathed in, tasting the fresh air.

He closed his eyes for a second.

He thought of the years of abuse he'd taken from Curtis, of being made to feel every bit of the runt he was physically.

He thought of how glad he was he'd never remembered his Dad; the stories he'd been told of how the man had knocked around his mother, striking her with big, powerful fists.

He thought of all the things Curtis had made him do, all the tasks and challenges he'd thrown at Lewis just to make Lewis prove his worth.

He was finally there.

He was a successful businessman now.

He inhaled the air again expansively, and gently patted his trouser pockets for his cigarettes and opened his eyes.

Lewis stumbled backwards slightly, coming face to face with the muscular customer from earlier in the day. The man's well-developed physique, the one Lewis had been admiring earlier, was now encased in an expensive-looking leather jacket over a fitted navy jumper. The messy hair had been brushed, the short fringe neatly swept to one side.

The smile had gone.

The eyes were cold.

The face was emotionless.

Before Lewis could say a word, or even move, Lucas dived forward, driving a pinpoint knee to Lewis's mid-section with incredible force. As Lewis hunched over, Lucas drove the point of his elbow to the back of Lewis's skull, driving the bone just under the curve and sending Lewis into a sea of darkness.

The Drayton body hit the ground, limp and lifeless. Lewis's face collided hard with the pavement, blood running from the top of his forehead, dripping down a motionless face.

Lucas scanned the deserted car park, the only sound being that of the few cars driving on the main road beyond the hill.

Lucas reached under Lewis's arms and dragged the limp body back through the doors, before locking the world out behind him.

CHAPTER TWELVE

The sun beat down on that day eight years ago, illuminating the incredible grounds of the Milner Estate gardens. The flowers were in full bloom, a mixture of blue, red and orange exploding effervescently in the green walls of the enclosing hedges. Birds flittered between the well-trimmed oak trees, serenading the world with their high-pitched songs. The recently cut grass emitted that fresh smell that's hard to describe. A few rabbits hopped around on one of the nearby greens, while a water fountain shot water into the air behind them.

Lucas stood with his hands in the pockets of his expensive, rented trousers. His neatly polished shoes planted firmly on the soft, green ground and he peered out at the beauty around him.

Patricia and Graham Bennett, his soon-to-be in-laws had spared no expense for their eldest daughter's wedding, the money saved from Graham's well-paid job as a civil engineer. They'd welcomed Lucas into their family, once they had got over the initial reaction and subsequent changes that it caused.

Graham had told him at the modest stag-do that Alex threw for him...

"The only thing a father ever wants for his daughter, is for her to find a man who will look after her. Keep her safe."

The drunken slap on the shoulder accompanying it gave Lucas all the confirmation he needed that her parents were happy with the decision Helen's heart had made.

The magnificent Milner Estate stood proudly within its beautiful surroundings, the substantial stone structure shooting up into blue skies. The windows were bigger than Lucas himself, the glass thick and spotless. Once belonging to a wealthy earl many years ago, it had been maintained through the generations and was now a wonderful attraction for weekend venturers.

On the other side of the stately home, a grand lake shimmered under sunshine, geese and ducks chasing each other in circles and hassling visitors for bread. The Milner Trust, set up decades ago by the philanthropic family, ensured that the acres of woodland surrounding the entire estate were well maintained and safe from destruction.

The place was a secret paradise.

A soft breeze filtered through, whistling inside Lucas's blazer. He adjusted his tie, the expensive suit hanging on his frame well, although he always felt uncomfortable in smart attire. He never felt he belonged in it.

Upstairs, in one of the guest rooms, Helen was having the finishing touches done to her hair, so much longer all those years ago.

It cascaded down from her head in large, blonde curls, like a waterfall overlapping itself several times over. Her make-up was modest, but done to the highest standard by the artist her parents had hired.

The dress, white with silver trim, hugged her figure tightly, her curves displayed wonderfully by the design. The train glided down, dragging behind her wherever she went like a ghostly shadow.

She looked like an angel.

Lucas's angel.

That was all he could think of when he turned to see her, her arm linked to her father's, nerves betraying her as she tried to walk confidently. The small room had been decorated with white lilies, Helen's favourite flower, fountaining from colourful vases atop small pillars. Rows of cushioned chairs lined both sides of the aisle, all laid out in meticulous symmetry. Many of the guests were there for Helen, family members and friends from days gone by, and all dressed for the occasion with not a hair out of place. Lucas's work colleagues were there too, sitting next to their own wives. The string quartet at the back of the room played effortlessly, their rendition of Helen's favourite piece of classical music weaving bird-like between the few gasps that the crowd gave at Helen's beauty.

Her eyes were fixed on Lucas.

He stood proudly at the front, his hands resting in front of him, his back straight and powerful shoulders tense. He shook Graham's hand as they arrived at the front, the father's eyes watering with pride and sadness at letting his little girl go for the final time.

Helen held Lucas's hand as they turned to face the minister and she squeezed it tightly throughout the entire ceremony. They spoke their vows to each other, Helen's voice breaking with happiness as she declared her love and devotion for the man before her. A tear formed that Lucas reached out and tenderly removed.

Alex, dressed in a similar suit to the groom, handed over the wedding ring when requested and Lucas held it in his hand tightly before placing it on the finger of the most important person the world had ever introduced him to.

The symbol of love that bound them together.
Suddenly, the entire room flashed white.
Lucas held the ring tightly.
Everything faded as it flashed white again.
Lucas was alone.

Lucas's fist clenched tightly around Helen's delicate wedding ring, the warm air of the night sky wafting around him as he returned to reality. Lucas looked out over the nearby farm; the animals had gone in for the evening and so he gazed out over the fields, his eyes losing the grass into the far darkness. Behind him, the lights of the batting cage burned brightly.

He held on to the ring, feeling every moment he'd spent with Helen, every 'I love you' they'd uttered during the eight years of happiness. He shut his eyes, the anger pushing his lids together hard.

He wanted to reach out and touch her face again.

To rest his hand on the small of her back as they ambled through the supermarket.

For her to push his nose up and oink at him one more time.

The sudden jingle of chains rattling against a metal fence made Lucas open his eyes. He let out a deep sigh, slid the wedding ring into his pocket and walked into the batting cage.

———

Lewis felt intense pain pressing against the front and back of his skull. It felt like a giant hand was crushing his brain and causing him to moan. He wanted to hold his head.

But his arms wouldn't move.

The ache in his shoulders caused him to open his eyes, his blurry vision and bright lights stinging all the way through his retinas. He tried again to bring a hand to his head and again was unable to do so. He winced at the sound of metal clanging against metal, and the cold bite of steel against his thin, breakable wrists.

'What the fuck?' he muttered, his words slurring over too much saliva dribbling over broken teeth and a quivering bottom lip. The throbbing pain bounced from the left side of his forehead to the back of his skull like a ping pong ball. His stomach felt like it had been hit with a mallet.

The world began to resolve before him, fine lines of

detail becoming clear. It took him a while to realise he was standing in the batting cage. A bright floodlight above had him in its beam, his eyes wincing and trying their best to look anywhere else. The cool air of the evening clung to his feeble body as he tried to step forward onto the mats.

His legs hit metal and his body fell back against the mats behind him.

His legs had been stationed apart by a few feet, both ankles wrapped in thick, industrial chains, the links veering off behind and firmly attached to the mesh fence of the batting cage. His small, muscle-less arms hung above him, the wrists chained together above his head. He couldn't move.

He heard the gated door to the cage open to his left, the silhouette of a figure moving in his peripheral vision.

"Hello?"

He heard the footsteps make their way around the divider separating the individual batting spots and there he was.

The memory filtered through his fogged brain.

Lucas closed the door.

He turned.

The customer...

The bright light burnt Lewis' eyes. Cold sweat slithered down the back of his neck. His face twisted in rage.

"You!"

Lucas didn't even bother acknowledging Lewis, instead standing ten feet away from him and looking at the control panel for the 'Pin Point' batting apparatus that Lewis himself had fawned over earlier. Lewis struggled, in vain, against his chains.

"Let me go you piece of shit."

Lucas raised a hand to his chin, casting an eye over the machine's controls with interest.

"You fuck! Do you know the fucking mistake you're making?"

Lucas coughed slightly, not even looking in the direction of the insulting tirade. His eyes lit up and he reached out with a steady hand and pressed a button on the underside of the panel. The machine opposite Lewis hummed into life, a mechanical yawn as it awoke from its slumber.

"You're a dead man. You hear me. A dead man!"

Lucas calmly inspected the machine while it rumbled into life, before slowly sliding his arms out of his leather jacket. He folded it neatly and rested it on top of the panel, the jumper he was wearing clinging tightly to his large frame. Lewis felt inadequacy join fear in his current state of emotion. Lucas cleared his throat and then took a few steps towards the shaking Drayton, sweat patches forming under his elevated arms.

"Unchain me you prick or I'll fucking kill you!"

The panic in Lewis's voice and eyes betrayed his attempt at intimidation. Lucas stared at him coldly.

"Your brothers..." the voice said calmly. "Names and addresses."

Lewis started laughing, nerves creeping in between breaths. He shook his head, looking up at his captor.

"Do you know what you've done? He chuckled some more. "Do you even know who I am?"

"You're Lewis Drayton," Lucas answered. "A member of the Drayton family, who apparently have this entire city running scared."

Lewis nodded along, an undeserved sense of victory on his face. Chains rattled against the fence.

"That's right. And that makes you a dead man."

Lucas raised his eyebrows.

"You know what we can do." Lewis said triumphantly.

"Do you know who I am?" Lucas asked, his eyes locked on his prisoner. Lewis seemed surprised at the question.

"Some prick who thinks he can make a name for himself? We've come across your type before."

Lucas took a few steps forward and Lewis swallowed nervously, sweat trickling down his bony spine. The humidity in the air suddenly felt thicker.

"My name is Lucas Cole. Two weeks ago, you and your brothers abducted my wife. You raped her. You killed her."

Realisation set in and Lewis's eyes grew wide with fear. The emotionless voice poured forward from the emotionless face.

"I know exactly what you and your brothers can do. Sadly for you, you have no idea what *I* am capable of."

Lucas let the words hang for a few moments, staring into the eyes of a man who had helped his wife die. Lewis couldn't find any words.

"Right. Your brothers. Names and addresses."

"Fuck you!"

Lewis drew phlegm up through his throat and nasal passage and spat it in Lucas's direction. It missed by a few feet. Lucas didn't react, staring instead at the pathetic runt in front of him.

"Okay. Let's have a play with this then, shall we?"

Lucas strolled back to the control panel, the instructions that Lewis himself had given him earlier in the day fresh in his mind. He pressed the 'sight' button and after a few moments, a red dot projected from the machine on the mat just to the side of Lewis's ribs.

"Now if I recall correctly," Lucas continued, "it's these arrowed buttons here that control the beam."

Lucas watched the red marker move slowly, following the light as he pressed on the keys. Lewis tried to jerk his body but the chains held him in place. The light came to a stop on his right knee.

"This isn't fucking funny!" Lewis screamed, terrified.

"Oh I agree."

Lucas pressed the 'release' button.

The machine kicked up in volume, the sound of one of the rock-solid baseballs being scooped up from the pile and loaded into the barrel seeming louder than normal. Without the hustle and bustle of the customers, the cage felt isolated. A place where no one would go. Where no one would look. Lewis fought against his chain, unable to muster the strength to free his leg of the red target.

The machine fired.

The ball exploded outwards, whistling through the night air and colliding straight into Lewis's kneecap. The impact caused the patella to instantly shatter, the pain erupting through Lewis's body making him scream furiously into the dark, like a werewolf at a full moon.

The ball bounced to the floor, rolling innocently off down the ramped floor and back into the line for recycling. Lucas watched patiently as Lewis's head arched over, his eyes watering. He was trying to breathe through his agony, his knee a bag of broken shards.

"Your brothers. Names and addresses."

"Fuck! Fuck!" Lewis whimpered.

Lucas exhaled disappointedly and returned to the panel. His fingers found the arrow keys again and swiftly brought the target to Lewis's left knee. What remained of his right one hung a few feet away. He pressed 'release' again.

Another white blur fizzed past, cutting through the calm, quiet night and shattering Lewis's other kneecap. Another resounding roar of anguish filled the cage and Lucas watched patiently as Lewis attempted to deal with the pain.

He thought of Helen.

Tears were now streaming down Lewis's face, his feet planted firmly on the ground. The weight of his body only added to the pressure on the sacks of bones that were once his knees. The shards ground within the skin.

"Please," Lewis begged. "Please stop!"

"Your brothers. Names and addresses." The tone was the same: calm and inflectionless.

"Suck my dick!" Lewis yelled in defiance, the pain racing up to his brain and nausea beginning to take hold.

"I'm not going to suck it."

Without even looking at the panel, Lucas manoeuvred the target until it was resting on Lewis's crotch. Lewis closed his eyes and winced, praying to a God who would, quite rightly, turn his back on him for the things he'd done.

"What did you say earlier? Oh yeah, if we turn this dial all the way up it'll come out like a rocket."

Lewis begged with his eyes as Lucas turned the dial, the power monitor increasing, the bars going from green to red and filling the screen. Lewis looked at the red dot on the zip of his jeans and more tears welled up.

"I suggest you tell me what I want to know, Lewis," Lucas said helpfully. "Otherwise this is really going to hurt."

"Please, just let me go."

The ball shot out at double the speed, the impact a sickening thud. Lewis immediately hunched over as much as his chains would allow and vomited onto his feet. He dry heaved through sharp breaths, the level of pain becoming increasingly difficult to bear. He felt the destruction of his testicles, the agony joining the current batch travelling from his knees up through his neurons to his brain.

"Lewis." Lucas waited.

Lewis couldn't articulate any words. The arrogant, threatening Drayton had been replaced by a broken, whimpering wreck. Lucas watched, feeling not one ounce of remorse. His hand had found its way into his pocket, his finger gently turning the wedding ring over and over. His face hardened, the memory of his dead wife hitting him like a slap in the face. He moved the target to Lewis's rib cage, just under his right armpit.

He fired.

The ball careered through the air.

The ribs broke instantly.

Lewis hung from his wrists, his knees no longer able to perform their duty now they'd been decimated. The ribs floated in his chest, the pain of internal bleeding now at the forefront. He sobbed for mercy.

Lucas responded by moving the red dot so it was painted over the bridge of Lewis's hooked nose.

"Your brothers, Lewis."

Lewis hung for a moment, the cage spinning around him in a hazy, black blur. The piercing light caused him to squint, the pain filling his body until he felt like he would burst. Hope had long since left him.

He shook his head, weeping as he did so.

When the round, solid ball struck Lewis' nose, the explosion it caused was impressive. The bridge instantly shattered, flattening against Lewis's gaunt, rat-like face. Blood burst through both nostrils, down his mouth and onto his shirt. Some of it mixed with the vomit on his feet. The impact caused a deep gash along his forehead, meeting his eyebrows at either side. Breathing was difficult, blood filtering its way down his windpipe.

"Okay! Okay!" Lewis begged, weakly. "Please, just stop."

Lucas removed his hand from the panel and admired his work. One of the people involved in the death of his beloved stood before him, the pain he'd inflicted entirely visible. Lewis was broken, in body and spirit.

Lucas felt nothing for him.

He strode over to the limp, grisly mess and placed two

fingers under a bloody chin. He tilted his head up, looking into the bloodshot eyes.

He saw fear.

"I don't really have any contact with them," Lewis managed, breathing frantically. "I try to visit them all the time, but they don't want me there."

Lucas stood firmly in place, waiting for more. Lewis was fading.

"They contact me when they need me, I swear to God!"

"Who does?"

""Tommy," Lewis swallowed, tasting his own blood. "My brother Tommy. He does everything for Curtis. Fuck knows why, the man is an animal. Tommy's the one who actually killed her."

Lucas leaned in close to Lewis, who was now trembling uncontrollably. The metal of his chains rattled above them.

"Her name was Helen."

Lewis began to cry, tears Lucas ignored.

"Tommy killed her – Helen," Lewis continued. "Harry says the two of them argued about it..."

"Harry?"

"He's the only one I still talk to. He buys coke from me. The guy's an embarrassment to the family."

"Was he there?"

Lewis nodded.

Lucas took a deep breath.

"Where can I find him?"

"At the club."

"What club?!" Lucas's voice broke with anger for the first time.

"The Hive. Curtis lets him run it, it's some crummy strip club. The card is in my wallet."

Lewis turned his head to the side, trying hard to breathe, to see himself through the pain. Lucas reached into the back pocket of Lewis's jeans; he gritted in pain as it jolted his broken knee.

Lucas opened the wallet and thumbed through it. He pulled out a few bank cards, which he dropped into the blood-infused sick pile at his feet. He found a few restaurant cards, offering special offers and free meals in return for stamps. They joined the bank cards.

He then pulled out a black card with electric orange writing. 'The Hive', with an orange outline of a woman leaning against a pole. He turned it, the address leaping out at him.

He pocketed the card, feeling it slide next to the wedding ring. The wallet splashed into the puddle below and Lucas then fished out car keys from Lewis's front pocket. He jangled them in front of Lewis, claiming ownership of the vehicle without saying a word or receiving any rebuke. The only sound was the hum of the 'Pin Point' machine. The air felt cooler as Lucas stared at Lewis, who was weeping to himself.

"Thank you, Lewis."

Lucas strode back to the panel, retrieving his leather jacket from the top of it. He held it in his hands, remembering the surprise as he pulled it from the bag that night in the hallway.

The look of excitement on Helen's face.

Her beautiful face.

"What have you done, Lucas?"

Helen's voice registered just louder than a whisper, the words floated around him. He felt her presence, the white smudges of her gown in the corner of his eye. He looked straight ahead, the misty vision of Helen staring a hole right through him. Her blue eyes, no firm edges to them, were fixed on his stern, blank face. He drew his lips into a thin, firm line, refusing to turn.

He shook his head.

She was gone.

"Hey!" Lewis's voice croaked, gurgling a small amount of blood.

Lucas ignored it as he pulled his leather jacket over his large, muscular arms. He pulled the jacket straight over his chest and stuffed the car keys in the pocket.

"HEY!" Lewis managed a scream.

Lucas looked at him blankly and turned towards the exit.

"I told you what you wanted!"

Lucas stopped, looking up at the night sky, Lewis hung from his chains, his body destroyed by Lucas's vengeance.

"You can let me go now."

Lucas turned, looking at Lewis one final time. The red dot from the scope still flickered on the centre of his crushed face.

"I never said I'd let you go."

Lewis's eyes burst with fear as Lucas switched the panel to 'Auto-fire'. Lewis yelled in vain as Lucas walked out of the batting area. He pushed open the mesh door and began his journey to 'The Hive'. He disappeared into the night. The machine roared into life, the loading mechanism working loudly as it loaded ball after ball into its chamber. Lewis tried to block out the pain, his knees were gone, his ribs shattered. Blood poured from his face. His chains rattled ferociously as he struggled for freedom.

The first ball loaded into the cannon.

The laser dot shone directly on his face.

Lewis screamed into the darkness of the night.

CHAPTER THIRTEEN

Starling had almost enjoyed his evening off.

He and Annette had lain in bed until the early afternoon and when she awoke from her sleep, she cuddled into him. They made love again, this time slower and more tenderly than when they'd collided earlier that morning. As she showered, Starling stretched between the bed sheets, wondering if it was too soon to propose.

The thought left his mind quickly when she returned, one towel wrapped around her tight, toned body and another around her hair. Her skin glistened.

"I want to go bowling," she declared, smiling at the handsome officer lying in front of her. He agreed and hopped in the shower himself before they left.

They played a couple of games, playfully arguing about Annette's need to raise the side barriers. Even with them up, she still bowled a pretty appalling game and faced many sarcastic comments, especially when Starling nailed a couple of strikes.

He led her by the hand down the street towards the car, deciding on a whim to take her to dinner before she had to dash back to her own flat to get ready for yet another nightshift. They sat across the table, enjoying delicious Italian food and sharing an intense conversation about the complexities of getting a mortgage in the current financial climate. When he dropped her off outside her block of flats, she leaned over and kissed him as hard as she could, grabbing his t-shirt by the scruff of the collar.

"Goodnight, handsome!" She winked at him.

He smiled back, waving as he pulled away to enjoy a relaxed evening of catching up on the latest TV show everyone at the station was talking about. She felt her heart flutter.

She was falling in love.

———

Starling visited his father the next morning, bringing him a few books that he'd requested but would probably never read. The weather on that Bank Holiday Monday was glorious and the friendly nurses allowed him and his dad to enjoy the well-kept gardens which sat behind Romford Hills Retirement Home.

They sat and played chess for most of the afternoon, his father's stroke not affecting his ability to wipe Starling out in just a few moves.

Starling cherished every moment of it.

The pretty blonde nurse, Kimberly, brought over his dad's medicine along with his lunch and, as accommodating as always, even prepared a sandwich for Starling. He gratefully accepted and shared the meal with his father in the sun.

He needed the time to recollect himself: the fury of Bailey's reluctance to chase the Draytons had made him question his career for the first time. He calmed down, ensuring he was relaxed when he was ready to tackle his night shift.

When he began his shift at ten that evening, things were quiet. He thought of Annette, his mind wandering to the feel of her naked body and the smell of her as she sat on top of him.

By eleven thirty, all hell had broken loose.

In a side street just off Kilburn High Road, Lucas rolled his recently acquired car to a stop. It was the main road which ran through the centre of the London Borough of Brent like an artery. The road was lined with streetlamps, the majority encasing the street in an artificial glow. Vehicles dotted the sides of the streets in allocated parking spaces, the roads themselves being relatively quiet and the residents all in their homes preparing to return to work after a rare long weekend.

The clock on the dashboard worked, however the bulb behind the numbers was dying a slow death. It was eleven fifteen and back in Harrow, baseballs would still be hammering the bloody cage where Lewis's head used to be. Lucas had expected an overwhelming rush of adrenaline to kick in afterwards: the act of killing a man should never be easy.

Lucas sat calmly.

He felt no excitement. No remorse.

Nothing.

He thought about Harry and how he could see 'The Hive' from where he was parked. The dreary, grey building was offensive just to look at. A tacky, neon sign sat above the door and almost seemed embarrassed to display the name. Either side of the single door were two burly bouncers, both on the overweight side who looked like they had seen better days. The beat of a dance song thumped through the walls.

Somewhere inside was Harry Drayton.

Lucas gripped the steering wheel with both hands, the thought of that man being involved in his wife's death making his knuckles turn white. The hard texture of the leather imprinted on his palms. The car smelt like stale cigarettes.

"Remember the good, baby."

Lucas's hard eyes flickered to the rear-view mirror. They met the unblinking stare of Helen, her eyes shining like two bright, blue marbles. He took a breath, looking down at his lap.

"You're not real."

He chanted it, repeating the words over and over, hoping they would have an effect on his wife's ghost. Helen's white gown floated around her, like tassels in a wind machine. Her words were almost echoing.

"Remember the good, baby," the vision repeated.

Lucas gripped the wheel again, closing his eyes and casting his mind back through his memories. He thought of Helen dropping a plate of hot sausages he'd just cooked one Sunday afternoon as they'd hosted a barbecue. He thought of her brushing her hair in the villa they'd rented in Gran Canaria four years before, the beaming sun setting behind the horizon through the window behind her. He thought of holding her arms at her side by the kitchen sink, and dabbing at her face with the foam from the washing up liquid as she playfully screamed.

He opened his eyes, staring into the mirror at the haunting spectre of his love.

"It was all good."

His words were broken, hanging heavily in the air. He took another deep breath, pushed open the car door and stepped out. He looked at 'The Hive' from across the street, the dark, gloomy structure calling to him.

He marched across the road, intent on killing Harry Drayton.

Helen had vanished from the back seat.

Officer Ravi Shah circled the roundabout, indicated and pulled off down the dual carriageway. Northwick Park hospital loomed beyond the trees to the left, the gigantic edifice fading into the night sky. He'd been part of the Harrow Response Team for over two years and had built up a reputation for being one of the toughest officers in the precinct.

Firm but fair.

Next to him sat Officer Daniel Carter, two months out of the Hendon Police Centre where eager new recruits were graduating more often, it seemed. Carter was a tall man which meant he carried his large bulk well. Shah, on the other hand, was always taking well-meant jibes, about his lack of stature, in his stride.

What he lacked in height, he made up with competence.

"So, what's the best arrest you have made?" Carter asked.

Questions like this were expected from new recruits. Their idea of policing was diving through windows with two guns and getting a medal from the mayor. Shah always enjoyed the naïve enthusiasm, knowing it would soon fade under routine calls to ungrateful members of the public and mountains of paperwork. He'd begun to wonder if they sent new recruits out with him so he could teach them that as soon as possible.

"All of my arrests have been personal favourites." He kept the car at a steady thirty. "An arrest is an arrest. Plain and simple."

"Have you ever had to throw down with someone?"

"Throw down?"

"You know, fight someone." Carter pulled his fists up and bobbed like an amateur boxer.

"Look, Dan, you do realise that just because you have the police uniform on and have a police badge, you haven't suddenly become John McClane." Shah said, his eyes squinting in confusion at the bright spotlight coming from over the hill.

"I know, I know," the young, eager officer replied.

They sat in silence for a while, Shah maintaining his gaze on the bright light peeking over the hill ever so slightly. He checked the time on the dashboard and tutted to himself. Indicating, he turned off the road, calmly swerving the car up the slip road that cut through the grass toward the driving range.

"Something's not right." He said, more to himself than the oblivious Carter.

"What about deaths? Seen anything gruesome?"

Shah pulled the car to a halt across the front of the Golf in Class entrance, not even bothering with a parking space. The floodlight illuminated the batting cage and as both men stepped out of the vehicle, a loud thud crashed against mesh metal.

"Have you?" Carter asked, irritating the senior officer with his persistence. Shah strode purposefully down the path leading down to the cages, his stab-proof vest rustling against his shirt.

"There's nothing exciting about dead bodies. All it means is bad news for someone and a shitload of paperwork. Okay?"

"Okay." Carter responded, his voice a shade of disappointment. "Why are we here?"

"I'm not sure yet.'

Shah walked confidently, hiding the nerves which had

begun to creep into his mind. This was Drayton territory and he prayed silently to himself that Lewis Drayton was just indulging in some late night swinging practice.

Another metallic thud echoed through the air.

It was so quiet apart from the distant humming of machinery constant in the background. Their police boots crunched on the stones beneath them as they approached the cages, the floodlight above burning its explosive gaze onto the first batting area.

Another thud, the ball rocketing so hard against the fence the entire cage rattled.

It was then, a few feet from the cage, when Shah noticed the blood hanging from the mesh like red stalactites. His eyes shot to the ground, blood pooling around the base of the cage, the floodlight providing it with a glossy, polished finish.

Shah ran to the cage door with the heavy-footed Carter in pursuit and he pushed it open with a forceful shoulder.

Both men stopped in their tracks.

Shah's eyes widened in horror.

Carter took a few steps back, hunched over and threw up the dinner he'd enjoyed a few hours before.

Another ball crashed against the cage, under limp arms that hung from red chains. The feeble body swayed gently, the clothes sticking to it and thick with blood. The legs, chained a few feet apart, rocked awkwardly and were misshapen at the knees. The floor was covered in a mix of vomit, blood and bits of skull.

Another ball shot out at an unmanageable speed, crashing against the cage where the head should have been.

Shah composed himself, his hand trembling as it reached up to the breast of his stab-proof vest and flicked on his radio.

"Control Receiving. Officer seven-seven-two. I need units at Golf in Class, Harrow. Send everyone. Fast!"

He waited, watched as another ball shot through the air, the impact resonating within him. He could only imagine the pain that had been experienced that night. He cast an eye over his shoulder, looking for his partner. Carter was leaning against the main building, his face pale and his legs shaking.

The image would stay with Carter forever. It was the harshest of learning curves. His radio cackled.

"Received. What's the situation?"

Shah watched another ball hurtle towards the recently deceased. He turned his head to the radio and spoke as calmly as possible.

"Somebody has killed Lewis Drayton."

———

Whiskey swirled around the glass as it poured from the bottle, facing the same fate as the three previous helpings. Fletcher didn't even bother putting the top back on the bottle, instead firmly placing it on the table next to him. The woozy effects of alcohol were beginning to filter in as his hands sloppily patted at the open packet of cigarettes. The smoke from his last one still hung around the sofa like an ominous raincloud.

A feeling of guilt had weighed heavily on his mind ever since the moment Lucas had left the night before. It wasn't just the Draytons he had put in danger, it was Lucas himself.

He sunk the whiskey in one gulp.

More splashed into the glass, his hand shaking as it gripped the neck of the bottle.

The old police radio sat on his side table, a thick layer

of dust wrapping around it along with the stale smell of a thousand cigarettes.

It suddenly burst into life.

"Somebody has killed Lewis Drayton."

The world went quiet.

Fletcher sat for what felt like an eternity, a mixture of fear and remorse dancing a waltz through his body. It was only when his sock began to feel wet that he realised he'd dropped the bottle of whiskey on the unvacuumed carpet, his favourite drink pooling around his feet.

He lit another cigarette, his thumb struggling with the wheel to ignite the flame.

As he drew the smoke in, he trembled, thinking of how ashamed Susan would have been. The idea of Lucas making a step he could not go back from was laid squarely at his door.

Drayton blood was on his hands.

He exhaled the smoke.

'What have I done?'

———

Lemar had been a bouncer at 'The Hive' for a little over two years. At forty-six years of age, his best days of bodybuilding were behind him. Still, he loomed over pretty much every sleazy man or workgroup who filtered through the door, their hands stuffed with notes and their minds fixed on other things. He had worked as a personal trainer for over fifteen years and was married with kids.

Then the cocaine addiction had started.

At first it was in small doses but soon his body relied on the substance and more money was thrown down the drug-induced drain. The wife, the kids, the healthy lifestyle had all left him, their memories fading with every sniff of white powder.

Now he was happy to spend his evenings here, working alongside Phil, the confiscation of his beloved drug from weak, pathetic customers becoming more regular. After throwing out the foot draggers at the end of the night, he would go backstage, trading a few hits from his newly acquired stash for a blowjob from one of his fellow addict strippers.

Phil, on the other hand, was nowhere near as tall as his partner, but was just as stocky. His large gut pushed the black shirt that he was required to wear to almost ripping point. Every night, he yearned for a customer to misbehave, to get in his face and challenge him. If there was one thing he loved in this world, it was smacking an arrogant little pervert in the face with his sledgehammer-like fists.

Both of them hated Harry Drayton, agreeing on many occasions that he was nothing more than a weasel. He had an awkward, lanky frame and a mop of greasy, black hair which sat scruffily on top of his head. The man was a disaster, relying on the two bodyguards he kept with him at all times to keep people in line. He demanded Lemar bring him the majority of the procured drugs from the evenings, snorting line after line in the private booth at the back of the club.

But they both knew what his surname meant and the weight that it held.

They never said a thing.

Phil was the one who noticed the man stride purposefully across the deserted main road. As he approached, Phil tried to position himself in a more imposing way.

The man didn't stop.

As he walked into the glare of the flashing neon sign, he appeared to Phil as a physical specimen. A challenge.

Lucas attempted to walk through the door when the bald, burly bouncer stepped in his way. The large, black bouncer, his dreadlocks tied back, stood a few feet behind, his hands resting on his hips.

"Hold up. Membership card."

Phil didn't so much as request it, but threaten him with it. Lucas stared him straight in his eyes. Phil could feel pure hatred radiating from the man in front of him. He made sure his hands were ready.

"Are you deaf? Membership card."

"I'm here to see Harry Drayton." Lucas's voice was calm, unflinching. The two door men looked at each other and then back at the man before them. Phil chuckled. This guy had guts, he would give him that.

"What business do you have with Harry?"

"*My* business." Lucas made to walk past and Phil stepped up to him, invading Lucas's personal space and making his first mistake. Lemar stood between Phil and the doorway, where an avalanche of dance music burst through.

"Listen you dozy cunt, I asked you a question. What fucking business do you have with Harry?"

Phil prodded a stubby round finger into Lucas's chest, pushing him back a step. Lucas looked down, the finger causing a small, greasy smudge on his prized jacket. His eyes flashed up, meeting Phil's after his second mistake.

Suddenly, the night seemed silent. No sound except the calm, stern words of Lucas.

"I'm here to kill him."

Phil immediately swung a fist at Lucas, but was too late. Lucas took a step to the side, sliding his arm behind Phil's neck and wrenching his arm upwards. The burly bouncer bent over forward, his arm aloft as Lucas pushed down on the back of his head with his forearm, his other hand wrenching his arm upwards by his thick, tattooed wrist. As Phil groaned in pain, Lemar took a few steps forward only for Lucas to stamp forward, the sole of the shoe connecting perfectly with the incoming kneecap.

His knee locked, the pain causing him to yell out, disturbing a few of the smoking customers situated round the side of the building. He dropped to his knee in the flashing beams of the neon sign, trying to gather himself as Lucas wrenched Phil's arm further upwards, the ligaments twisting and detaching themselves quickly. Phil struggled, still hunched over, blindly swinging his left arm back across to try and attack his captor. Lucas brought his elbow down hard on the back of Phil's skull, sending a shock wave of pain through his spine. In one fluid motion, Lucas spun Phil to his right, driving the top of his skull into the crumbling, brick wall surrounding the doorway.

Phil dropped to the concrete below, motionless. Blood escaped from the deep gash caused by the impact.

"Get the fuck out here, now!"

Lemar held the radio in his hand, screaming into it as Lucas approached. It was the last thing Lemar would remember as Lucas sent him to sleep with a hard knee to the side of the head.

Both men lay motionless, their silent pain alternately brightened and darkened by the sign above the door. The music roared a loud welcome to Lucas as he continued his journey and entered 'The Hive'.

The inside was as depressingly unwelcoming as it was outside, the narrow bar area brightened by a single light hanging from a low ceiling. The music pumped out of speakers placed around the entire venue, and through the bar it opened out into the main stage area. There were two of them, small and elevated above the floor and guarded by metal poles, eager punters leaning on them with their heads resting on their hands. On the stage, Sapphire, the main attraction of the club, slid down the pole, her exposed breasts bouncing as she came to a stop. She wore a thin, glittering thong that had a few notes hanging out of it and as the music echoed and the customers cheered, she began to ease it off.

In the private booth at the far end of the room, Harry Drayton arched forward, sniffing another line of cocaine from the table, whilst two of his employed strippers sat either side of him, running their hands over his thighs and his crotch. The bottles on the table were numerous and, combined with the drugs, meant that nobody at the table was mentally themselves.

The booth was a circular chair cut into the wall, the seats covered in leather cushions for comfort. Either side of the entrance were two bodyguards, employed by Curtis to keep Harry safe and out of trouble.

Lucas walked through the bar area, ignoring the offer of a drink from the scantily-clad barmaid who clearly made more in tips. The music drew him to the main stage, the lights flashing as Sapphire, now completely naked, bent over for the leering crowds of men who had gathered at the railings, throwing money and demanding more.

A fist flew at Lucas and he immediately threw up a forearm, deflecting it and responding with a jumping knee to the ribs. The bouncer, drawn to Lucas by Lemar's final call before unconsciousness, stumbled back a few steps, allowing his partner to charge. Lucas span to his left, grasped the back of the bouncer's shirt collar and directed his head to the metal railing edging the empty stage. The impact was loud, in pain and volume, and everyone in the vicinity turned. The customers watched on with enthusiasm, whilst Sapphire scrambled naked on the stage floor, trying to collect her earnings.

In the far booth, one of the bodyguards told Harry to leave, watching as the young Drayton couldn't string together a coherent trail of thought due to his intoxication. Whilst he waited for Harry to move slowly, scrambling over the unhelpful strippers, the other bodyguard ran to join the action.

With the music rattling the dimly lit club, Lucas dropped the unconscious man against the stage and planted his feet firmly on the floor. The other bouncer, feeling the pain surfacing in his ribs, re-approached, throwing wild punches, all of which Lucas blocked with maximum efficiency. He then delivered a hard side kick to the man's upper thigh, thinking back to the technique Alex had shown him. As the bouncer's balance deserted him, he stumbled to the left, where Lucas connected with a sickeningly powerful right hook. The bouncer fell to the stick, hardwood floor with his jaw instantly broken.

Lucas looked down at the two bouncers, feeling nothing but the drive to find Harry and marched past the customers who all backed away, their fear obvious. The bodyguard, dressed in a black suit, had a knife in his left hand, his mission to stop Lucas clear. He lunged at Lucas who instantly dropped his shoulder, the blade cutting the air beside his stern, focused face. He instantly grabbed the man's wrist with both hands and then lifted his back into the man's body. With the momentum of the lunge, the bodyguard flipped over Lucas and slammed his spine against one of the thick oak tables that were nailed to the floor for safety reasons. The impact was as brutal as it was quick, the bodyguard hitting the hard floor head-first as he dropped. The customers had begun to cheer Lucas on, nobody applauding Sapphire as she hastened her exit from the stage, notes hanging from her folded arms.

Harry witnessed the attack, his face somehow creating a new shade of pale from fear. He managed to scramble out of the booth, falling over the little step and then stumbled towards the fire exit door. Lucas approached the final bodyguard, who pulled his hands up, revealing his boxing training. Lucas manoeuvred into a defensive stance and blocked the first few jabs. As the bodyguard propelled forward with a right hook, Lucas cut him off with an uppercut that connected with the underneath of his chin. Blood, saliva and teeth spewed out of the man's mouth like a fountain and he fell back against the table where Harry had been seated moments ago. Bottles toppled, like sandcastles falling into the sea and the two strippers screamed in terror. Before the bodyguard could get to a vertical stance again, Lucas connected with a hard right, sending the man crashing face-first into the small step, before rolling onto the floor, his face a crimson mask.

Lucas looked at the two strippers, who huddled in fear screaming for help. He looked back at the customers, many of them awestruck by the sheer efficiency of his fighting. The music still pounded out of the speakers like a tribal drum, the lights flashing. The scene of destruction flashed into sharp relief one second, then was gone the next.

Lucas took one final sweep of the venue, the four bodies lying either motionless or writhing in severe pain.

He straightened his jacket and marched out the fire exit door.

———

A thin mist of rain had mixed with the wind and it blasted Harry in the face as he burst through the back door. His shirt swung untucked from his trousers, his jacket stained with alcohol. The panic of being chased was amplified in his head due to the amount of drugs circulating through his body. His steps were uneven, his legs wobbling as he stumbled across the car park towards the red Porsche he'd parked under the only working lamp post. The light beamed down on his escape route as if from the heavens themselves.

His hands fought his trousers until they found the pocket, trembling as they entered and pulled out the keys.

The sound of the door opening and closing behind him inspired Harry to pick up the pace, however one foot ignored the other and they collided, sending Harry to the hard, concrete floor. His keys spilled from his hands, sliding a few feet ahead. The air was damp, mixing with the tears beginning to fall down his cheeks.

Footsteps echoed in the car park, closing in on Harry as he pushed himself up, blood easing out of a cut on his knee.

He managed to scoop up the keys from the ground but fell against the door of his car. He fumbled around, the keys slipping around his fingers like a wet bar of soap as he hurriedly tried to find the correct one.

The footsteps came to a stop behind.

Harry took a deep breath, then made an effort to wrestle hold of the fear.

"Look man, I don't know what this is about or who the fuck you are but please, let's just...

Harry spun around fast, the keys flailing out of his grip like claws. He swung them at Lucas's face as hard as he could.

Calmly, Lucas reached up and grabbed him by his thin, flimsy forearm. Harry's eyes burst with horror as Lucas spun him around, and with his hand firmly grasping the back of Harry's skull, drove his head into the car window. The faint wailing of sirens could be heard in the distance, merging with the muffled thumping of the club's music.

Harry hit the ground silently, followed by a downpour of glass that glistened like rain in the single beam of light from above.

CHAPTER FOURTEEN

"Fuck!"

A TV monitor crashed against the bright, cream walls of the 'Odds On' betting shop, the screen shattering and collapsing to the floor followed by trickles of glass. On the other wall, the bracket from which it had originally hung swung from one final screw; all the others had been ripped out along with the monitor.

Curtis Drayton angrily observed the monitor fall to the floor, anger pumping through his body like an overdose. His face was a shade of pink, the fury changing his complexion. He breathed heavily as he tried to control the rage that had surged through him as soon as Tommy had taken the call.

Usually, he would have revelled in the fear a police officer would have had knowing he was about to call the Draytons. The squirming, pathetic man of the law. Blind rage had removed all traces of pleasure.

He may not have liked or respected Lewis, at times even hated him. But he was family. The family he had protected from their father all those years ago and a part of the family he'd built into an empire running London.

Lewis was his property and his property had been destroyed.

Tommy stood with his large, vein-riddled arms folded, his back resting against the long counter running the length of the shop. His apparent calm about the situation was only adding to Curtis's fury, a whirlwind of explosive rage in a fine, tailor-made suit.

Sat on the high stools were two lackeys, names that Curtis couldn't remember and didn't care about. They were hired by Tommy to do errands that neither of them wanted to do.

You could have heard a pin drop but for Curtis's breathing.

He angrily paced the room, glass cracking under his Italian loafers as he turned to his younger brother.

"You find this guy, okay, Tommy? You find this motherfucker and you kill him. YOU KILL HIM!"

Tommy raised an eyebrow at the command then returned to the phone, his hulking hands skimming the smart phone screen. Curtis angrily snatched it and hurled it at the wall. Another downpour of technology scattered the floor. Tommy, stone-faced, turned to Curtis.

'Some prick thinks he can attack our family. Our family!' Curtis ranted, still pacing. His voice echoed in the silent shop. "I want him, I want his family and I want his family's family. You hear me?"

"Calm down!" Tommy soothed.

"Calm down? CALM FUCKING DOWN?" Curtis almost chuckled. "He killed our brother, Tommy!"

"Yeah, he killed Lewis." Tommy pushed himself off the counter. "But let's face it, Lewis was a piece of shit embarrassment to this family. Always has been. If anything, this has saved us a job."

"So, what? You're on this prick's side all of a sudden? I should fucking kill you right now!"

Tommy took a few steps forward towards Curtis, both men burning holes through the other's eyes. Tommy encased Curtis in his hulking shadow. His voice was low and quiet.

"You really want to go down that road with me, Curtis?"

Curtis's face distorted into a hideous scowl and he turned from the intimidation of his brother, taking slow steps to the other elevated table. Tommy stood, hands on his hips.

"Look, we're not the only people in this city capable of things like this. You remember the amount of bloodshed when Flanagan and his boys tried to take Wood Green?"

Curtis snorted, his mind racing back to the Irish brothers who'd tried to muscle in a few years ago, selling their cheap heroin at even cheaper prices. The streets of Wood Green were stained with more than just blood after Tommy had taken it back.

"I say we wait until morning, wait until we hear from Ashley about what's going on and we go from there."

Tommy's suggestion appeared to fall on deaf ears, Curtis staring at a blank patch of wall, no one daring to imagine what was circling his mind. The two lackeys sat silently, obediently, like attack dogs. Tommy crunched over glass to his elder brother.

"But, believe me, Curtis. When we find this piece of shit, and I promise you I will. We'll make sure he feels every second of his death."

Curtis turned slowly, almost unnerved by the cold vengeance hanging in his brother's words. He took a breath and stood up, straightening his tie. Wrestling back control.

"Just bring him to me."

He nodded at his brother, then powerfully stepped over

to the other table. The hired muscle immediately sat to attention: Curtis felt the power returning.

"Call some of your boys. I want protection for Matt, Harry and Ashley and I want it now. Wherever they go, your boys follow."

"Matt won't like being babysat," Tommy interjected.

"Fuck Matt!" Curtis turned, snarling his words. "He will do what he's goddamned told!"

Tommy shrugged his brother off, who turned back to the blank, fear-filled faces under his employment.

"Go on then."

The two men quickly slid their chairs back, the screech of the metal shrill like a bird chirping. They exited through the door quickly, Curtis watching them leave with a twisted snarl.

"I need a drink."

He stalked slowly towards the door to his office, looking at the broken mess of technology on the floor and making a note to have it cleaned. Tommy had pulled another phone from his pocket, his thumb fanning over the bright screen.

"Want me to call the others? Let them know what's happened?"

"Yes, do it!" Curtis replied. "Tell them to keep their eyes and ears open. Also, make sure you keep trying Harry. He never answers his phone."

"That's because he is usually flat on his back and completely fucked."

Curtis chuckled, pushing open the door to climb the stairs to his impending drink. Tommy raised the phone to his ears.

———

Harry woke up flat on his back and completely fucked. He didn't know it straightaway, his eyes wearily forcing themselves open to be greeted by a sharp brightness from a lone bulb. The room smelt damp and dusty, the surface he laid on was hard and unforgiving. His arms were outstretched above his head, bound by metal around the wrists. Cable clips, the plastic staples used to tack wire to the wall, had been hammered to the wooden desk between his fingers, separating them at the knuckle as if he was doing an elaborate wave.

His head throbbed with pain, and it was joined by the feeling of blood sticky in his naturally greasy hair. He tried moving his feet, but, again, his joints met nothing but metal.

An echoing sound of whistling filled the room behind him, bouncing off the walls and making it impossible to pinpoint.

"Hello?"

No answer, although the shuffling sound of footsteps and drawers being opened caused Harry to make the attempt to turn his head.

"Is somebody there?"

His words trembled, his fear laid bare. He retraced his steps, the throbbing pain of a head injury and the aftereffects of a lot of cocaine and alcohol not helping his task. He remembered being at the club, Tiffany, the newest stripper, rubbing him off under the table whilst he took another line.

He remembered a panic, bouncers and bodyguards rushing.

He remembered the shrieks of terror, the crash of a body on a table.

The man in the leather jacket.

His body tightened immediately, his breathing became difficult through panicked thoughts and sharp exhales. The man in the leather jacket, who had been picking apart his trained protectors as if they were nothing.

In the car park. Falling over. The footsteps. The wild slash of the keys.

He remembered the man grabbing his arm with considerable strength.

Then black.

Harry tried to calm his breathing but only ended up crying.

Chills had danced up Lucas's spine as he'd pulled into the gravel car park, specks of rain randomly dotting the windscreen. The Porsche was a nice drive, the car handling like a dream through the empty streets across London. The journey from Kilburn to Bermondsey was almost eight miles, although even at eleven-thirty at night, the A5 was a beehive of activity and bright headlights.

Lucas had laughed as he'd stopped at a red light, only for a police car to pull up beside him. The officers looked across, seeing Harry lying back in the chair, completely motionless. Lucas had removed the remainder of the glass from the window he'd introduced to Harry's skull and leaned his elbow on it casually. Lucas intimated to them that Harry had had one too many, rolling his eyes and shaking his head. One of the officers smiled before they drove off as soon as the lights changed, obviously with more important matters to attend to. Something they had in common with Lucas.

As he'd pulled the Porsche to a stop in the car park, he'd felt his stomach flip. Strung across the doorway in an x shape was black and yellow police tape. The warning sign fluttered in the wind which painted the door with a fresh coat of rain drops.

This is where it happened, he told himself.

The police had explained to him where they'd found her and researching the location online hadn't been difficult. He winced as he imagined a terrified Helen being hauled from a car, dragged across this very gravel and taken inside. His throat began to overlap on itself, the imminent feeling of throwing up taking over as he thought of the sick, depraved bastards as they'd their hands over his wife. He hunched over and dry heaved, no sick, no saliva pouring forth.

Only pain.

He composed himself, finding relief in the crispness of the cold moisture sitting thickly in the ever increasing wind. The area was silent, the industrial park an arena of isolation. Many of the units or offices were boarded up, 'for sale' signs littering the parking lot.

This place was a graveyard.

A place where lives came to an end.

He was in the right place.

Lucas wrenched the tape from the door frame with one easy swipe before using a full force kick to rattle the flimsy lock off its hinge. The door swung open, a waft of damp and neglect almost knocking him over. Lucas took a deep breath and then entered the dark.

As he stepped inside, he willed his eyes to adjust to the room, with a vague awareness of furniture and objects pushed against the wall. As he walked in further, something slapped gently against his face.

A light switch.

He pulled the string and a single bulb buzzed into life.

Squinting, he saw a lone sofa in the room, out of place with the freshness of its quality. Scanning around he noticed a large workbench in the far corner of the room and then a sight that made his fists clench.

A dried patch of blood staining the floor.

He knew it had belonged to Helen.

He pushed his grief aside and heaved the sofa to the shadows encompassing the circular beam and then made light work of hauling the bench into its place.

Now the bench had Harry Drayton secured to it, with nowhere to run and no excuses. Lucas remained silent, opening up the drawers in a tool storage unit, the metallic implements jingling as he rummaged through them.

"Help me!" Harry increased the volume.

Lucas sighed and slowly walked over to the bench, his footsteps inviting dust to rise from the floor in small clouds. He reached the end of the table, strolling around it slowly until his eyes made contact with the fearful Harry.

"Do you honestly think I'd take you somewhere where anyone might be able to hear you?"

Lucas raised his eyebrows, awaiting a response. The horrified expression was the only answer he needed. He returned to the darker outskirts of the room, leaving Harry to ponder his fate while he rifled through more tools until he found what he'd been looking for. They had seen better days, the rust clinging to the metal like fungus.

Harry's voice was as weak as he was.

"Look man, I don't know who you are, but I got money. Yeah? I can get you money, drugs, women. You name it."

Lucas remained silent as he returned the man's side, his hands gripping his findings but hiding them from Harry's view.

"What do you want?" Harry exclaimed in naïve hope.

"I want to tell you a story." Harry looked at Lucas in puzzlement. "There was a man who, let's say, strayed from the path. For years he was doing things, feeling things and thinking things that no one should. For a long time. A long, dark time.

"But then, at the age of twenty one he meets not only

the most beautiful woman he has ever seen, but also a reason. A reason to live in this world like everybody else does. Also a reason to lock away all those bad thoughts and feelings, and to get himself back on the path. A reason just to wake up in the mornings."

Lucas almost smiled, reminiscing about the splendour of his dearly departed. That look quickly vanished as he turned and stared straight at the tear-stained face of the man on the bench.

"Then two weeks ago, she was abducted, beaten, raped and killed by your, soon to be deceased, family." Lucas leant in, his face a few inches from Harry's.

"So when you ask me what I want, I think you can answer that for yourself."

"I'm sorry," Harry murmured quietly.

"What?'

"I'm sorry. I'm so sorry."

Lucas closed his eyes, taking a calming breath. When they opened, the calmness had been replaced by the purest form of hatred.

"You're sorry? For what? For taking the only woman I've ever loved and putting her through a living hell? Tell me Harry, how many other women have you and your brothers killed that you're sorry for? Huh?"

Harry tried to look away, but the restraint meant he could only turn his head so far. All he could see was darkness. Lucas leaned over again.

"Answer me!" His voice portraying the threat that ignoring him would bring.

"Loads, okay? Loads. I don't know how many. It's Curtis, you have to believe me. The man is twisted. Something went really fucking wrong a long fucking time ago."

"What do you mean?"

"I mean he has this real fucked up need to feel powerful. Every chance he gets, he tries to shit on people. Talk down to them. It's happened to every one of us. His ego feeds off it. That's what happened to your wife."

"An ego boost? Listen to me Harry, my wife did not die because some pathetic man needed to feel like a king." Lucas hated even saying it. "She died because you and your family made the conscious decision to take her."

"I told you, man. It was Curtis. He's the one you want."

"Oh, he is. And he will be held accountable for his actions."

Lucas finally pulled up his hands, placing a large hammer and a blunt, rusty chisel on the table. Harry wriggled against his restraints to no avail.

"As will you."

"I said I was sorry."

"And I believe you are. But not for what you did, just that I found you."

Harry wept, his pathetic sobs not even registering with Lucas as a reason for pity. His hand slid inside his jean pocket, the cold feel of the wedding ring reminding him of why he was here.

Every step he'd taken, each one leading him further beyond the point of no return. They would never stop hunting him, especially as by now they would have found the remains of Lewis Drayton, strung up and left to die like the animal he was.

Lucas firmly squeezed the ring one more time, before reaching to the bench and picking up his recently-acquired tools.

Starling pushed young Adrian Helms through the station doors, the arrogant kid dragging his feet to make things difficult. Starling had dealt with the young offender before, this being the third time in the last year he'd arrested the eighteen year-old. He had tried compassion, warning the slightly-built wannabe street gangster exactly how many husbands he would have in prison but it never seemed to register with him.

Now he'd decided to bring him in, book him and let the family decide whether or not to press charges. If so, it would be interesting to see how a Crown Court would perceive his third strike for burglary.

He pushed the smart-mouthed offender to the check in desk, when suddenly the imposing frame of Sergeant Bailey appeared through the glass double doors to the left.

"Starling. With me."

Starling obliged, leaving Adrian in the capable hands of the desk officer. Bailey strode at an alarmingly fast pace for a man of his size, hurtling through the corridors like a one-man stampede. Starling struggled to keep up.

"Everything okay, Sarge?" Starling asked over loud thudding of police boots.

"No, it's not okay." Bailey opened the door, inviting Starling in first. "You could say a hell of a lot of shit has just hit a very big fan."

They entered the main office of the station, none of the desks being manned. Officers working the nightshift were assembled in the conference room, none of them there a few days earlier when Bailey had chewed Starling out in front of everyone.

Starling was grateful for that fact.

As they'd entered, Bailey strode to the front, immediately commanding everyone's attention with his authoritative approach. Starling stood, arms folded across his Met vest, at the back of the room.

"Right, listen up!" Bailey stood in his usual stance: legs apart, fists on hips, and a cold gaze panning the room. "I'm not going to beat around the bush. Lewis Drayton is dead."

Excited murmurs passed around the room like a quick-fire game of Chinese whispers.

"We don't know who did it, or why it was done. What we do know is it was a methodical and violent attack."

"How was he killed?" Officer Marsden sensibly asked.

"He was strung up in a batting cage, tortured and then left to be somewhat decapitated by an onslaught of baseballs."

Stunned silence can sometimes be louder than any reaction. Bailey nodded agreement with their shock.

"Not exactly a robbery gone wrong, eh? I've spoken with the Captain who stated that any station within what is now being called the 'Drayton Zone' is to treat this as top priority."

"I thought we were supposed to ignore the Draytons?" Starling asked, immediately regretting it. Judging the look that Bailey gave him, he knew he was right.

"Starling, things change. The Draytons have been informed of the murder and now we are preparing for what may be a very volatile retaliation. Now we don't know if this was gang- or business-related. Hell, it could just be the fact that the family are a bunch of arseholes. The bottom line is, we need to establish any connections between anything that could have led to this."

The room of officers obediently scribbled in their notebooks. Bailey gave them one final look before he marched to the door.

"Let's nip this one in the bud before it starts."

Just as Bailey was about to leave, the young desk officer appeared in the doorway, slightly out of breath.

"Sarge?"

"Yes?" All the officers turned to attention. Starling

pushed himself from the back wall, his focus on the young officer.

"I just got a call from Sergeant Patel from Brent."

"I know him, he's a good man."

"He said that there was an attack at 'The Hive' nightclub this evening. Six men were badly beaten and the owner, a Harry Drayton, is missing."

Starling exhaled, realising the situation had just got a whole lot worse. The officers all looked at each other and another game of Chinese whispers instantly began.

Sergeant Bailey only needed one word to convey his reaction.

"Shit!"

―――――

"Harry, I want you tell me about Curtis. Now if you tell me what I want, then things will be easier for you. If you lie to me, or I think you're lying to me, you'll suffer more pain than you have ever imagined. Is that clear?"

Lucas relayed his instructions from the head of the table, Harry's hands splayed out a few inches away from him. Harry didn't respond, his weeps had grown in volume and regularity.

"Harry, I suggest you respond."

Harry sniffed, hope was leaving him fast.

Lucas brought the hammer down with the full force of his upper body, the metal swinging in his right hand. The left hand held the chisel, the blunt, jagged edge pressing against the bottom of the left index finger.

The connection was perfect.

A spray of blood and Harry's severed finger fell away from his hand. He screamed in agony, blood pouring from the wound. Lucas swept the finger from the table with the hammer, like it was a dead insect.

He felt nothing.

"Harry, where can I find Curtis?"

"I don't know!"

Harry was answered by another hard strike from the hammer. This one sent the chisel through flesh, muscle and bone until it dented the wood underneath. Harry screamed through his tears, the pain burning into his hand like a blowtorch. Lucas flicked the finger to the floor where it dropped near the other one, splattering fresh blood to join his wife's.

"They don't see me ever. I swear! I swear!"

Lucas knew Harry was in too much pain to lie. He picked up Harry's blazer which he'd hung on the nearby cupboard, along with his own leather jacket. He tore the sleeve off with minimal fuss, bunched it up and pressed it against the flowing blood pouring from Harry's hand.

"How do I find him? What about Tommy?"

"Ask Lewis. I only see him to buy my drugs. That's it."

"Lewis is dead."

"What?" Harry's words were getting weaker, only spluttering out of his pale face. He was turning as white as a sheet through the blood loss.

"I killed him earlier tonight."

Harry began to cry, not through pain but through sheer terror. Realisation was kicking in, outweighing the shock and he again tried to fight his restraints. The chains held tight; Lucas had ensured he'd trapped his prey perfectly. Lucas pressed the chisel to the thumb.

"Harry, how do I contact them?"

"You could try Matt? Or Ashley?"

"Who are they?"

Harry lay silent.

"WHO ARE THEY?!"

Harry's thumb came off just as cleanly as the previous two digits, the top of the bench being painted red with the young man's blood. After losing the thumb, Harry fell into an almost dream-like state. He began to float out of his own body, looking down to see his physical self being tortured by this maniacal avenger.

Harry's body gave the required information to Lucas, telling him exactly where he could find more members of his family, who would experience a similar fate. Harry watched as Lucas thanked his body, before taking the chisel to his throat, pressing it against his Adam's apple. With three thunderous whacks of the hammer, the chisel drove through Harry's windpipe until it cracked into his spinal cord.

Harry drifted away, the final view he had was of Lucas walking into the darkness and a metal chisel standing upright from his own neck, blood pumping out like a burst fire hydrant in an American street.

―――

"And that I like some company."

Lucas remembered that morning, Helen nibbling his ear and then giving him a display of her naked body before disappearing into the bathroom.

He remembered how he'd joined her, making love to his wife under the hot, heavy bullets from the shower above.

The sink forced out some orange liquid, trying to pass it off as water.

Lucas held his hands underneath, washing the stains of revenge from his skin.

He thought of Helen, that morning three weeks ago when they were so in love.

For a brief moment, he remembered what it was to be happy.

CHAPTER FIFTEEN

Matt Drayton took a final drag on his cigarette before flicking it against the wall of his brother's betting shop. The cold of the night was not in the rain beginning to fall, but drifting on the wind that carried it. He blew the smoke out of the side of his mouth and stepped up to the door.

Locked.

He reached out without even looking to the metal panel on the side of the wall, pressing an oil-stained finger on the button. A buzzer rasped, signifying his arrival. He stood patiently, looking at his reflection in the glass door.

He didn't look like a Drayton. That always pleased him, his African mother's gene's immediately setting him apart from the rest of the clan. His dark blue overalls were coated in dry oil, battle scars from another long day at the garage he ran in Brixton. Although Curtis owned the business and used it to store and distribute copious amounts of cocaine, he left Matt to his own devices.

Through the glass, Matt saw Tommy emerge from the door to Curtis's office, nodding his hello. Keys jangled from a fist that had broken many a man.

The door was unlocked and Matt wasted no time pushing through.

"Hello to you too!" Tommy said, slamming the door shut and twisting the key.

"Do you want to tell me what the hell is going on?" Matt stormed into the centre of the room, noticing the space on the wall where a monitor had once hung.

"Curtis wanted to make sure everyone was okay."

"Why? Because Lewis went and got himself killed?" Matt said, sympathy absent from every word.

"Because I fucking said so."

Curtis stood in the doorway, the stairs behind him disappearing up to his office. He glared at his half-brother, taking measured steps into the room. Curtis's tie was loose, hanging to the side of an open collar. A half-filled glass of expensive scotch was clutched in his hands.

"Well, all due respect Curtis, I'm a big boy. I can look after myself."

Curtis continued his entrance, smirking appreciatively at Matt's comment. Tommy took his usual position, leaning against the counter, phone in his hand.

"You don't like me, do you Matt?" Curtis didn't look at him as he asked.

"Not really."

"Even after everything I've done for you?" Curtis finished his drink calmly, his fingers clenching the glass tumbler.

"It is what it is, Curtis. I run the business and I run it well. I also make sure your party powder gets cut and sold and I make you a shit tonne of money. So what do you want me to do? Bow when you walk in a fucking room?"

The glass hurtled across the room, skimming Matt's left shoulder. It burst into hundreds of pieces as it collided with the fresh wall space from the hurling event earlier that evening.

"YOU SHOULD OBEY ME!"

Matt took a step back, Curtis's immaculate teeth gnashing the words like a rabid pit bull. Tommy barely flinched, thumbing through the numbers on the screen in his hand.

"I'm out of here." Matt angrily made for the door. But Curtis stepped across, cutting off his route.

"Sit the fuck down!" Curtis's eyes were wide, full of unpredictable violence.

As his two brothers stood nose to nose before an impending outbreak of fists, Tommy selected 'Harry' from his contact list and calmly raised the phone to his ear.

Blood dripped onto the cold concrete floor, dyeing the dust around it deep red. Each splatter resounded around the room, sliding down from the puddle of blood pooling around Harry's lifeless body, while the single lightbulb shone a glaring spotlight on Lucas's handiwork.

Lucas turned the tap, stopping the flow of rusty orange water and then dried his hands on the remainder of Harry's blazer. He replayed the events of the evening in his mind, how he'd set off a chain of events that would only escalate. How he had revisited a side of himself he'd thought was long since locked away.

How he'd kept his promise to Kelly.

They'd screamed for help.

They'd begged for mercy.

They'd died in agony.

Creeping doubts began to sneak into his thoughts, the fingers of Helen's memory attempting to reach out and show him what he was doing.

A buzzing sound sliced through the silence.

Lucas shook the thoughts clear, his ears trying to hone

in on its origin. It buzzed again, the sound of plastic rattling against a solid surface.

He slowly walked to the table, the motionless corpse lying within a deep red outline. Harry's pocket shook, the vibration of his mobile phone rumbling loudly against the wood. Lucas carefully slid his hand in and pulled out the device, drops of blood falling to the table.

The name 'Tommy' flashed on the screen.

His fist clenched beyond his control.

He took a deep breath and raised it to his ear.

"Harry, why the fuck do you never answer your phone? We have been trying to reach you all evening!" Tommy said with measured anger.

Curtis and Matt stayed inches apart, their eyes locked on each other. Tommy stood patiently, concern spreading across his hard face after a few more moments of silence.

"Harry?"

"Hello, Tommy."

The cold, calm words of a stranger had Tommy standing straight, his eyes widened with worry. He pushed himself away from the desk as his brothers watched on with intrigue.

"Who is this?"

"I think you know." Lucas said calmly, his breathing soft. The room was silent, the dripping blood the only audible company. Lucas stared at the lifeless body before him.

"Listen, let me speak to Harry, okay?" Tommy's voice conveyed little concern. "Let me speak to him and we can talk this out. We can handle this like men."

"Men?" Lucas chuckled. "Tell me Tommy, what kind of men abduct a woman, rape her and then leave her for dead? Tell me!"

Curtis's Italian loafers shook the room as he stomped across the betting shop. He violently snatched the phone from his brother's hands, before turning on his heels and walking back to the middle of the shop. He thumbed the screen, amplifying the conversation through the speaker phone.

"Listen here you fucking piece of shit. You're a dead man."

Saliva hung from Curtis's mouth, his words spraying venom around the room.

"Hello, Curtis."

Lucas gritted his teeth, holding back the sickening feeling brought on by hearing the voice of the man who raped his wife. He took a deep breath, his powerful arm holding the phone in place.

"Do you realise the mistake you've made by messing with my family? Do you?" Curtis threatened, as he laid the phone down on the table surrounded by him and his siblings.

"I'm fully aware of what I'm doing, Curtis. It's YOU who hasn't realised the mistake YOU'VE made by messing with mine."

The calmness of Lucas's voice caused the brothers to trade concerned looks, the lack of fear completely new to them. Curtis tried to wrestle it from the mysterious voice.

"Fuck you!"

No response.

"This is my fucking city! Every fucking street, every fucking building, every fucking person. Do you really think you'll survive the next twenty four hours after killing a member of my family?"

"Members."

The word stopped Curtis in his tracks. Tommy stared at his older brother.

"What?"

"Members, Curtis. Members."

Lucas walked a few steps forward, bursting from the

shadows and into the light surrounding the blood splattered desk. Harry lay still, a memory of the world.

"If you're calling to speak to Harry, I wouldn't hold your breath."

"If you've done anything to my brother, I swear...'

"I killed him. Just like I killed Lewis."

Both of Curtis's fists crashed against the table, the phone rattling on top. Matt sat quietly on one of the elevated stools, the smoke from his cigarette dancing up towards the bright lights. Tommy stood solemnly to the side, his mammoth arms folded across his broad chest.

"But he told me everything I needed to know, Curtis. Before he choked on his own blood, he told me all about you. About Tommy and Matt."

The two brothers looked at each other, acknowledging the threat. Veins were screaming against the skin on Curtis's temples.

"About Ashley."

"Don't you fucking threaten my sister."

"Oh it's not a threat, Curtis. It's a long way past that."

Curtis snatched up the phone, his hand shaking through a mixture of fear and anger. Matt stubbed his cigarette out on the table and dropped it to the floor. It rolled into the pieces of the broken phone.

"If you want what's left of Harry, I just activated his Phone Finder. Modern technology really is incredible nowadays."

Curtis looked at Tommy, who nodded, indicating his understanding of the application. Lucas continued.

"I'm sure you'll recognise the address, Curtis. My wife's blood is still on the floor."

"You're in a very dangerous place, my friend," Curtis warned, trying to calm the shakiness in his voice.

"You have no idea. You are going to regret ever laying a finger on my wife. All of you."

Lucas's mouth pulled into an infuriated scowl, his nostrils flaring up with rage. His free hand rested loosely in the pocket of his jeans, fingers wrapped around the wedding ring he held so dear.

"I'm coming for you all."

He squeezed the ring, remembering the beauty he'd once held in his arms. Remembering how she'd been taken from him.

"One by one."

Lucas disconnected the call and gently threw it onto the blood-soaked body before him. He pulled his leather jacket over his shoulders and took a final look at the carnage he'd caused. His heart ached knowing that Helen had once been here.

He strode out of the light, into the darkness of the room. The door opened and then moments later, sent a violent slam echoing around the estate.

The line went dead and Curtis walked away from the phone, his hands pressed against his head in frustration. It was a foreign feeling to not feel in control and he took calming breaths as he pulled his eyes shut. Tommy ended the call on his phone, slipping the device back into his pocket. Matt flicked the butt of his cigarette to the floor and pushed himself off the chair, smoke drifting up around him. He strode to the door silently.

"Where do you think you're going?"

Curtis didn't move, his voice resonating as if from a statue.

"Back to my life. Just stay the fuck out of it!"

Before any response was thrown, Matt unlocked the glass door and threw it open. He'd disappeared into the dark of the wet night before it even closed.

Curtis rubbed his temples, extending every effort to stay calm.

"I swear to God one of these days I'm going to kill him!"

"Matt's his own man, always has been. But unless we deal with the problem at hand, you might not even have to."

Curtis spun, his eyes open, shooting daggers at his brother. Tommy's calm demeanour stoked fires of anger within him.

"You think I'm going to let this guy lay another finger on a member of this family?"

"Calm down."

"Calm down? Did you even listen to this guy?" Curtis gestured wildly with flailing arms.

"Yes I did. And do you know what I realised, Curtis?" Tommy waited, not expecting a response. "He was calm."

Curtis looked at his hulking sibling, awaiting further elaboration. Tommy obliged.

"This isn't some idiot stepping out of his comfort zone. This is a man who knows exactly what he's doing. He knows what we did." Tommy shook his head. "He is going for the throat, Curtis. He won't stop and that's why he's calm. He knows he can't afford to not be."

"So what do we do?" It surprised Tommy to see his brother so distraught now they were alone. The lights of the room burnt down on them both.

"Well I'm going to call Ashley, let her know what's going on. Hopefully she can find out where this is with the police tomorrow, there's no way this won't be priority number one by the morning."

"Just make sure she's safe. I want ten people shadowing her at all times until this is over."

"No problem." Tommy replied reassuringly.

Curtis's shoulders hunched forward and he took a few

slow steps towards his brother. He patted him on the side of his enormous bicep before trudging towards the door to his office. He looked at the shattered shards of phone on the floor, his head down.

"You think I'm scared don't you?"

Tommy didn't answer as he retrieved his phone from his pocket. Curtis turned, his face interrogating Tommy as it landed on him.

"No. You think I deserve this."

"It was only a matter of time before something came back on us."

Curtis only stared at him, the emotional weight of the evening visibly taking its toll on him. Tommy returned the look, the phone ready to dial in his hand.

"This man has killed members of our family, Curtis. I won't let that go."

Tommy's voice was direct and full of purpose, a promise of vengeance that seemed to awaken Curtis from his fearful shell.

"Good."

Curtis nodded and then straightened the tie that hung loosely from his shirt collar. He stomped over to the door, wrenched it open with one twist of the handle. Before he ascended the stairs, Tommy, holding the phone to his ear, called after him.

"Just remember, Curtis. We killed a member of his too."

―――

The park within the metal fences of Soho Square was dark, the street lights turned off and the gates closed. Near the white pavilion, a sneaky homeless man shuffled across the muddy grass to a bench, ready to lie a drunken head down for a horrible night's sleep.

The wind swept through the grounds, rain coating everything in a fresh, wet skin.

The stone face of the King Charles II statue was drenched, droplets careering down its smooth cheeks like unstoppable tears. The black world around it dulled the look of the statue, no longer the stark white which it appeared in daylight. The only light filtering in from a few street lights outside the fence parameter.

Lucas stared up at the statue, the rain wetting his hair and the wind blowing it in any direction it chose. He wanted to feel something, some sort of judgement for the horrors he had created that evening. The pain he had put those men through.

He thought he would find it in the eyes of a statue that meant so much to him.

His fist swung gently by his side, squeezing the golden circle that had once lived on his wife's finger.

He closed his eyes, his mind thumbing through its archives until it settled on their first date.

―――

The two of them were standing where he was now, the rain falling just as heavily but warmer.

Maybe it had been just as cold, only Helen's presence had made the temperature irrelevant. Her voice was soft, almost angelic.

"I don't care how much trouble I get in to, Lucas. It's my life."

He'd always loved her stubbornness, even more so when reflecting upon it.

"It's your career though, Helen. You don't want to throw that away for a waste like me."

"You're not a waste!"

Her face was beautiful, even in anger. The rain fell on them, neither feeling anything except the birth of their love.

"And if I have to leave my job, move to another hospital in another town then I will."

Lucas smiled, remembering the words. How much she'd meant them.

"As long as you come with me."

Lucas had looked at her, shocked that she could feel that on their first date. She would always say, the six months she'd spent with him before their first date was when she'd fell in love with him.

When she'd saved him.

"You can't do that." Lucas replied, shaking his head in disbelief.

"I love you, Lucas."

The words had shaken Lucas, even though the years had passed and they'd got married. Hearing her say those words for the first time, her declaration of love dancing over raindrops, suddenly reminded him of what he was avenging.

"I love you, too."

She'd taken a few steps and then had pushed herself up on her toes. Their lips had locked for the first time, an act that would happen daily but would never waver in passion.

They stood and kissed, the rain falling around them.

The statue of King Charles II had witnessed it all.

———

Lucas slowly opened his eyes and felt the rain on his face. Drops ran down from his hair, some even scattering down the back of his jumper, trickling down his defined back.

He took a few deep breaths, controlling his heartbreak as he stood in the spot where it had all began.

Suddenly, the angelic voice ghosted across the air behind him.

"What have you done, Lucas?"

Lucas stared straight ahead, tightening his mouth to stop himself from responding. He told himself she wasn't there, that she wasn't real.

"Lucas. Look at me."

Lucas took a moment and turned. His eyes squinted in the onslaught of rain, peering through at what appeared to be the love of his life. Only it wasn't quite, her gown floating against the arc of the wind, her hair smudging into the light that surrounded her.

It was almost Helen.

But not complete.

Her eyes clung to him, not once stopping to blink. She reached out an arm, no true definition to the fingers at the end of the hand she put to his cheek.

"I miss you, Helen." Lucas knew he was saying it to himself.

"I miss you, too." The words didn't feel authentic, instead feeling like they'd come from a previous memory.

The pair stood for a moment, as they'd done all those years ago. Charles II bore witness once again.

"You have to stop this, Lucas."

"I can't."

"You have to." Her voice sounded broken, the words not resonating as loudly. The rain echoed off the ground like chattering teeth. "Otherwise they'll come for you."

Lucas closed his eyes, wishing, beyond anything, that he could feel the hand she'd raised to him. Feel her fingers on his face just one last time. His fist squeezed tightly, encasing her wedding ring in his fingers

"Then I will kill them."

Lucas opened his eyes, the rain falling in the dark around him.

He stood alone.

AN EXTRACT FROM 'LIFE ON THE BEAT: MEMOIRS OF A THIRTY YEAR POLICE OFFICER.' BY PAUL FLETCHER.

I'll never forget that moment.

The words of Officer Shah rang through my police radio, my evening companion, and hung in the air alongside the multiple clouds of cigarette smoke and stench of whiskey.

"Somebody has killed Lewis Drayton."

Suddenly, the world around me became very real. I'd lived an existence ever since my beloved Susan had left me, but not one that I could ever truly recall. I would eat meals I couldn't taste and iron shirts out of habit. I would encase myself in my work, not wanting to exist in a world without her.

Suddenly, that world became apparent.

I knew the moment those words had filtered through, I was in a world where people experience a variety of pains and agonies, all of which were unique. Those words spoke to me because I knew exactly what had happened.

Lucas had killed Lewis Drayton.

Murdered him in cold blood.

And how did I feel?

Not a day goes by that I don't wish that a physical manifestation of cancer would appear in this world, so I could corner it in a room and batter it to death for the lives it has taken. Not just my dear

Susan, but the life where I exist as a father and a grandfather that was snatched away from me.

Every single person who has lost someone will know that feeling.

That desire to be able to hold the responsible party to their actions and beat them into submission. I would do it gladly.

Alas, the horror that took my wife and stole my means of existence is a prolonged evil. An evil that this world will one day, hopefully, conquer. To this world, my wife is just another number on a long list claimed by that destructive force.

Lucas knew exactly who was responsible and made them face the devastation they'd caused. Whilst my colleagues danced around in a wild panic at the news of the death of Lewis Drayton, Lucas rampaged through Drayton territory and claimed another.

How did I feel about it?

Numb.

Because I knew, when I'd looked into his eyes when they'd buried his wife that this had been coming. In hindsight, I should have warned the police, or at least made them aware of what I knew about Lucas.

How his mind worked.

The things he'd done.

But all I could think about was how badly I wanted to face cancer in a fist fight and I kept my mouth closed. Lucas was a good man and had had his life ripped from him.

He deserved to have his vengeance.

Lucas suddenly went straight to the top of the Metropolitan Police's most wanted list. Interviews were held with close friends and work colleagues from the quaint village where he and Helen had lived happily. It truly is a beautiful town, however ever since the war between Lucas and the Draytons, a dark cloud hovers over it.

I myself had the pleasure of interviewing Alex, Lucas's best friend and trainer. He didn't tell me anything I didn't already know.

"*They loved each other dearly.*"

"*I haven't seen Lucas since the funeral.*"

"*He couldn't possibly have done this.*"

I believed every word he'd said apart from that last sentence. His eyes betrayed him.

He knew what I knew.

Lucas was more than capable of committing those atrocities that night in London, where Drayton blood washed over the streets and their numbers diminished.

He would prove it again, just twenty four hours later.

CHAPTER SIXTEEN

Starling sat in the far corner of the back row of chairs, the cheap plastic offering no support for his back. His hair sat scruffily on his head, his face dark with stubble. He lifted the cup to his lips and took a large gulp of hot, black coffee, hoping to battle the exhaustion. The dark bags under his eyes countered his attempt.

Other officers filtered into the conference room, the rows of chairs filling up with his bemused and shocked colleagues. He noticed Officer Boulder as he walked in, nodding a silent hello. Officer McCarthy hobbled in, his usual smile replaced with a look of horror and Starling knew he'd been told of the night before. Those who had just started their shifts were murmuring their disbelief.

"Who the hell would kill a Drayton?"

"It has to be a gang attack."

"He beat up six men."

Starling closed his eyes and let his head tilt back. It had been a night verging on the unbelievable and he longed for Annette. He had tried to picture her blonde hair as she snuggled into him on the sofa, her eyes locked on an episode of America's Next Top Model. How soft it was when he ran his fingers through it, how beautiful it smelt when she'd just washed it.

His nose began to twitch, almost as if she were next to him then and there.

She had messaged him earlier, apologetically telling him she had a family crisis to attend to with the brother he was yet to meet. After the night he'd just had, Starling wasn't looking forward to getting into an empty bed.

Starling was interrupted by the ground-shaking stomps of Sgt. Bailey as he stormed through the door, his broad shoulders demanding a walkway which his officers provided. Starling opened his eyes, immediately noticing the urgency in the usually stern-faced Sergeant. The whispers and murmurs died down as Bailey made it to the front of the room, the board behind him still displaying the beautiful smile of Helen Cole. Starling wondered why.

Paul Fletcher quietly walked to the front too, standing awkwardly to the side of the room as Bailey rubbed his strong jaw with a powerful hand.

"Right let's cut to the chase. For those who are still here from the night before, you know what's happening. To those who have just arrived, listen up."

The room went silent, a sea of eyes fixed forwards.

"Last night, Lewis and Harry Drayton were both murdered in two separate attacks. I'm not going to sugar-coat it; whoever did it, wanted to make them suffer." Bailey let the room scribble down notes, a number of pencils scratching on several pads. "Now so far, we have reason to believe that these events are linked. Evidence suggests it was one man. CCTV at 'The Hive' nightclub shows the suspect easily fighting through Harry Drayton's security before Harry himself was abducted. He turned up ninety minutes later with several fingers missing and a chisel through his throat. Before that, Lewis received an army of baseballs to several points of his body before being decapitated by an avalanche of them."

A few murmurs spread among the audience. Starling watched, envying the officers who hadn't been on duty through the night.

"We need to contain this situation before it escalates. Contact has been made with the Draytons. We managed to speak to Tommy who politely told the police they didn't want to be involved with our investigation."

"What does that mean?" A young officer, whom Starling had never formally met, spoke up.

"It means the Draytons are going to burn this fucking city to the ground to find this guy themselves."

Again, wild murmurs and questions excitedly flew around the conference room. Starling stretched his back, the plastic seat wreaking havoc on his spine. He focused on Fletcher, standing at the side of the room with an old file rested in his arms.

Bailey stood patiently to let the officers compose themselves, understanding the excitement which accompanied a situation like this. Fletcher could appreciate it also, having spent many nights of his long career in the same situation. He stood and observed the room: smart uniforms, rapid-fire questions, and a buzz of excitement. Bailey's hands rested on his hips as he waited.

"Who on earth would want to attack the Drayton's?" a question flew out from the room.

"I can answer that one.'

All heads turned to Fletcher as he pushed himself slowly from the wall. He could feel the confused stares of the room locked on him. Bailey strode to the side with his arms folded.

Fletcher coughed nervously and ran a hand through his thin white hair.

"Eighteen years ago, probably before most of you were

even thinking of joining the Met, I attended a crime scene I'd never forget. Three teenaged boys, no older than sixteen, had been brutally beaten at a foster home. They all kept saying the same thing. They all kept saying 'We all knew he was crazy.' The foster parents came home to find the three boys in such a state and were terrified that the fourth was missing. What they should have felt guilty about was that they never stopped it from happening."

Empty expressions faced Fletcher; he sensed they were not following. He adjusted his glasses and flipped open the folder he'd been clutching, looking down at the printed words.

"Apparently, the missing child had been played a shit hand from birth. Drug-addled mother, a father who was never there. Eventually the social services placed him into care. Throughout the three other houses in which he'd been previously placed, he never quite fitted. Very withdrawn. This obviously made him a target for other wayward kids with a temper and for drunken parents who never felt a true connection to him. The boy took more beatings than Audley Harrison."

A few sniggers around the room which ceased as soon as Bailey scowled.

"I know we've all heard this story before. Run of the mill, scum of the earth kid, never had a chance. But unlike the usual ones who act out because they grew up at the bottom of the barrel, he was different. He educated himself. He taught himself patience. He prepared himself for violence."

Before any questions could be thrown out, Fletcher continued, his confidence growing as he took a few steps to the board behind him. Helen's beaming smile still illuminated the room.

In the back row, Starling began to feel uneasy, as the pieces began to fit.

"Eventually, the day came when he snapped back. The three boys – two of whom are now inside and one of whom is unaccounted for, were tied down and beaten with a cricket bat. No words were spoken. Not one shred of remorse. At fourteen years of age, he systematically beat them to within an inch of their lives. He then walked out calmly, his shirt covered in sweat and blood. He walked through the doors of this police station. They led him to a room and he sat in front of me and told me what had happened. He told me everything.'

The uneasy silence echoed off the cheaply painted walls of the conference room. Fletcher reached into the folder, pulling out a sheet of paper that he held face down on top.

"He begged me to put him somewhere where those violent urges, the need to make this world beg for forgiveness, would all go away. He told me he never enjoyed it, nor did he feel an ounce of guilt."

Starling sat up straight, his back screaming from the plastic chair.

"He told me that sometimes the bad people need to see what bad truly is."

A hand shot up amongst the crowd. All faces turned to attention and Officer McCarthy lowered it, his words carrying the heaviness of his Irish accent.

"What the hell does this have to do with anything?"

Fletcher shook his head. He turned and tapped the photo of Helen with his knuckles.

"This woman here, whom the Draytons raped and killed, was his wife."

Realisation swirled around the room, nervous voices murmuring inaudible phrases. McCarthy sat back in his plastic chair, silent. Fletcher lifted the sheet from the folder, a photo of a handsome man, his smile rich and genuine. A snapshot from a heartfelt memory.

He stuck it to the board, next to the beautiful wife he'd lost. The happy couple together one last time.

Fletcher turned and faced the room, holding their complete attention.

"Lucas Cole."

The name was written in several different handwriting styles in similar notepads. Starling felt his fists clench, a surge of guilt and anger rendering his knuckles white.

"The reason this gets worse, is that, after Lucas came to me, he was tried and he was sentenced to the London Institute of Mental Health for an undetermined amount of time. They pumped him with the standard medications, listened to him from time to time. He never improved but he never worsened. For eight years, he merely existed as another name on a list that people had given up on.

"Until one day, Helen Murphy began her internship, a bright and beautiful girl, who was on the path to becoming one of London's top psychotherapists. Instead, she fell in love. I remember it vividly, I used to drop in from time to time, to show Lucas that the world hadn't given up on him. I don't know why – I guess eventually, you get sick and tired of seeing people treated like dirt. He told me about the moment he'd first seen her, how the world suddenly wasn't screaming at him to leave any more. He felt that he had a reason to talk to people. A reason to get better, and a reason to live.'

'So he got better?' a voice jumped from the seated audience.

"Not better, no. He just stopped. No violence. No outbursts. It was as if there was nothing to get better from. It wasn't exactly by the book, but it worked. And she fell in love with him just as quickly, much to the disapproval of her superiors, as you can imagine. Eventually they agreed to release him on the grounds that he was no longer a danger to anyone. They relocated to a sleepy village called

Brinscall in Lancashire. She started up a private practice with an old university friend and Lucas got a job as a mechanic and spent his spare time being trained in the discipline of Muay Thai by his best friend, Alex. We've contacted Alex, who hasn't seen or heard from Lucas since he buried his wife.'

"So what does this all mean?" A young, brunette officer asked, aware that most of the guys looked at her with a hint of lust.

Bailey stepped into the centre again.

"It means we need to catch this man before this gets a hell of a lot worse. We have interviewed his work colleagues back home, his few friends. No family apart from the in-laws who didn't want to talk about it, which I'm not entirely surprised about."

"What do we know?" Boulder, ever efficient, offered.

"We do know that he hasn't been seen in Brinscall since Helen's funeral. However he did withdraw eight thousand pounds from his and Helen's savings account on Saturday. We've checked CCTV for both Preston and London St. Pancras station for the entire weekend and nothing. His car is still parked outside his house in Brinscall, so unless he was given a lift which we doubt, we can assume he took a coach. Howson, Jeffers, I want you both running through all the major coach companies that travel either direct to Preston or link to Preston.'

The two officers, both middle-aged and world weary, nodded as they scribbled down their orders.

Fletcher looked on, his heart slowly throbbing as the feeling of failure set in. He could see the station all those years ago, his hair darker and thicker, as a gangly fourteen year-old boy sat across from him.

Blood stained his hands. His shirt.

His eyes were wet from tears.

Fletcher had promised him he was safe now. That he

would make sure he would never go down such a path again.

He had failed.

"Do we know where he's staying?" a voice brought Fletcher back to the room. Bailey shook his head.

"No we don't. Baker and McGuire have been checking with the leading chains: Premier Inn, Travelodge and so on, but nothing. We can assume, that if he's taken out that amount of cash, he's using it. No cards means no trace. Also, the chain hotels require ID and, as Fletcher has said, he seems to think about these things.'

"B&B's?" Officer Hatton, the pretty brunette, suggested.

"I'd say it's likely. I want you, McCarthy and Dobbs to start filtering through websites. Rooms to let, bed and breakfasts, the lot."

"That's like chasing a small needle in a big, fucking haystack." McCarthy sneered.

"Then maybe we'll get lucky!' Bailey raised his voice. The room shook and all conversation stopped. "Bottom line people, we have very little to go on right now. I want the rest of the Draytons shadowed. Jensen will be delegating the babysitting. If you're selected, don't get too close, we aren't exactly high up Curtis Drayton's Christmas card list right now. If we're lucky, then maybe we can catch this psycho before he goes off again."

The officers nodded in unison.

"Get to it."

On those words, the officers all stood, the teams wandering off together with an unmistakable buzz of excitement swarming around them like bees. Starling stayed seated, his eyes transfixed on the back of the chair in front of him.

Fletcher approached Bailey, lowering his voice.

"With all due respect sir, Lucas isn't a psycho."

"I'd say what he did at the batting cage begs to differ."

"Sir, he's a man who was exceptional at violence when pushed. I'd say he's been pushed as far as possible."

Bailey looked at Fletcher, his eyes betraying the confidence he'd projected to his officers.

"So what are you saying, Fletcher?"

"Sir, this is only going to get worse."

"It's just one man."

Fletcher turned and looked at the board, at the smiles that he'd never see again. He looked the sergeant dead in the eyes.

"One man with a reason."

Starling pushed himself up off his chair, the room empty apart from the Sergeant and Fletcher who were talking quietly at the front. The weight of last night's pandemonium hung from him like a medallion.

He needed his bed.

He wanted to see Annette.

He exhaled deeply, knowing she wasn't going to be there when he got home. He could get in his car and drive to Romford Hills Retirement Home and spend some time with his Dad, but it wouldn't do any good. He felt exhausted but, worst of all, he felt guilty.

He had willed something to happen that night. He didn't believe in fate or karma, or the idea that you need to be 'careful what you wish for'. But he still felt guilty.

What made it worse was he had seen the look in Lucas's eyes when he'd come back through that hospital door. That tell-tale aura of vengeance hanging around him like a spectre after he'd said goodbye to his wife for the last time. He'd let his sympathy cloud his judgement and now two people were dead and London was on the verge of a Drayton backlash. The last thing he needed was his father catering to his ego.

Bailey's boots echoed as they clomped towards the door.

"Haven't you got a girlfriend to go home to?"

Bailey stood by the door way, gesturing for Starling to leave.

"Sir, surely if this guy is targeting the Draytons then we should have more than one person shadowing them?"

Bailey sighed and pushed his glasses up as he rubbed the bridge of his nose in frustration.

"Look, Starling, it's been a hell of a night. I really don't need my directions being questioned, okay?"

Silence between them. Fletcher shuffled slowly to the door as Bailey, again, gestured for Starling to exit. He approached his Sergeant, his head shaking in disappointment.

"But we don't even know if they did it?"

"You were the one the other day who was banging the Drayton drum, saying that we needed to go after them."

"That's because I'm pretty sure they did it."

"Then what the hell is your point?" Bailey's voice rose, a reminder of his seniority. A few heads in the office turned with interest.

"Just because we think they did it, doesn't mean they have. And that sure as hell doesn't give somebody else the right to take the law into their own hands."

"I know what the law is, son. You'll do well to remember that."

"Lucas Cole has killed two members of a violent crime family, sir. I feel like we should be doing more."

"A lot of the guys in the station wouldn't agree with that."

"Fuck the other guys!"

"OFFICER STARLING!" Bailey lifted one of the plastic chairs and slammed it down, the metal legs clattering loudly. Fletcher took a step back and Starling took a breath.

"I'm sorry sir, it's just..."

"Just nothing. You're a good kid, Starling, and a fine officer. I know the Draytons are the scum of this earth and I would like to see them all sitting in a cell, ticking the years off a calendar. However, this is the real world and we do what we can and we do our best.'

"Yes sir." Starling said quietly, defeated.

"Right now, we don't have a lot but we'll hunt Lucas to the ends of the world if we have to and hope we find him before they do. So let's be ready, see what his next move is and go from there."

Bailey had simmered down, his authoritative demeanour had returned and he reached out and gave Starling a strong pat on the side of the arm.

"What if his next move is the same as his last?"

'Then you can give me a big, fat, fuck off 'I told you so'."

Bailey smiled, for the first time in hours and Starling found it surprisingly irritating. He drew his lips shut and stormed past the Sergeant, aware that their already strained relationship would need even more repairing. Maybe if he caught Lucas, then this would all be put behind them. Bailey had a reputation for holding a grudge from time to time and Starling cursed himself as he headed to the locker room for arguing - yet again - with him. As he got to the door, he checked his mobile phone.

Annette had sent him a text.

Hey gorgeous. Just waiting for my brother now. Hope you're okay, sounded like a rough night. I have ten mins if you want to talk? Smooches. Xx

Starling could once again smell her shampoo, his heart fluttering slightly at the thought of hearing her voice. To tell her everything that had happened, how he felt responsible but knew he wasn't. How he couldn't imagine the pain of losing her like Lucas had lost Helen. He turned from the locker room door and headed to the car park entrance, the phone already trying to connect him to the woman he was becoming ever more dependent on.

The oak desk had cost over five thousand pounds and sat proudly in Curtis Drayton's office. The value was diminishing every second as he pushed the blade of a knife into the polished wood, nuzzling a deeper cut as he twisted it.

Dry, maroon specks still clung to the blade.

The warm, comforting feeling began to flow back through Curtis, reminding him of a time when he took charge of a situation and protected his family. A feeling he wanted again, having spent a sleepless night in a blind fury.

Two of his brothers had been viciously slain.

He closed his eyes and took a calming breath. He remembered all of those years, missing school to earn a living by running drugs for local dealers. He recollected all the evenings where his father took his own inadequacies out on him in a downpour of insulting tirades and wild fists. The conversations with a crying Ashley, her face strained with horror as she tended to another bout of their father's wrath, dabbing blood-soaked towels to his beaten face.

He remembered Mr Hamilton, the naïve PE teacher who'd taken Tommy under his wing and introduced him to boxing. Whenever Curtis came to collect his younger sibling, Hamilton would try and convince him to join. To learn how to protect himself.

How foolish, Curtis had thought, a man trying to take Curtis from a world he'd never understand.

Why be the one who throws the fists?

Curtis chuckled upon his recollections, the knife slowly twisting into the oak, shreds of dust pinging up and landing beside the glass of expensive scotch.

He looked at the blood which decorated the blade like a tattoo. He smiled.

———

Billy Mulgrave had run a series of drug rackets in East and South East London for over twenty years. A highly feared man, he ensured his business was large in scale, but small on people. He kept the company of only three men, entrusted with keeping certain people away from his door. Like Curtis, he had people willing to pull a trigger or take a few years in prison to stay in his good books. But his trust only belonged to a few.

That night, six years ago, he sat around the table in his office with the trusted men. Jack Grigg, Steve 'The Hand' Nickson and of course, the hulking figure of George Drayton. The rain clattered against the window as they discussed business, Mulgrave handing out instructions with quiet authority.

The door flew open.

Before anyone could react, Lewis, Harry and Matt Drayton stormed into the room. Years had passed since George had last seen his offspring and his shock at seeing his boys as young men proved fatal. The three Drayton boys held up their pistols, aiming them directly at those seated.

"What the fuck is this?" Billy Mulgrave yelled, pushing himself up from his chair.

A powerful hand latched onto his shoulder and, the now muscular, Tommy drove him back down into his seat with a thud. Despite the pistol aimed at him by Matt, the unwanted outcome of a loveless affair, George tried to get to his feet.

"Tommy?"

He extended his arms, yearning for a hug from this specimen that used to be his little boy.

Tommy swung a hard right hook, cracking his father straight across the jaw. The oldest Drayton fell back into his chair, not even saying a word. Mulgrave went to object, however the echo of footsteps approaching the door caused all attention to refocus.

"You little cunt," Mulgrave's face twisted in fury.

Curtis walked in, his suit as immaculate as always, even then. His brown hair, fuller and longer. He smiled an evil grin at the crime lord, not one ounce of fear in his body.

"Harry."

Curtis motioned with his hand and his youngest brother eagerly handed him the gun, his body shaking with excitement and cocaine.

"You think you can get away with this, you little prick!" Mulgrave tried to stand again, his attempt immediately stopped by another hard shove from Tommy standing behind the chair. Curtis smirked again, scratching his eyebrow with the nozzle of the gun.

"This is my city now."

Curtis extended his arm fully, the gun lining up perfectly with the wrinkles darting across Mulgrave's head. His eyes widened in fear but before he could protest, Curtis pulled the trigger.

The gunshot rang around the room as the bullet pierced Mulgrave's skull, blood erupting upwards like a crimson firework. The once-feared gangster fell back against the chair, slumped over and then fell to the floor, limp and motionless. Blood pooled around the table. Curtis dropped the gun on the table and then snapped his fingers.

While Matt held the gun on Jack Grigg and 'The Hand', Lewis and Harry pulled the men's arms behind their chairs. Lewis and Harry each pulled a roll of masking tape from their jacket pockets. They wrapped it around the men's hands, excessive amounts until neither of the two could move.

George sat motionless, watching the boys whom he had brought into this world take others from it.

Tommy immediately walked around the desk, the three seated men frozen in fear. Lewis handed him one of the rolls of masking tape and then, from his coat pocket, he removed two plastic bags. Without a word, he wrenched the plastic bag over Jack Grigg's head, and then wrapped the masking tape around it as he struggled. He gasped and strained, air a commodity he was fast relinquishing. Before Grigg had died, Tommy had sent 'The Hand' to the same fate.

Curtis watched emotionlessly. He glared at his father, the man who had subjected him to such relentless violence. Now he could watch.

He could see what his handiwork had created.

"Now then," Curtis smiled. "I think we are long overdue a father/son chat, aren't we, George?"

George looked his eldest son in the eye, turning away quickly when he saw nothing but hatred staring back. Strong hands wrenched his arms behind the chair, the ripping of masking tape following as Tommy secured him to his seat. Curtis's eyes didn't move.

"For what it's worth, boys, I loved you all. Every single one of you."

"Well I can tell you what that's worth. Absolutely fucking nothing!"

George looked at his son again, trying to apologise with his eyes. Curtis smiled casually.

"The one thing you did do right was you taught me that in this world, the only way to survive is through violence."

"I never intended that for you or...."

George was cut off by a humiliating slap to the face. For a moment, the rage that haunted Curtis's youth flashed in his eyes.

"You never intended? Never intended what? Huh? To beat me till I bled every night? To scare that whore of a mother away, for her to leave us with you?" Curtis's voice broke slightly, the pain and emotion from all those years and all those fists pushing as hard as they could.

"I'm sorry."

The apology was feeble.

"So am I."

Curtis reached into the inside of his jacket and pulled out a knife. The blade shimmered in the light, the handle feeling heavier than usual in his hand.

George took one final look around the room, at his children. He could understand why Ashley didn't want to be there for this, but the idea that all of his sons wanted a front row seat to his execution made him realise he deserved it.

Matt looked slightly uneasy with the situation and slowly backed towards the door. A shake of the head from Tommy stopped him. Lewis watched intently, Harry snorted another fingertip of cocaine. Tommy stood, casting an imposing shadow over the father he'd hated ever since he could remember.

Curtis leant forward, his grip tightening and, looking his father in the eye, slowly pushed the blade into his stomach.

George's eyes widened, a moan of pain was instantly shut off by a strip of masking tape from Tommy. Curtis held his gaze and with a cruel smirk, twisted the knife.

Blood seeped from their father's stomach, the warm, red liquid changing the colour of his shirt quickly.

Curtis pulled the knife out.

Muffled groans of pain filled the room and Matt turned and stormed out. Tommy nodded at Lewis, who followed. Harry chuckled and raised his middle finger at his dying father before being ushered to the door by Tommy.

"You coming?"

Tommy didn't get a response. Curtis sat, staring at his father as life began to puddle out of him, mixing with the blood from Mulgrave, the hole in his head still trickling. Behind Curtis, two bodies slumped forward, faces hidden behind the bags that had killed them.

George gasped for air, for life, his head tilting to the side as the world around him grew dark. Curtis reached out, pressing the bloody knife against his father's cheek and raising his eyes to meet his.

"Look at you. You're pathetic."

They were the last words George Drayton ever heard.

―――――

"Curtis. Are you listening to me?"

Curtis shook himself free of the memory, the knife

twisting deep into the table. Oak dusting had spread around the blade. Across the room from him sat Ashley, dressed immaculately as always with her hair brushed neatly.

"I heard you."

"This guy, if it is him, they don't think he'll stop."

Curtis rubbed his eyes with the palms of his hands, the lack of sleep catching up with him quickly.

"I spoke with him, Ashley. He isn't going to stop. He knows what we did and he's coming for us."

Ashley adjusted her blouse nervously as Curtis picked up his glass, downing the remaining scotch, letting it burn the back of his throat.

"So what are you going to do?"

Curtis slammed the glass down.

"Me? I'm going to find him and I'm going to make him beg me for death."

Ashley shook her head.

"What?"

"Nothing."

"WHAT?" Curtis repeated, his voice exploding with rage.

Tommy looked up from the sofa on the far side of the room as Ashley cowered slightly. The tiredness hung in bags under Curtis's eyes, but the fury burst through.

"I'm going to go."

Ashley quickly pushed herself up out of her chair, but before she could even drape her designer handbag over her shoulder, Curtis was up. He stormed round the desk, shaking the room. Ashley only got two steps before he angrily grabbed the back of her hair and pulled her back as hard as he could. The base of her spine clattered into the desk, shooting a pain through her that made her scream. Tommy leapt up from the chair as Curtis wrapped his murderous hand around her throat.

"You think I won't kill him for what he's done?"

"Let me go!" her words choking from her throat.

"Curtis. Let her go." Tommy stood calmly to the side.

"No, not until she says what she wants to say."

Ashley looked at Tommy, begging for help. Curtis wrenched her face back to his.

"Don't look at him. Look at me."

"Curtis. Let go of her throat."

'You look at me Ashley with such disdain, yet I'm the one who makes damn fucking sure nothing happens to you. I put you in that fancy flat, where you fuck this new boyfriend that you are too ashamed to introduce to us. You are just as involved in this as we are, so maybe you should show me some goddamn respect or I'll feed you to the fucking wolf myself."

Curtis shoved her back against the desk, relinquishing his grip. Ashley hurried to Tommy, tears streaming down a face frozen in fear. Tommy wrapped an arm around her, burning a hole in his brother, who poured himself another glass of scotch.

"I never wanted any of this to happen," she said meekly between sobs.

"Just get out," Curtis said quietly, taking a sip from the fresh glass, the feeling of inebriation wrestling control from the exhaustion.

"I'll handle this. You go." Tommy smiled at her.

Ashley dabbed at her eyes with her jacket sleeve and nodded. She readjusted her skirt, wincing at the pain emanating from her back. She hobbled towards the door and then stopped.

"You're a monster, Curtis."

"Yeah, well just remember, Ash. You're the one who keeps feeding me."

Ashley shook her head in disgust as she turned and stormed out of the door. Curtis raised his eyebrows, taking another large sip. Tommy sighed, pulling up a chair.

"Tommy, if you ever tell me what to do again..."

'What, you're going to put a gun to my head? Because that really worked last time didn't it."

Curtis smirked.

"You got boys following her tonight?"

"Yeah, I told you. It's sorted. Gave Shane and one of his boys a shooter each. Just in case."

"If they kill him, I will murder everyone they care about."

"Curtis, we just need him dead."

Curtis stared at his brother, angered by his calmness. His lack of fear.

"I need him alive. This city needs an example of what happens when it crosses me."

"Then let's find out more about him."

Curtis raised his eyebrows, the alcohol aiding his confusion. Tommy stood up, towering over his brother.

"She said it was Fletcher who knew everything about him, right?"

"That old bastard. He still alive?"

"Apparently so."

"He was a pain in the arse. Like a fucking boy scout."

"Well, he seemed to know a hell of a lot about Lucas Cole."

"He won't tell us anything."

Tommy grinned.

"I can always change that."

CHAPTER SEVENTEEN

It wasn't so much as sleep, more a continuous flash of Helen's face. Her smile. Her tears.

Her screaming for help.

Lucas checked out of the Lindthorpe Bed and Breakfast promptly at noon. Mrs Lindthorpe tried to exchange niceties about his stay but Lucas tiredly mumbled his thanks and left, his sports bag over his shoulder.

Last night's clothes, soaked in blood, were in a black bag hidden beneath those he had packed. He would dump them in a bin at the first opportunity. Wearing a fresh pair of jeans, shirt and his leather jacket, he stepped out into the midday air of the city. London was alive with foot traffic as he wandered down Oxford Street. The hard-at-work were now free for their lunch break, scurrying into fast food shops without a concern for their fellow pedestrian.

Black cabs shot through red lights, narrowly avoiding crossers whilst cyclists were doing their utmost to become even more despised.

Lucas hadn't missed this place at all.

After buying a coffee at a nearby Costa, Lucas found a

bench on a side street and took a seat. As the world whizzed by, he thought about how his had imploded. How an act of cruelty had led him back to this moment with two deaths on his hands.

It reminded him of pack mentality. How in a large herd, even the smallest animal could seem powerful. However, once separated, they will always show themselves to be rich in cowardice.

The fear in both Lewis and Harry Drayton's eyes had given credence to that. They had both begged for their lives, happy to give up those they deemed 'family' in the faint hope of maintaining their meagre existence.

That was the difference between the Draytons and Lucas.

They would gladly sacrifice those they hold dear.

Lucas would sacrifice it all just to see her again.

The spring air dropped a few degrees, sending a cold chill rattling through the city. A few light drops of rain fell, one of them landing right on Lucas's skull with a cold splat. It shook him from his thoughts and there she was.

Sitting beside him, her white robe floating as if she was sitting in a wind turbine. Her blonde hair glowed brightly, light reflecting from it. Her skin shone, her blue eyes piercing him with no pupils.

It wasn't Helen.

But it was.

"You need to go home, Lucas."

Her voice boomed slightly, as if said softly into a microphone. Only he could hear it.

"There is no home."

He grimaced, knowing he was talking to a shaded memory of his wife. He wanted to remember her, but it was never complete. Never fully her.

He cursed himself that he couldn't make her whole. Blamed himself that he hadn't been able to protect her.

With one hand wrapped around the warm, cardboard coffee cup, his other slid into his pocket, the cold feel of her wedding ring greeting his fingers. Her voice echoed again.

"Our home. Where we lived our lives."

He shook his head. The rain began to fall with a little more might.

"You don't get it, do you?"

Lucas stood up, his action mirroring the rise in his volume. A few passers-by shared concerned looks, stepping away from him as he yelled at a seemingly empty bench.

The vision of Helen didn't move. She stared into his soul.

"There is no home, Helen. There is no you. There is no us. There is nothing there for me anymore."

Lucas took a few steps to a nearby bin and disposed of the cup. He stood for a few moments, taking a few deep breaths, the calming effect of the rain etching its way into his body. She was still behind him, he could feel it.

"I don't know what else to do, Helen."

"You could stop."

He turned, her words louder and she was now standing a few feet from him. She hung in the air, the spectre of her dancing on the wind which breezed through. The rain never touched her.

"I can't."

"Everything we did, baby. Remember how far you've come."

"That was you." Lucas shook his head in defeat.

"That was us."

"There *is* no us anymore. Not in this world."

The vision of Helen flickered slightly, as if she was appearing on a broken TV screen.

Lucas slowly lifted his face to the rain. He felt the small, delicate pelts of water and let its refreshing calm wash over his body again. There was so much he had to do before eight o'clock. He had to find another place to stay for the night. He had to buy some new clothes, some industrial strength cable wire and some alcohol.

He opened his eyes, lovingly staring at the fading memory.

"They took you from me, Helen. They snatched you from this world and it meant nothing to them. I know I can't bring you back."

Lucas took a few steps to the bench and reached down for his bag. He brought it up over his wet hair, letting the strap drop over his muscular shoulder. He looked into the sharp, blue eyes once more, they swirled like whirlpools.

"But I can't just let that go."

Helen evaporated into the rain as Lucas turned and headed back to the high street, his feet splashing in puddles on the pavements of London.

———

Ashley had left the family betting shop as soon as she could and stepped out into a not unexpected downpour, aggravated that it would ruin her hair. She scurried quickly to the underground station a few streets away, juggling the notion of calling her boyfriend if only for the comfort of his voice.

No, it was too soon to let him into the crazy that was her family. He would never understand.

It was a little before three so the train itself wasn't packed, yet she still felt claustrophobic. The guilt of feeding that woman, like so many others, to her brother began to shackle her like a straitjacket. How could she have been so cold?

That poor woman, only a few years older than she was, ripped from what had been described as an ideal life with a husband who very evidently loved her. All because Ashley felt obliged. Because Curtis had this terrifying need to feel powerful. She didn't even realise she was crying until a fellow passenger, a scruffy looking old lady handed her a tissues.

She smiled a thank you as she dabbed mascara from her cheeks.

By the time she had arrived at Canada Water train station she had decided to block it from her mind. Yes, what she'd done was wrong, however it was a necessary act to survive within the Drayton family. All the other brothers had fallen in line and she was just following suit.

But it was the last time. She was certain of that.

It was time to focus on her job, focus on her blossoming romance and to focus on building a life that wasn't tainted by her name.

Lucas Cole wouldn't reach her, Curtis would never allow it. Despite his horrifying nature, he ensured his family was protected, her more than most.

She exited the station, turning left towards the Hamden Trading Company, a large ten-storey building on the outskirts of the trading epicentre that was Canary Wharf. Surrounded by student accommodation, the building was slightly out of place but Ashley enjoyed being away from the plethora of slick guys with too much money and not enough manners.

She walked beyond the building, noticing the police car sitting out the front on the other side of the road, with a peculiarly attractive police officer seated in the front, boredom etched across his sullen face. On the near side of the street, a black Fiat Punto sat with two men watching her in the mirrors. She recognised one as 'Tombs', a muscle bound letch who worked for her brother.

Both cars were there for her protection, just with different ideas of what it entailed.

She walked past, her head down, not wanting to even acknowledge what was happening, lest it remind her of the part she had played. She took quick steps, her high heels clicking off the wet pavement as she silently cursed her decision to not bring an umbrella.

Soaked through, she entered the small, privately owned sushi restaurant at the end of the street. She waved hello, her regular custom greeted with smiles as she ran her delicate fingers through her wet hair.

She needed to wash it before her next romantic rendezvous.

She sat at the booth, ordering some Salmon and Cucumber Maki and some prawn Nigiri. As she twiddled the chopsticks in her left hand in eager anticipation, she removed her Kindle from her bag, returning to her novel. She wouldn't start her shift at Hamden Trading until six, however she would go in at five to catch up on any work missed. With the recent upgrade to the servers, the team that she proudly managed would be working well into the night ensuring the systems responded to the server change and that the trading applications never faltered.

At ten minutes to five, she settled her bill, put away her novel and walked out into the rain which had softened over the last ninety minutes. She felt better, that things would be sorted by the end of the night. Her brothers would make sure nothing ever happened to her.

So content was Ashley that she walked straight past Lucas Cole as he stood in the alleyway opposite her building. He watched intently as she scurried between fast moving traffic to enter her workplace.

———

It hadn't been too difficult for Lucas to find another room for the night. After ambling through London for almost an hour, he eventually paid seventy pounds cash to check into the Luxury Hotel just off Gower Street. The rooms were anything but, the dank colour scheme making the room feel smaller, and the cleanliness of the bed was suspect. The cupboard-sized bathroom had been lazily sprayed with multi-purpose surface cleaner, but hadn't been wiped properly. The hard aroma of disinfectant enclosed in the room like a secret.

Still, it would do.

For the rest of the afternoon, Lucas had wandered around the Brunswick Centre, an arcade of shops littered between eateries and chain restaurants. He bought himself a new jumper and a baseball cap from River Island, changing into it by the counter, much to the delight of the young girl behind the till. He stuffed his now-redundant shirt in his sports bag, which would soon be followed by a large bottle of vodka which he'd bought from a nearby newsagents.

Walking past the Tesco Express opposite Russell Square station, he decided to stop in and purchased a set of tea towels.

Before continuing his walk towards Holborn, Lucas ventured through a sea of umbrellas and shoulder barges into Russell Square itself.

The park, which would be so vibrant and busy in the coming summer months, was almost deserted, the only people those using it to cut through to other streets.

Just like Helen had.

He stopped, looking around at the beautifully maintained grounds, the small café with nobody sitting outside. The water feature, the centre piece of the square, was in full flow, but its impact was emasculated by the rain. Lucas closed his eyes, sending himself back to that night.

He could see Helen running, sheer panic on her face.

He could imagine Harry and Lewis, laughing and

grabbing at her as Harry had described to him before he'd died, as they'd chased her hurried steps with large, foreboding strides.

His fists clenched.

Upon leaving the park, Lucas walked straight up Southampton Row, beyond Holborn Station. He continued through the avalanche of tourists until he came to the Tool Hire shop. Within five minutes, he was walking out with twenty metres of industrial grade cable that was wrapped and stuffed in the bag, along with a pair of navy overalls.

He made his way to Canada Water via the Jubilee line, after walking to Waterloo Station and taking in the sights of Big Ben and the London Eye while crossing a rain-battered Waterloo Bridge.

There was some beauty left in this city, he'd thought, however his mind refused to allow him a moment to appreciate it. Not when real beauty had been lost here.

He'd waited for only twenty minutes outside the front of Hamden Trading, when, just as Harry had told him between screams of anguish, he spotted Ashley scurrying across the road and through the glass doors, speaking an unheard greeting to the security guard.

Lucas noted the police car and couldn't quite determine if the officer was asleep or not.

He noticed the black Punto, but safely assumed they would not know exactly who they were looking for.

He had already hidden a carrier bag in the alleyway, behind a badly dented dustbin sitting in front of a darkened doorway. The doors were chained shut and strewn in graffiti.

As Ashley disappeared into a lift, he casually picked up his sports bag and walked across the zebra crossing, his feet hitting the wet, striped road in time with the chimes from the traffic lights.

None of the occupants of the two cars paid him any notice, as he entered the large block of student halls that sat next to the Hamden Trading Company, separated by a thin alleyway.

They also didn't notice when he stepped out fifteen minutes later, without his sports bag or baseball cap.

―――

"What a day, darling."

Fletcher always greeted the smiling image of his wife hanging proudly on the hallway wall. A photo taken on a whim, when the two of them had taken a trip to the New Forest. There she was, leaning against a tree, her summer dress hugging the figure she kept well into her fifties. Her hair was just showing signs of a grey tinge.

The smile looked as vibrant as the day he'd met her all those years ago.

Fletcher meandered into the front room, dropping his jacket onto the back of the sofa and making a beeline to his kitchen counter. There sat the half empty bottle of Jack Daniel's, his trusty companion, and he knocked a small glass back in one tilt.

The fiery liquid burnt his throat, causing him to cough slightly, the flames helping to burn away at the guilt. Two men had been brutally slain because of him. Lucas was now wanted for murder. And to make it worse, the most dangerous family he had ever known were out for blood.

The day had been an endless wave of paperwork, the two murders causing all kinds of mayhem within the police station. Many young officers, bored of routine house calls and vandalism cases were like kids at Disney Land, buzzing with excitement as more information unravelled. Fletcher had sat stiffly all day, his stomach in knots as he wondered how long before they pulled the thread hard enough to trace it back to him.

He would likely die in prison if they found out what he had done. He would never get a chance to meet Laura. Hold her. Kiss her. Love her.

Another swirl; his glass was refilled and his feet had led him to the sofa, the well-worn carpet flattened from years of the same journey. He collapsed into the chair, dust lifting off like a morning fog.

The house, like himself, missed Susan's touch.

He reached up, fondling his coat until he retrieved his cigarettes, lighting one up and letting the smoke filter slowly into the dusty clouds engulfing the room. He shot a look at his desk, the untouched laptops and the fading dream of writing a memoir looking back him with pity.

Another night, drinking and smoking until sleep claimed his consciousness, awaited him.

With his free hand, he removed the manila folder from his jacket, the file on Lucas Cole that twenty four hours ago was doing nothing but gathering dust and taking up space. Now it was hotter property in the office than the latest Dan Brown novel.

He dropped it onto the table, hiding cigarette butts, piles of ash and water rings from the world.

From Susan.

How had he let the house get into such a state? He looked at the clock; it was almost twenty to eight. The next door neighbours had two young children, so the idea of vacuuming would have to wait until tomorrow.

He had another glass of Jack Daniel's instead.

The beating on the front door startled Fletcher to the point that he dropped his cigarette on the carpet. Quickly composing himself, he picked it up and stubbed it out in the overflowing ashtray, sending even more butts scattering over the desk.

He straightened his shirt, realising he still had his security pass hanging from the lanyard around his neck. He tossed it onto the empty pages of his memoir marked 'I'll start tomorrow'.

As he walked to the door, he promised himself he *would* start tomorrow. He promised himself that he would fix the house up, and make it a home Susan could be proudly displayed in. He would stop smoking too.

He opened the door, his usually friendly smile freezing halfway through. His eyes widened.

"Good evening, Paul."

Curtis Drayton, despite having aged in the years since they'd last seen each other, still had a smile that would send a shiver down your spine. Fletcher almost shuddered. Their eyes met, the dark almost pupil-less eyes of Curtis looking straight through him. Sharply dressed in an undoubtedly custom made suit, Curtis barged his way past Fletcher and into the house.

Fletcher looked up at the man-mountain that was Tommy, his arms rippling, struggling to burst from the captivity of his t-shirt sleeves. The rain fell gently behind Tommy, small patters like someone delicately shaking a maraca. Fletcher stood to the side and Tommy offered an empty smile of thanks as he walked through and into the Fletcher family home.

He closed the door slowly, pressing his hands against it and trying to control his breathing. He stood straight, taking a glance at Susan once more, then followed the two Draytons who had commandeered his front room.

As he walked in, he saw Tommy standing over his desk, shifting through papers covered with loose notes and indecipherable scribbles. Curtis was standing by the fire place and Fletcher felt a dangerous fury rise up like a volcano within him as he saw what he was holding.

The photo of Susan on holiday.

"Is this Mrs Fletcher?"

"Please put that down."

"You're very hostile, Paul."

"Just put it down."

Curtis smirked, even letting a small chuckle drift from his lips. He slammed it back on the mantelpiece a little too hard, making it wobble and fall back from its stand. Fletcher took a step to correct it, to return his beloved to her rightful position, but a powerful hand from Tommy shot out, latching onto his shoulder like a mechanical vice. Before he could even relax, Tommy guided him to the single chair and shoved him down. He hit the cushions with a thud, daring not to move again.

"W-w-what do you want?"

Despite his best efforts, Fletcher couldn't hide his terror, something he knew Curtis would enjoy.

He was right.

"I want to have a little chat, Paul."

Curtis lazily opened the drinks cabinet, scoffing at the number of cheap labels housed inside. He pulled out two glasses and slowly walked to the coffee table. He tutted mockingly at the state of it, before placing the glasses down and topping them both up with the bottle Fletcher had been enjoying earlier. He handed one to Fletcher, ignoring Tommy who had given no indication he was remotely interested in one.

Curtis sat on the edge of the coffee table, a few feet from the panic-stricken face of Fletcher and smiled.

"To good health."

He raised his glass. Fletcher didn't move. The glass shook in his hand. The whiskey sloshed.

"Cheers."

Curtis knocked it back, shaking his head in disapproval.

"Wow. That is awful. I didn't realise the police pension was so bad these days."

"I get by." Fletcher responded, his eyes flickering to his cigarettes. Curtis followed his gaze.

"Would you like a cigarette, Paul?"

He handed one to the retired officer, even leaning forward to light it for him. Fletcher never took his eyes off him.

"Would you mind if I had one?"

"Be my guest."

"Very kind." Curtis smiled, sliding a cigarette out of the box, holding it within his crooked smile. Tommy remained like a statue as a second plume of smoke engulfed the room.

"Right. How do I find him?"

The question whipped through the smoke and caught Fletcher by surprise.

"Who?"

"Don't bullshit me, Paul. Where do I find him?"

Curtis's smile had gone. The friendly, mocking tone had abandoned his voice.

"I'm sorry, Curtis. But I don't know..."

'WHERE THE FUCK IS LUCAS COLE?'

Curtis snatched the glass of whiskey from Fletcher's trembling hand and hurled it as hard as he could at the mantelpiece. It smashed just above the photo of his daughter's graduation, the picture coated in a downpour of cheap glass and cheaper liquor.

"I don't know, I swear."

"Oh come on, Paul. Don't treat me like one of those dozy smack heads you used to harass. I know he has been to you, of course he has. You were the only person to believe his little sob story all of those years ago, weren't you?"

"Excuse me?"

Curtis forced a smile, a bad attempt at covering his

frustration. He took another pull on his cigarette, the orange tip illuminating. He let the ash fall on the carpet.

"Lucas had a shit life, boo hoo. He beat people up, sob. He got put in a mental home, shagged his doctor and they lived happily ever after. Now I know he has been here and Paul, I think that you set him on his little mission."

"Curtis. I honestly don't know what you're talking about.'

Curtis leant forward, rubbing the bridge of his nose with his fingers. Tommy stared at the coffee table, intrigued by the folder that sat atop the neglect below.

'This is useless. I would have thought that a highly decorated man of the law such as yourself would have had the bollocks to admit to such a bold move.'

"The same way I thought a man like you wouldn't need to rape and kill women to make himself feel like a big shot."

Curtis sat back slightly, almost in admiration. Fletcher's body shook in fear but he did his best to control it.

"Whoa. Calm down, Paul." Curtis leant forward. His smile evaporated. "It's like you're trying to hurt my feelings."

Fletcher let smoke drift from the side of his mouth, feeling the fear escaping within the white cloud.

"Bollocks that you have feelings."

"I don't know. I'm feeling pretty fucking angry right now." Curtis took another drag, more ash falling to the carpet. "Some prick is out there, killing members of my family, Paul. So, before I really lose my rag, and even worse, before Tommy does, why don't you tell me where I can find him and I promise I'll make it quick, before we have any more carnage.'

"It's not carnage.'

Curtis tilted his head in aggravation.

"Excuse me?'

'It's not carnage, Curtis." Fletcher sat forward a little, noticing the worry that was slowly etching itself across Curtis's face. "Carnage implies there's no control. Wild. That's not what this is. He knows exactly what he's doing and that's what scares you the most.'

"Fear isn't a trait that I have time for."

"Well make time for it."

"Careful, Paul."

Tommy had slowly circled the room to the coffee table and he reached down and lifted the folder, the pages detailing Lucas and his life resting in the palm of his hands.

The conversation continued around him, words echoing in a smoky tomb.

"No, Curtis. I think for the first time, it's you who needs to be careful. Lucas isn't some ill-advised crack addict or a street urchin trying to make a name for himself. He's someone who knows violence better than you and your brother here."

Tommy's ears picked up and he turned.

"Is that so?"

'Yeah, that is so.'

Tommy looked at Curtis and smiled.

"Sounds like my kind of guy."

'Shut up, Tommy.' Curtis snapped. Tommy rolled his eyes and continued reading. Curtis took a final drag on the cigarette.

"So he's a violent guy with a vendetta. I've seen it a million times, Paul."

'Not like this. Not like Lucas. You go around pushing everyone and eventually someone will push back with all they have."

'I will kill him, Paul, for what he's done to my family.

Fletcher leant forward, his eyes meeting the dark coal

like spheres of Curtis Drayton. He could see behind it, there was a genuine fear. Lucas had kept his word.

"What he's doing, you mean?"

Curtis raised his eyebrows in confusion.

"Because by my count, Curtis there are still four of you left."

Curtis suddenly shot forward, grabbing Fletcher by his right forearm. Surprisingly strong, Fletcher began to struggle until Tommy stormed around the sofa and planted both hands on his shoulders, pinning him to the chair. He leant down, his lips a few inches from the old man's ear.

"Don't move."

Curtis held up the cigarette he'd finished, the tip of the butt still lit, the final shards of nicotine sizzling off into the world.

"When this is all over with and he tells me that you helped him as he begs for his life, which he will, I will be back here."

Curtis brought the cigarette down onto Fletcher's forearm, the smell of singed hair and burnt skin filling the air. As Fletcher let out a howl of pain, Tommy's murderous hands clamped over his mouth.

The young kids next door would not be disturbed by the noise.

Fletcher breathed heavily, his brain shooting out thunderous signals of pain. His skin roared with a fiery fury. Curtis leaned in, his face an ugly twist of a raging scowl.

"I will reunite you with your wife, piece by piece."

Curtis stood, re-buttoning his blazer before stomping towards the front door. Tommy rolled the manila folder into a long cylinder and gently tapped a pain stricken Fletcher on the top of his skull.

"I'm keeping this."

Fletcher waited for the front door to close and he immediately darted to the kitchen. The cold water couldn't burst from the tap fast enough as it connected with the red, burning patch of skin on his forearm. He stood for ten minutes, as instructed for a burn, with the water slowly numbing the pain and restoring his mind to normal.

He thought about all the plans he'd made for tomorrow, how he was going to turn his life around.

He sat on the sofa, poured another drink, lit a cigarette and ignored them completely.

CHAPTER EIGHTEEN

Ashley sat in the small kitchen on the thirteenth floor of the grand Hamden Trading building, looking out of the large windows that let the outside world in. Rain drops clattered gracefully against them, racing each other down the glass and into oblivion. She had enjoyed a nice, hot cup of coffee, chatting with a few colleagues who hadn't envied her night shift.

At five to six, she gathered her bag and left the kitchen, walking down the long corridor towards the open plan office where her night would be spent. The elevator door opened as she approached and she quickly ducked into the nearby stairwell as Peter Masters stepped out. As nice a guy as Peter was, his attraction to her was obvious and sometimes made for uncomfortable moments outside of work hours.

'Just tell him you have a boyfriend now!' She told herself, smiling at the thought. How she wished she could have run into her boyfriend's arms after her family ordeal earlier. After a few moments, she re-emerged into the hall, pretending she was just arriving.

She almost collided with Mary Reid who was waiting for the elevator.

"Sorry!" She realised who it was. "Hey Mary. How are you honey?"

Mary hadn't been herself, not since the horrible news of the death of her friend. Ashley could barely force herself to smile, the guilt trying its best to wrestle out and confess her role in it all. Mary however, did manage one.

"Tired." Her usually bubbly, round face was crestfallen, evidence that a few weeks of solid crying can change a complexion. Her usually vibrant curls hung from the side of her head like morbid curtains.

"I know it's hard." Ashley gently rubbed her friend's arm.

"It's crazy," Mary began to well up, her voice cracking as it struggled with the memory. "It was only a few weeks ago I saw her. I should have booked her a cab."

The struggle was pointless and Ashley put a reassuring arm around her friend as she sobbed.

"It wasn't your fault."

"She just wanted to get back to the hotel. To speak to Lucas and..."

Her words trailed off, replaced by heavy breathing in a futile attempt to regain composure. Ashley felt cold, knowing this poor woman was shouldering blame that rested with her and her repulsive family.

"I know she did. She loved him and was happy. At least take comfort in that."

"I hadn't seen her in so long."

"I remember you telling me."

"I'm sorry. I must look a right state."

"Don't be silly, honey. You know you can talk to me about it whenever you like."

The lift dinged its arrival and the doors slid open. Grant

Bishop, another member of Ashley's team walked out, grunting a hello and steering as clear as he could from the emotional traffic jam in the corridor. Mary dabbed at her mascara-stained eyes with a tissue and stepped into the lift.

"Thank you, Ashley."

"What are friends for?"

They shared a warm smile, the doors cutting it off as they collided. As the lift embarked on its journey downwards, Ashley let out a large exhale. For a brief moment, she hated herself. The pain caused by her wasn't just reserved for Helen and Lucas. The ripple effect of it had travelled throughout the lives Helen had touched. She thought of Helen's life up north, whether she'd had parents who were sobbing over baby pictures or siblings who didn't know whether it would be okay to laugh when they saw each other next. She shook it from her head, telling herself again that it was all about survival in the Drayton family and survive she had.

Her watch said it was three minutes past six. She silently cursed her lateness, pushed through the double doors and went to work.

Lucas went for a wander for the next few hours, stopping at a nearby café to purchase a coffee which this time wasn't haunted by a heart-breaking vision. As he walked the streets, he noticed a box van that parked in the alleyway behind the Hamden building. He could only assume they were there for him. The young police officer was still sitting in his patrol car, the windows covered in rain drops like watery freckles.

The black Punto by the alleyway still hadn't moved.

The entrance to the student halls that neighboured the building was a beehive of activity, students rushing in and out, returning from lectures or heading for another night of cheap drinking. It certainly hadn't been as busy when he'd entered it earlier. The sun was dying out, its glow fading as thick clouds began to dominate the evening. Streetlights burst into light, illuminating patches of thoroughfares.

At a quarter to eight, Lucas saw what he'd been waiting for and duly dumped his now empty coffee cup in to a nearby bin.

A young student exited the building, cupping his hands to his mouth. Smoke drifted up from his young features until it lost itself in the rain. His messy brown hair was pushed flat by his hood.

Lucas looked back to the front of the building.

The young police officer was looking downwards, a blue glow lighting up his face as he lost himself in one of the latest mobile phone game addictions.

Lucas waited to cross the road as a black cab whizzed by, followed by sprays of water from the wet tarmac. He hurried across and the student only looked up in acknowledgement when Lucas asked him if he had a lighter.

He handed it to him.

Lucas then asked him for something else.

———

Officer Patriski sighed, the completion screen flashing in front of him telling him he'd completed yet another level on yet another pointless game. It seemed that every week there was a new 'must play' app available that spread around the station like wildfire.

He'd been sitting outside the building for the last four hours and nothing had happened. He cursed his eagerness, getting caught up in the whirlwind of excitement which had snared everyone in light of what had happened.

Someone was killing the Draytons and he offered to stake out the building. He wanted to be the first on the scene should Lucas turn up.

But as the minutes had turned into hours and the excitement had faded to boredom, he began weighing up the likelihood of Lucas Cole being an idiot. Of course he wouldn't walk straight into an arrest. He may be a man on the edge but he didn't appear to be a fool. Not from the evidence of how he'd systematically taken out several men and butchered two members of the most notorious crime family in the country.

There was a moment of marginal excitement, when he reported in that a black van had pulled into the alleyway and a Punto with two men had been sitting outside the building for as long as he had.

Again, disappointment when he was told to stand back as it was just Curtis trying to protect his sister and the last thing they wanted was to antagonise a grieving Curtis Drayton.

Only two hours left until he could go home, he shuffled uncomfortably in the driver's seat, his Met Vest hanging from his slight frame awkwardly.

The next level had just loaded when he was startled by a knock on the passenger window. He took a moment to collect himself and shook his head while winding down the window.

"You just gave me a heart attack."

"I'm sorry." The young student apologised, his hood now stuck to a wet patch of brown hair. The aroma of cigarettes filtered into the car from his clothes.

"It's fine. What's the matter?"

"Sorry to be a pain, Officer, but there's a homeless man in that alleyway over there.'

He pointed but Patriski struggled to see the hand through the raindrop-laden windscreen.

"He asked me for money. Of all the people to ask, a student?"

"Being homeless isn't a crime."

"I know. And I wanted to help. So I reached into my pocket and pulled out my phone as it was in the way and the bastard snatched it out of my hand.'

'He forcibly took your phone?" Patriski managed to hide the smile, but his eyes gleamed with excitement.

"Yeah. I tried to get it back but he told me he would beat the shit out of me if I came near him."

'And he is still there?'

'Yeah. It happened, like, a minute ago. Thank God you were here."

Patriski thought carefully. He badly wanted to get out of the car, but it was against his orders.

"I'm not supposed to leave my vehicle. I am here on another call."

"He's right there," the young man said desperately, again pointing out of Patriski's line of sight.

Patriski sighed. It was five minutes before he needed to give his half hourly update, but his hands found their way to the radio sitting proudly on the breastplate of his stab-proof vest.

"Control Receiving. Officer one-four-two. On scene at Hampden Building. Just an update for the call. Sitting here and it's all quiet."

Both of them waited in silence, the only sound the rain drumming against the windscreen like fingers on a table.

"Received," abruptly shot from the radio.

Patriski turned back to the young student.

"Right. Let's make this quick."

The student nodded and stepped away from the window as it closed. He was already halfway across the road when Patriski closed the car door behind him. He looked up and down the street, rain slapping against his face with a cold repetition. He jogged across the road as the student disappeared into the alley.

———

Shane Meehan sat in the passenger seat of a black Ford Transit, the paintwork shimmering in the light from the streetlamp. Rain hammered against the body of the vehicle, echoing hollowly. Shane had known Tommy Drayton since they'd been kids, growing up in the same gyms together and sparring daily. Despite being a ferocious fighter, Shane had called time on his fighting career five years earlier, tendonitis in his left knee making a full recovery impossible.

He was an asset to the Draytons, however, his bulky frame and vicious fighting style meant he was perfect to call on when they needed someone taken care of. His ginger hair was shaved almost to the scalp and his thick, orange beard gave the impression his head was upside down.

"Any news?"

Carl Finch, hands on the steering wheel, looked at Shane who shook his head.

"Not yet." His accent was thick, almost indecipherable.

Finch nodded, his long brown hair bouncing. He wouldn't argue or complain, not with Shane or the Draytons. They'd cancelled a gambling debt he owed them, in return for jobs such as this and he was determined to cling onto his addiction-obsessed life for as long as possible.

The smell of marijuana wafted through from the back of the van and Shane turned abruptly, his powerful neck muscles throbbing with anger.

"What have I told you fucking pricks about smoking when we're working?"

Tyrell and Stan, nicknamed 'The Marley Boys' for their

dark skin and braided hair leant forward through the thick cloud of smoke, like genies emerging from a lamp.

"Calm down, bruv," Tyrell said, his bearded face smiling uneasily.

"Don't you tell me to calm down you little prick. I'll come back there and knock bash the living fuck at a'ya."

"Yo Shane, you always so uptight. Take a hit of this shit."

Stan, the younger and slimmer of the two, handed the spliff up towards the enraged Shane with the hands that had stabbed sixteen people in the name of the Draytons. Tyrell smiled his lazy grin, the last thing a number of people had seen before receiving a bullet to the skull.

Shane snatched it with a powerful hand and crushed the entire thing in a shaking fist. He didn't so much as flinch as the burning rock was extinguished against his skin.

The 'Marley Boys' watched on with impressed horror.

Shane stared at them for a few seconds and then slowly returned to his seat. He reached into his jacket pocket, pulling out the .93 Beretta that Tommy had given him. The other gun was with 'Tombs', sat in the Punto on the other side of the building. He pulled back the safety, checking the chamber in full vision of Stan and Tyrell. His eyes flicked to the rear-view mirror, boring holes into their reflections.

"If I smell that fucking stuff again, Lucas will be receiving two less bullets. Understand?"

The two men nodded, trying their hardest not to show fear.

But they were scared. Everyone was scared of Shane Meehan, and tonight, he guaranteed to show Lucas Cole why.

The other .93 Berretta sat loosely in the palm of David 'Tombs' Tombley's hand. It didn't feel right, like it should be heavier. A former bodybuilder who had met Tommy Drayton at a local gym years earlier, Tombs had found steady work for the Draytons since.

He'd even took a shine to their sister, Ashley, for a while but was told to back away by Curtis as he held a butchers knife to Tombs' throat.

Tombs, as his dear old Dad would say, 'wasn't the sharpest knife in the drawer.' But he was big, he was strong and he was loyal.

Loyal to his Dad until he'd lost his battle with pancreatic cancer.

Loyal to the Draytons, who paid him well and kept him out of prison.

And he was loyal to whoever he was ordered to protect. He recalled that night a few years back, when he'd had to shadow Lewis Drayton when he ran a coke deal in Shoreditch. He'd sat and waited in the car, assured by Lewis that he would be back in five minutes.

As soon as six minutes flashed on the basic Casio stopwatch he wore on his tree trunk-sized wrists, Tombs went looking for him.

He found Lewis on the ground between three middleclass bearded guys, an avalanche of finely polished shoes raining down on him.

It took less than twenty seconds for Tombs to render two of them unconscious and break the third one's collar bone.

The Draytons had paid him handsomely for his loyalty then and were willing to pay handsomely for it tonight.

His loyalty to Ashley.

Beautiful Ashley Drayton.

'Yo Tombs, what you make of that?'

Chris Hiller, an old friend of Curtis Drayton and a

man happy to let his psychotic need to hurt people aid his friend's family, nudged the large man in the passenger seat.

He motioned at the wing mirror with his eyebrows and the behemoth beside him slowly turned to see the reflection. They saw the young policeman leave his car, jog across the road and then slowly walk towards the alley behind them, casually sliding his hands into the top of his Met vest.

Tombs shrugged.

"Well, keep your eye on it, big man."

Chris smiled at Tombs; he'd always liked him. It would be a pleasure to maim Lucas Cole with Tombs by his side.

They sat in the car and waited.

The rain continued to fall.

Officer Patriski walked slowly down the alleyway, the smell of rubbish overflowing in the bins exacerbated by the wetness of another spring night in London. He tucked his hands behind the breast plates of his Met Vest, his arms loosely hanging. He wanted to look casual, approachable, anything to calm down an erratic homeless person who would undoubtedly be hostile.

As he ventured further down, he could barely make out the student anymore and, of more concern, he couldn't really recall what his face had looked like.

Where was this homeless man?

Had he made a mistake?

"Hey kid, where is he?" Patriski called out, wondering if he should go further. Suddenly, a hand grasped the back of his vest and pulled it back. The vest crushed against his chest, locking his hands in place.

'UNHAND ME THIS INSTANT!'

Patriski struggled, but his captor held on with incredible strength and then struck a quick, yet painful knee to the back of his legs. He fell to his knees, scratching uncomfortably against the wet concrete.

"I'm really sorry, Officer," Lucas apologised.

He reached down with his free hand and unclipped the radio from the breast plate of the safety vest, which was now his reason for captivity. He slid the radio into the back pocket of his jeans, and then struck the officer with a hard elbow strike to the back of the skull. It would have been worthy of winning any Muay Thai bout.

Patriski's world faded to black.

Lucas dragged the unconscious man into the doorway and then gently lowered him to the cold, wet alley floor, the body shrouded in dark shadows. It had hidden Lucas well enough.

Lucas took a few steps out, calmly looking around the alleyway, trying to peer through a sheet of rain. The young student approached him, a large smile adorned on his face.

"That was insane," he chuckled.

"Here." Lucas handed him two fifty pound notes. The student gratefully accepted them, stuffing them into his jean pockets before the rain got to them.

"Is he dead?"

Lucas shook his head confidently and then took a few steps to a dented dustbin he'd visited earlier. He opened the carrier bag he'd stuffed behind it, pulling out a bottle of Vodka. The student's eyes lit up.

"Are we celebrating?"

Lucas chuckled, surprising himself with how long it had been since he had last laughed. He handed it to the student.

"Hold this." He reached back into the bag and pulled out a few rolls of thin, industrial strength cable, which he tucked into the back of his jeans, resting them against the back of his leather jacket. His hand disappeared into the plastic once more and returned with a packet of cheap tea towels. The student watched, puzzled as Lucas removed one of the tea towels and stuffed it into his pocket. The others went back in the carrier bag, which he tossed against the wall. They hit the floor with a muted slap.

"Vodka."

The student quickly handed the bottle back to Lucas, who snapped the lid off. The alcohol fumes exploded into the air around them, catching them both by surprise. Whatever this stuff was, it was strong. Lucas looked up at the student and smiled.

"If I were you, I would stay away from here tonight."

"Hey, I have a hundred quid to spend. I won't be back until the morning."

"Good. Make sure of it. There are going to be a lot of police here and that poor sod over there is going to be trying to remember who led him down here.

The student shrugged, stuffed his hands into the pockets of his hoodie and then scurried up the alleyway, disappearing into darkness. Lucas watched him evaporate into the night, knowing he would never see him again. He retrieved the tea towel from his jacket pocket and poured the pungent alcohol over the fabric. He then rolled one half of it up into a tight wrap and carefully fed it into the top of the bottle. It took a few attempts, but with methodical patience, Lucas managed to slide it in. He held it under his jacket, ensuring the rain didn't interfere with the alcohol.

The fumes raced upwards, hitting his nostrils. He walked slowly back to the main road, his eyes adjusting to the brighter London street. He noted the police car sat across the road, knowing the occupant was forcefully sleeping in the alley behind him. The Punto was still in place, twenty yards from where he was standing.

Lucas spun back into the alley, leaning with his back

against the wall. He took a moment to remember the wonderful smile on his wife's face when he'd surprised her with an extra Christmas gift last year. How they'd playfully fought on the bed because he had 'won' Christmas, something she vowed he would never be able to do.

All of it a memory.

Helen resigned to the archives of a life he didn't want anymore.

With one hand holding the bottle under his jacket, his other rammed into his jean pocket. As his fingers grasped around the lighter, he felt the cold touch of Helen's wedding ring. His faced tightened in a vengeful scowl and he felt ready.

He needed to be quick.

He needed to be accurate.

He pulled the bottle out and the vodka-laden tea towel swung lazily, heavy with fluid. He clicked the lighter a couple of times, teasing it to spark into life. On the third click, the flame arrived, dancing in the wet and windy night air. Lucas touched it carefully to the cloth. The flames spread up the cloth with a chaotic beauty and Lucas quickly ran out into the street. The yards between him and the car dwindled rapidly, and as he approached the back tyre, he gently tossed the flaming bottle over the roof of the vehicle.

It crashed onto the bonnet of the Punto, shards of glass bursting out onto the road, chased by flames exploding into the night sky. The flames engulfed the bonnet of the Punto instantly, flickering wildly as they spread around the front of the car with a burning fury. The car shook in panic as the driver's door opened, Hiller struggling manically with his seatbelt, trying to escape the oncoming inferno. The passenger door flung open and Lucas ran as fast as he could towards it.

Tombs leant forward, about to exit the car. Before his

foot touched the pavement, his eyes met those of Lucas Cole for a mere instant. Lucas grabbed the door and slammed it back, crushing Tombs' head against the car. He slumped forward, motionless, hitting the hard, wet concrete with a thud. He didn't move, blood trickling from the side of his skull.

Hiller was oblivious, having won his struggle to free himself. He now stood in the road, his panic stricken face darting from left to right, trying to decipher what had happened. Lucas kept low, shuffling around the side of the car which was slowly losing itself in the fiery grip. Hiller fumbled for his phone, wanting to alert Shane and the others. When he looked down at the screen, Lucas sprang into action.

He grabbed Hiller's arm, locking his grip tightly, and then rammed his head as hard as he could into the driver's window. He pulled Hiller's head from the shattered pane, shards of glass and drops of blood scattering over the wet tarmac, and then with a surge of strength, hoisted him up and slammed him onto the Punto's bonnet.

Hiller's back collided with the red-hot metal, and he screamed in anguish as the flames surrounded him. He rolled off onto the floor, his clothes burning, his skin scalding as the flames spread down his jacket and his jeans. Lucas walked across the road, the rain hurtling towards him with no respite, the door to the Hamden Trading Building a few feet away.

Chris Hiller rolled on the floor, the puddles doing their best to help him squash the flames that danced on his body with painful joy. They eventually extinguished themselves as the rain fell. Hiller had already passed out from the pain.

The security guard, who had seen the flames burst into the sky from across the road, was racing back to his desk to the phone when the door flew open, the whistling of the wind and the cold, wet air whipping through the door accompanied by Lucas.

"Don't even think about it."

Lucas's voice boomed, echoing in the plush marble corridor. The security guard, the same one he'd seen silently welcome Ashley to the building, froze on the spot. Lucas strode towards the desk, wet footprints left on the clean floor like soggy bread crumbs.

The security guard slowly, with minimal movement, pressed the nine button three times, but before the call could connect, Lucas slammed down the phone with a firm hand. The other wrapped around the back of the guard's head, driving him face down onto the hard oak.

The security guard rolled off the desk and on to the floor, his nose broken and his mind blank.

Lucas pressed the button for the elevator, which opened immediately.

Ashley Drayton was on the thirteenth floor.

He pressed thirteen and the doors closed.

CHAPTER NINETEEN

"What the fuck is happening down there?"

"Oh my god!"

"Someone call the police."

"Already doing it."

"Is that man on fire? Oh my god he is!"

"Is it a terrorist attack?"

"Someone call the police, for God's sake!"

"I think Peter is!"

Ashley's office was a beehive of panic-stricken activity, her whole team standing against the windows overlooking the chaos below. The Punto was still ablaze, a thick, grey beanstalk of smoke swerving up to meet the rain clouds.

Ashley tried to remain calm, not wanting to alarm her team any more than they already were, and briskly walked back to her desk. The spacious, open plan office was over two thirds empty, only the six of them knuckling down for the nightshift were present. As she rummaged through her bag, the other five were still witnessing the chaos below, loudly voicing their theories and worries.

"Hey, you okay?"

Peter flashed his overly affectionate grin as he leaned

over her desk. She started slightly, then smiled politely back.

"Yeah, sorry. I'm just a little flustered, that's all."

"Is it what's going on downstairs?"

"Yeah."

"Well, you're safe here." He gently rested a hand on her shoulder, and she shifted slightly.

"I know we've worked together for a while, Peter. And I really do think you're a terrific guy."

Peter realised where Ashley was leading him and quickly retracted his hand followed by an empty display of male pride.

"Hey, Ash. I was just checking that you were okay. I wasn't, you know, trying anything."

"I know. But I know we've had a few moments in the past and I want them to stay there. I have a boyfriend now and it's getting pretty serious.'

"Since when?"

Before Ashley could answer, the double doors to the office flew open violently. They swung round forcefully and slammed into the wall with an attention-commanding bang. Everyone turned, shocked and confused as the unknown man walked in, his footsteps leaving wet prints on the cheap carpet. His short brown hair was messy, water drops falling from his fringe and down his stern, handsome face. Water clung to his leather jacket. His deep, brown eyes were locked on one person.

Ashley Drayton.

Her co-workers moved cautiously from the window, walking slowly together, grasping onto the notion of safety in numbers. Ashley froze with fear, her eyes beginning to water as she began to contemplate the inevitable. His voice was as terrifying as she had imagined.

"Everybody out."

He raised his arm and pointed a threatening finger straight at her. Rainwater fell from his sleeve.

"Except her."

Lucas took a few more menacing steps towards the group, his muscular frame becoming more apparent as he approached them. He walked past a few of the empty banks of desks, his eyes not leaving hers.

She could feel the hatred he carried, for her and her family.

For the things they had done.

For what they'd taken from him.

Peter, with the foolish notion of trying to bend the situation to his benefit, took a few steps towards the oncoming Lucas.

"Look mate, I don't know who you think you are, but you can fuck right...."

Before Peter could finish his idle threat, Lucas swung a rock solid right hook, connecting fully with Peter's jaw. The impact echoed through the office, a few screams from the co-workers followed. Peter stumbled backwards, falling onto his backside. His jaw swung loosely from his skull, broken and useless. Lucas looked up at the group again, his eyes narrowing in on Ashley who hadn't moved from her seat. A horrified hush filled the room.

"Everybody out, NOW!"

This time, the request was received with frantic movement, Ashley's co-workers scrambling quickly for their coats hanging on the nearby coat rack, the ladies retrieving their handbags from their desks. Grant Bishop shed his usual hostility to haul a disorientated Peter to his feet, draping his arm over his shoulder and walking him slowly to the door.

Ashley remained in her seat, staring her pleas of forgiveness at the emotionless widower before her. He took two more steps toward her. Large, wet footprints indented the carpet.

"This will be a lot easier for both of us if you stay seated."

The double door to the office slammed closed.

Starling was seated in the interview room with Officer Carter, recounting the moment the young PC had seen Lewis Drayton's headless corpse. Carter was a strong witness, giving great detail at the barbaric crime scene he'd stumbled upon. However, it all felt kind of trivial.

Starling knew this was Sgt. Bailey's way of warning him to stop questioning him in front of the other officers. It had happened twice over the past few weeks and Starling knew that if he wanted his career to progress within the Metropolitan Police, there wouldn't be a third.

He thanked the young PC for travelling in for the interview, the stocky officer only too happy to oblige. Starling walked back through the office, past the empty desk of Paul Fletcher. He stopped for a moment, recounting the story Fletcher had told them earlier that morning. About the violence and trauma of Lucas's past. Although everyone knew what a distinguished career Fletcher had had within the Met, it had never occurred to Starling that at some point Fletcher had been right where he was.

He continued walking through the office, looking for a spare hot desk to log in and type up the statement. He nodded a goodbye to Officer Murphy as he slid on his jacket and limped to the exit. He found a free computer and sat down, dropping his notebook in front of him and adjusting the seat accordingly.

"That was quick."

Sgt. Bailey was standing a few desks down, staring disapprovingly at Starling, who leaned back in the chair.

"He just recounted what had happened that night," Starling replied.

"Well we already had his main statement when it was taken before. Not really too much more to add."

Starling held his tongue, he knew Bailey was trying to get a rise out of him and he wouldn't let him. If he wanted to be out on the street catching Lucas Cole, the fastest way was to play the game, fall in line and prove to Bailey he was wasted in the office.

Bailey grunted and began lowering himself to his seat when Officer Hatton rushed in. Even in a panic, she exuded a genuine beauty. Her brown hair, tied in a ponytail, bobbed behind her.

"Sir, we've had reports of a fire on Lowton Road."

"Then tell them they have the wrong service. We aren't the fire brigade, Hatton."

A few sniggers from other officers, all wanting to remain in Bailey's good books as he sat back in his leather chair. Starling rolled his eyes.

"I know, sir. But Lowton Road is where the Hamden Trading Building is located."

Instantly, Bailey and Starling both shot to their feet. A few of the other officers turned with interest.

"Officer Patriski radioed in fifteen minutes ago to say everything was fine, but we haven't since been able to make contact with him since."

Starling was already halfway to the door as the Sergeant began barking out orders, ordering all available officers to rush to the Hamden Trading Building. No one was to enter until he got there and his request for an Armed Response Team was granted.

Within minutes, the rain-soaked streets of London

were awash with blue flashing lights and the high pitch squeals of wailing sirens.

Shane drummed his fingers on the dashboard, shattering the silence of the van with his rhythmic tapping. Tyrell sat silently, his eyes chasing a plastic bag being swept up in the rain addled wind outside. Stan was asleep, silently waiting to be woken. Carl Finch shuffled restlessly in the driver's seat, bored and in need of a smoke.

"Can you sit still?"

Shane didn't so much ask, as tell him. Finch smiled apologetically, fishing his cigarettes from his jacket pocket. He stepped out of the car, fumbling with the zipper of his jacket, as the wet chill of the spring evening slammed into him. He struggled against the wind to light his smoke and then leaned against the van as he exhaled the carcinogenic smoke.

Shane watched, shaking his head at what he believed was a pointless habit. He held the gun up to the light, admiring the polished barrel and the damage it could cause.

"Yo, Shane. Let me hold that."

"Fuck you, Marley. I ain't giving a dumb fuck like you a gun. Think I'm stupid?"

"Why you always gotta come at me with that dumb bullshit?"

Shane spun round in the seat, pointing the gun at Tyrell who held his hands up in surrender. He looked to Stan hopefully, who was lost in his own dream.

"How about you just shut your goddamn mouth until this night is over. If Tommy wanted you to be strapped, you would be."

Tyrell nodded in agreement and Shane slowly turned

round in his seat. Finch rapped his knuckles on the window. Shane ignored him, but on the second rap he turned, his agitation obvious.

"What do you want?"

Finch beckoned Shane out of the car. He sighed, but as soon as he kicked open the passenger door he understood why.

Sirens.

The howling calling card of the Metropolitan Police was echoing through the streets of Canada Water, ripping through the downpour. They grew in volume and numbers by the sound of it and Shane slowly jogged down the alleyway.

The first thing he saw was the flames, frantically reaching skywards with long, fiery fingers. Second, he noticed Hiller, face down and motionless on the floor. Tombs was nowhere to be seen.

A panicked contingent of people raced out of the building, screaming and animated. The blue flashing lights were beginning to cast their repetitive glow on the buildings further down the street.

Shane raced back to the van, thumping the side of it to wake Stan. Tyrell exited, joining Finch as he raced to meet Shane.

"The fucker is here. Tombs and Hiller are down."

He cocked the gun and motioned to the fire escape hanging off the side of the building like a metallic arm.

"Up we go."

———

Ashley sat facing the window, her wrists and ankles bound with brown postage tape. She could see the blue lights flashing in the distance, like an over the top Christmas tree. She was willing them to arrive as soon as possible. She sniffed back her sobs, her tears staining her cheeks with black strips of mascara. The chair had wheels, but she knew it was pointless to try and move.

Lucas stood to the side of her, casually leaning against the side of one of the desks. In his hands, he was unrolling lengths of industrial cable which he'd removed from the back of his jeans as soon as they were alone.

She could see why Helen had fallen for him. He was classically handsome, his strong jaw covered in stubble. His body, wrapped in wet clothes and a fine leather jacket, was impressive. But his brown eyes, they conveyed a hatred and a pain that she could never put into words.

When he'd spoken to her, his words had been stern but his tone soft. Almost gentlemanly.

She realised that this was a good man, pushed to violent measures by the deeds of her and her family.

A living embodiment of karma.

"You don't have to do this, you know?"

She looked up at him, her stained eyes pleading for mercy. He looked at her blankly, stretching the cable out with his hands.

"I know. What I should be doing at this time is sitting on the sofa with my beautiful wife, hammering through another few episodes of Game of Thrones."

He stretched out the last of the roll of cable before picking up the other. He unravelled a little, before tightly knotting the pieces together. He pulled it tight, ensuring its strength and then proceeded to keep unravelling.

"The thing is Ashley, I can't do that."

"I know and I am so sorry."

"And the reason I can't do that," Lucas said, ignoring her apology, "is because you and your family took her from me."

"It's Curtis. He makes us do these things. Ever since we were young, he protected us, but he's demanded complete obedience and respect. He is the one who took your wife."

Lucas shook his head, raising his eyebrows at her. She knew he knew. Her head dropped, realisation setting in. The street below the window alternated from dark to bright blue, the sirens screaming up at them from the pavement below.

"Harry told me everything."

She looked at him, tears splashing down to her blouse with black spatters. Lucas leant forward, meeting her stare full on.

"Everything."

"That's all I did, I swear."

"It was enough."

Lucas reached the end of the cable wire and then bent it over on itself. Creating a hoop, he then tied a loose knot where the wire connected with itself.

"Mary told me that her friend was coming down for the weekend." Ashley stared ahead, almost confessing out loud, more to herself than Lucas. 'She said she was excited that you weren't going. Not because she didn't like you, but because she was going to have a girl's night in. I've known Mary for a few years, I know where she lives. So I passed it on to Curtis and he made the boys make the arrangements.

"Mary had told me that Ashley was staying at the Hilton and I asked her how far it was. 'Just a little walk through Russell Square' she told me. I guess that was enough."

Lucas stood patiently, waiting for more. Ashley took a few deep breaths.

"I spoke with Curtis this afternoon and he's scared. You have done something I've never seen anyone do and that is to make him panic. I've seen how much this has ruined your life."

"My life is not important. It was Helen's life that I cared about and your family ended that. So no amount of apology or begging will change what has to happen."

Ashley nodded, her face scrunching up as the tears returned. Her mind wandered to her boyfriend and whether he would ever have loved her like Lucas had his wife. Lucas dropped the hoop of wire on the desk and then, carrying the long stretch of cable with him, approached a metal filing cabinet. He knelt down and fed the cable through the hinge hole on the side. As he pulled it through and began to tightly fasten the cable together, Ashley watched two more dark tears fall onto her shirt.

Sgt. Bailey stepped out of the car as it came to a stop, the rain bulleting into his face with a freezing welcome. Lowton Road was frantic with activity. Five police cars had parked up outside of the building, blue lights flashing wildly. A fire engine had also made its way to the scene, fire fighters tending to the flaming car, the fire having spread to the interior. Two paramedics, their ambulance parked across the alleyway were tending to the burns of an unconscious man in the middle of the road.

It was pandemonium, and Bailey shook his head as he witnessed it.

Police officers were out in full force, their high-vis coats protecting them from the torrential downpour. Two of them directing traffic to turn around as the road was not open for business. Three officers were searching for Patriski, his car abandoned outside the building. He noticed Officer Hatton talking to a rather panicked group of office workers, one of them with his arm draped over his colleague and looking in a sizeable amount of pain.

"Is he in there?"

Bailey turned as Starling strode purposefully towards him, trying to figure out if the young officer was trying to provoke a response.

"We don't know yet."

"Sir, permission to go in and see?"

"Not until the Armed Response unit gets here."

"But what if it's too late?"

"Remember your rank, constable!"

Starling gritted his teeth and took a few steps to the side, not even the cold drops of rain being enough to calm him down. Officer Hatton motioned to a paramedic who'd arrived in a second ambulance. Immediately, the young medic approached the office worker in agony. The pretty officer hurried over.

"What's the news?"

"It's Lucas Cole, sir. And judging by what they've told us, he is really pissed off."

Bailey flashed a look at Starling, who stared back with a willingness to act. Bailey turned back to Officer Hatton. A few officers had gathered around for an update, their uniforms and coats dripping wet.

"We wait until the Armed Response get here. Until then, I want every fucking exit of this building covered."

A few of them dispersed, rushing down the side alley of the building, past the fire escape. A radio message was struggling to be heard over the noise, requesting a paramedic in the adjacent alleyway for Officer Patriski.

Bailey looked at Starling, with a victorious smirk on his seasoned face.

"The bastard has nowhere to go now."

———

Susan sat across from Fletcher, wearing the beautiful summer dress that was archived in his memories. She reached out to stroke his hand, telling him he'd made the right decision. None of this was his fault.

He looked at her, asking her what he should do.

"No one enters the building until Armed Response arrive. ETA two minutes."

He looked at her, puzzled.

"Cover the exits and wait for further orders."

Suddenly, the entire image of Susan sitting at the table, the sun beaming behind her, was pulled away and Fletcher sat up straight on his sofa.

His shirt was damp, the upturned glass of Jack Daniels he had fallen asleep holding was empty. The room stank of cigarettes.

The police radio crackled again. It was Sgt. Bailey's voice.

"Get Patriski in a goddamn ambulance. What's the location of my response unit?"

Fletcher dropped the glass and began to wrestle his arms into his jacket, the raw burn on his forearm shooting out a painful reminder that he ignored.

"Currently on Harper Lane. ETA at Lowton Road, one minute."

Fletcher's keys rattled in his hand as he raced through the front door, the rain pelting around him as he dashed to his car.

Lucas strode back across the office, running his hand on the cable, following it back to the desk. He peeked out of the window to the street below, the frantic activity illuminated in bursts by blue lights.

Ashley was sobbing quietly, her head hanging as far as her neck would allow. Her blonde hair reminded him of Helen, the way it sat neatly on her head. He slowly reached into his pocket and pulled out her wedding ring. He looked down at it, remembering his hand shaking as he'd slid it onto Helen's finger, a smile of pure love radiating from her as he did so. All doubts that he had of going through with this, of avenging her were quashed by that smile.

He closed his eyes and clenched his hand into a fist, refusing to let go of that wonderful memory.

"I have to, Helen."

Ashley looked up, her face evidently tired, the skin hanging from her skull, exhausted. She looked at the man before her, his face pain-stricken as he squeezed his fist harder. The grief that had been caused by her.

The grief that had led to this moment.

"You don't have to, Lucas."

His eyes opened and he turned to Ashley, a renewed hope on her weary face.

"You could let me go and we could work this out."

Lucas closed his eyes again, slowly returned the ring to his pocket and he shook his head.

"Please, I am begging you not to do this."

"Begging?"

Ashley nodded enthusiastically.

"The police are downstairs and there's no way out if you do what you came here to do. But together, we can talk to them. Try and help you."

Lucas looked away, his eyes peering through the speckled window at the skyline of London. Bright lights all the way to the horizon. Blue lights flashing with boring repetition below.

He looked back at Ashley.

"Did my wife beg?"

"Excuse me?"

"My wife. Helen. When your brothers were chasing her, did she beg them to stop?"

"I don't know.'

"Or when Tommy lured her into the false safety of a cab, locking her in and attacking her. Did she beg then?"

Lucas's voice became strained with emotion, the words slightly breaking as he recounted the horrors his wife had suffered. Ashley teared up again, shaking her head hopelessly.

"When Curtis raped her and then had Tommy push a blade through her stomach and through my unborn child. Did she beg then?"

Ashley looked around the room, everything blurring behind her veil of tears.

"I don't know, Lucas. I don't."

Lucas's face tightened into a scowl of pure hatred.

"If you hadn't said anything, my wife would still be alive. I wouldn't be here. This all started with you."

Lucas hoisted up the hooped end of the cable and draped it over Ashley's head so it hung around her neck. She tried to struggle, but it made no difference. Lucas returned to the loose knot he had tied earlier and tightened it until was almost pressing into the skin of her neck. He lowered himself down to her face, their eyes both rich with pain and regret.

"It's your fault my wife is dead."

Ashley sobbed a few more times, her stained cheeks plastered in more tears. Metres of the cable lay loosely on the floor, like a meandering scribble between the filing cabinet and Ashley's neck. Lucas stared out to the world one more time and then hauled Ashley out of her chair, holding her by the collar of her blouse. Her eyes widened with fear. Urine ran down the inside of her leg. She somehow coaxed the courage to speak.

"Would it make any difference if I told you that I hated myself? That I am so sorry?"

Lucas stopped for a moment, realising the terror that

encased this young woman was his doing. A flash of Helen lying on the bed, moments after she'd passed away, hit him, a large bloodstained sheet covering her stomach and the baby he would never hold.

His face wrenched into a painful snarl.

"None."

With all of his might, Lucas took a step to the window and with both arms he lifted Ashley off of the ground. His arms violently swung to the side and he hurled her against the large pane of glass.

Thousands of shards joined the downpour of rain as her tiny frame clattered through it, the flashing lights illuminating all of them as they sparkled and fell hurriedly to the ground. Ashley saw the bright lights of London one last time as she flew out into the night sky, feeling the calming cold of the rain. The ground below rushed up towards her at a thunderous pace.

The cable followed her out of the window, the pile diminishing as it whizzed by Lucas's feet. Eventually the file cabinet shunted slightly and the cable snapped tight.

Ashley hung from the side of the building, her feet swinging as she died instantly.

The rain and wind shook her body as it swung in the night sky.

CHAPTER TWENTY

Thousands of shards of glass twinkled in the glowing blue flashes of the police lights as they hurtled towards Lowton Road, like a thousand fireflies losing their fight with gravity. Officers and civilians ran for cover, as they crashed against the pavement, exploding into thousands more pieces that threw themselves around with reckless abandon.

Voices of despair rang out; horrified gasps of disbelief and cries of terror drowned out the sirens, as all eyes were transfixed to the side of the building.

Ashley's body hung motionless, gently swaying in the bullying shove of the wind.

A large van with the words 'POLICE' skidded to a stop near the cars and out stopped Sargent Marshall, a burly man who carried himself with genuine threat. He was wearing a bulletproof vest, a thick, navy helmet and held in his arms the police authorised MP5SFA3 semi-automatic carbine rifle. He scouted the area, raindrops sticking to his visor until he saw Sgt. Bailey.

"Bailey."

"Marshall."

"This is turning into a goddamn war zone. He's just thrown that woman out a window.'

Marshall followed Bailey's meaty finger pointing to the building; the sight of a woman, hanging from her neck at someone's barbaric will, caused his eyes to thin with rage. He reached to the radio on his vest, his deep voice booming into it.

"Everyone get ready. We're going in. Locked and loaded boys."

Marshall nodded confidently at Bailey, before turning on his heels and stomping back through the chaotic street to his van. He thumped a powerful forearm against the side of the truck, which rocked slightly as the team inside readied themselves to breach the building. The Police Officers watched with intrigue, many of them caught up with the excitement of the evening. Others looked genuinely mortified at what was unfolding before their eyes.

Bailey stood in his usual stance, his hands on his hips as he watched the preparation, already playing out the conversation he would have with the Chief Inspector about why Lucas Cole was shot dead on this very evening.

Starling stood a few feet behind him, the rain dripping from his hair and into his dishevelled face.

Bailey spoke into his radio.

"I want two paramedics in behind the response team. We need to bring that poor girl in from the cold as soon as possible." He turned his head, his eyes meeting Starling's. "This ends now."

"Will they shoot him?" Starling asked, peering up at the building.

"If they have to. My money is on he won't come quietly."

"But he should be arrested for the crimes he has committed."

"And he will. But these boys won't mess about."

Starling looked over at the van; its doors were pulled open and twelve armed and ready officers jumped out in twos, their uniforms padded and their rifles at the ready.

"He needs to be arrested. Not killed."

Bailey turned furiously.

"HE JUST NEEDS TO BE STOPPED!"

Starling shook his head in disgust.

"Fuck this!"

Starling shot past the Sergeant with an impressive pace, darting past the armed team and crunching over the glass covering the ground like glittering pebbles. He heard Sergeant shouting his name, cursing it to high heaven as he burst through the door and into the foyer of the Hamden building.

Lucas felt the time stop as Ashley crashed through the window. He saw her collide with the glass, the cable flicking behind her like a cruel dog lead. As she connected with the glass, every tiny crack became apparent, spiralling out from her like a thick, white spider's web. As she smashed through, the wind swept in, surrounding Lucas with a chill that was as cold as his actions. She disappeared out of sight, followed by droplets of flashing blue glass.

When the cable tightened, he turned and marched back towards the double doors that he'd burst through earlier.

"It's over, Lucas."

The voice ghosted through to him, drowning out the wails of sirens and screams of panic from the broken window. He continued walking, stopping by the door and turning his head back to see her.

She floated a few feet away, eyes burning like two blue flames.

"Not yet."

He clenched his dangerous fist and then thumped the small pane of glass covering the fire alarm. The shrill, clanging of the alarm engulfed the building, ringing wildly through the corridors on all of the empty floors.

"They're coming for you, baby."

He knew she was right. With the amount of officers there were at the front of the building, it made sense they would have the back covered. They may have even run into problems with the occupants of the black van.

"It's over."

Lucas turned and took a few commanding steps, his face a mere few inches from the glowing apparition of his wife's.

"No. Not while there's still breath in my body."

Her face begged him to stop, the blue eyes pleading with him to give in. He took a final glance at her and then stormed out into the corridor. The screen above the elevator side scrolled the words 'Not in Service – Fire Emergency'. It would inconvenience the police, although he could hear the faint clambering of footsteps on the first few floors as he opened the door to the stairwell. He jogged down the corridor, past the toilets, past a small, quaint kitchen and pushed open the Fire Exit door.

As he did, a gun was pointed straight into his chest.

Starling raced to the lifts as he ran past the deserted desk in the centre of the lobby, his fingers inches away when the fire alarm rang out above him. He silently cursed, knowing he had to keep moving before he was hoisted back by the Armed Squadron who were scuttling towards the main doors. Behind them, standing in the street, he knew Bailey was already writing his obituary.

He scanned the large room until he saw the stairwell door, kicked it open and then began climbing the mammoth amount of stairs, knowing full well his protective vest, utility belt and rain-drenched clothes were only going to make it harder.

He climbed as quickly as he was able to.

———

Shane had been waiting on the thirteenth floor of the rickety, metal fire escape for a few moments, the gun hanging loosely in his hand. Finch stood just to his right, leaning against the wall with a garrotte wire in his hand. Stan stood on the other side of the door, a pocket knife shimmering in the rain as it twitched in his fingers. Tyrell was a few steps behind Shane, standing further down the wet, metal staircase so he couldn't push past. The small walkway could barely hold all three of them and should Lucas try to run, Shane knew he wouldn't have the space to be able to get through them all.

Tommy had been very strict with his words.

"Do not kill him. But feel free to hurt the bastard."

Shane wasn't going to pass up the chance of scoring some brownie points with Curtis and he was sure delivering the murderous little prick with a few broken bones and a couple less pints of blood would do just that.

The narrow alleyway that they stood in was encased in shadow, the only lights those glowing from the windows on the building opposite. A similar fire escape hung crudely from that building also, wet and rattling in the wind.

There were no armed men on that one, however.

Suddenly, Shane heard footsteps approaching at an alarming rate and he took a step back from the door and held the gun up.

It swung open, shielding Stan from the view and Shane pointed the gun right into the solid chest of Lucas Cole.

He pulled the trigger.

Lucas instinctively swung his left forearm up and swiped the gun-wielding hand to the side. Shane squeezed the trigger, but such was the speed at which Lucas had reacted, his gun had already moved.

The bullet ripped a hole through Finch's neck, blood spraying out like a fractured water pipe.

As he fell to his knees, coughing and spluttering blood, Lucas struck Shane with a hard right uppercut to the stomach and in one fluid motion, swung his elbow up and connected with a crushing blow to the bridge of his nose. He could feel it shatter, blood spraying down the sleeve of his leather jacket.

Shane stumbled backwards towards the metal stairs, Tyrell a few behind him, and Lucas thundered forward with a powerful teep kick, the sole of his shoe making a colossal impact with the centre of Shane's chest.

The blood-covered Irish man flew down the steps, his huge frame colliding at full speed with Tyrell who tried to step to the side. The impact sent Tyrell into the railings, his legs hitting them hard and he flew back over them.

He hurtled quickly to the wet, cold pavement that welcomed him to the afterlife.

Stan, seeing his best friend fall to his death, pushed the door to the side, screaming at Lucas as he lunged at him with his knife. The blade cut through the rain drops and caught Lucas across the cheek, slicing a cut that trickled blood. Lucas quickly responded by grabbing Stan's arms, the fighting training that he had and Stan lacked became instantly apparent. He twisted the wrist so the knife fell, clanging through the grates of the platform and tumbling down the metal steps below.

He connected with a brutal knee to Stan's ribs, and as

he hunched over in pain, Lucas lifted his knee again and ferociously drove it into Stan's face. Stan stumbled back woozily, his eyes watering at the pain his face was screaming. He sloppily threw a lame kick in Lucas's direction which was caught with ease.

Holding the leg straight, Lucas brought his elbow down on the knee cap with all of his weight. He felt the knee cap snap with ease, the blood instantly spraying up the inside of Stan's jeans as it ripped through the skin.

The howl of anguish shot through the night sky like a wolf at a full moon.

He pushed Stan backwards, and he slumped hard against the metal railings, the pain becoming too much as he went silent. Lucas felt the metal structure shaking, police officers who'd been greeted by the falling body of Tyrell had begun to race up the fire escape.

Lucas took a few deep breaths, knowing he had only one shot at his escape.

A concrete-like fist caught him in the cheek.

He stumbled back as Shane, his face a bloody, distorted mess stepped forward, rocking Lucas's ribs with another furious punch. Lucas tried to respond with one of his own, but Shane blocked it, catching Lucas again with another body shaking swing.

Lucas shook off the weariness and Shane, standing straight with his fists up, looked every bit the boxer. He unleashed a barrage of fists at Lucas, who blocked them all by raising his forearms above his head, keeping his face protected by his elbows. Shane roared with anger, ducking down and launching his shoulder into Lucas's hard stomach. They fell back a few steps, the small of Lucas's back colliding hard with the wet, metal barrier.

Shane's hands found their way to Lucas's throat, and he pushed as hard as he could on them, arching Lucas's back further over the railing, the world below beckoning him down with cruel fingers. The police officers further down noticed them hanging over the edge of the structure, Lucas could make out the crackle of a radio.

As breathing became a struggle, Lucas looked up into the deranged eyes of Shane, the man's face dripping blood from the wreckage of his nostrils. Lucas gritted his teeth and managed to stamp out with his foot, catching Shane in the shin. His attacker momentarily relaxed his grip to rebalance allowing Lucas to push up, his forehead colliding with the remains of Shane's already obliterated nose. As Shane stumbled back, Lucas pushed himself up, shook away the pain and then ran at Shane. He leapt upwards and grabbed the back of Shane's skull. He then tucked his knees up, so they rested just under Shane's chin and then dropped hard to the metal ground, dragging Shane face first with him. His spine slammed against the hard steel, rain drops leaping upwards like they were celebrating.

Lucas heard the crack of bone above him and he watched as Shane limply slid off his knees and onto the metal grate they shared.

Shane's eyes were open and his body showed no signs of movement.

Finch coughed a final, blood curdling grasp at life and then laid to rest alongside Shane. Stan was alive, but shock had sent him into a world beyond. Somewhere on the pavement, thirteen storeys below, Tyrell had painted the pavement red. Lucas hauled himself to a vertical base, straightening his blood-stained and rain-drenched jacket.

His cheek stung, a small trickle of blood rubbing off on the back of his hand. His ribs ached, still absorbing the impact of furious Irish knuckles. He gently rubbed his throat, trying to reopen the airway that Shane had tried his best to close. He rolled the lifeless Shane down the stairs, his large body colliding with each step, the metal platforms shaking under his weight.

Lucas looked over the railing, catching a police officer's gaze from a few floors below. The officer yelled up, a warning presumably, but it struggled to be heard through the overbearing onslaught of noise the night held. Lucas looked across at the building opposite, the fire escape that was similar in design but wasn't strewn with the motionless bodies of criminals. He took a deep breath and slowly backed away from the railing, through the fire exit door and back down the corridor.

Starling cursed himself as he climbed up to the seventh floor, furious that he hadn't spent more of his free time maintaining his fitness. He was in good shape, worked out regularly, but his stamina level was worse than he'd expected.

He felt an irritating stitch burrow into his side as he clambered more stairs; three sets of seven stairs separated each floor, each one becoming harder to scale than the last. Below him, he heard the clatter of twenty-four police boots strategically making their way up the first few flights, the Armed Responses equipment shuffling as they moved.

Starling rounded the bannister on floor eight, feeling the sleeves of his police shirt sticking as sweat poured from him. He carried on, scaling the last few flights two steps at a time. Lucas was here, on this floor and he was going to arrest him before anything else could happen.

Before he was shot and killed by the Police, more than likely becoming a martyr to people who have lost someone they love.

Before Lucas managed to kill another member of a family that could very well burn London to the ground while the Met sat back and watched.

Starling was going to stop all of that from happening.

If only he'd realised this back at the hospital, when he'd looked Lucas in his eyes and saw only pain and vengeance.

Starling's boots landed on the thirteenth floor and he quickly pushed himself through the door into the corridor. He looked to the right, the windows of the door providing a peep hole into the office where Ashley hung sickeningly from the window.

He looked to his left and there he was.

Lucas Cole.

He stood halfway down the corridor, rain drops falling from his blood-stained jacket onto the carpet. Beyond him, the fire exit door was open, a rectangle of wind and rain sweeping through into the building.

"Lucas Cole. You are under arrest for the murder of…"

Lucas ran towards the door.

Starling gave chase.

Lucas strode through the door, into the whipping wind and rain and then leapt. He landed his right foot onto the railing and then launched himself off. No sooner had he left the railing that Starling collided into it, stopping his momentum from carrying him over.

He watched in amazement as Lucas hurtled through the night sky and Starling instantly raised his radio.

"He jumped. He fucking jumped across. I repeat, Lucas Cole has jumped across to the opposite building."

Starling let go of his radio, the Met vest falling back against his chest. He looked through the drizzling fuzz of the night at the motionless bodies that littering the stairwell, and at the blood running down through the gaps in the metal platform. A few police officers were painstakingly making their way up the stairs, stepping over the substantial barricade of a man who lay on the bottom step.

Starling slammed his hands against the metal railing and yelled.

"FUCK!"

The world whipped by Lucas as he sailed through the air, watching as the metal staircases began to zip up and out of his line of sight.

He heard nothing but the whistling of air. His stomach felt like it had turned inside out and then leapt up towards his windpipe.

He collided hard with the metal railing, the pipe crashing into the side of his ribs. Lucas felt his ribs break instantly, and his arms straightened as he hung from the sixth floor platform. With all his might, he pulled himself up, groaning at the agony as he hauled his weight over the railing and dropped onto his back on the platform. He lay there for a moment, allowing the magnitude of what he had just done to sink in and then gradually pulled himself up. He looked up at the Hamden Trading Building, seeing the young officer slam his fists into the railing and project a profanity into the night sky.

He took quick, shallow breaths; the impact of collision had driven the air out of his lungs. His right side ached completely, his broken ribs rattling inside his body. He slid his leather jacket off uncomfortably and wrapped it around his hand. Lucas punched the window in the wall in front of him, the glass shattering easily and falling to the floor inside. He eased himself through the window, chuckling at the difference between this entrance and the one he'd made when he'd visited the building earlier.

Both his feet crunched down on broken shards and he removed the jacket from his fist and rolled it into a tight ball.

He stuffed it under his shirt, like a fat costume, and then made his way down past two doors to the janitor's cupboard which he'd had ensured was unlocked earlier that evening.

The moment Starling's voice screamed from the radio, Bailey had barked his instructions to his officers. They embarked on the neighbouring building immediately, a number of the students who lived there greeting them in the corridors as they investigated the commotion in the streets.

Under instructions from Bailey, Officer Hatton pulled the fire alarm, instigating a building evacuation. The Armed Response team filtered out of the Hamden Trading building, following each other with choreographed precision as they took their places, divided evenly between both sides of the steps leading up to the glass entrance of the building.

Students filed out of their dorm rooms, some of them barely dressed and many of them loudly complaining about the disturbance. When they saw the armed officers, those complaints died down.

Also in the building on each floor were members of the campus cleaning crew, employed to clean the dorm hallways and kitchens in the evenings as the students themselves couldn't be depended on for upkeep.

Dressed in their navy overalls and holding cleaning materials, many of them didn't speak English and they just filtered out with the students.

Hatton continued up the stairs with a few more officers, cautious that the murderous Cole was somewhere in the building. They opened the stairwell door to the sixth floor and slowly fanned out. A few more students emerged from their rooms, zipping up coats as they passed.

They searched the entire floor, Hatton inspecting the

shattered glass from the broken window that Starling had reported Lucas had broken into.

The only thing they found of note was an open janitor's cupboard which for some reason housed an empty sports bag.

Sgt. Bailey stood and watched from the street as students filtered out through the doors, he wanted them away from the building before the armed officers swept the building clear. He had been in regular contact with Officer Hatton, who was impressing him with her calm nature and sense of responsibility. They hadn't located Lucas yet but he was in there.

Bailey was looking forward to putting him in the back of the car and sending him off to a lifetime in a cell.

"What's happening?"

Bailey turned in surprise.

"Fletcher? What the fuck are you doing here?"

"I heard the radio transmission."

"Whatever," Bailey dismissed it. "We got him."

"Lucas? Where?"

Bailey pointed at the building, where students continued to pour out, along with some more navy-clad cleaners.

"He jumped across. The man is a maniac and he's trying his hardest to get away."

"He jumped?"

Bailey nodded. He pointed to the Hamden Building, up towards a broken window where a woman's body was being hauled back up through the gap.

"He hung that poor girl from the window and then according to Starling, he jumped from one fire escape to another. Can you believe that?"

"Starling? He went in?"

Bailey's face flashed with a grimace. His uniform was soaked through.

"He did. I'm waiting for him to get back down here so I can stick my foot up his arse."

Fletcher looked around at the chaos, the overbearing feeling of guilt weighing on his mind. All of this for Lucas, and all because he gave him a name.

Because the police hadn't done anything for Helen.

He watched the flood of students congregating on the nearby street, a rush of excitement spreading through them all as they watched armed police officers tactfully enter the building.

He saw a large number of cleaning staff, some of them smoking and discussing the events with puzzled expressions.

So many people were on the street. The majority of the officers were in either of the buildings.

Fletcher realised he was holding his breath and only relinquished it when he was almost certain that Lucas was long gone.

As the excited chatter of students filled Lowton Road while they filed out of their homes, one of the cleaners slowly ambled to the outside of the sizeable group of people. Dressed in navy overalls that did little to hide his large gut, he drew his baseball cap down over his face, blocking out the cold rain. He trod carefully around the group, making sure to stay on the outside.

Amidst the excitement and confusion, the portly cleaner quietly slinked off down one of the side streets, out of the eye-line of any police officer.

He walked slowly at first, but once he rounded the next corner, his pace quickened until he was a safe distance away from the flashing blue lights and the thrilling police stand-off.

Lucas stopped and removed his baseball cap, welcoming the refreshing downpour on his hair.

He unzipped the overalls, stepping out of them and tossing them into the green bin sitting on the side of the road. He pulled his leather jacket out from under his shirt, flapped it open and swung his arms lazily into it, his ribs groaning with pain.

Lucas briskly walked across the road and turned onto the main strip of shops. He immersed himself with the pedestrians there, carefully looking around for any sign of law enforcement.

He made his way to the nearest tube station and got on the first train to anywhere.

———

Starling had stood on the fire escape for a few minutes, willing himself to relive the moment again but to be just a few seconds faster.

He couldn't fathom leaping like Lucas had just done, finding it almost disturbing that the man's grief could lead him to take such a drastic risk. Or that it could lead him to hang that poor woman for the world to witness her death.

He went back into the building, already sure that Bailey would make an example of him for breaking rank. Starling didn't care; he didn't want to build a career based on doing the wrong thing. He would take his licks and he would pick himself up and be better for it.

Maybe Bailey would even respect him for it.

He dismissed that notion as a joke and followed the few police officers who'd entered through the stairwell door. They'd pushed open the double doors, revealing two paramedics standing by with a wheeled stretcher. Two other officers were carefully standing by the shattered window, their boots planted firmly on the glass-ridden carpet. They were gently hauling in the cable, hand over hand until one of them could reach his arms under the lifeless ones belonging to Ashley Drayton. They pulled her delicate body through the window just as Starling pushed through the doors himself, walking past empty rows of desks that would normally be humming with activity.

They laid her down on the stretcher, the paramedics discussing with the various emergency servicemen what had happened.

Starling looked at her and immediately felt his world collapse. His heart began to beat at a furious rate, slamming against his ribs as his mouth began to taste the vomit that was trying its level best to escape his mouth.

He dropped his radio on the floor, his feet dragging, the energy needed to lift them sapped from him.

His face went a ghostly white as he stared at her, tears worming from the corners of his eyes and slithering down his already wet cheeks.

He tried to hear his father's voice, wanting to hear that he had done well. But he couldn't locate it.

He didn't deserve it.

He stared at the young woman as the paramedics wheeled her past him.

Everyone else saw Ashley Drayton on the stretcher.

He was the only one who knew her as Annette.

CHAPTER TWENTY-ONE

Ashley was led through the double doors to a resounding silence in the street. Her body, covered in a sheet, lay motionless on the stretcher as the two paramedics wheeled it between the police cars to their ambulance. Officers stood solemnly, watching the person they were there to save be carted off to the after-life.

The swathes of students mumbled to each other, many visibly shocked at having witnessed a dead body.

A life had come to an end tonight on a rainy night in London.

Bailey stood still, a resounding look of failure etched on a tired, stress-riddled face. Fletcher lowered his head in respect. Although she was a Drayton, Ashley was never one who'd registered on their radar. Yet she'd fallen to the same fate as two of her brothers had and with Lucas still at large, Fletcher was sure she wouldn't be the last.

Sgt. Marshall ordered his team back into their van after they'd emerged from the student halls, all of them walking dejectedly, carrying fully-loaded weapons that wouldn't be used tonight. The two Sergeants nodded a goodbye to each other and the van took off, quickly followed by two ambulances, one carrying Ashley's corpse and the other taking Officer Patriski to hospital as a precaution.

Bailey rubbed the bridge of his nose in frustration, the radio call announcing three bodies on the stair well and the remains of another on the ground below meant an awful lot of paperwork. Adding that on to Ashley's death and the fact Lucas had gotten away, this was turning into one of the worst nights of his career.

He knew it would be swiftly followed by the worst morning too, as he was sure that Chief Inspector Hurst would be in for a report.

Bailey and Fletcher stood silently in the rain, as Officer Hatton emerged from the building, carrying the sports bag.

"Good job tonight, Hatton," Bailey said, not looking at her.

"Thank you, sir."

She smiled her beautiful smile at Fletcher, who returned with one that he was sure was of significantly less appeal.

Bailey sighed heavily.

"I will catch him, Fletcher."

He turned and looked at the old, retired officer, who couldn't offer a response. Bailey drew his lips tight and looked around, a sudden determination to shut the scene down and get as many of his officers away from here as possible.

There was one officer in particular he wanted as far away from there as possible.

———

Starling had stood completely still while they rolled the stretcher past him, heading to the lift. A ghostly, pale statue of a man. Two officers, both of them male, asked if he was all right. He didn't respond, words refusing to leave his body.

They eventually gave up, leaving Starling alone in the room. This was where she'd worked, where she'd come every night while he was out on the streets. She'd tell him how she would look out over the night sky, wishing she could fly through the stars to where he was.

It was why he'd called her an angel.

He slowly trudged towards the large void where a window used to be, the gusts of wind scattering the glass remains around his feet. Life suddenly felt worthless, the idea of having this love for someone and to not have them around anymore swam around his brain.

He could just dive through, fall towards the ground and let the earth have him.

It would be so easy. All of this pain, this sense of abandonment would just wash away, taken by the rain in its random quest to attack the earth.

But it wasn't her fault she was gone. She was taken from him.

His fists clenched, the wind and rain sneaking into the building and dousing him with a renewed sense of clarity. Annette, no... Ashley, was so scared of the life she'd lived she couldn't even tell the man she loved her real name. Ashamed of it, although it was the acts of others that had shrouded it with fear and hatred. She didn't want to expose him, a young police officer, to the world and family she'd belonged to.

She had loved him too much.

A few more tears were shed before Starling launched a pain-drenched roar of anger into the night sky. Officers below looked up, wondering what the noise was and preparing themselves for a second death.

He didn't jump.

He turned and strode back towards the elevator in the hallway, hell bent on the idea of retribution

As he emerged on the ground floor, he noticed that the cars and flashing lights had diminished in numbers, the remaining few on clean-up duty. He slowly made his way through the lobby, one of the officers mentioning something about him being 'crazy' but Starling didn't respond. He pushed the glass doors and walked directly towards his car, parked with a wheel up on the curb, the driver door still open.

He didn't even notice as Bailey broke away from a group of officers.

"What the hell did you think you were doing?"

Bailey stepped in front of him. Starling took a calming breath. His words radiated menace.

"That girl is dead."

Bailey scoffed at the tone. Fletcher looked at the young officer, worried about his demeanour. He looked like a man lost.

"So, what, is this you giving me your 'I told you so'? You deliberately disobeyed an order and..."

Starling angrily reached up and grabbed his superior officer by his Met vest. He shook him angrily, pulling his face close to his. The Sergeant and the crowd of officers and remaining students looked on, shocked.

"That girl is dead because of your failure to act."

"How dare you put your hands on me?"

Bailey slapped Starling's hands away from his chest and steadied himself for a conflict. His eyes red from the tears, Starling stared back at him. He reached into his back pocket, pulling out the leather clad police badge that he carried at all times.

He slapped it forcefully into the Sergeant's chest.

"Fuck you!"

Starling barged past Bailey, ignoring the barrage of

threats of disciplinary actions as he trudged through the rain over to his car. None of it mattered.

Not anymore.

He got in and slammed the door, not even looking back. Wanting this entire event to end and never be returned to.

He finally understood what Lucas Cole was doing. What it was like to have the woman you loved snatched from you by a monster.

He vowed to handle it exactly the same way as Lucas too.

He started the ignition and drove off into the rain.

Daylight cut through the curtain the following morning, awakening Lucas with a thin strip of brightness across his eyes. He eased himself up, his ribs rattling in his chest and screaming for attention.

He had slept.

For the first time in weeks, Lucas had slept without being constantly haunted by a vision of Helen, her outstretched hand begging for his help and him never quite being able to reach for it.

He hadn't dreamt at all.

He pushed himself out of the bed, stepping over yesterday's clothes and turned on the light in his bathroom.

It still hummed with the thick stench of disinfectant.

Bruises had begun to form down the side of his muscular body, a horrible purple shade introducing itself. The pain was trying its best to be overbearing. Lucas leant in close to the mirror, inspecting the cut running up his cheek. The dark red line sliced through his stubble, but it would heal.

He turned on the shower, the water bucking a few

times before jetting out in a constant stream. He let it fall over his body, the sounds of the outside world drowning out as it fell over him.

After what seemed an age, he shut off the water, wrapped a towel around his waist and strode to the window. He stared out, half expecting a sea of police cars to be surrounding the Luxury Hotel, guns trained on his window.

There was nothing.

On the small desk in the corner sat his wallet and key card. On top of those, Helen's wedding ring.

He slowly bent down, groaning with pain as he lifted his clothes piled messily by the bed. He carefully got dressed, wincing as he lifted his shirt over his head.

He checked his wallet, which was still packed with plenty of fifty pound notes, and decided to buy himself some new clothes.

He pocketed it and then held Helen's wedding band in his hand.

He knew she would have hated what he was doing. Somehow, somewhere, she was trying to reach out, to get him to stop.

He hated not listening to his wife.

He slipped the ring into his pocket and headed for the door, knowing he would continue not to.

———

"You tell me how a man, who, by all accounts, is a nutjob, managed to escape from almost thirty officers in the middle of the goddamn street."

Chief Inspector Malcolm Hurst sat in the make-shift office, his long, limber frame making the room even smaller. His thick, grey brow was furrowed, the frown directed at a rather meek Bailey who stood respectfully in front of the desk.

"Sir, I can assure you, we covered all the exits and..."

"And he still got away?'

"We hadn't anticipated that...."

"He still got away?"

Bailey's head dropped.

"Yes, sir."

The Chief Inspector shook his head, slamming a hand forcefully down on the desktop. Pencils leapt into the air and clattered back just as quickly. Bailey felt like a fool.

"How many dead?"

"That's three Draytons now, sir."

"And the others?"

"Three dead from last night, sir. One has been identified as Shane Meehan, a close friend and confidante of the Draytons. Apparently, he was a childhood friend of Tommy Drayton."

Hurst raised his eyebrows unenthusiastically.

"Oh brilliant. So our guy isn't content with just picking off family members, he's going for childhood friends too? What's next? Dig up the Drayton's family dog and take a piss on it?"

Bailey knew better than to laugh. Hurst sat back, his long neck twisting in annoyance.

"Look, Robert. You're a good man and a damn fine Sergeant. Work with me here. What the hell are we going to do about this situation?"

"I have men working double-shifts to locate this son of a bitch. Every contact, every possible lead but he leaves no trail."

"He's smart." Hurst said, almost with admiration.

"He's dangerous."

"That, we agree on."

"I've got officers stationed outside Auto Repair where

Matt Drayton works and two unmarked police cars either end of Brixton High Street. They have Lucas's photo tattooed on their brains and will cut him off he makes a play."

"Brixton High Street?" Hurst asked, raising his eyebrows.

"It's where Curtis's betting shop is sir. If Lucas shows up then they send an emergency transmission and we have an Armed Response Unit on him within five minutes."

Hurst shook his head firmly.

"No, pull them back. We are about as welcome as a fart in an elevator with the Draytons at the moment. Let's not trample on their turf."

"But sir, we can take him on the street if we have to."

'No.' Hurst shook his thin head, the mop of grey hair swaying with the motion. "Let them think that we're letting them handle it. Pull your men back a few streets. Have a plain-clothes officer somewhere in the vicinity but that's it. I don't want another repeat of last night. Do you know how much arse kissing I've had to do to fix what happened?"

"Again, sir. I'm sorry."

"It was a complete clusterfuck. Footage was recorded on a number of student's mobile phones of a young woman hanging from the side of her office block."

Bailey had no response, taking his beating on his powerful chin. Hurst sighed, pushing himself up on his long, spindly legs. His uniform hung from his thin frame.

"Fix this, Robert. For both our sakes.

"Yes, sir."

Hurst strode with authority over to the Sergeant, extending a slender hand. His fingers frayed like the legs of a praying mantis. Bailey took it, shaking it firmly. Hurst even afforded him a smile.

"If it does go tits up, at least we won't have the Drayton problem anymore."

"Every cloud, eh Sir?"

Hurst chuckled, patting the Sergeant on his meaty arm and then walked out the office. Bailey exhaled, telling himself it could have been worse. He could have been relieved of his duties. But he knew he was highly regarded by the high-rankers in the Met: his reputation preceded him.

Catching Lucas, and ending what was becoming an execution of the Drayton family, would be the making of his career. The only worry he had, was the retaliation from the Draytons and the fear they might target his officers, due to their ineffectual attempts at stopping Lucas so far.

He was worried what their reaction to their loss would be.

He left the office to return to his duties, not realising he wouldn't have to wait long to find out.

It had been a long time since Curtis had shed a tear.

He had trained himself to never show any emotion, not since those nights all those years ago when his father would berate him, strike him with hard rights and belittle him constantly. He refused to allow himself to show fear, or to show emotion.

To show weakness.

When he and Tommy had returned to 'Odds On' after visiting Fletcher, he'd felt good. He had a spring in his step; he was about to wrestle control of a situation and that would undoubtedly end with him leaving Lucas to die. He may have killed Lewis and Harry, but in the long run, they had been a burden which Curtis had felt obligated to carry. Without him they'd either have died long ago or would now be spending their lives trying to survive in a prison cell.

He sat at his desk and poured himself a glass of his finest scotch. It was only when Tommy had told him that he couldn't reach either Shane or Hiller that he began to worry.

Tommy received a phone call just after half past eight.

Ashley was dead.

Every precaution Curtis had taken had been systematically eliminated, some of them permanently, while his sister was killed publicly. Hanged like a piece of fucking meat in a butcher's shop window.

Tommy had left him that evening, telling Curtis he would demand the body so they could give her a proper burial. Tommy was just as furious, maybe even more so as he'd also lost his friend, Shane, in the chaos.

When Curtis was finally alone, he slumped in the comfy, leather chair behind his expensive oak desk. He drank the finest scotch like it was tap water.

He cried until he lost consciousness, the alcohol stealing him away from the painful reality for a few hours.

It was midday the following day when Tommy woke him.

"Get up."

Curtis mumbled, the alcohol still affecting every sense and his brain feeling like it was swelling in an ever-shrinking skull.

"Come on, Curtis. You're no fucking use if you let it get to you."

"He killed Ashley."

His words were mumbled feebly and his hand wearily reached for the almost empty bottle. Tommy rolled his eyes unsympathetically, swiping the bottle away before his fingers had grasped it.

"Give me the fucking bottle."

"You need to shower and you need to wake the fuck up.

"I'm going to kill him."

Tommy nodded, stomping angrily to the drinks cabinet and shutting the scotch away.

"Not like that, you're not."

Curtis looked at him, his eyes red from the alcohol and his apparent grief. Tommy looked healthy and awake as always, like nothing had happened. He folded his colossal arms across his chest, staring at his older brother.

"While you're sitting around here, drinking and crying yourself to sleep, Lucas is still out there. He killed our baby sister and the way you're going to repay him is by cowering in here like a pussy?"

Curtis's rage flashed, his face snarling as he pushed himself up.

"How dare you fucking speak to me like that?"

"Like what? Huh?"

Curtis wobbled slightly as he tried to manoeuvre himself around the desk, reaching out to steady himself. Tommy didn't move a muscle.

"It was your guys who failed to protect her. It's a good thing he killed Shane otherwise I would have skinned the prick alive!"

Tommy didn't so much as flinch.

"Do you even care that he killed her?" Curtis screamed in his brother's face. His breath carried the fiery after-stench of alcohol.

"Of course I care. And I care that he killed my friend."

"Well you have a funny way of showing it!"

Curtis stumbled across the office, yesterday's suit hanging roughly off his body as he hazily made his way towards the drinks cabinet. He pulled it open, only for a forceful hand from Tommy to slam it shut.

"Just because I'm not drinking myself to death or

crying my eyes out, doesn't mean I don't care. I want this piece of shit dead for what he's done."

"Then at least fucking act like it!"

"I am."

Tommy reached behind his back, pulling the manila folder out from his back pocket. He slapped it down on the oak desk, a few pages sliding out from its side. Curtis looked at it in confusion, trying to command his brain to focus.

"What the hell is that?"

Tommy stared at his brother.

"Payback."

Curtis shook his head, dismissing Tommy as he walked back to his desk. He raised his palms to his eyes, angrily rubbing them to try and wake himself completely. He pulled the cord for the blind, the wooden slats colliding together and whipping up to reveal the sunshine that the day was affording the city.

There was no rain today.

"Have you spoken to Matt?"

"Yeah, I called him last night."

"And?"

"He's furious."

"So he should be."

"Furious with you."

Curtis turned, his face almost portraying a look of pain.

"When is he getting here?"

"He isn't," Tommy shook his head. "He said he didn't give a fuck what you wanted, he's better off on his own. If Lucas comes for him, so be it."

"He said that?"

'Mmm hmm. He also said that he was strapped and he would gladly put a bullet between the eyes of the man who killed his sister."

"No, I'm the one who will kill this bastard." Tommy shrugged. "You tell Matt....'

"He isn't listening to us anymore, Curtis."

Tommy watched as his older brother collapsed into his chair, resting his head in his hands. His elbows rested on the table a few inches from the folder.

"I still want him shadowed."

"That's already taken care of. I also have a few more watching the shop."

"I don't need protection."

"Lucas tore through six men last night. He broke Shane's neck. I'm not taking any chances."

Curtis sighed, the throbbing vengeance of a night of drinking had emerged and he needed some fresh air. Tommy opened the small fridge that sat under the drinks cabinet and retrieved a bottle of Evian. He handed it to his older brother before picking up the Lucas Cole file and slapping it in front of him once more.

Curtis sipped the water, the room finally beginning to emerge into clarity. He could feel himself finally awakening, a sickening rage-fuelled grief burning within him.

Lucas had killed his sister.

He downed the rest of the water in a few gulps and crushed the plastic bottle in his hand, tossing it hard against the wall. His brother stood idly by like a musclebound statue.

"I want this prick to suffer beyond reason."

"Me too."

Curtis met his brother's stare and nodded. He looked down at the manila folder, flicking it open to see A4 pages covered in letters, his brain not yet ready to register them as words.

"What are you suggesting?"

Curtis looked at his brother, the cold expression that he returned was oddly sinister.

"An eye for an eye."

Tommy slid a few pages off the table before tapping one of them. Curtis leant forward, straining himself to read it. After a few moments, a sickening smirk etched itself onto his lips.

"Go and bring the car around."

CHAPTER TWENTY-TWO

Stacks of files and folders were piling up on Fletcher's desk, creating mountains of paperwork. He watched as officers came and went, dropping more off faster than he could file it. The station was in a frenzy, the death of Ashley Drayton and the assault on the lowlifes on the fire escape had caused Bailey to return to ruling with an iron fist.

Complacency had almost cost him his job.

It had cost Ashley Drayton her life.

Fletcher picked up a report from Officer Mills, the young officer with an attitude to match. He scanned the first few lines with expert eyes, immediately correcting the spelling mistakes. He shook his head, these young officers seeing the paper trail as a waste of time. They wanted to be out there, hunting Lucas Cole.

They all wanted the glory of slapping cuffs on his wrists and ending his crusade.

Fletcher dropped the poorly-written report onto his desk and rested his head on his hand. He gently massaged his wrinkled temple, feeling his thinning grey hair float over his fingers.

"Hell of a night, eh?"

The unmistakable thick accent was followed by Officer McCarthy's welcoming smile. It certainly was welcome, as the office had been carrying the vibe of a funeral parlour ever since Fletcher had walked in.

"Here you go, lad. Black."

McCarthy handed Fletcher a plastic cup, the piping hot coffee looking like a watery shadow. Fletcher raised his eyebrows in a way of thank you, sat back and took a sip. McCarthy leaned against his desk casually, almost flooring an Everest of police reports. He flicked his eyes over them, his mop of ginger hair flapping as he shook his head.

"Jesus, Fletcher. You sure you don't mind doing this for free?"

"It's what I'm here for."

"I know, but come on. Most people spend their retirement gardening or watching daytime TV. I wouldn't even sentence a scummy teenager to do this."

Fletcher chuckled, thankful for the much needed release.

"Well Patrick, somewhere in here there'll be something of value. It's just a case of rooting through, filing it correctly and ensuring the right stuff goes to the right people."

McCarthy shifted uncomfortably, the metal brace around his knee evidently causing some pain.

"Well, judging by last night, it may take a lot more than a fancy report to stop this bastard. The man is a lunatic."

"I'm not too sure about that. He seemed to know exactly what he was doing."

Fletcher wondered if he sounded too defensive, but if he did, McCarthy didn't seem to notice.

"That poor girl. Hanging like a goddamn set of Christmas lights for the world to see. If that ain't gonna piss those damn Draytons off, I don't know what is."

Fletcher felt the stinging burn on his forearm, knowing

full well that the Draytons were angry. He, like everyone else in the station, was preparing for the backlash. McCarthy shook his head again, a forlorn expression on his chubby face.

"That poor girl," he repeated. "All because of her name."

"We don't know that." McCarthy raised an eyebrow in Fletcher's direction. "I mean, let's not forget what they've done."

"Ay, but do we have proof?"

"Lucas seems to be pretty certain."

"Lucas?"

"Lucas Cole."

"I know who he is. You just seem to be being a little bit casual with it all."

"Look, I knew Lucas a long time ago. I saw what he went through. I know how much Helen meant to him and I know how much this has hit him. I was at Helen's funeral."

"Well then, if you know him so well, what the hell was he trying to prove by murdering that poor girl last night?"

Fletcher shuffled in his seat, struggling to shake off the feeling that he was being interrogated. McCarthy's face was always friendly, but his big eyes stared through him. Fletcher took a sip of his coffee, trying to find the best way to word it.

"They took away his family and there was nothing he, nor any of us, could do about it."

Fletcher took another sip, looking down at the pile of papers scattered across his keyboard.

"And he is just repaying them in kind."

McCarthy huffed to himself, taking a few moments to process it. Fletcher looked at him cautiously, wishing he was wading through the mountains of papers. Eventually, Officer McCarthy pushed himself up, hobbling slightly as he headed to his desk. He looked back at the retired, older volunteer.

"I still don't think you'll find anything useful in those papers. Have you seen the level of intellect around here?"

Fletcher smiled.

"Well if you want, you could always go out and catch him yourself?"

"With this knee? I have more chance of winning Ireland's sexiest man than catching him."

McCarthy walked around the corner, the sound of Fletcher chuckling growing quieter behind him. He ventured slowly, limping to take the pressure off his leg and yearning for his chair. As he took it, he looked up at the imposing frame of Sgt. Bailey, who was waiting with his arms folded.

"Well?" Bailey kept his eyes on the corner, ensuring Fletcher didn't sneak round. McCarthy sighed.

"I don't know, Sarge. I don't know."

———

The Bentley coasted at a steady speed up the M1, Tommy keeping a safe distance behind the car ahead. His broad shoulders encompassed the entire driver's side of the car, his hands gently resting on the wheel.

He sat in silence, his eyes straight ahead as he watched the road frantically disappear beneath him.

Curtis sat in the back, his head down.

After Tommy had read him the riot act earlier he had taken it upon himself to freshen up. He showered, followed by a shave. His thin, brown hair was combed neatly, a small amount of wax keeping it in place, despite the wind whipping in through the crack in the window.

He raised a hand to his mouth, taking the cigarette in his lips and inhaling a long, slow drag. The paper sizzled as it reduced, turning to ash. He held it up to the window and tapped it, allowing the ash to dance freely over the motorway behind them.

He had picked out one of his best suits and an immaculately ironed white shirt. He had chosen a red tie, the colour of pain, which was secured to his shirt by a silver tiepin.

In his other hand was his Beretta.

He took a final drag on his cigarette and then flicked the butt out the window, it taken by the wind instantaneously. There was no rain today, but the black clouds above looked ominous, as if a storm was approaching. Curtis could relate, his anger simmering on the edge of a violent eruption.

He held the gun out, turning it slightly with admiration. The metal gleamed, the nozzle was well polished. He dropped the ammo clip from the handle, ensuring the expensive, hand crafted bullets were in their rightful place. Once he had done a register, he snapped it back and pulled back the safety.

"Let's not let that go off in here, eh?"

Curtis didn't offer a response to his brother. He sat back in the seat and tilted his head to the window. The world whizzed by, fields and trees reduced to green blurs. Everything reduced to nothing more than smudges of colour that didn't register with him.

They could have been anywhere.

He closed his eyes, immediately seeing the fear in Ashley's eyes as he held her by the throat. The sheer terror on her face as he threatened her. His own little sister.

He wondered if the same look had been present when Lucas had wrapped that wire around her neck. If she cried, begged for mercy.

If she'd prayed for Curtis to save her.

A life of looking after his family, keeping them away

from the people who could hurt them or interrupt the expensive lives he had built for them.

All of it ruined by one man.

Curtis gritted his teeth, the very thought of Lucas bringing his fury to the surface.

"How much further?" He asked, not looking at his driver.

"A few hours."

Curtis nodded and returned his gaze to the dashing fields, thinking about death.

"See you tomorrow, fella."

Matt nodded as Sam waved his goodbye, walking out into the drizzling evening and disappearing into a world of traffic and street lights. The sun had begun its decent just after six, with the moon overlapping and taking control of the sky. It had been a long day at Auto Repair, Matt had been elbow-deep in a car bonnet for the entire afternoon. Sam had been out back, stocktaking.

Matt looked around the garage as he pottered over to the shutter: everything was in its correct place which made him smile. He was proud of the business he'd forged for himself despite Curtis's constant interference.

Matt was a damn fine mechanic and word was beginning to spread.

He stood in the garage's entrance way, the metal shutter above his head clattering in the wind as rain collided against him. He spotted the car up the street, knowing full well Curtis wouldn't listen to him and would send some of his guys round.

He noted the police car too.

He sighed, knowing that if Lucas decided to show up they would be of little use. He was safer on his own and he reached behind his back to the band of his overalls. The handgun sat tightly against the small of his back, fully loaded and ready to eradicate the killer of his sister.

He turned the lights off on the shop floor and the building went dark.

A few moments later, the police officer would see Matt emerge from the darkness, insert his key in the shutter control box and lower the grated metal to the ground. He then padlocked the door to the control panel before quickly moving through the dark evening cold to his BMW 5 Series. It roared into life before shooting up the street and taking a right.

It was followed by both cars that had been watching him.

As they disappeared out of sight, Matt turned the lights of the garage back on, chuckling to himself.

He wished he could see the look on the policeman's face when the car went all the way back to his flat only for them to discover that he wasn't driving it.

His friend Kyle had been more than happy to run diversion, making them think they were doing what they were supposed to. When he got out of the car at the other end, Kyle would drop the keys through Matt's letter box, give the police and Curtis's shadows the middle finger before heading off home again.

Curtis would be livid, which amused Matt greatly.

Besides, he still had work to do.

He walked back through the spacious shop, treading around the Ford Fiesta which had decided to test the durability of an oak tree at full speed. The fact the driver had survived had shocked him, such was the crumpled state of the vehicle. He pushed open the 'Private' door and walked out into another room, the metal shutter open and leading on to the alleyway beyond. Rain clattered down on the pavement outside, echoing loudly inside like someone shaking dice in a cup.

Pavel was zipping up his leather jacket, his motorbike facing the doorway and the engine purring. Matt nodded a greeting before walking to the large desk to his left. It was pressed against the brick wall, where tightly wrapped blocks of cocaine were stacked neatly across it.

Curtis had used this room many years ago as a storage facility for his narcotics and Pavel was one of his most trusted delivery men. Matt didn't even know his last name, but he knew from rumour that Pavel's loyalty had led to the deaths of a few people.

The seat of the motorbike was open and Matt tossed one of the thick, white slabs to the driver. He caught it, patting it gently and then dropped it into the secure space. He slammed the seat down, locking it in place.

"You know where you're going?"

Pavel nodded, his dark green eyes staring straight at Matt. He pulled his black helmet down over his head, the visor open to maintain eye contact.

"Drop it off, pick up the cash and then bring it back here. Then we can settle up and get the fuck out of here."

Pavel nodded again, a muffled agreement that Matt couldn't understand. The large man then straddled the bike, his powerful, leather clad legs swinging over and he got into position. Matt gave a lazy salute and then turned back to the table, organising the next few blocks for tomorrow's delivery.

The gun stuck out from the back of his overalls.

The rain continued to pelt the ground outside.

The motorbike roared into life.

———

As the engine echoed from inside, Lucas pushed himself up against the wall. He could see light bursting out from under the shutter and moments ago had heard Matt barking out orders. The rain trickled down the back of his neck, his whole body drenched.

His arm hung loosely at his side where he clutched a thick, metal pole he'd found in the skip further up the alleyway. It was heavy, and with Lucas's ribs cracked and throbbing with agony, he questioned if he could even swing it.

Everything felt like it was beginning to slow down. Each rain drop flashed before him like a small, shimmering star before dashing to the ground and shattering gloriously. The wind howled like a lone, pain-induced groan from the earth itself.

The roar of the motorbike sounded like a lion standing before its pride.

Lucas's other hand rested in his soaking pocket, wet fingers gently moving the wedding ring around its denim prison. He pictured his wife, her beautiful face as he ran his fingers over it and told her that he loved her.

That smile.

The bike roared again and the driver pulled off. The bike shot towards the rainy world surrounding the garage and as he passed the threshold, Lucas slapped his other hand onto the pole and then swung it with all his might, ignoring the searing pain that roared from his ribcage.

The metal crashed through the visor, shattered glass went flying in the air with a concoction of rain water and blood. The driver shot backwards off the bike, crashing hard to the dry ground inside the garage. Blood poured from the helmet, pooling quickly across the clean floor. The bike carried on for a few feet before toppling to its side and sliding across the wet pavement until it collided with a large crash into the brick wall opposite. Shrapnel exploded into the alleyway as Lucas burst into the garage.

Matt swung round the moment he heard a sickening crack and watched in awe as Pavel's body hurtled back and stopped motionlessly in front of him. Within a few seconds he then came face to face with Lucas Cole, drenched head to toe from the violent downpour outside.

The metal pole, shimmering in the light as it dripped rain drops onto the bloody, glass covered floor swung in his hand.

Matt reached for his gun, pulling it from the back of his overalls and drawing it up to shoot the man who had been butchering his family. Before he could, Lucas swung the pole, the unforgiving metal connecting forcefully with the side of Matt's knee.

They both felt it shatter.

Matt dropped to the floor in agony, the gun sprawling out of his grasp and sliding into the bloody debris. He held back any screams of anguish, instead refocusing, survival instincts taking over. He reached forward, his fingers gently grazing the handle of the gun.

Lucas crushed his hand against the concrete floor with another violent swing of the pole.

This time Matt screamed in agony and he retracted his hand now hanging loosely from his wrist. The bones slithered inside his skin, loose and free. Glass hung out the back of his hand, gleaming in the light like jewels.

He fell back, colliding with the desk and the illegal bricks atop shook.

He took a few deep breaths, ordering himself to manage the pain and to face the inevitable like a man. Incredible pain shot around his brain but he calmed himself, safe in the knowledge that it would all be over soon.

He opened his eyes and Lucas stood a few feet away, pointing his own gun at him. He chuckled.

"Well, fuck me."

He shook his head weakly, before searching his pocket with his functioning hand. The other laid motionless on his thigh, misshapen and bleeding.

Lucas stared at him, his brown eyes radiating pure hatred. Matt could feel it without even looking up.

He fished his cigarettes from his pocket, sliding one out with one hand and popping it in his mouth. He then found his lighter. He clicked it a few times, engulfing the end of it in flame.

Lucas stood watching, the gun dead still in his hand. The rain danced on the wind behind him.

Smoke filtered up from Matt as he leaned back against the desk. He looked at Lucas, a forlorn expression on his face.

They both knew what was coming. Matt Drayton had to die.

Matt took another pull on his cigarette and both men watched the smoke twirl its way upwards.

———

"Well, keep working at it. Seriously. Every evening just shadow-box. You need to nail the technique before you nail the power."

Alex smiled at his young student, a sixteen year-old who had found a new lease of life since he began attending the Muay Thai classes a few years ago. Alex loved to see how the discipline could not only change someone's ability but also their whole way of life. It's why he loved doing what he did.

The young student nodded and then quickly walked across the matted dojo to the bench where his bag rested.

Alex watched him as he collected his things, the posters of 'Discipline' and 'Control' proudly decorated the walls. The young lad slipped through the doors and Alex took a moment to stretch. His muscular arms reached upwards and he arched his back, feeling the strain of three two hour lessons pouring out of him.

He slowly walked over to the mats, picking up the few remaining shin guards that he'd brought out for the evening session.

As he collected them in his arms, he thought of Dianne back at home, her feet up and radiating a glow that only comes with pregnancy. Her hand slowly stroking the solid bump growing with every day.

He smiled, embracing the idea of parenthood as every day drew it closer. He opened the door to the storeroom and stepped into the dark. There was no need to find the light switch, Alex knew where every piece of equipment lived and he followed his memory to the container filled to the brim with safety equipment.

Footsteps.

He arched his head to the door, but his view was restricted. He heard hard shoes clatter against the wooden floor serving as the entrance to his dojo.

"Give me a minute!" he called out, stuffing the shin guards down with the others before pulling the lid down firmly.

"Alex Thornley."

The voice boomed across the room and invaded the store cupboard, the words thick with a London accent. Alex marched out.

"Sorry sir, but the dojo is closed."

Alex emerged into the bright lights of his dojo and stopped in his tracks. Across the mats was a well-groomed man wearing what he could tell was an expensive suit. His red tie exploded against his crisp white shirt. His arms hung at his sides, hands clasped behind his back. His dark brown eyes locked on Alex.

Behind him, a much larger man slowly closed the door to his workplace, ensuring they were completely alone. His arms pulled the sleeves of his polo shirt to their physical limit and the rest of it clung to an impressive frame.

"I'm not here for a fucking lesson."

Alex didn't respond as the suited man's face snarled in his direction. He knew who was standing before him. The police had been to see him after the reports had come in that Lucas had brutally murdered two of the people rumoured to have been involved with the death of his wife.

The officer had told him of the family's stature, of what they were capable of and why any information he could give them would be invaluable. Alex took a few steps onto the mats, each step shrouded with caution. As he did, the hulking sidekick took a few steps forward also, stretching his colossal arms behind him and then cracking his neck. Alex knew he was a fighter just by the way he stood.

The two of them stared down, roughly eight feet of padded matting the only thing separating them. The man in the suit took a few steps to the side, his stare still latched firmly onto Alex.

Alex raised his arms up, his fists clenching and he bent his elbows. He slid one foot in front of the other, knee slightly bent as he prepared for the onslaught.

As the larger man took a few steps towards him, a gunshot rang out around the dojo that encased the noise and expanded it.

Alex felt the bullet rip through his thigh, the burning pain following as he collapsed to the mats, blood spraying out in a wild pattern. He refused to make a noise, biting his lip as he winced in agony.

"What the fuck?" Tommy angrily turned to his brother, who held the gun proudly in his hand.

"I didn't come here to watch you two girls dance now, did I?"

Curtis smirked at his enraged brother, before turning his attention back to Alex. The gun swayed in his hand as he ordered his brother to find a chair. Alex slowed his breathing down, maintaining calm as the pain flowed from his leg in a steady, constant stream of blood. He knew there was no point calling for help.

He knew why they were here.

He closed his eyes and thought of Dianne, her radiant smile and the beautiful bump.

CHAPTER TWENTY-THREE

"I imagine Harry and Lewis begged for their lives, huh? Lewis definitely."

Matt slouched against the desk, the cigarette delicately poised in his functioning hand. His other lay lamely on his leg, a mishmash of broken bones and shards of glass. The smoke danced gracefully upwards to the tube lights that hung symmetrically from the ceiling above.

Lucas didn't answer as he twisted the cap of the red, plastic petrol container and began to casually flick the pungent liquid over the nearby work bench.

"Deep down that's what people do, right? Whatever they can to survive."

Lucas stopped in his tracks, the petrol sloshing in the canister as he turned to face the floored Drayton. He studied his face and found the expression disturbing. It wasn't fear or hatred. It wasn't desperation.

It was acceptance.

"Is that why you did it?" Lucas's voice was cold, his words punching like a verbal boxing glove.

"Did what?"

"Chase my wife and lure her to a fate that no one should face."

Matt shook his head in disgust, taking a deep drag on his cigarette. The smell of petrol was growing and he carefully stubbed it out on the concrete beside him.

"I did it because I'm weak."

Lucas stared at him, his eyes urging him to continue.

"That's why we all did it. Time and time again." Lucas wasn't even sure if Matt was confessing to him or to himself. "Curtis had always been there when we were growing up. I don't know exactly what our piece-of-shit dad had done to him, he would never say. But whatever it was, it left a scar that no amount of time could heal. It changed him.

"Over the years he just became this monster of a man who craved power. Oh he was generous. The golf range, 'The Hive', this place. He paid for it all and gave us the keys. I guess when you look back on it, it wasn't really worth it."

Lucas stared at Matt, who began fishing another white cigarette from his box. There was no fight in him. Lucas poured more petrol out, this time over a small, wooden kitchen table and the matching chairs. The liquid slapped against the wood in thick, random splashes. As the canister finished, he dropped it to the concrete with a loud clang and began unscrewing the cap of another one. The smell grabbed his nostrils and clung on for dear life.

"Worth what?"

Matt took a deep pull, the smoke floating over his thoughtful face.

"Our lives."

Lucas nodded, agreeing with the words of a man he was there to kill. A few more clouds of smoke rose gently into the room.

"The man had people willing to take a bullet or do time

for him. For our name. I guess even though we were family, we were just the same. He wanted to feel powerful and he got us to bring him women like he was ordering a fucking pizza."

Petrol splashed the body of an old motorbike sitting in the corner of the garage, its only use gathering rust.

"I hate you for what you did to Ashley, but she was just the same. She would see these girls, these 'easy opportunities' and send them our way..."

Matt trailed off, shaking his head as he recollected the vile deeds of days gone by. Lucas poured a trail of petrol out into the centre of the garage floor and then tossed the empty canister onto the already doused workbench.

"Your wife deserved better than what we did."

Lucas watched as the remorseful man took a final puff and then carefully extinguished his cigarette beside the other. He looked up at the vengeful widow before him.

"And we all deserve to die."

The two men locked eyes for a moment and a silent agreement was shared. This had to happen and both of them knew it. Matt drew his functioning hand across to his other pocket, fishing out his mobile phone. He lazily held it upwards and Lucas's shoes sloshed in the petrol as he strode forward. He calmly took it, sliding it into his own pocket to keep Helen's wedding ring company. Lucas took a few steps to his left and bent down, spraying rain drops into the petrol that shimmered on the ground.

He picked up the gun that Matt had so desperately scrambled for.

"You called the police that night, didn't you?"

Matt looked up at Lucas, the pain surging from his shattered hand and mangled knee evident in his eyes. He nodded slowly, knowing it would do little to change what was coming.

"You tried to save her?"

Matt shook his head slowly, his eyes closed.

'I tried to give her a fighting chance. I knew how it was going to play out. Same as the other girls. I thought they may be able to save her if they got there in time."

Lucas slowly rubbed the thick stubble on his wet chin, the gun hanging loosely in his other hand. He looked around the room, the fumes surging at him with a forceful potency.

He pulled the clip from the bottom of the gun and flicked a bullet out. It spun in the air, splashing as it hit the petrol slowly absorbing the ground beneath them.

"Every woman you took.

Another bullet.

"Every life you helped end."

Another.

"Destroyed countless others."

Three more pinged from his hand, bouncing recklessly into the room behind him.

"I have killed your family for what they have done to mine."

Another splash.

"And I will finish the rest of them."

He flicked one more bullet until only one, solitary piece of silver sat in the clip. He slid the clip back into the gun, clicking it into place. Standing roughly nine feet away from Matt, he slowly bent down and placed the gun on the floor. One bullet left.

One chance at an easy way out.

"You tried to give her a fighting chance. Consider this yours."

Matt's eyes began to water, the realisation that his life was about to come to an end shaking his body. He nodded at Lucas, accepting the offer and Lucas nodded in return. He then reached into his pocket and retrieved the lighter he had expensively procured from yesterday's student and rolled the metal wheel.

The flame danced within its small, metallic armour and Lucas tossed it casually onto the workbench. Flames immediately engulfed the wooden top, flickering and swaying with violent beauty.

Lucas saw them spread down the legs and burst across the floor of the garage as they flickered with mesmeric grandeur. He turned and briskly walked towards the sanctity of the rain, the sting of the fresh air in his lungs most welcome.

The room sweltered, the heat from the flames beginning to cause serious discomfort to Matt who knew he had no chance of following Lucas out of the door.

His body would be turned to ash and would wash away like the stain on the earth he'd become.

He thought of karma and how he'd always known a day would come when he'd face the horrors his family had bestowed upon others.

The world would always restore the balance. This was his.

He painfully pushed himself forward, his clothes thick and heavy with petrol. As he dragged his limp, broken leg through the petrol, the flames quickly pounced on him. They spread across his back and he gritted his teeth as his skin began to burn.

A few more feet and the pain was becoming excruciating, his skin charring as the fire began to dominate him.

Smoke billowed out from the garage, the thick black clouds being carried by the harsh winds of London.

He reached out with his good hand, the flames encasing his sleeve as he did.

His fingers clasped onto the gun.

As Lucas walked hurriedly down the alleyway towards the main road, he heard the unmistakable echo of a gunshot. He stopped for a moment but then continued his march, as the fire grew in stature behind him.

―――――

Alex spat blood onto the mats as his jaw rocked from another meaty right hook. Tommy shook the impact of the punch from his wrist as he stepped away. Curtis sat on a chair opposite, as Alex hung slightly to the right of his.

"Where can I find him?"

Alex sniffed, swallowing the blood swashing around in his mouth. He sat back up, lifting his battered face up to meet Curtis's.

"I don't know."

There was little fear in his voice or in his eyes. It riled Curtis who nodded to his brother. Another face-shaking right hook, another spray of blood slapped against the mats.

"You're beginning to try my patience, Alex." Alex wobbled on his seat but straightened himself. "Again, where is he?"

Alex stared at Curtis, the cut above his eye gently dribbling blood down his quickly bruising cheek. His other eye was already beginning to swell.

"Are you scared, Curtis?"

"You are really starting to try my patience."

"Because if this is some sort of attempt to impose your power or dominance, you do realise that it's failing?" Curtis scowled in his direction. "All it's doing is revealing your desperation."

Tommy took a step forward, his lethal arm primed and ready to swing again. Curtis held up a hand, stopping his destructive brother.

"Enlighten me, please."

Alex chuckled slightly before drawing up the blood in

his mouth and spitting it to the side. It crashed on the mats and flared out across it.

"Do you think that attacking me will stop him?"

"Not exactly."

"You're right. It won't. There is more to Lucas than you know and if you think you're playing a game of 'my violence can beat your violence' then you've already lost."

Curtis shuffled uncomfortably on his seat, the gun resting lazily in the hand on his lap. Tommy stood behind him, arms folded and back straight.

"So what, he is some sort of crazed psychopath? I've already gathered that much."

"Oh he isn't crazy. Not at all. We used to discuss why he needed to curb it, why he needed to train and why he sought an outlet for what was inside him. When you go through an upbringing like Lucas's, when your only way out was to fight, it's very difficult to turn off.

"Lucas was adamant he wouldn't go back to the person he was, or to feeling angry all the time. Not when he had the life he never believed imaginable."

Curtis lit a cigarette, snapping his metal zippo lighter shut. He leant forward, shrouding Alex in the smoke he exhaled.

"We all have a bad past, mate. You can either run from it or embrace it."

"Is that what you did, Curtis? Embrace it? Use it as an excuse to rape and murder women?"

Curtis smiled proudly, the disgust in Alex's voice amused him.

"I used it to build a future that revolved around me. And one that will end with Lucas joining his wife again."

"I'm sure he has his own mapped out. You're right, he did run from his past. However, unfortunately for you, you have made him confront it after all these years and that's why you're here and that's why you're so scared.'

Curtis blew more smoke into the brightly lit dojo as his eyes bellowed with rage. The blood on the mats shimmered.

"I'm not scared of violence. I've been around it my whole life."

"Not like this, you haven't." Alex swallowed more blood, his thigh throbbing with pain and pumping blood down his leg. "Violence is like a storm. It's a natural occurrence that causes untold damage. It can rip everything apart – lives, families, everything. And like a storm, sometimes violence can have so much power behind it, it becomes unstoppable. Admirable in the sheer, unrepentant chaos it brings."

Curtis dropped his cigarette to the floor and stamped his expensive, Italian shoes on top of it.

"It becomes a thing of beauty."

Alex held Curtis's stare as well as he could with the swelling obscuring his vision. Curtis ran a hand nervously over his jaw, looking around the room. The bright lights illuminated the well-maintained dojo, everything sat in its rightful place. On the wall, the large posters took centre stage, displaying their message proudly. Curtis scoffed at them. Alex continued, defiant to the end.

"So you do whatever the hell you want with me. I won't beg and I won't die an unhappy man. But it won't save you Curtis. It won't stop what's coming for you."

Curtis returned his attention to Alex, the lack of fear in the man causing him to angrily stand up. The chair flew backwards, almost crashing into his imposing brother.

"You can spew all the high and mighty bullshit you want, it's not going to change anything. Lucas is going to die a slow, painful death and I will be the reason for it."

Alex felt the pain ringing in his jaw, in his head. He tried to smile.

"I would say you got the wrong person who's going to die, but you got the reason right."

Curtis, snarling and snapping like a rabid dog, leant forward, mirroring Alex's eye-line. His rank breath stank of the odour of a hundred cigarettes.

"You think that because you've given him discipline and control, he'll survive? These fucking principles mean nothing."

"I never gave him control."

Curtis stood up straight, the gun hanging at his side. He raised his eyebrows in slight confusion.

"What?"

"I said I never gave him control." Alex looked up, forcing himself to battle the pain to make eye contact. "I gave him discipline, sure. I trained him, taught him to channel it. Direct it. But it was Helen who gave him the control. His Helen, who you took from him. You let him off his leash."

"And I will put him down."

"Everything that's happened, Curtis, is on you. You may not believe in discipline or control. You may not believe that you could ever be afraid or that you're even mortal. But you should believe in the fact that laying a finger on her was the biggest mistake you ever made."

Alex quickly alternated his glance between the two brothers, blood trickling across his vision.

"It will be the end of both of you."

Curtis tilted his head back in frustration, taking a long, hard breath. Tommy stood silently, staring at the battered man in the chair. Alex began to feel the woozy from blood loss, feeling his mind beginning to spin along with the room whilst his body wouldn't move. He shuffled slightly, willing himself not to fade to black.

He heard feet shuffling ahead of him, the blurred

vision somehow deciphering the black shoes that moved closer.

He heard the click of metal and moments later he felt the cold, circular press of it against his forehead.

He leant against it, whatever it was pressing against his blood-covered head held his balance. The steely grip of unconsciousness began to wrap its fingers around him. He heard an echo of a voice.

"An eye for an eye."

Alex took a deep breath, his vision distorting and relaying nothing to him. All he could see was the beauty of his wife, that wonderful moment when she'd told him she was expecting his child.

They were sitting together, he kissed her gently and their fingers interlocked as they rested their hand on her stomach, the warm home that surrounded their child.

Somehow, despite the pain, a smile formed on his face.

Curtis pulled the trigger.

The entire station fell silent when the news filtered through. With the search for Lucas now at the top of every priority list, it didn't take long for word to reach London.

To reach Bailey.

Fletcher had been seated in his front room, the radio crackling as he sunk another glass of Jack Daniels in the smoky room. When the notification of Alex's murder filtered through the airwaves, Fletcher felt his skin turn cold. The grey hairs that adorned his now wiry, wrinkled arms stood to attention like miniature grey soldiers.

The entire Metropolitan Police Service had been waiting for a reaction. They didn't know how or when, many officers even fearing it would be one of their own who would suffer

Drayton vengeance as Lucas picked off their family members. Some of them worried about the threat towards the higher-ups, like Chief Inspector Hurst who'd been seen recently on TV, unfaithfully dispelling the myth of a vigilante in London.

But it had been worse.

Much worse.

An innocent father-to-be, whose only crime was to be a friend to a man done wrong. A man who would never get to hold his new-born baby, or watch them grow. Memories that Fletcher began to cherish tenfold from that moment onwards.

He sat the glass down on his coffee table and turned the radio off. The silence in the house made him feel ill at ease. He sat still for a few moments, remembering the discussion he'd had with Alex at Helen's funeral.

Alex had been incredibly charming without being arrogant, his smile magnetic. When his wife, Helen's best friend, broke down as the coffin was lowered into the earth, he'd shouldered her pain. He loved his wife dearly, and in turn had been loved by many people.

Now he was gone.

Murdered.

Without thinking, Fletcher pushed himself up from the beaten sofa, a trail of dust swimming aimlessly through the air behind him. He slid his arms into his jacket and snatched his car keys from a neglected pile of memoir notes. He raced through the door, propelling himself through the rain to his vehicle.

Lucas had to know.

He drove carefully through the London night, his windscreen wipers rhythmically swiping back and forth, clearing his line of sight. Everything looked the same. Each street was indistinguishable from the last in the darkness of night and the sheeting rain.

Fletcher drove on autopilot.

As he stopped at a red light, he tried to downplay the surging feeling of guilt chipping away at his conscience. He had given Lucas the Drayton name.

He had set the course.

If he'd just held strong, not allowed his emotions to take over then maybe this wouldn't have happened. So many deaths, in such a short space of time. Innocent people brutally murdered in the horrendous concept of vengeance. Lives obliterated by association.

All because of him.

Paul Fletcher: guilty of murder.

The lights flashed green and Fletcher put his foot down, the car shooting forward in a spray of water and leaving the idea of responsibility behind. He drove for the next few minutes in complete silence, not even comprehending listening to his increasingly gnawing conscience. The gate to Soho Square was chained shut as he pulled up to the curb outside it. It hung off old hinges and shook in howling, wet wind which burst through the evening. Fletcher vacated his car, locking it with the fob as he approached the metal gateway. Rust clung to the metal bars like a fungus. Beyond them, the world was black.

Fletcher grasped two of the sharp, slippery bars at their peak and placed a foot on the metal beam that ran along the bottom of the fence panel. He then hoisted himself up, planting a shaky foot on the slick metal beam at the top, the rainwater playing mayhem with his balance. He hauled himself over the protruding metal spikes and fell to the ground on the other side.

Cursing his age, he stood upright and ventured into the darkness, pulling his coat tight to his body for warmth. His footsteps crunched on the gravel pathway. The looming presence of a pavilion grew to his right, the whiteness of the painted bricks reflecting the small fraction of moonlight cast upon it. Fletcher followed the path, his footsteps slowing and grinding to a halt as he reached the intersection.

All paths in the park ended here.

The King Charles II statue, rich in history and beauty, years of wear and tear only adding to its awe.

Lucas Cole stood a few feet from the stone figure, his head down, allowing the cold rain to wash over him. His rounded shoulders hung slightly, his leather jacket glistening in the moon-stained rain.

Fletcher took a step, his foot crunching on the stones below.

"What are you doing here, Fletcher?"

Lucas's voice was barely audible, carrying an irritation from being interrupted. He didn't move a muscle.

"I needed to find you."

"If you've come to stop me, you're wasting your time."

Fletcher took a tentative step, his eyes squinting to form Lucas entirely in his vision.

"I haven't."

Lucas nodded, his short, wet hair flicking extra droplets into the night sky. He looked up at the statue, his hands firmly in his pockets.

"How did you find me?"

"Give me some credit here," Fletcher offered a light-hearted chuckle. "' used to be a detective. Besides, this is your statue, right? Yours and Helen's?"

"It was."

The past tense hit Fletcher harder than he would have imagined. Despite all the violence and carnage since he'd last seen Lucas, all he felt was his grief. Lucas wasn't murdering his way to a happy ending. He was simply lost within his grief, navigating through his pain through the only means he knew how.

It was hurting him to grieve.

It was hurting Fletcher just to witness it. His trail of

thought was broken by Lucas's solemn voice. The rain hissed around them, beyond that, the faint whisper of a howling siren.

"Helen used to say to me that I never deserved what happened. That I was a good person in a bad world."

"There's truth in that."

"She used to say that I was a good man."

Fletcher took another careful step.

"You are."

"Am I? Every step of this she's been with me. I see her every single moment I close my eyes, every corner I walk around. She's there, but it's not her. I can never recreate my wife with all of her beauty. I knew her better than anyone but to try and envisage her would do her an injustice."

Lucas shook his head, peering into the enveloping nothingness.

"Every time I see my projection of her, I can hear her begging me to stop. I know she's right, Fletcher, but I don't know what else to do."

Fletcher took another step forward, his trousers clinging wetly to his legs. He thought about extending a comforting hand, but withdrew quickly.

"I've done some terrible things. Bad, bad things."

Lucas turned on his heels to stand face-to-face with Fletcher merely a few feet away. He read the concern on Fletcher's face and registered its sincerity.

"How the hell can I be a good man?"

Before Fletcher could open his mouth, Lucas took a step to the side and trudged lazily away. He passed the old, trustworthy visitor who span around in surprise.

"Remember what you told me all those years ago, Lucas?"

He stopped in his tracks. He turned, his head looking over his shoulder, his face strained with the realisation of the acts of violence of the past few days.

Fletcher took a few steps towards him.

"Sometimes bad people need to be shown what bad really is."

The two men nodded, a silent bond of trust that had been generated all those years ago. Another time in Lucas's life that had been haunted by violence and a deep sense of isolation. Lucas nodded again, Fletcher's words almost reaffirming what he was doing. Before he could leave, Fletcher spoke again.

"But, like I said before, the Draytons will come at you with everything they have."

Lucas would regret ever asking what he meant. As soon as Fletcher mentioned that they'd received a phone call from Officer Chamberlain in Brinscall, he knew. The same officer who'd informed him of his wife's demise was-again the bearer of an unspeakable horror.

The closest thing Lucas had ever had to a brother.

The one man that Lucas had trusted with his life.

Fletcher continued, the details only adding to the sheer brutality of the ending of his best friend's life.

Lucas turned and stared up into the dark sky, searching for anything to distract him from the facts before him.

Alex was dead.

It was his fault.

And as the wind swept around him and the rain pelted him with cold, relentless drops, Lucas shed a tear for the first time since Helen had died in front of him.

AN EXTRACT FROM 'LIFE ON THE BEAT: MEMOIRS OF A THIRTY YEAR POLICE OFFICER.' BY PAUL FLETCHER.

It's always the innocent people who get caught in the crossfire. It has to be one of the biggest clichés in the history of language. It sits proudly on the list alongside 'If you love them, let them go' and 'Time heals all wounds.'

However, it is based in truth.

Clichés are founded on the back of truthful experience. The reason they're mocked by some people is because nobody wants to fall in line anymore. Everyone wants to believe that their experiences are unique, that they have somehow carved out an individual niche in the universe and that their world spins on a slightly different axis to others.

But everyone deals with the same problems.

Heartbreak. Anger. Grief.

These are the guarantees we all face at some point in our lives. But we all feel that, when we face them, we do it differently. God knows I thought I was on my own, and I cut the world off when I watched Susan fade away. But let's face it, it's a cliché to shut the world off when you don't want to deal with it. The lone struggler, dealing with his feelings the only way he knows how.

Lucas falls into that category. He just dealt with his own feelings a little differently to how I did.

Let me make it clear to you all now, as I sit here casting my mind back over those crazy few weeks, when the worldwide view of right and wrong was skewed, that Lucas was not innocent.

Helen was.

Alex was.

Lucas was one of the people who got dragged in by the ripple effects caused by brutality. As was Starling. Good men who were broken by the beastly acts of others and let down by those people they relied on for protection.

But the things they did in retaliation were NOT innocent.

Helen was ripped from this world in a way that should be unimaginable. Alex was murdered because he knew her.

Because he knew Lucas.

As I've said, I had the pleasure of speaking to Alex after Lucas's introduction to the Draytons and he told me he didn't think Lucas had done what we'd reported. He did however, say he thought Lucas, would be capable of it. He knew both Lucas and Helen so well, his time with them spent in a cocoon of smiles and laughter.

Did he deserve to die because of it?

A family man, who'd spent his entire life living by strict principles and a dedication to a discipline. Happily married to a wonderful woman, and ready to become a father to his first child and help mould a person for the future.

Alex did not deserve to die.

The cliché once again showing that, despite the eyes that roll when it's spoken, it's heavily bathed in truth. His poor wife, Dianne will forever remember the image of that night, discovering her husband's lifeless body. Every time her daughter, who I hear is doing well, asks what her father was like, she will only have one image of him.

The dead, lifeless stare looking up at her.

Another person who didn't deserve the pain that hangs from her shoulders like an evil cloak.

Cliché or not, it's like I said.

It's always the innocent people who get caught in the crossfire.

CHAPTER TWENTY-FOUR

All the excitement of the 'Lucas Cole Manhunt' had almost evaporated from the station once the details of Alex's murder filtered through the offices. Fletcher could visibly see the effect it had on the hard-working officers; the feeling of failure in a situation that had got out of hand long before.

A father-to-be with nothing but good intentions with a long list of people willing to say kind words about him. A man who'd been a rock in his community, who'd committed himself to charity event after charity event, cruelly sent to the afterlife because of a friendship.

Bailey informed the officers through a couple of briefings, explaining how Dianne had been in the kitchen, warming up the stir fry meal she'd prepared for her husband, walking slowly around the kitchen with her hand on her protruding stomach. Their child snugly curled up within her, growing with every moment as they took their shuffling steps towards parenthood. A car had pulled up outside and a faint sound of shuffling up the garden path had made her feel warm and safe.

It was when she heard the second slam of car doors,

followed by the roaring engine as it sped off down the street, that she became concerned. Peering through the window, she could see her husband's feet lying across the steps, his legs stretched out as he sat against the door. As she opened it, her worst nightmare fell at her feet.

Alex's body slumped over the threshold, his lifeless eyes staring up at her. There was nothing behind them.

Blood trickled from the bullet hole in his head.

The police had turned up within minutes, called by the neighbours who had heard the pain-stricken screams from the Thornley house. They found her sitting by his side, cradling his head and weeping uncontrollably, begging him to wake up.

A renewed sense of urgency now radiated from the officers, the need to catch Lucas had taken a new turn. Fletcher realised that many of them had been caught up in the romance of his whole crusade.

A man wronged and doing what was necessary in the name of the wife they took.

It was all so poetic.

But now, an innocent man had been delivered to his wife, with a bullet through his skull and a message sent loud and clear.

This was Lucas's fault.

It was Fletcher's fault.

A man who had been so polite when Fletcher had attended Helen's funeral and again when he'd called about the first set of Drayton murders. The guilt weighing down on him made the menial tasks of the office admin a struggle. Every file now felt like it was made out of solid concrete. Every step through the office felt like he was walking in thick tar.

Bailey had lost his usual impervious swagger, instead respectfully delegating responsibilities to his officers. Officer Starling had still not reported in since his rash outburst that night outside the Hamden Trading building. No word had filtered in on whether he had officially resigned, but his colleagues offered the notion that seeing that young girl die in such a brutal way had hit him harder than they would have thought.

Whatever it was, something had enraged the young man and Fletcher silently worried about his well-being.

He slid his fingers under his glasses and gently massaged the bridge of his crooked nose.

All he wanted was to return home and continue his abandonment of his promise to stop drinking. A glass of whiskey was all that was getting him through the day.

Dianne had made the arrangements quickly, the funeral was to be held on Sunday morning in the same place that her best friend had been buried. Where, only a week prior, she'd stood, tears in her eyes, watching someone important to her be committed to the earth.

She would repeat it again.

Fletcher sat at his desk, his head in his hands as he imagined how alone she must feel. Her husband murdered, her best friend taken from her. Lucas missing.

The only light in the young woman's life would be mothering a child, but she would be forever reminded of the brutality of Alex's murder when she looked at it.

He had set the chain of events in motion.

It was his fault.

Lucas had said very little after Fletcher had told him of his friend's demise. He shed a tear, nodded his head and then walked off into the downpour. Fletcher had called out after him, saying he would take Lucas home to pay his respects.

He got no response.

The search continued throughout Thursday and Friday to no avail. No trace of Lucas. No more violence. No more Drayton death. Speculation mounted that Lucas had stopped his vengeful quest on account of Alex's death. Others speculated that the Draytons had found him and the Metropolitan Police would be receiving another dead body soon.

A few rumours of suicide also rose to the surface.

Fletcher knew differently. He knew that Lucas was locked away in a dark corner of London, blaming himself for another loved one's death.

He had kicked the hornet's nest, yet it was his loved ones who got stung.

Fletcher spent the whole of Saturday avoiding his memoirs, even taking a wonderful stroll through Regent's Park. The weather decided to treat him to a bright day, the sun painting London in a beautiful spring glow. Families gathered on the fields to build fun-filled memories, a few runners in numbered vests trotted by as they ran for a good cause. The ducks glided aimlessly down the vast stream shimmering in the sun's mighty rays.

He had hoped he would see Annabelle sitting on the same bench, book in her hand as the beautiful granddaughter, who he'd never met, played innocently nearby.

The bench was empty and he felt farther from his family than ever. He had been a pitiful father, weak when his daughters had needed strength. Now he had, indirectly, been the cause of another child growing up without a father. The sight of the empty bench seemed to darken his walk, the sun not feeling quite as bright anymore.

He willed the rest of the day away until the streets turned dark, street lights bursting into action and illuminating the world for the London population.

At eight o'clock exactly he got into his car and drove carefully through the London traffic until he arrived at Soho Square. The gates were still open, the public curfew had not yet been reached.

The King Charles II statue sat in its usual spot as the centrepiece.

In front of it stood Lucas.

Moments later, Fletcher pulled away, heading out of London towards the motorway, beginning the long, silent journey to Brinscall, in a car that radiated nothing but vengeance and guilt.

———

The crying had stopped a few days ago.

Starling stared into the mirror with red, strained eyes and didn't recognise his reflection. His jawline was now coated in dark stubble and his blonde hair scruffy. He hadn't showered since that night.

He hadn't done anything since that night.

Annette was dead.

The bags under his eyes aged his young face which twisted into a hate-filled snarl. Standing in the bathroom of his flat, wearing just his black boxer shorts, he angrily threw a fist at the wall. His knuckles struck the white tiles, the impact sending a sharp crack across his bone.

He took a few steps back, grimacing at the throbbing pain and picked up the bottle of vodka he'd brought in with him. Never usually one for drinking, Starling had found a refreshing companion in the clear liquid. He unscrewed the red cap, letting it drop onto the filthy bath mat and bounce near his feet.

He took a large swig. The burning was a wonderful release.

As the alcohol sloshed around inside his stomach, Starling could feel the pain of Annette's demise leap to the surface. The one person who'd made him forget about anyone else, the one person who'd made him feel loved in this world.

Taken from him.

Taken by Lucas Cole.

Just the thought of the name released an uncontrolled barrage of expletives, Starling cursing the man and wishing him dead. A clearer mind would maybe have prevailed, however the intoxication was leading Starling down a path of anger.

He could see in Lucas's eyes how much pain he was suffering that night when Helen had died. That he wasn't going to accept her death and move on. Starling saw it, but did nothing.

Now she was dead.

He could have stopped it.

A drunken hand lazily reached into the shower cubicle and flicked the button. Water crashed out of the shower attachment, sprinkling Starling as he eased out of his shorts. He climbed in, vodka in hand and let the water wash over him. For a few moments, he felt free. Free of all the pain and the guilt that had enveloped him for the last days.

He closed his eyes and saw Annette.

Her beautiful smile as he told her how gorgeous she was. The intensity in her eyes as they made love. The cold lifeless expression on her face as they'd hauled her corpse up through the window.

Starling stumbled slightly, his back slapping against the wet tiles. He slowly slid down the wall, his knees bending until he connected with the shower's floor. Next to him sat her shampoo. She would never be back for it.

He felt his eyes watering as he raised the bottle to his nose, reminding of the beautiful aroma of her hair as she would lie in his arms.

Nothing mattered anymore. He hadn't been to see his dad, unable to face looking at the lost shell of the man whom he used to look at with heroic awe. He hadn't answered any phone calls from work, knowing that when he thrown his badge at that useless bastard, he'd thrown his career away.

Everything he'd wanted in life, eradicated in an evening.

He took a few more gulps of his vodka and sat in silence, allowing the water from above to fall on him as he finally made a decision he never thought he would.

The engine slowly rumbled to a quiet stop and Fletcher turned the key in the ignition. The car sat neatly against the curb, the small brick wall surrounding Lucas's house running alongside it. Fletcher yawned, feeling the stiffness in his back from the long drive.

Lucas sat in the passenger seat, his head resting against the window and his eyes closed. He'd slept almost the entire journey, the draining effect of more grief finally taking over his body. His hand was balled into a fist as he clutched something that Fletcher couldn't see, as tightly as possible.

"Lucas."

Fletcher's voice was gentle, a soothing calm for Lucas to stir to. He blinked a few times, gathering himself and remembering where he was. He sat upright, stretching his arms and rolling his shoulders, aches and pains easing away. His ribs shot a harsh twang of pain through his body.

"We're here." Lucas looked at Fletcher, who returned a warm smile. Lucas looked out of the windscreen, his eyes cautiously flicking towards the building before them.

The Cole residence.

He took a deep breath, waves of memories crashing over him as he viewed the home he and Helen had made for themselves. It now sat as nothing more than another building, cold and empty with no shred of life peeking through.

No one lived here anymore.

He unclipped his seat belt and pushed open the passenger side door of the car. The chilled air of the night swept in, slapping Lucas awake.

"Lucas."

He turned in his seat, one leg out of the car as Fletcher adjusted uncomfortably.

"I guess it would mean nothing if I told you I was sorry. For everything that's happened."

Lucas forced a small smile.

"Thank you, Fletcher."

He extended a hand, one that Fletcher knew had been responsible for more death than he'd wanted to remember.

"For everything."

Fletcher took it, shaking it firmly and feeling the sincerity in Lucas's gratitude. They nodded their goodbyes and Lucas stepped out onto the road he'd trodden every day for eight years. The car purred into life, its headlights illuminating the road ahead as Fletcher slowly pulled away and Lucas watched the car until it had disappeared to the right at the end of the street.

He stood still for a few moments, the wind whirling around him as he forced himself to open the small gate and enter the garden. Someone had been there to cut the grass, Kelly he assumed. It smelled fresh, and small piles sat sporadically around the lawn. His steps felt lumbering: he heard each one as if he were treading on balloons.

He entered his key and slowly pushed open the door.

The moonlight shone brightly behind him as he stood in the doorway, casting his impressive shadow into the hallway.

He took a few steps in, expecting Helen to greet him at

the door to the living room, her makeup off and her hair wet. She would give him a sloppy kiss, her mumbled greeting inaudible as she crunched on popcorn. She would then dart back into the front room and he would follow her in lovingly, seeing her drop to the sofa in her dressing gown and turn her attention to the last five minutes of a reality TV show that he would never understand the appeal of.

But there was nothing.

A hollow silence hung eerily in the air.

He closed the front door and leant against it, taking a few deep breaths before slowly wandering into the front room.

There was no reality TV show.

No beautiful wife enjoying every minute of it.

The room was tidy but was missing any sense of life. This used to be his home, yet he felt no connection to it anymore. The days where this was the only place he'd wanted to be had ended when Helen had died. He slowly walked past the small side unit, the shelves filled with books, all of which had once rested in Helen's hands as she consumed their words. Along the top, photo frames were arranged neatly, snapshots of a life that had been so wonderful.

The two of them dressed up as Frankenstein and his bride for Hallowe'en one year.

Helen panicking at a pottery wheel on their trip to the south of France.

The two of them kissing on their wedding day.

He gently reached out, running a finger along the top of the frame, forcing himself to remember how beautiful she'd looked.

How beautiful she'd always looked.

"Lucas."

He turned sharply, her voice ghosting into the room and out of it just as quickly.

There was no one there.

No loving wife.

No ghostly, imperfect vision either.

He carried on perusing the photos, stopping in his tracks as he picked up the final frame.

With boxing gloves proudly displayed, he and Alex were standing side by side. They were both smiling, sweating after what he remembered was a particularly vigorous sparring session.

They were both smiling.

Alex was always smiling.

Lucas frowned, remembering the reason he was back home and slammed the photo down angrily. The impact rocked the unit, other frames toppling over. He went into the kitchen, remembering the rich aromas wafting through when Helen indulged her interest in cooking. He stood in its doorway, watching as she busily navigated her way from the stove to the chopping board. A cooking book lying open, ingredients thrown wherever there was space. She would get so flustered, always panicking that she was doing it wrong but it had always tasted so delicious.

He smiled to himself, remembering the time Helen had accidentally set a tea towel on fire and screamed her head off thinking she would burn down the house. He had simply walked in, thrown it into the sink and turned the tap on much to her self-deprecating embarrassment.

The kitchen was empty. The only sign of life was from the shadows of the outside trees rustling in the wind.

He took gentle steps back through to the hallway, a vision of Helen running towards him in her underwear to give him his morning 'present' on their anniversary.

His shoes clomped loudly while climbing the stairs, walking past a few photos from Helen's youth, a time of her life he hadn't been a part of.

Her young, pretty smile as she stood with her proud father when she graduated.

Her and Kelly on a see-saw in the garden of her family home.

This house used to be full of a life that itself was filled with love.

Now it was empty.

He pushed open the door to the bedroom and there she was. Sitting at her dressing table, gently brushing her face with the oversized blusher brush. Her hair was pinned back with the small, metal pins that Lucas would find in every corner of the house and jokingly complain about. She was wrapped in a towel, her smooth legs shimmering as droplets of shower water ran down them to her delicate feet.

Her phone was in the speaker dock he'd bought her for a birthday one year, playing one of the latest indistinguishable pop songs.

Wherever she was going, she was going to own the room with her beauty.

Lucas stepped across the rug that they'd picked out together and rested his hand on the back of the empty chair. Bottles of perfume and stacks of make-up products lined the circular mirror, a thin sheet of dust resting on top of it all.

He felt his heart throb slightly as he stared at the empty chair, its vacancy reiterating her absence from his life.

"Lucas."

The voice whispered again and he turned, but was quickly aware he was alone in the room. This room, where they'd lie together every night, where they had made love countless times. Where they had lain lazily on Sunday mornings when he didn't train, putting the world to rights and making big plans for their future.

Where the child he would never hold was conceived with the wife he would never touch again.

He reached out across the dresser and his hands slid around the small jewellery box. Kelly had returned it to its rightful place when he'd left and he held it closely against his chest. The jewellery inside rattled loudly as he lifted it. With slow, heavy steps, he made his way to the well-made bed and sat down. His ribs ached.

Very slowly, he opened the lid of the box, the small, plastic ballerina flicking up like a jack in the box and began her pirouette. The musical chimes rang out and Lucas broke.

Tears rolled down his cheeks, losing themselves in the thick stubble. He stared at the miniature dancer twirling slowly and he sat and thought of Helen. How this small box had meant so much to her that, even now, it adorned her dresser.

She was gone.

Alex was gone.

With a trembling hand, he slowly raised the plastic box and rested it on the dressing table next to the small pen and pad that Helen had used to make the large number of lists that she'd loved so much and that he'd ridiculed her for.

He picked up the paper and pen and sat for the next half an hour, his hand scribbling away.

He then fell back on the bed and slept one last time where he was always happiest.

The jewellery box played him a night long lullaby.

CHAPTER TWENTY-FIVE

The first thing Dianne heard on the worst day of her life was the drumming of rain against the window above her bed. She slid a tired hand over her stomach, cradling the bulge of her baby and holding it close. Her other hand fell on the empty side next to her, her skin touching the cold, unruffled pillowed.

She wept for over an hour.

She lay in emotional anguish for as long as possible, wondering how she would cope not just with the day, but with carrying on with the rest of her life. How could she raise their baby when 'they' had been reduced to just her?

She stared through teary eyes at the photo of her and Alex proudly displayed on the bedside table. His arm around her, his peculiarly attractive smile owning the entire shot.

"I miss you, baby."

Eventually, she calmed herself with the thought of making him proud, and showing him that she was strong, and that she would honour him today by holding it together. She pulled herself from the sanctity of their bed and shuffled to the bathroom, the soft kicking of their baby reminding her that there would be a life beyond this day.

A life which had been irreparably destroyed by the actions of others.

She turned on the chrome taps of the bath and the let the cascading flow fill up the tub while adding some Radox. As it gradually filled to the top, she brushed her hair, its brown strands swaying freely with each stroke.

She then de-robed and looked into the mirror, amazed at how holding this life within her had altered her body so much. She desperately wanted to hear Alex's upbeat voice, telling her how beautiful she looked despite her constant complaints about the effects pregnancy was having on her body.

She bathed leisurely, allowing the warm water to wrap itself around her discomfort. More tears as she recalled the times her and Alex had sat in the same tub together, their naked bodies entwined as they spoke about the future.

She already missed him but she knew it would only get worse.

He wasn't perfect. He spoke too much. She chuckled at the memory of him having an answer for everything.

There were no answers anymore, only questions.

She wandered back into the bedroom with a towel wrapped around her, the bulge of her child testing its width.

"How are you, sweetheart?"

Dianne's mother stood in the doorway of the guest room, her black jacket sitting over a white shirt. She'd come to stay with her only daughter as soon as the news of Alex's murder had reached her, remembering what it was like when she'd lost her own husband. She'd always loved how protective of her daughter Alex had been and keenly felt his absence in the house.

Dianne smiled sheepishly before treading small, wet footprints to her bedroom where she shut the door.

The hearse would be arriving within an hour, to make their way to St. Joseph's church. Floods of people with black ties and sad faces would witness her burying her husband in the cold ground.

They'd say all the right things, and make promises to be there for her. They'd also curse the world, offer their condolences and all of them would be genuine. Then afterwards she would bring them back home for the wake, trays of nibbles begrudgingly prepared by her mother whilst they all rehashed the memories of times when Alex had lightened their lives.

But none of it would bring him back.

She wept silently as she eased into a black dress. Then, sitting at her dressing table brushing her hair again, she decided mascara would be a mistake. The emotional tides of the day would inevitably hide her behind a black, streaky mask.

She yearned for Helen, her best friend, to be sitting next to her and say how everything would be okay.

But she was also gone.

Everyone she'd cared about had been taken from this world within a week.

That included Lucas, although the very thought of the man caused her tears to turn from sorrow to hatred. She understood Lucas's pain, the sheer turmoil of having your soul mate wrenched from you like a page torn from a notebook was unmanageable.

Yet it was Lucas who had guided that hand to Alex.

She gritted her teeth, hating herself for hoping the police caught him soon before he or anyone else got hurt.

She finished attaching the black fascinator to her hair, the mesh net draping over her eyes like a thin curtain.

Her mother called up the stairs, informing her that the car was outside.

She stared lifelessly into the mirror, her face a ghostly pale. Her eyes were bloodshot, tears finding their way to the edge of her eyelids before diving off to splash onto her cheeks.

She glanced at the photo of Alex one more time, smiled through the, pain and then slowly lifted herself towards the door, to say goodbye to him for the last time.

Curtis waited patiently on the cobbled courtyard of the crematorium, his eyes fixated on the brightness of the colours bursting from the flowers lining the immaculate grounds surrounding the old building. Standing under an arch, he sheltered himself from the rain while pulling on a cigarette, sighing as he exhaled.

Ashley's coffin had looked so small, you would have been excused for mistaking it for a child's.

The service had been brief, Curtis refusing to allow any speeches to be made about his sister and insisting on a small audience. Tommy had been the first to get up after the pointless sermon given by the local priest, his hulking frame wrapped in a smart, black suit. He strode purposefully to the small, pine box and touched it with kissed fingers. He then dropped a rose on top of it and marched out, shocking Curtis with a rare show of emotion.

As his brother stormed out of the side entrance into the courtyard, Curtis had waited for the small gathering of other mourners, all dressed in their black best, to say their final condolences. He gazed at the box, refusing to say a final goodbye to the little sister he'd always loved dearly.

Refusing to take responsibility for her death.

After a few moments, he rose from his pew, taking

measured steps to the front where her body lay entombed in pine. The crematorium smelt of fresh flowers, even with the odour of death surrounding him.

He said a silent goodbye, making a solemn promise that he would send her killer to the afterlife as soon as possible.

The priest attempted to console Curtis with his words, but Curtis followed his brother; as words of forgiveness and salvation fell on deaf ears.

Now he stood under the archway, his cigarette disintegrating to ash which caught the wind and fluttered across the cobbled stones. The rain pelted the concrete, his mind wandering to Ashley's body, swinging from the London skyline with the same rain crashing against her.

He clenched his fist, crushing the burning embers of the cigarette's remains to his skin and then sharply unclasping as the pain tore through him.

The butt fell to the ground.

People around him were sobbing, their compassion and weakness in front of others drawing his immediate disdain.

Tommy stood silently, allowing the weather to engulf him in a calming wetness.

Lucas was a resourceful man, he would give him that. No doubt he would have found out somehow that he had put a bullet through his best friend's skull. That he, Curtis Drayton, despite Lucas's avalanche of vengeance, had been able to hurt the man even more for what he had done.

Soon, Lucas would come for him.

And Curtis would keep his promise to his sister.

As the clock struck midday, Tommy pulled the Bentley into the garage behind 'Odds On', the front of the shop dark and locked, the shutters pulled down. Sunday was usually one of their busiest days, feeble addicts racing in to bet on the 'Super Sunday' football in a hope of actually achieving something. Winning a bet to them was like being 'chosen'.

Curtis scoffed at the idea, all too happy to line his pockets with their desperate cash.

They trudged in through the back door, their fine, Italian loafers squelching with rainwater. Curtis needed a drink and was almost through the door to his office staircase when Tommy's voice broke the silence that had been held since they'd collected the remains of their sister in an urn.

"Who the fuck are you?"

Curtis stepped back into the shop, as Tommy stomped to the back door where a young man, his face worn and ragged, had stepped in. Rainwater dripped off his coat as he stood nervously, begging Tommy to wait as the hulking Drayton grabbed him by the scruff of his jacket and slammed him against the door frame.

His blonde hair dripped water down a fear-stricken face.

Curtis gave him a minute to explain who he was and what he wanted.

A minute later, Curtis began formulating a plan.

―――

"You call me if you need anything, okay?"

Dianne's auntie squeezed her tightly on the door step, her hands rubbing Dianne's aching back. A few days earlier, Alex's body had been dumped where they were standing. It felt like treading on his grave and she stepped back into the safety of her home.

She leant against a wall, letting out a huge sigh. The final guest had left and she rested her hand against her bump, wishing she could cradle her child.

"Here you go, dear."

Her mother walked in from kitchen to the quaint front room, clasping a mug of piping hot tea. Dianne smiled and waddled to the leather sofa, dropping down with a thud as her mother collected the last of the paper plates used for the finger buffet and dropped them in a black bag.

Dianne had a sip of tea, cradling the cup with both hands and enjoying the rich flavour.

"Leave it, Mum," she smiled appreciatively. "It can wait until later."

She knew her Mum was just trying to keep busy, the weight of losing her son-in-law had caused her a great deal of pain she refused to reveal to her daughter.

It was something Dianne would forever be thankful for.

"I just don't want you overdoing it."

"I'm fine. Trust me."

"It was a beautiful service," her mother said, plumping up some of the sofa cushions.

"It really was."

"Alex would have been proud. You were so brave."

Dianne smiled into her mug, knowing that wasn't true. She'd planned on saying a few words, wanting to let the world know how much she was hurting and how deep Alex's absence would run.

But she couldn't.

Having either him or Helen there would have helped. But now they'd both moved on and she was alone.

She felt a small kick in her stomach.

Well, not *completely* alone.

"Right, its three o'clock," her mum stated with purpose. "I'm going to have a shower and then how about the three of us get out of here?"

"Where?"

"Anywhere, my dear. Let's just see where we end up."

"That sounds great."

Dianne's mother gently squeezed her knee, before

pushing her, slightly overweight frame off the sofa. As she strode to the stairs, she loosened the pin in her auburn hair, which gently fell around her shoulders. Dianne sipped her tea as footsteps disappeared upstairs, shortly followed by the locking of the bathroom door.

She closed her eyes, allowing her thoughts to race towards Alex, his defined arms reaching out to wrap around her. He would hold her so tight, and any worry would slowly fade.

Her safety had gone.

She was startled out of her thoughts by the doorbell. She opened her eyes, looking around the room to locate what had dared stir her from Alex's embrace. The only noise she heard was the water crashing against the shower wall, echoing softly somewhere above her.

She tried to return to Alex.

The doorbell chimed again

She looked up, noticing a figure looming behind the window of the front door. She immediately cowered in her seat, praying that her mother would race down to open it. Or, miraculously, Alex would stride out from the kitchen and send whoever it was away.

The doorbell rang one more time.

She sighed.

Placing the tea down on the neat, vintage coffee table, she managed to pull herself up with help from the arm of the sofa. She took a few steps towards the door, shaking at the memory of seeing Alex's dead body fall over the threshold.

She opened the door and saw the next worst thing she could have imagined.

"Lucas?!"

Her shock was obvious. Her voice shook as she said his name, her eyes wide with disbelief, eyes which cloaked a raw hatred. Lucas stood a few feet from her, his feet planted in the spot where she'd seen her family die. A death he was responsible for. He wore a white shirt with a black tie underneath the leather jacket she'd witnessed her dead friend buy for him.

He shuffled uncomfortably, unsure of what possible words he could say that could offer any comfort to a woman grieving for a loved one. The rain rattled gently around him, the drops not registering with him. Before he could say a word, she raised her hand and cracked a firm slap across his face.

"How dare you?"

He looked back up at her, his bristle-covered cheek throbbing and glowing red.

"How dare you come here?"

"Dianne, please...."

"Do you know what you've done?"

Tears of fury leaked from her eyes, reinforcing her decision against the mascara. The remaining shards of Lucas's heart broke when he saw her pain.

"I am so sorry..." His words were quiet as he struggled to believe them himself.

"No, Lucas. You don't get to apologise!" For the first time since she'd cradled Alex's lifeless body, Dianne felt strong. "You don't get to turn up here and say you're sorry. This is Alex's home and he can't come back here because of you."

"Bad people did this to your husband."

"And why's that? Because he was a bad person? Because he deserved it? Of all the people in this world, my Alex was the best of them!"

Lucas looked down at the ground, understanding the verbal barrage he was receiving was deserved.

"Or was it because of *you*, Lucas?!" Her finger jabbed his chest. "All because you couldn't handle the cruelty of this world and now it's taken another person."

"Alex was my best friend."

"He was my husband. Don't you dare fucking tell me that you're hurting, Lucas. I know Helen was taken from you and it hit us all. You more than most, and I understand that. But Alex, he had nothing to do with it."

"I know..." his words trailed off feebly.

"All he was, was your best friend. He was there for you from the beginning. When everyone questioned Helen's decision, that it was too big of a risk, Alex saw through it and treated you like family."

Dianne took a pause, inhaled deeply and willed herself calm. The last thing she wanted was her neighbours seeing her losing her composure.

"Fact is Lucas, I know what you're going through. You want the person responsible for destroying your life to face up to the things they've done. But that is the job of the police."

Lucas shook his head, looking up at the clouds that returned his gaze with more rain drops.

"It is, Lucas. But you decided that wasn't good enough. The things they say you have done. I mean, are you even you anymore?"

He turned a heart-broken gaze at her.

"Are you even the man Helen loved anymore?"

"I just couldn't stand the idea that Helen could be struck from this world and no one batted an eyelid."

"But they did, Lucas. We all did. We all grieved and we all cried. We celebrated her memory and not a day goes by that I don't shed a tear for her."

She stared at him, her hatred trembling at a man she had once held so closely in her life.

"But she's gone. And because you couldn't handle that, Alex is gone too. His child will grow up never knowing him."

She rubbed a hand over her stomach, the bump pushing against her black dress.

"Because of you."

Lucas's head dropped, his hands stuffed into his pockets. He thought of all the conversations he'd had with Alex when they trained, remembering the excitement in his friend's voice as he spoke of his impending fatherhood. The little things, like teaching his child to tie their shoe laces, seemed so exciting with Alex's enthusiasm behind them.

It would never happen now.

Dianne broke the silence.

"I want you to leave."

"Dianne.

"*Leave!*"

Lucas looked at his friend's widow, a woman he'd shared so many happy memories with. Her eyes radiated a disgust that would never be repaired. Her large, dark eyes leaked tears without fluttering, the water trailing down her pale cheeks.

"I will make them pay for what they've done. I promise you."

Dianne scoffed a pitiful chuckle.

"Don't you get it Lucas? I don't want you to. Helen wouldn't have wanted this either."

The words hit Lucas, a truth he'd kept locked away from confronting. Helen had spent years talking to Lucas about his past, about all of the anger and fury he'd felt from the years of neglect and mistreatment. The way he'd handled the boys at that foster home, how he'd seen violence as his only means of respite.

She'd helped him to control those thoughts, to see that confronting life's challenges with violence meant that no matter the outcome, you had already lost. She'd encouraged his training with Alex, another person who'd only ever had his best intentions at heart.

Now both of them had been taken from him.

He tried to look for another avenue but there was only one path.

One that Helen would turn away from in a second.

Dianne took a step back into the hallway, allowing the heat from the house to welcome her with its warm embrace.

"Goodbye Lucas."

The door began closing.

"I hope I never see you again."

The door slammed shut in his face. Lucas stood still, captive in another cage of loneliness. A few weeks ago, he was sitting around a table with the three people he cared for more than himself. They'd toasted to him, having whispered discussions about the family he didn't yet know he was about to begin.

All of it, gone.

The door had slammed shut, not just on his condolence, but on his last link to a life that could pass as normal. The wind whipped up around him, his black tie flickering below like a black flame. He took one last, loving look towards the house and then slowly walked back down the stone path, the little slabs poking through the grass in random fashion.

He needed to keep calm. Alex's death was an attempt to unnerve him, a retribution for the way he'd rattled the Drayton cage.

He was so close to finishing what he'd set out to do.

To keep his promise.

Discipline and control. That's what he told himself. As he walked down the street, reciting the lessons that Alex had spent years beating into him, Dianne stared from her window.

Hard, painful tears flooded from her eyes as she watched the broken shell of the man she'd known slowly shrink away into the distance. She knew she'd never see him again. It pained her to see him in such a way, despite all of the hard work Helen and Alex had done.

He knew only violence, and only violence awaited him.

She looked at the photos on the table underneath her elegant bay window. Her hand began to shake as she slowly picked up the one from her wedding day.

Alex looked so handsome, so happy.

Dressed in a matching smart grey suit was Lucas. They had their arms around each other's shoulders, cigars hanging from genuine smiles. She dropped the photo to the floor, the glass shattering on impact.

The photo slid from the frame and across the floor.

Alex would have forgiven Lucas, it was the type of man he was and one of the reasons she would love him until the day she saw him again.

She couldn't forgive Lucas. But she could try to save him.

She reached for her mobile phone and moments later, asked to be put through to the police.

CHAPTER TWENTY-SIX

"I'm sorry."

Lucas's words hung in the air momentarily before the wind grabbed them and whipped them away. The rain had dropped in velocity, but a light drizzle still swept through the grounds of the cemetery. It should all have been so familiar and Lucas hated the fact he didn't remember a single detail of the place.

The church itself sat a hundred feet to the left, a magnificent structure of white brick and stained-glass windows, its crucifix cutting into the darkening sky with a mighty pride.

The grounds themselves were well maintained, the freshly cut grass providing a thin icing over squishy mud. Trees overhung the pathways, cutting through the grass, the first signs of blossom threatening to emerge to brighten the dullness of the overcast sky. Somewhere in the distance someone was muddling around a gravestone, clearing away debris which had desecrated the permanent resting place of a loved one.

Lucas stood still, allowing the silence of the afternoon to take control. All that could be heard was the wind, his tie, jacket and hair all fluttering backwards as it pushed against him. He winced as his shattered ribs reminded him of their condition.

"I promise I'll make this right."

Again, words that nobody would ever hear.

Before him, a makeshift wooden cross spiked up from the ground, slowly rocking back and forth with each gust. Speckles of rain scattered from the wood to the grass below it. A fresh rectangle of upturned mud lay in front of the wooden emblem, recently piled in on top of his friend who'd been committed to the earth only hours before.

A friend he hadn't had a chance to say goodbye to.

Flowers adorned the burial plot, with a wreath that spelled out Alex's name resting against the cross. A few petals, ripped by the elements, fluttered away.

Lucas admired them all, the beautiful colours and gorgeous arrangements, chosen by those who'd loved Alex as a final goodbye. He'd also visited Helen's grave on the way to the spot, sitting for half an hour in the cold and the wet, staring at a stone emblazoned with her name.

The ground was still relatively fresh, the mud clear apart from the small bouquet of roses he'd purchased on his way in.

The red flowers had rocked mournfully in the wind as Lucas gently kissed his fingers and ran them over the letters carved into her memorial stone.

He missed her more than he could bear.

And now, here he was, looking down at newly turned soil. A few weeks before, they'd spent their time discussing the future and now it was nothing but mud. A life, ended cruelly, and the remains stored away from the living.

He reached slowly into the inside of his leather jacket and produced the phone which Matt Drayton had offered him just moments before his death.

With a scowl, he thumbed through the numbers and then lifted the now wet mobile to his dripping ear.

The phone only rang twice.

"Well I know this isn't Matt, don't I?"

Curtis's voice sent a shiver down Lucas's spine, his fist clenched of its own volition. The calmness of the man, the tinge of arrogance in his voice only added to the fury.

"Tell me, Lucas. How's Alex? Still dead?"

"You've taken everything from me."

"Have I?"

"This needs to end."

'Hmmm, I don't know Lucas. The way I see it, you're still two up on me aren't you? You're just lucky I don't come back up there and send your little friend's wife and kid to meet yours."

Lucas gritted his teeth, the very idea of anything happening to Dianne and her unborn child made him shudder.

Curtis sipped his drink, letting out a satisfied sigh at the end of it. Tommy leant against the counter, his suit stretching as his bulky arms crossed against his chest.

"I'm tired of killing people. I only have two left.

"And I only have one."

The two men let the silence speak, agreeing on the solution without using words. Curtis finished his drink and slammed the glass down on the counter.

"My door is open, Lucas. If you want the address, I have this nifty little app called Phone Finder. You may remember it?"

Lucas stared at the ground, the tilled soil sitting freshly above grass level. Below it, his best friend, murdered by the man at the other end of the call. He felt his fist clench again.

"I'm on my way."

The phone line went dead before Curtis could retort and he snarled viciously at the screen. He scanned the apps on his phone, activating the location device to beckon Lucas to him.

To his death.

He reached for his glass, cursing under his breath upon the realisation that it was empty. He pushed himself from the stall, shooting a glance at Tommy.

"Make some calls, get some of the boys round here. I'm not taking any chances with this prick."

"This is everyone," Tommy stated, motioning to the room. Curtis raised his eyebrows and turned his head. Two men sat at one of the high tables, smoke pouring from the cigarettes both men were enjoying. Curtis recognised one, Mark, an ex-security guard who Tommy had used a few times for debt collecting. The other young man, known as Banner due to his ridiculous temper that drew comparisons with the comic book character 'The Incredible Hulk', sat beside him.

Behind them, on a single chair against the wall, the young man who'd emerged earlier sat silently, rain still dripping from his nose while he warmed himself up with the coffee Tommy had begrudgingly made at Curtis's order. He turned back to his brother.

"Really? Where the fuck is everyone else?"

"Dead or inside. Plus, people ain't exactly lining up to help us out at the moment."

"Since when?"

"Since Lucas started killing us off."

Curtis shook his head in rage, looking back at the dwindling numbers of his army. He felt his control ebbing away.

"Well, once we gut this piece of shit I want the names

of everyone who backed out and I'll give them something to really be afraid of.'

Tommy rolled his eyes and Curtis took a few intimidating steps up to the young intruder. He saw the fear in the stranger's eyes: he ran a hand through his wet, blonde hair.

It made Curtis smile.

"Seems that we're going to need you sooner than we'd thought. Get your arse home, gear up and get back here."

The young man nodded nervously, fumbling with the mug as he set it down on the floor. As he got up and made a few steps towards the door, Curtis reached out and grabbed his shoulder, spinning him slightly.

His face was a mask of sheer terror.

"If you fuck this up, you are as good as dead."

The young man nodded frantically and hurriedly shuffled through the door and into the rain.

Curtis basked in the young man's fear.

The wind carried fragments of blossom with it, colourful leaves dancing erratically through the cemetery grounds. The rain had picked up, water spotting against the screen of the phone as Lucas memorised the address.

It was time to meet Curtis.

He shut the phone down and slid it into the pocket of his jacket, his black tie flailing rapidly as a strong gust blew through.

"Are you happy now, Lucas?"

He stood still, the sound of the voice turning his entire body cold. He shuddered, knowing she wouldn't quite be her.

"All this death?"

He turned, his face revealing the pain caused by the

words. There she was, almost floating before him, her white gown emitting its own source of light. The rain fell around her, yet the vision remained dry.

"It should never have come to this. Never. I should have been beside you. I should have been there with you in London."

"No, Lucas." The ghostly voice was tinged with an unnatural echo. "You should have accepted what happened. I begged and I pleaded with you not to pull down every wall we'd worked so hard to put up."

Lucas shook his head in desperation. He slowly reached out a hand towards hers, the tips of her fingers were smudged and hanging in the air like smoke.

His words were quiet as he looked at them.

"I had to."

"Why?"

"All I ever did was love you, Helen. Every day with every part of me. But because of the actions taken by bad people, I will never get to see you again."

Lucas looked up from her fading hands, his eyes meeting the swirling blue gems sitting back in her slowly-fading face. They latched onto Lucas with a pain-stricken stare.

"That's why I had to pull the walls down. To put things right."

"And this is right?" She pointed a spectral finger towards the ground that encased Alex. "Alex is dead."

"I never meant for things to get so out of control."

"But they have, Lucas. There's only one way this will end. You know that."

Lucas nodded his head sheepishly, his eyes watering at the realisation of her words. His hand dipped into his jean pocket and returned with a small, gold ring in its palm. They both looked at it as the rain splashed against Lucas's skin.

"When I gave you this, I promised you I would love you until the day I die."

Her arm floated forward, rain falling either side of her hand as it hovered above his. He looked at her, his heartbreak plastered across his face.

"It's a promise I intend to keep."

His hand balled into a fist and he turned on his heels and made to exit the cemetery. Helen stayed where she was, her eyes fixed on her husband.

"Please don't go, Lucas. If you go you'll die."

He stopped, and turned back to look at his wife's image one last time.

"Then I'll die fighting. I'm going to make someone else give a damn that you're gone."

Lucas continued his march, his footsteps trudging through the squelching grass. Helen watched on, seeing her husband grow smaller and smaller as he disappeared towards a destiny she'd never wanted for him.

"You were enough, Lucas. You always were."

Her words were empty, disappearing alongside a thousand raindrops. The mud covering Alex's coffin was now thick and damp, locking his body away for an eternal rest.

Helen vanished.

Lucas got to his car, wet and heavy from the downpour. He turned the key and pulled out, heading for London.

Fletcher could barely keep his eyes open.

His desk was awash with files, loose papers and a few empty mugs that had half helped when they'd been filled with coffee. He shuffled a few papers on his desk, trying to wake himself a little as he let out a large yawn.

The long drive home had been uneventful, the roads

had been clear and the only deterrent had been the patches of rain falling in random showers.

When he had finally arrived home, it was a little past four in the morning and he longed for the days when he and Susan would sleep in on Sundays before enjoying a walk through a village she'd recently discovered outside of London. They would stroll through, their arms linked, taking in the narrow, cobbled streets and the old, Victorian houses. Lunch would be delicious, usually from a quaint, family-ran eatery that would be one of the cornerstones of the community.

How life had changed.

He adjusted his position on his seat, his back aching from hours of driving. His mind wandered to Alex's funeral, wondering if Lucas had even attended or not. Either way, Lucas was home now and hopefully he could find peace.

"Jesus. You look like you have been dragged through a hedge backwards by your bollocks."

Fletcher cast a tired glaze upwards, seeing the beaming smile that usually accompanied the thick, Irish accent. McCarthy hobbled up to the desk, his knee still causing him serious discomfort which was evident with each step. Suddenly, the noise and hustle of the office broke through and Fletcher felt involved in the day again.

"I didn't sleep too well," Fletcher lied, not even sleeping the night before and treating himself to several glasses from a new bottle of Jack.

"Aye, me neither," he winked. "Mrs McCarthy saw to that."

Fletcher chuckled politely, the thought of his large colleague in the act wasn't an image he particularly cared for. McCarthy looked over the mess which Fletcher claimed was a desk and shook his head.

"Anyway, look alive. Bailey wants to see you in Interview Room A. Said it was urgent."

"Really?" Fletcher's caution evident in his tone. "What for?"

"How the bloody hell should I know? No one tells me anything round here."

Fletcher nodded, easing himself up from the chair and battling the stiffness in his spine. He straightened his tie and tried to flatten some creases on his unironed shirt. He walked through the office, watching McCarthy struggle with lowering himself into his chair. He walked past the locker rooms and the toilets, before approaching the white door to the interview room. A few officers walked past, politely smiling at the old retiree who then rapped the door with a gentle knock.

"Come in!" Bailey's booming voice returned from within and Fletcher obliged. He slunk in through the door.

"Hello, sir."

"Fletcher. Please, close the door and grab a seat."

Fletcher did as he was asked. Bailey sat opposite him, a mug of tea on the table and a manila folder next to it. Fletcher painfully lowered himself into the plastic chair, knowing full well it would only add to his aching back. Bailey opened up the arms to his glasses and slid them over his stern face.

"You look shattered, Fletcher."

"Rough night."

"I see. Well, I just wanted you to know that we've found him."

"Who? Lucas?"

Bailey nodded, his powerful arms crossed over his police uniform.

"When?"

'Dianne Thornley rang to inform the police that Lucas had visited her after Alex's wake earlier this afternoon.

She said he tried to apologise but she wasn't having any of it."

"Did they arrest him?" Fletcher asked, worried that the concern in his voice was too obvious.

"'No. He'd already left by the time she'd called. An Officer Chamberlain then led a search of Lucas's old residence and found a pile of worn clothes on the floor so we can assume he's been home. Other things recovered were a jewellery box that was lying on the bed, alongside a handwritten note.'

"What was in the note?"

"We're still waiting for the report."

"So where's Lucas now?"

Bailey unfolded his arms and leant forward, his biceps bulging against the short, white sleeves of his uniform.

"We don't know. The police are searching the village and keeping an unmarked car outside his home. Fresh flowers have been recovered at the grave of his wife, so we can assume he's been to visit her."

"When he went to pay his condolences to Alex?"

"Makes sense."

Fletcher nodded in agreement, trying to mask the concern he had for Lucas's freedom. It would only be a matter of time before they caught up with him.

Bailey brought him back into the room with his commanding voice.

"Now, the question that I had, was how did Lucas know what had happened to Alex?" Fletcher shuffled uncomfortably. "Questions have been asked and no one up there has had any contact with the man since Helen's funeral over a week ago. No one knows where he's been or where to find him. Yet he turned up the day of the funeral."

"I don't know, sir. Maybe he just wanted to go home?"

Bailey stared at Fletcher, his gaze unrelenting.

"I did a little digging once we got the call earlier this afternoon of his sighting and asked them to search any nearby CCTV cameras to try and identify him, see how he's travelling et cetera et cetera."

Fletcher sat very still, a little impressed with Bailey's detective work but becoming increasingly aware of how alone he was in the room. The walls felt a lot nearer to him, the door further than he recalled. Beyond the mirror, he wondered how many sets of eyes were locked on him. Bailey opened his folder, lifting a sheet of paper.

"Imagine my surprise when this was taken from a Shell garage, just outside of Brinscall at two minutes past two this morning."

Bailey slid the sheet across the desk, as Fletcher slipped on his own spectacles. It was a grainy black and white image relaying the courtyard of the station. Three petrol pumps stood empty, nothing but a few oil stains before them. The fourth pump was in use, a grainy outline of a figure holding the nozzle to the car. Any identification was impossible due to the poor image quality.

The car however, was a little clearer and was identifiable as a new model Ford Fiesta.

"Look at the license plate."

Fletcher didn't need Bailey to instruct him. He had already noticed it and knew why he'd been called into the room. Bailey sat back in his chair as if he was awaiting a response.

There was none forthcoming.

The car belonged to Fletcher and they both knew it. Fletcher gently rubbed his forearm, the pain of the burn had evaporated a few days before but the skin was still charred. Bailey sniffed and then placed his hands on the table.

"What were you doing in Brinscall last night, Fletcher?"

Fletcher sat silently. He could try muster up a lie, but he knew the process here. Anything he said would be used against him. Bailey grunted, clasping his hands together.

"The way I see it Fletcher, is you just so happen to be leaving Brinscall in the early hours of the morning the day Lucas turns up for a funeral. So I'm led to believe that you drove him there last night. Didn't you?"

Again, Fletcher remained silent, staring at the incriminating evidence before him and wondering how long he would last in prison. Bailey got up, looming over the old man with his awesome stature.

"But even still, you would have had to have been able to make contact with Lucas. Let him know what happened and arrange to meet for your journey. Which then leads me to the question as to how he knew who we suspect had killed his wife."

Bailey slowly walked around the table separating them until he was beside Fletcher. He placed both hands on the desk and leant down so he was close to Fletcher's ear level.

"If you have helped him in anyway Fletcher, I will find out. So anything you tell me right now will help me to help you when that time comes."

Fletcher sat still for a few moments, trying to control the panic creeping into his breathing. Bailey was regarded as one of the best interviewers, his reputation for getting the truth out of people one of the reasons he was such a commanding Sergeant.

"How can I find him? Or how is it that you make contact with him? Tell me before the Draytons decide to avenge another family member he's killed. I can't help him and I can't help you, Fletcher, if you don't give me anything."

"I haven't done anything wrong."

"Then what have you done?"

Bailey sat on the edge of the table, looking down at

Fletcher who slowly twisted the lanyard that his ID card hung from. Bailey waited for a few more moments of silence to pass before he stood up, sighing deeply.

"Fine. You're suspended pending an investigation. Give me your ID and then please leave the premises."

Fletcher quietly pushed the chair back and stood up quickly, his back tightening and causing him to wince. He lifted the lanyard over his thin, grey hair and placed it in Bailey's outstretched hand. He headed for the door.

"Fletch. Everything always comes out in the wash. You know that as well as I do."

Fletcher opened the door, turning back to look at the Sergeant who was willing him to respond.

"I've done nothing that I can see as wrong."

Bailey nodded.

"I hope that's true. Otherwise I can't help you."

Fletcher walked through the door and headed back to his desk, ignoring the muffled voice of McCarthy as he passed. He collected his coat and made a speechless exit towards his car. Bailey sat in the interview room, looking at Fletcher's ID badge. He looked at the photo of a man he admired, but could never trust again.

He tossed it onto the table and then sat back, his hands pressed against his head as the toll of the last few weeks washed over him.

He awoke half an hour later, thanking his lucky stars no one had caught him grabbing a quick power nap.

Starling had finally got round to shaving. A small, red rash burnt his neck but he felt a little more human. When he'd walked in through the front door of his flat, he'd dripped rain drops over the small pile of unopened letters on the doormat. It was the first time since Annette's death that he hadn't been drinking, the sobriety giving way to an uneasy confrontation with his grief.

The love of his life had been murdered in cold blood.

He discarded the bottle of vodka sitting on his coffee table and headed straight to the bathroom. He shaved and showered, wanting to look every bit the policeman that he knew he was. He'd promised to protect people to ensure those who broke the law were brought to justice.

He'd believed in those words ever since the day he'd uttered them with his hand over a bible, swearing himself into the police force before a room full of strangers and a very proud father.

Now he would reinforce them one more time.

He pulled on his uniform, feeling incomplete without the police badge he'd discarded in his emotional turmoil. Bailey would take him back, he was sure of it. They may not see eye to eye, but he was a damn good officer. The Metropolitan Police needed good officers.

He strapped on his stab-proof vest, realising that his lack of sleep and food had made him weaker and that the vest hung heavier than before. He would pull himself out of it. He would get himself back on track and it would all begin tonight.

He left his flat and pulled away in his car within minutes.

Tonight would be the night that he stopped Lucas Cole.

As he drove towards Brixton, he tried to remove the cold, dead eyes of Annette staring up at him from the floor of her office. She'd had the vacant look of someone who'd been erased from the world.

He gripped the wheel in anger until his knuckles shone white.

A few hours passed, the sun had retired for the night and now rain fell along Brixton High Street, illuminated by the bright moon overlooking the world. He glanced at the clock.

Eleven o'clock.

He sat with his eyes transfixed on the street ahead, the pavement clear and the only building with any signs of life was the 'Odds On' betting shop. Although closed, the lights still burnt behind the windows.

Starling ran a hand through his blonde hair and then clicked on his radio. He listened to the voices of his colleagues, all of them out on their respective beats, a few reports of a fight breaking out in a nearby pub.

A car pulled into up to the curb a few spaces behind him. He stared into the rear view mirror, his fingers turning the volume dial of his radio until he sat in silence.

All he could hear was the rain clattering against the body of his car.

The door opened in the reflection and Starling felt a jolt of rage as if he was struck with a cattle prod.

Lucas Cole stepped out and onto the street.

He looked up and down the road, looking for signs of anyone or anything out of the ordinary. Starling recognised him immediately, remembering how powerful the man had looked when he'd barged into the hospital a few weeks back, his life and loved one fading away within minutes.

Before sympathy settled in, he envisaged Annette begging to this man before he'd thrown her to her death.

Lucas crossed the empty road, his footsteps splashing through small puddles in the uneven tarmac. Starling slowly opened the door to his car, ensuring he made no noise to alert Lucas, who was striding towards the door of the Drayton property. He slunk along the side of his car and then lightly jogged across the road, keeping his footsteps light even in his hulking police boots. He stopped as he approached the cars in front of the shop, as Lucas approached the glass door.

"Lucas Cole!"

The man spun on the spot, locking eyes on Starling. He recognised him, something that Starling was hoping for.

"You're under arrest."

"I remember you."

"Put your hands on your head and face the wall."

"You were at the hospital. You were the one who found her."

"I said put your hands on your head and face the fucking wall!"

Lucas took a few steps nearer the cars that separated them and Starling reached towards his belt, his hand clasping the CS Spray he was obliged to carry.

The street was eerily quiet. Only the sound of the rain and the distant traffic could be heard as the two men stared at each other.

"This has got nothing to do with you."

Click.

Lucas stood dead still at the unmistakeable sound of the gun safety latch being removed. A moment later, he felt the cold, hard steel of a gun pressing against the back of his head.

"Easy does it."

Tommy Drayton held the gun in a firm, strong grip at the end of an outstretched arm. His muscles pulled his polo shirt tight, his finger resting gently on the trigger. Lucas stood still, a realisation of defeat spreading across his face.

Starling thought he would enjoy it more.

"Let's get inside, shall we? We'll catch our death out here."

Tommy slowly walked to the side, the gun pressed to Lucas's skull as he turned around. Two other men stood either side of the door, one of them pointing a snub-nosed shotgun directly at Lucas's stomach. The other, looking vigilantly up and down the street, held a Beretta in his hands. As Lucas took small, careful steps towards the door, the lookout leant forward and opened the glass door. The man holding the shotgun went first, carefully walking backwards into the shop, his gun locked on Lucas with every step.

Lucas entered, the bright lights causing him to squint uncomfortably, but he gradually adjusted. Four large tables, each flanked by long-legged stools inside a rather elegantly decorated shop. Large screens were mounted on the wall. Tommy entered behind, his hand steady as he held the gun, guiding Lucas in. Starling then hurried in behind, rain water dripping from his Met vest. The lookout took one last glimpse and then shut the door, locking it in place and then operating the control box to bring down the shutter.

Within moments, the world was shut out.

A moment later, Lucas felt a sharp pain emanating from the back of his skull, as Tommy clubbed him with the butt of the gun.

His world went dark before he hit the ground.

CHAPTER TWENTY-SEVEN

The irritating pain of someone slapping his face brought Lucas back to reality. Another firm palm connected with his face and his eyes opened. He was leaning forward, his arms held back behind him as he felt two separate pairs of hands clasped on either arm. Mark and Banner stood behind him, locking his arms in place.

"Wake up, sunshine."

Lucas lifted his head, to be greeted by a playful smile from Tommy Drayton. The man had the stature and swagger of someone who knew how to handle himself, fitting Harry's description of him perfectly. Lucas didn't have to wait long to discover how powerful he was as Tommy clobbered his stomach with a vicious uppercut from his mighty right hand.

Lucas felt the air leave his body and his shattered ribs jingle. He heaved and Tommy grabbed his hair and lifted his head with a hard tug of his hair.

"That was for killing my sister."

"Enough, Tommy!"

The voice made Lucas's stomach turn. He'd heard it over the phone, screaming vile threats with an uncontrollable rage. He saw the smart, well-polished shoes step into view and, as he raised his head, his vision climbed up the tailor-made suit until he locked eyes with Curtis. They were black, emitting an evil Lucas would have only reserved for the devil. His short, thin hair was neatly brushed and his smile was one of a victor.

Lucas tried to lunge for him, but he was held in place. Banner even twisted his arm, the tendons in his shoulder stretched almost to breaking point. Lucas succumbed, staring at the man who'd raped and murdered his wife.

"Well, well, well, Lucas Cole. Just the man I've been looking for."

Curtis calmly stood a few feet away, not even attempting to hide the smugness of his victory. He slowly removed his blazer and rested it on the nearby desk.

"What was it I told you?"

Before Lucas was allowed to answer the rhetorical question, the two captors pulled Lucas's arms back to straighten him. Curtis threw a violent right hook, his fist colliding with Lucas's jaw with a thunderous crack.

"Oh yeah. I told you that I'd get you, didn't I? And what would I be if I wasn't a man of my word?"

He swung another punch, sending a spray of blood shooting from Lucas's mouth. His two henchmen locked him in place, refusing to remove him from the punishment. Tommy stood calmly, arms folded. Starling looked around nervously, every moment only adding to the regret he was now starting to feel.

Curtis then hammered a hard punch straight into Lucas's rib cage, his detached bones thumping around inside his body. He coughed, more blood splattering the floor, but he did not make a sound.

Curtis scowled, slowly removing his expensive, gold cufflinks and rolling his shirt sleeves up his arm. Lucas closed his eyes, his resignation of failure etching away at him.

"See, Lucas, I know what the world is like. People want to make out that you can find happiness in this place; that you can walk through it with the sun shining and the birds chirping. But you and I know the truth, don't we?"

Curtis took a step forward and propelled his whole body weight into his next strike. Lucas's head snapped back on the impact, his nose a broken mess. His legs weakened slightly and the two men held him in place as he slumped forward. The blood dripped slowly to the floor.

Starling watched on, wishing he could retract the worst decision he'd ever made.

"Life hands people shit from the start. I know all about your life, what happened when you were younger. The bullying, the beatings, the poor little tyke who just needed a cuddle. Seriously, I was touched."

He nodded to the henchmen who, once again, held Lucas steady. Then strengthened their grip as he slumped forward again after another hate-filled fist connected with his hard stomach.

"Nobody cared, right? They didn't when I had the same fucking hand dealt to me. But do you know what makes us different, Lucas?"

Lucas coughed, feeling blood filling up his mouth. He spat it on the floor, right in the direction of a snarling Curtis. His words were quiet, but he looked Curtis straight in the eye.

"I don't need to rape women to feel like a man."

Lucas closed his eyes in preparation, knowing that the next fist was imminent. He was right, and Curtis struck him with his final punch, breaking a few of his knuckles on Lucas's jaw.

The man swung, almost unconscious in the arms of the two henchmen. Tommy hadn't even flinched, watching intently from his spot against the counter. Starling could feel himself shaking, his vengeance had clouded his judgement and now he was watching a man get beaten to death, knowing his life would never be the same again. Curtis, his hand swelling by the second, slowly paced in front of his fallen nemesis.

"The difference between us, you piece of shit, is that I embraced it and played my hand perfectly. I used it to take control of this fucking city. All you did was hide behind doors until you relied on someone to take you out of it."

Curtis turned and nodded to Tommy, who stepped away from the counter. Lucas, with blood trickling from above his eye joining the mass dripping from his nose, hung from the hands behind him. He heard the man's footsteps.

"You're not the only one in the room who has lost their partner, Lucas." Curtis pulled Lucas's head up by his hair, lifting his eye line towards Starling, the nervous looking Police Officer who'd ambushed him earlier. "Ashley was his girlfriend. He wanted to make sure you also got what was coming."

Curtis turned towards Starling, his fingers still roughly latched onto Lucas's hair.

"You want to give him a few?"

Starling looked anxiously around the room, shaking his head. He could feel vomit trying to escape his body, tunnelling its way up his throat but he managed to stop the flow before it reached freedom.

Curtis shrugged and let go of Lucas, his head feebly flopping forward again. Blood dripped from his facial wounds onto the tiles below.

"You killed three of my brothers, Lucas."

Tommy approached Curtis and reached into the back pocket of his jeans. From it, he pulled the large, vicious blade that had ended Helen's life. He handed it to Curtis.

"You killed my little sister."

Curtis spoke through gritted teeth as he clasped his fingers tightly around the blade's handle. He took a few steps towards the blood-stained man who had done so much damage to his family.

"I know Helen meant the world to you, Lucas. She was your reason for everything. Your control. I'm sure you have been poring through memories, remembering everything about her."

Curtis leant forward, his mouth next to Lucas's ear. He swung weakly.

"Thing is, mate, I don't even remember what colour her fucking hair was."

Curtis lunged forward.

A burning sensation roared from Lucas's side, as the knife ripped through his skin. The blade pushed in as Curtis held it with as much force as he could. Blood began to seep around the blade and Lucas gritted his teeth, refusing to give Curtis the satisfaction of his pain.

He breathed heavily, counting down the moments in his head until he could see Helen again.

Starling watched on in horror. Curtis's eyes were wide and filled with a crazed delight. Lucas wobbled in the grip of the two men, his face a beaten mess, his shirt stained with blood.

Curtis pulled his arm back, revealing the knife that was now red and dripping with Lucas's blood. Blood oozed from Lucas's side and he dropped to his knees. Mark and Banner relinquished their holds, slowly stepping away as the blood trickled out onto the floor.

Curtis proudly stepped back, handing the knife back to his brother. He began to slide back into his blazer as he turned to Tommy.

"Take him downstairs and get rid of him."

"In my gym?"

"Yes, in your fucking gym. I have business to attend to." He nodded his head in the direction Starling, who cautiously watched the two brothers.

"What the hell do you want me to do with him?" Tommy looked at the dying man, crumpled on his knees before them.

"Whatever you want. I've done my part."

Tommy shook his head in frustration, before treading through the blood towards Lucas. He slid the knife into his back pocket and then reached down with his massive arms and pulled the fading Lucas to his feet. Lucas groggily stood, feeling the life pouring from him as the blood trickled from his stab wound, staining his jeans red.

Starling swallowed the vomit that had snuck up his throat, knowing he needed to remain calm and just get out of the shop. Everyone else seemed completely unmoved as Lucas was marched to the door.

Curtis straightened his tie and then stepped in front of Lucas one last time. He reached out, placing two fingers under Lucas's blood stained chin and gently lifted his face up. He looked into his increasingly vacant eyes.

"Look at you. You're pathetic."

Curtis smirked at Tommy who pushed the crestfallen Lucas forward. He hobbled towards the door, his hand pressed firmly against his side, the gun Tommy held prodding against his leather clad spine. Each step was harder than the last and he felt the fight leaving him with each passing second.

He had let Helen and Alex down.

Mark pushed open the door to the gym and Tommy forced Lucas through it, the beaten avenger leaning against the wooden bannister as he disappeared down the wooden stair case. Tommy followed behind and Mark closed the door.

For a few moments, the only noise that could be heard was the decreasing echo of their footsteps. Then silence.

Curtis lit a cigarette and triumphantly blew the smoke into the shop. It floated around the room like a cloud, hovering over the drips of blood leading from the door and back to the small puddle which had already fallen from Lucas. Curtis watched as Mark and Banner sat at the other desk, the latter lighting a cigarette as Mark began shuffling a deck of cards they'd been tossing back and forth earlier that evening.

They had done well tonight and with the rebuilding job Curtis had on his hands, he ring fenced them as being integral.

Tommy had been right. He had lost his grip. People would question how hard his grip was on the bollocks of London, especially as one man had managed to rip a hole through his empire and leave four of his family members facing a trip to the after-life.

As ironic as it was, considering he had just consigned Lucas to death, he was exactly the type of man Curtis would have wanted by his side.

He shook the image from his mind and took another long drag on his cigarette, the ash tumbling lightly to the floor.

His eyes locked onto those of Starling, who looked pale and increasingly uncomfortable.

Curtis enjoyed it.

"So," he said, approaching Starling, doing his best to present himself as intimidating. "You're the one who was fucking my sister, eh?"

Starling looked up, surprised by the question and was met with a firm stare from the head of the Drayton household. He mumbled nervously, trying hard not to show his fear despite the display of unrelenting brutality he'd just witnessed.

Curtis shrugged, hurrying him along.

"Well?"

"I-I-I loved her."

"Aww." Completely insincere. "That's sweet."

Curtis dropped the cigarette to the floor and stamped on it, crushing the flaming embers into the laminate flooring.

"I really did!" Starling said, painfully.

"Did you ever wonder why she never told you who she was?"

Curtis walked over to the bench again, picking up his cigarettes and lighting another one, enjoying the harsh, burning sensation as it clipped the back of his throat. He shook his empty glass in Mark's direction, turning away as the young man obliged and raced up to his office for a refill. Curtis then pulled out his custom designed Beretta from the inside of his blazer, holding it up to the light before returning it.

Starling wasn't sure if it was all a show for him, for him to witness what he was now expected to become.

"Did you?"

"Did I what?"

"Jesus fucking Christ. For a pig you ain't half shit at the whole listening thing."

"I guess she didn't want me to go running when I found out what her last name was."

"And why would you run?" A perverse pleasure clung to Curtis's words. Footsteps thudded down the stairs as Mark re-emerged, a full glass of scotch in his hand.

Curtis accepted it without a thank you.

"I wouldn't have." Starling finally responded.

Curtis stopped the glass halfway to his mouth, surprised.

"You wouldn't have?"

Starling shook his head, gambling at the wisdom of his

response. He reminded himself of what he had just witnessed, that the man before him had killed countless people and that Lucas Cole was facing the end of his life just a few feet below them.

"I would have tried to adjust."

Curtis chuckled, almost spitting his drink out as he took a large gulp. Starling smiled nervously.

"That's a good one." He chuckled some more. "Adjust."

"I would have made it work."

"Listen, mate. There's no adjusting on this side of the fence. You don't just make things work and sweep things under the rug."

"I loved Ashley, not the life she came from."

"You mean the life where she hand-picked girls for her brothers to bring to me? That life?" Curtis shook his head, taking another sip. He looked like he'd just won the lottery such was his celebratory demeanour. "Did you know that once, probably before you were on the scene, some woman pulled the fella she had her eye on in a club. She called Tommy, and after I gave her the once over, Ashley called to make sure she was dead?"

Starling felt his fists clench, a sudden rush of anger bursting through him at the accusation. He controlled himself somehow and Curtis smiled like a spoilt child playing with a new toy.

"Lighten up, Ollie."

He raised his glass at the regretful policeman, winking patronisingly at him. The deck of cards flicked rapidly as Banner shuffled them on the other side of the room. His shotgun lay on the table alongside an ashtray with a half burnt cigarette releasing smoke into the air.

Starling cleared his throat, straightening his back and standing firmly.

"'Like I said, I didn't love the life she had. I just loved her."

"So you came to me because you knew that I would take care of the situation?"

"In a way, yes."

"In a way?" Curtis's voice flickered quickly to irritated.

"Look, I wanted Lucas dead. It's funny, I watched him in the hospital room when he was told his wife had moments to live. I'd never seen pain like it."

Curtis smirked, taking a sip of drink as a liquid pat on the back. Starling felt his anger bubble again.

"Then, when he walked back out of that room, he was a different man. Any emotion he'd before had been struck off. Like someone had entered the playlist of his emotions and had deleted them."

Starling shook his head, re-treading the steps that had brought his enjoyable and well-planned life to this moment.

"But when I saw Annette's, sorry, Ashley's body, when they'd hauled her back in from the rain, I understood. I understood why he wanted you and your family dead. Because seeing her eyes open but her beauty gone rendered all my other emotions useless."

Curtis finished his glass, the ice clinking softly as he placed it down on the bench.

"I just wanted the person responsible for her death to go the same way."

Starling said the words to the floor, his head hanging low in shame. What would his father think? A man who'd boasted to everyone within earshot about the upstanding police officer his son was? Now here he stood, face to face with one of the most notorious criminals London had known and working alongside him to end another man's life.

This was not the path he'd wanted.

Curtis showed little sympathy as he walked towards him.

"Well he's dead now. For everything he's done and taken from us, he's gone the same way as everyone else. And if it's any consolation to you, Ollie, you helped."

The look on Starling's face told him it was not.

"But that's all done now, so now we need to discuss exactly what this means going forward. I could use a drink."

Curtis wrapped his arm around Starling's shoulder and the two men slowly walked through the shop towards the door leading to his office staircase. Curtis looked over at the two card players.

"When Tommy's finished playing with his food, tell him to come upstairs would you? We need to talk."

Mark nodded but didn't look away from the wonderful hand he'd been dealt. Starling stared at the pool of blood on the floor and could only imagine what Lucas was going through.

"See Ollie, the way it works is: people in this city, they fall in line. When I say jump, I don't want them to ask how high. You understand? I want them to just jump higher than they ever fucking have. Now I'm sure I'm all over your station, people always looking at ways that they can bring me down. I imagine right now, what with Lucas's irritating rampage, that opportunity is brighter than usual."

He smiled at Starling, who felt the unease of the man's forearm draped across his shoulder.

"You work for me now and that means that cannot happen. It won't take long. Once Tommy posts Lucas back to the police, body part by body part, the press will soon get the message."

Curtis stopped a few feet from the door. He turned and stood in front of Starling, adjusting his blazer lapels and locking his jet black eyes on the young officer.

"This city will be afraid of me again. I promise you that."

Starling sighed. He envisaged Annette's blonde hair against his face, the intoxicating aroma of her shampoo filling his nostrils. Her pretty smile flaring up unwillingly at his lame jokes.

Her heart-breaking giggle.

She was worth this. He told himself again. No matter what she'd done.

She was worth this.

"Now you've already proven to me that I can trust you. You played your part tonight to perfection and I am kind of impressed. You're a natural."

Starling felt Curtis goading him. He knew he couldn't rise to it.

"Now, like I said, the police are probably going to try and make a move and I need you to make sure that doesn't happen."

Starling was too busy looking at the floor, wallowing in his own self-hatred and wonderful memories of a love lost, to notice that Curtis had slid his hand into his blazer.

"What do you need me to do?"

He looked up, his eyes widening in horror at the gun that was in Curtis's hand.

They grew even wider at the sadistic, calm stare that sat on Curtis's face.

"I need you to die."

The explosion of the gun as it shot the bullet out rang around the shop like a firework. The bullet ripped through Starling's neck and slapped against the wall behind him, embedding itself in the plaster.

It was followed by an erratic splattering of Starling's blood.

Starling stumbled backwards, gargling as the blood

pooled out from the hole in his throat, more of it falling downwards and slowly filling up his lungs.

His eyes searched Curtis for any strands of help.

There were none.

He fell to the ground, coughing and spluttering, a scarlet pool quickly surrounding him.

Mark and Banner shuffled their cards.

"A dead cop is a hell of a message."

Starling heard the words trail off and footsteps ascending the stairs and growing quieter.

He stared at the ceiling tiles, the long bright lights that sat in their brackets.

As the blood gushed over his fingers that clasped to his throat, he tried to picture Annette a final time.

He slowly faded from consciousness.

CHAPTER TWENTY-EIGHT

Fletcher slammed the front door behind him with such force as he stomped into the house that the photo of his beloved Susan swung on its hook.

He refused to look at it, out of shame.

Thirty years as one of the most respected men to wear the Metropolitan Police uniform; it was all undone in one act of sympathy. He knew that helping Lucas had been a bad idea at the time, but he could see the man's need for vengeance. The pain that was locked around his body and slowly crushing him.

Now, as he walked through the dark hallway and into the equally dark living room, he would have to face the consequences of the events he'd set in motion.

He unzipped his coat, tossing it onto the back of the dusty sofa and rocking the living room as he marched his way to the kitchen. The house stank with the aroma of stale cigarettes, the plug-in air freshener by the doorway fighting a losing battle as its batteries slowly died.

He could relate.

He pulled the cord inside the kitchen doorway, the light

flickering a few times before casting its fading light over a dirty kitchen that was used sparingly. On the side was a bottle of Jack Daniel's, a third of its contents gone with the rest about to go the same way. He pulled open the cupboard above the sink and removed a dusty glass tumbler.

He ran it under the sink, the water crashing against his hand and forearm and his mind jumped back to a few nights earlier when he'd stood in the very same spot shaking after the Draytons had left.

His arm would be forever scarred from the night he'd defied them.

He shut off the water and scooped up a tea towel, sloppily drying the glass before slamming it down on the worktop.

A desperate hand reaching for the bottle.

Unscrewing its cap.

The whiskey cascading into the glass.

Fletcher hurriedly slapped around his pockets, located his cigarettes and retrieved the box. He pulled out a thin roll of nicotine and lazily tossed the box onto the side. It slid and rebounded off the bottle of Jack.

He placed the cigarette between his lips and before he lit it, he wondered what Susan would think.

Chain smoking. Alcoholic. Estranged from their kids. His grandkids. Destined to spend the last of his years rotting in a prison cell.

She would have been so ashamed.

But what did he have left?

What could he possibly have to offer the world when he had nothing to offer himself?

He clicked the lighter and as he drew it upwards, his eyes gazed over the fridge.

Christine and Annabelle's childish faces smiled from the photo, both of them dressed like princesses. Susan sat between them, the make-up they'd painted onto her face, making her look like a clown.

It was one of his most cherished memories.

He was still a father. He could still be a grandfather.

His eyes roved back through the living room to the desk sitting in front of the bay window, the curtains drawn to keep the world out of his business.

He let the cigarette drop to the floor.

With a quick scoop, Fletcher poured the whiskey down the sink. The rest of the bottle followed.

A few minutes later he walked into the living room with a hot cup of coffee in hand as he approached the masses of papers that reminded him of a job he'd never go back to. He pulled the chair back and sat down, placing the mug of coffee to the side and lifted the lid on the laptop.

As it booted up, he shifted through the random scrawlings, trying to impose some degree of order.

He leant over and switched on his police radio, turning the volume down to no louder than a whisper, the world of crime quietly providing the backing track as he began typing, allowing his memoirs to flow from his fingertips.

Lucas stumbled off the final wooden step, tumbling forward and landing onto the firm mats carpeting Tommy's gym. He breathed heavily, the pain of his stab wound doing its best to keep him grounded. He received a firm kick in the ribs.

"Get up!"

Tommy stood above him, the gun casually swinging in his hand. Bright lights burst from the ceiling, illuminating the gym with a polished glow. Everything was meticulously placed, every weight lined up properly, the two benches in alignment by the mirror on the far wall.

Lucas could barely register anything, his vision swirling as colours and shapes merged into one another. He pushed himself upwards, blood trickling down his face and splashing onto the mats.

It joined the small puddle from the hole in his side.

He staggered to his feet, swaying slightly, his head spinning. The firm metal of a gun prodded him in the spine and he slowly took an aimless step forward, his feet dragging across the mats.

Tommy took measured steps behind him, his quiet voice not suiting his hulking frame.

"It was always going to end this way, Lucas."

More shuffled steps. Lucas could barely see out of his right eye, the swelling from Curtis's cheap shot was covering his eyeball. Blood eased itself from the opening above, trickling down his swollen cheek.

"Don't get me wrong, there were a few moments when I thought you might actually pull this off, that I'd be another Drayton for you to tick off your sheet. But ultimately, I knew it would end like this. Deep down, you did too."

Lucas couldn't answer, his breath struggling to filter in and out of his lungs. He wanted every step to be towards Helen, for her to be waiting for him with her arms open and a smile on her face.

Soon, he told himself.

"Now Curtis - Curtis is all show. I mean he *is* an evil fucker, but most of it's for show. The whole high and mighty thing he did with you up there; that was for him as much as it was for you. You've shown him something recently that no one ever had before. That even he can be vulnerable."

Tommy prodded Lucas forward a few more steps, a large black structure manifesting in Lucas's eye line. Blood slowly dripped from his side and to the mats below.

"And I really don't think he can handle it. I don't. He likes the fact that you, the public, the police all look at him like he's the devil. He feeds off it. It's allowed him to build an empire that for a long time has been untouchable. Until you came along."

The black structure grew, looming over Lucas like a dark wall. He wondered if it was the pathway to the other side, knowing the things he'd done would not lead him towards a lighter after-life. His foot clipped against a step.

"He is actually terrified of you, Lucas. I've never seen fear in the man like the way you put it in him. The way you came after us, the relentless thirst for vengeance. The violence you put our family through. It shit him up. He's probably up there right now, begging I put a bullet in your head and set you on fire so you don't get back up."

Tommy chuckled, shoving Lucas forward. His shins hit the step and he fell onto another hard floor. The floor beneath him shook slightly, echoing the noise of his impact.

"Me? I'm actually kind of impressed by it all."

Tommy stepped up and through the door to the black MMA cage which had housed hundreds of hours of his life.

"I mean, you don't believe in the chaos of it all. You're like me. You believe in the violence. The truth within the violence and how people react when it comes for them. You either face it or you flee it. Either way, it'll get you. Curtis would flee. If he didn't have me or the now dwindling numbers around him, he would have fled from you a long time ago."

Tommy slammed the cage door shut, locking them both within the octagon structure. Lucas slowly crawled away from Tommy, reaching the black, mesh wall of his prison. He pushed weak, bloody fingers through the holes in the metal and pulled his battered body to its feet.

Tommy looked on with a glint in his eye. He tossed the gun towards the door and began stretching his arms.

"He underestimated you. I think we all did, really. However the time has come, Lucas, for this whole journey of yours to end. But before that I want you to know something. Yes, I did kill your wife. But it wasn't anything personal. It just had to be done."

The fence of the octagon reached all the way up to the roof of the gym, the panels connected by thick padded beams in each corner. Tommy slid the knife that had shed the blood of the man before him and his wife, and stabbed it into one of the padded beams with great force.

"Alex. Well that was just retribution. I mean, there have to be repercussions."

Lucas heard the words as he straightened up, his broken chest pressing against the cage. The calm in the voice as it relayed the murders of those he held dear made him shake with an anger he could barely muster. Tommy continued.

"You killed my friend. You killed three of my brothers and you killed my little sister. I can't let that slide."

Lucas pushed himself off the cage, turning feebly as he struggled to stay up on weary legs. His face was unrecognisable, the damage from Curtis's fists evident in the blood and bruising. His nose was crooked and broken, wheezing slightly as he breathed. Blood had covered the entire front of his shirt, with more of it dripping from his favoured leather jacket.

His life was slowly escaping from the hole that had been cut into his side.

Tommy stared at him as he limbered his shoulders, stretching out his neck before raising his fists as if ready for a competitive fight.

"I would have loved to have fought you at a hundred percent."

With that, Tommy burst forward with staggering speed, launching himself into the air as he swung down a violent right fist that slammed into Lucas's cheek. Lucas stumbled back into the cage fence, a tooth zipping out his mouth and crashing to the mat in a bloody splat. Tommy weaved slightly, like a professional boxer, before sending a hard, pinpoint left hook into Lucas's midriff. He collided again with the fence, the little air in his body shooting out of him like a cannon.

He tried to stay on his feet, the power and energy that had brought the other Draytons to their death had left him. He tried to pull himself up straight as Tommy stalked him slowly, like a lion about to catch its dinner. As soon as Lucas planted both feet firmly on the mat, Tommy lunged forward, his legs pivoting as he raised a hard knee that shattered into the broken ribs.

Lucas hit the cage again, rebounding off the black chain links behind him and Tommy thrust the bone of his elbow into the side of Lucas's head.

Lucas hit the mat hard, blood and rainwater spraying off him on impact.

Tommy stood on the spot, loosening his arms as he bounced on the spot, his enjoyment evident. He hadn't even broken a sweat and he watched gleefully as Lucas slowly pushed himself up again, his refusal to die admirable.

The broken widower weakly clambered to all fours, his arms shaking under the weight of his own body. Tommy stamped a hard boot down onto his spine, pinning him to the mat. A few more crunching stomps hammered Lucas's back, each one driving the air and will to fight from him.

Soon he would be with Helen.

Soon.

Tommy reached down with powerful arms, wrenching Lucas up by the scruff of his leather jacket. Tommy shoved him backwards, his legs like jelly as he collided with the padded beam between two panels. He stayed standing and tried to raise his fists, but the agony of his crushed ribs and the burning pain of his stab wound meant that he could barely muster anything.

Tommy responded with a jaw shaking uppercut that sent Lucas tumbling backwards and he watched with pride as the man responsible for killing his sister turned in the air and landed hard on his chest in the centre of the cage.

Lucas was finished.

As the mammoth man paced around his prone body, Lucas felt himself beginning to shut down. The pain was subsiding in his abdomen, the loss of blood beginning to create an almost soothing calm.

He closed his eyes, saying a silent goodbye to the world.

Tommy checked his knuckles, they were split from the impact of the punch and he carelessly shook the blood off of them.

"You know, you make a lot less noise when I punch you in the face than your wife did."

Lucas's eyes shot open.

Lying directly in front of him, Helen's face was turned up to meet his with burning blue eyes. Tommy's words resonated with both of them.

She stared at Lucas with a determination pouring from her pupilless eyes.

"Get up."

Her words echoed louder than before and Lucas remembered why he'd done what he had, why he'd come back to London.

To kill those responsible for the death of his wife.

He blinked and Helen was gone.

All he could hear was the pacing footsteps of the man who'd killed his wife and had beaten him to the verge of death.

Tommy was waiting for him.

With gritted teeth, Lucas pressed both hands down against the mat and pushed, his back rising upwards until his knees slid forward. Then, despite the pain that was squeezing his insides, he rose to his feet, his legs feeling firmer as he stood before Tommy.

The Drayton looked impressed. Lucas's eyes conveyed only hatred. Tommy met the stare, the two men reaching an understanding that this was it.

Tommy stepped forward and swung a right, but Lucas threw up an arm and blocked it immediately, then sent Tommy a few steps back with a hard right hook to the nose. His eyes watered and he felt its sting but he shook it off, throwing another punch, this time with his left hand.

Lucas dodged it, took a step to the side and cracked Tommy in the side of the jaw with a brutal straight right. He stumbled to the side, trying to swing a firm kick towards Lucas, who grabbed his leg, pulled him inwards and shattered Tommy's nose with a ferocious head butt.

Tommy hit the mat, blood pouring down his shocked face. Lucas wobbled on the spot, his wounds trying their best to overcome him as he raised his fists again.

Tommy needed no further invitation.

He pushed forward, throwing a few hard rights that collided with Lucas's broken body, before he swung one towards Lucas's jaw. Lucas dodged, grabbing the arm at the wrist, before ploughing an elbow back along the arm into Tommy's jaw. The blow rocked Tommy, before Lucas held his grip on the wrist firmly and twisted it, so Tommy's arm straightened out.

He then thrust his elbow down on Tommy's forearm with the remaining strength he had.

Tommy's radius shattered, the forearm bending backwards as Lucas clutched his wrist firmly. Tommy roared in agony, before pushing Lucas away with his left hand. He took a few steps in retreat, his right arm hanging loosely, the wrist pointing in the wrong direction as the bone swung from its clean snap.

As Lucas took another step towards him, Tommy loosely swung his left, but Lucas grabbed it, stretched it, then ducked down and rammed his shoulder upwards into the bone.

It snapped as brutally as the other had.

Lucas relinquished his hold and Tommy stumbled backwards, his forearms shattered. His bloody face stared at them, the shock and the pain taking him out of the cage as he stood blankly, staring downwards. He was launched backwards by a firm teep kick that Lucas somehow mustered the energy for.

Tommy collided with the cage and Lucas, with his last burst of strength stepped forward quickly, pulled the knife that protruded from the pad and then lunged at Tommy.

He pinned him against the fence and their eyes met as the knife plunged through Tommy's skin and deep into his stomach.

Tommy's eyes widened, the bloody faces of the two men mere inches apart. Lucas stared at Tommy with disgust, pushing his entire weight into both hands that held the knife inside him.

Tommy choked a little and coughed, blood pouring from his mouth.

He began to shake, the knife ripping into his internal organs and slowly shutting him down. Lucas's arm shook with the pressure and he imagined Helen lying on the floor, beaten and attacked by Curtis and watching helplessly as Tommy approached with the very knife he now held.

He relinquished one of his hands from the blade handle and willed it into his pocket. He clenched his fingers around the wedding ring, his symbol of Helen, and squeezed it tightly.

He then pulled the knife across, the blade ripping open Tommy's stomach, before stepping away.

He didn't look back as Tommy dropped to his knees, a waterfall of blood pouring from his abdomen followed by his shredded insides.

He collapsed forward.

Lucas dragged his feet forward, the willingness to see this through to the end pushing him towards the door of the cage. He grasped the metal and lowered himself gently, the pain reminding him that his time was approaching fast.

He reached a tired, weak arm towards the mat and clasped his fingers around the handle of Tommy's handgun.

With the firearm hanging loosely from his grasp, Lucas pushed open the cage door and slowly descended to the gym floor.

He followed his own trail of blood back towards the wooden steps, as Tommy's corpse began to engulf the cage in a sea of his blood.

CHAPTER TWENTY-NINE

Curtis took the most expensive bottle of scotch from his cabinet and strode merrily across his large, well decorated office to his desk. He spun the bottle in his hand and was a step away from whistling. The glass was set down and he watched as the golden liquid flowed neatly from the neck of the bottle.

It tasted just as warm as it looked.

He exhaled his relief.

His fingers danced along the top of his desk to a small, well carved oak box with a smooth velvet lining. Housed within were his finest cigars, which, when lit, tasted almost as delightful as his scotch.

Curtis poured another glass and then walked around the desk, followed by a cloud of thick, grey smoke. He dropped into the leather chair and leant back, the padded cushions providing the comfort that he felt was well earned.

Sitting there, enjoying the luxuries the life he'd built had bestowed upon him, he knew Lucas Cole was likely dead. Tommy wouldn't take any chances with him, more than likely opening him up a few more times with the knife before removing the body from the premises.

The world was almost back to how it should be. He would need to adjust, four of his family members were brutally slain and at some point he would have to accept that it was his actions that had drawn Lucas towards them. But they'd known the consequences of his requests, knowing full well that he didn't set them up with the businesses they ran for everything to be above board.

In fact, he needed another release.

Having Tommy capture a woman for him, to see that fear in her eyes as he walked towards her while she was bound and exposed would top the evening off completely.

He took a sip of his drink, contemplating whether Tommy would cater to such a request.

A few puffs of the cigar sent a thicker, darker cloud up to the spotless fan hanging down from the painted ceiling.

Curtis stared at the knife on his desk, placed neatly on its stand, the very knife which had ended his father's life and had set him on his pathway to domination. He decided that another stand would be acquired to proudly display the knife which had defeated Lucas Cole.

He reached into his blazer and removed the Beretta, the nozzle still warm from the bullet that had ended Starling's life.

Curtis felt nothing, pleased to remove the man of the law from his life as quickly as he'd entered. His sister deserved better than a fucking policeman. She deserved better than to be hung from the window for the world to see.

Curtis had ensured that both of those problems had been eradicated.

He took a final sip of his scotch and then checked his watch. It angered him when Tommy decided to take his time with things, his usual efficiency sometimes swept aside for his more sadistic urges.

He sighed.

He wanted to discuss the way forward, maybe ask Mark and Banner to run the golfing range and The Hive while they recruited a few more men to the cause. He wanted to discuss it now.

With one hand, Curtis carefully poured himself another glass of the golden, luxury beverage, whilst the other thumbed through the screen on his phone. He shut off the Phone Finder app as it had served its purpose wonderfully.

He called Mark.

He answered on the first ring.

"Yes, sir?"

"Give Tommy a shout will you. Tell him to stop touching Lucas up, kill the prick and get his arse up here."

"Yes, Sir."

Curtis dropped his phone on the desk and smirked at the obedience he demanded from men like Mark. He toasted himself, for ending Lucas Cole and for the beginning of his re-structure.

A few moments later he stood to attention, with a panic shaking his body and an expression of fear gripping his face.

The commotion he heard, the crashing of bodies against tables, the yelling that followed and the gun shots told him two things:

Tommy was dead.

Lucas was alive.

Curtis looked around his office, trapped by the only escape route leading straight down to the warzone. He wished Tommy was there, he would always handle a situation that could potentially get out of hand.

He was dead. Curtis knew it.

With his hand shaking, Curtis picked up his gun and tried to decide where in his office he could possibly hide.

Mark had hung up his phone after Curtis's request and had slapped his cards down on the table. Banner held his close to him so Mark couldn't catch a glimpse of them and then reached over his shotgun to tap his cigarette in the increasingly full ashtray.

Mark shot a glance at the body of Starling lying in the middle of the shop, aware that he would be requested to mop up the glinting pool of blood around it. He didn't mind, he knew he'd be made once he'd helped Curtis through this evening.

He'd be one of the few men left standing, one of the people who'd helped Curtis avenge his family's deaths.

Curtis would never forget that. Mark would never let him.

Starling shuddered slightly, a faint gasp resonating from his motionless body as he clung to the last few strands of rope.

Mark smirked, he hated the police and it gave him pleasure to watch this young pig die.

He reached for the door and as he pulled it slightly, it suddenly swung at full speed, cracking him square on the eyebrow. He stumbled back, his face colliding with the side of the raised bench as Lucas kicked the door open.

As Mark fell to the ground, Lucas stumbled through, his body trying its best to function and keep him standing. The cigarette dropped from Banner's mouth in shock and moments later, he reached for the shotgun by his side.

Lucas had somehow mustered the energy to lift his arm, the gun hanging lazily in his palm. He gripped it and pulled the trigger.

The bullet flew through the side of Banner's skull, ripping out through the cheek on the other side of his head. The flesh tore open as the metallic ball burst through, followed by an explosion of blood and teeth which rattled against the table and scattered across the floor like a box of tic-tac's.

Banner slumped from his chair and was dead before he hit the ground. The shotgun clattered to the floor beside him.

Lucas took a few stunted, shuffled steps forward but was then falling as Mark tackled him. He wrapped his arms around Lucas's knees, dropping him to the ground and then climbing on top of him. His eyebrow was gushing blood, the misshapen cheekbone giving the indication that it had cracked against the desk. With a chance to become the man to kill Lucas Cole, Mark batted away Lucas's feeble attempts at defence and clamped both hands around his thickly muscled neck.

He began to crush his fingers inwards, pushing down on Lucas's windpipe. Lucas stared up at him, his bloody wreck of a face gasping for air as his weak, lifeless arms tried to fend Mark off.

He just didn't have the strength. He had come this far, but this was it. His fingers pressed against the thick, short metal barrels of the shotgun.

The room was blurring.

Oxygen couldn't get through.

The blood loss was increasing.

Mark pushed down with his full weight, his eyes wide and wild.

"Just die"

Lucas pulled up the shotgun and with his last remaining effort, pulled back the trigger.

The noise shook the entire betting shop, the buck of the shotgun pushing it back into his already shattered ribs.

The spray of bullets connected just above Mark's top lip, eradicating the upper part of his skull. Similar to blowing dust off the top of an old book, it simply sprayed the entirety of his face into the air. His eyes, nose, head, all reduced to nothing but blood and pieces of flesh. Brain fragments rained back down from the ceiling which now sported a fresh coat of red.

The remainder of Mark fell forward on top of Lucas, the body twitching as the nervous system shut itself down. Lucas managed to push him to the side, a thick, current flow of blood pouring from the space where Mark's face had used to be. The once immaculate floor of the betting shop was now a slippery pool of death.

Lucas took a few moments to force air back into his lungs, refuting the idea of allowing Helen to take him with her and leave the world behind.

There was still Curtis.

With a groan of sheer agony, he pushed himself forward, sitting up and looking at the two dead bodies that had been added to his rampage. Both of them lay motionless, blood pouring out from two very different gunshot wounds.

Lucas felt nothing for them.

Across the floor, he saw the statuesque body of Starling, lying in his own blood, his chest expanding and relaxing with a fatal irregularity. He hauled himself forward, his hand still clasped around the snub-nosed shotgun and he crawled across the floor, his hands dipping in and out of the blood of men he'd killed as he scrambled forward.

A gut wrenching gurgling sound hummed from Starling as he drowned slowly, his lungs almost full of his own blood. He couldn't feel the pain anymore.

Lucas eventually made his way to his side, dropping back and sitting next to the young officer. Despite the deception, he knew he was looking at a man who'd tried to save his wife. Who'd done everything he could to try and keep her in this world.

A man who hated him for killing the woman he'd loved.

He understood, knowing what it was like to be driven mad with the rage of vengeance, wanting the violence gifted to a loved one to be returned to its vendor ten-fold.

Starling's eyes radiated nothing but fear, a scared acknowledgement that he was about to die.

Lucas reached a broken, blood-covered hand forward, expelling more of his precious energy to reach out and clasp his hand over Starling's. The dying police officer gripped it, squeezing it as if he was clutching to the edge of a life boat.

He choked a little, drops of blood jumping from his open mouth before falling back in and inevitably pouring through the hole in his neck.

His pupils were dilating.

Lucas offered him a comforting smile.

"I'm sorry."

His words tumbled out and he wasn't even sure that the young man had heard them. His blonde hair was thick and matted, his own blood styling it however it saw fit.

Outside, the rain crashed against the metal shutter that contained them.

Starling heard the words and with his penultimate act on this earth, he squeezed Lucas's hand as a way of acceptance.

Lucas nodded his gratitude. With his eyes locked on the last face he would see, Starling weakly lifted a quivering hand to the radio that clung to his Met vest. His fingers, stained a dark red, fumbled over the device until they'd found the red panic button.

He clicked it.

Bailey was standing with his hands on his hips, conveying a feeling of irritation as Officer Hatton stood before him.

"So, nothing then?" His question was blunt and uncaring.

"I'm afraid not, sir. Officer Chamberlain says they've swept his house for a second time and they've had round the clock patrols of the village. They've asked everyone on the few surrounding streets but nothing."

Bailey tutted and shook his head. Hatton sympathised with the pressure he was under.

"No one has seen Lucas Cole, sir."

Bailey reached a powerful arm backwards, scratching the small of his back. He felt tired, the power nap he'd stolen after admonishing Fletcher had only exacerbated his need for sleep.

"So what do we have then? He was there, but now he's not. Is he back in London?"

Hatton diverted her delicate face towards her notepad, her brunette ponytail swinging freely.

"Umm, we're not sure, sir. His car has gone. Chamberlain checked the itinerary from the last sweep and it's missing. So common sense dictates that he's taken his car."

Bailey's eyes lit up hopefully.

"Do we have the plates?"

"Yes, sir."

"Then I want them circulated to every goddamn police district between here and Brinscall. He will show up somewhere and I want us to know the second that happens."

Hatton nodded, her youthful exuberance almost too much for Bailey as he ignored the perils of middle age trying to ensnare him. She turned and marched off towards an empty desk, a renewed purpose in her step.

"Hey, Hatton."

The young officer turned, her immersive green eyes locked on him with intrigue. It was a rare occasion where Bailey showed the world his smile.

"Good job."

She smiled and immediately tried hard to disguise it. She then disappeared into the hive of activity in the office beyond. Bailey let out a deep sigh, his eyes straining, trying to remind him of his exhaustion.

He removed his glasses and rubbed them thoroughly, trying his best to remove any thoughts or feelings of stopping.

He needed to catch Lucas Cole.

This whole situation had got out of hand. As he slid his glasses back on, he trudged with lumbering steps to the briefing room, to the large wall of evidence that had been amassed over the previous few weeks. There would be nothing new waiting for him; he was merely using it as a distraction.

The thought of digging into Paul Fletcher's background, a police officer he'd had nothing but kind words and admiration for, was not a job he looked forward to. The idea of rummaging through the facts and finding the inevitable guilt was hard to stomach. The man would be arrested, his long, highly decorated career with the Metropolitan Police would be tarnished, maybe even forgotten.

The old man wouldn't survive in prison, but if the facts held together then there was no alternative.

He, Robert Bailey, would send Paul Fletcher down for his remaining years.

The very thought erupted in a spasm of anger as he walked through the door to the briefing room and in one powerful swing, he pulled a plastic chair from the row and hurled it across the empty room. It clattered into a number of others, the crash echoing out of the room and arousing the attention of a number of hardworking officers.

Bailey stomped over to the board, looking at the photos of the dead Draytons, the maps with the circles drawn around them and the post-it notes with details scribbled across them.

It told him nothing.

"Where are you, you son of a bitch?!"

Bailey muttered the words to himself, his eyes locked on the photo of a smiling Lucas. He knew that the man would probably never smile again.

He didn't even know if he was still alive.

Suddenly, knuckles rapped gently against the door. He turned sharply, his eyes narrowing in on the young radio operator, Cheryl, who he had only ever spoken to a few times. She was a lot smaller than he remembered, her ginger hair hanging in a short bob beside her concerned face.

"What?"

"Sir, we've just had notification of a panic button being pressed."

"Then act upon it. Send officers to the scene immediately and ensure I get a full report as soon as they arrive."

He turned back to the board, scowling hateful eyes at the array of evidence that had so far failed to bear fruit.

Cheryl coughed slightly.

"Sir, the radio was last signed out by Officer Starling."

Bailey spun round, the mention of the name grabbing him instantly. He hadn't seen the man since that fateful night for Ashley Drayton, when he'd thrown his badge away in disgust and marched away in the rain.

The man was finished as a police officer.

"Why the hell is Starling radioing in a distress call?"

He loomed over the young operator, who cowered

beneath his intimidating frame. A few officers peeked up from their desks, intrigued by the conversation.

"I don't know, sir. Officers are on their way to his location."

Bailey marched through the doorway, heading for his desk to retrieve the rest of his essential gear before he headed to his patrol car. Cheryl scurried after him, her high heels clomping on the tile floor.

"Sir, that's not all of it."

He turned to her, his eyes begging her to tell him.

"The location is coming from two-eight-four Brixton High Street."

Bailey's voice left him. He knew that address without even having to think. Starling was in the Drayton's betting shop and he was under threat. Regardless of what the man had done or his lack of respect, he wasn't going to leave one of his men to the wolves.

He leaned in towards Cheryl, his voice low.

"Get every available unit heading to that location. Get me an Armed Response team waiting for me at that location immediately. Go. Now!"

Cheryl scuttled off, clicking her way through the office as fast as she could. Bailey slapped his cuffs and baton onto his belt and then wrenched his arms into the sleeves of his luminous coat.

"Everyone not dealing with a life or death, follow me right fucking now."

His voice boomed across the open plan office and the majority of the officers leapt from their desks, rushing after their superior as he jogged down the corridor, and bursting out into the pouring rain.

He ran to his car and was pulling away within seconds. A fleet of flashing lights and sirens followed, howling through the London night in the blue glow they provided.

The only light in Fletcher's flat was the desk lamp illuminating his desk, its glow lighting the newly organised piles of notes. The laptop hummed slightly, as the fifteenth page of the recently typed memoir finished at the end of a well-written paragraph. The lights of the screen shot out towards an empty chair.

The moment the location was announced on the radio, Fletcher darted to the sofa to retrieve his coat.

He was still putting it on as he raced through his front door into the downpour.

Starling's hand didn't leave the radio.

His fingers clasped it tightly in their final moments, his other hand wrapped around Lucas's. His eyes stared directly upwards, the beaming lights from above reflecting in their lifelessness.

The gurgling had stopped. So had the pain.

Lucas grimaced as he looked at the young man, drawn into a world he'd tried to keep at bay. He had tried to do the right thing, by Helen, by Lucas, even by the Draytons. All it got him was the love of his life taken from him, followed by his senseless murder.

Lucas understood the betrayal. He had slaughtered the woman Starling had loved. He would be drenched in hypocrisy if he couldn't relate.

He gently reached a shuddering hand forward, his fingers delicately stroking the eyelids downwards, shutting out the light and allowing Starling to drift off towards those whom he had loved and lost.

He could go to Ashley.

With a grunt of anguish, Lucas pressed the shotgun to

the floor, using it for support as he pushed himself back to his feet. His legs trembled under the pressure of supporting his body.

He felt loose and dizzy, the loss of blood leading him towards a final goodbye.

He fought against it.

There was still one more thing to do.

He reached into his pocket and pulled out Helen's wedding ring, his link to the love that this whole crusade had been for.

He squeezed it with a blood-soaked fist.

With slow, pain-riddled scuffs, he trudged to the doorway that led up towards Curtis Drayton, the shotgun hanging loosely from the other.

CHAPTER THIRTY

Each footstep took longer than the last. The weight of each clomp was exaggerated by the echo of the stair well as Lucas slowly climbed it. Curtis heard each step grow louder, ducked down by the side of the door frame with his gun trembling in his petrified grasp.

With every footstep, Curtis winced, wondering what it would take to kill this man. The gun shots told him that Mark and Banner had been killed, two more useless obstructions obliterated by this unstoppable tide of vengeance that was now climbing the steps with calculated, measured steps.

Curtis didn't know that, with each step, a weaker foot followed, a thicker bloodstain remained. Never had a situation arisen like this, where Curtis was left to fend for himself. Not since all those years ago, when his bastard of a father had beat him senseless. Even then, he knew he had his family behind him.

They proved that the night they'd gutted George like a fish.

Now he was alone. The only way to freedom was through the man who would die trying to kill him.

The gun rattled in his hand and he tried to control his breathing. Crouched down beside the door to his office, he was hoping to welcome his assailant with a bullet to the skull as he entered.

Having forged a life off the deaths of others, Curtis had begun to feel immortal. His own life had never been in danger and without his siblings around him, he sat in genuine fear.

Another step.

Curtis checked that his gun was loaded.

The footsteps stopped. They'd reached the top of the staircase. Lucas was on the other side of the door that Curtis had closed in a panic earlier.

The handle turned slowly, the mechanism creaking slowly under the pressure.

The door gradually glided open.

Lucas darted through the door and Curtis opened fire, unloading four bullets at the movement before him.

Lucas's leather jacket, the final gift his wife had got him before she was senselessly eradicated, flopped to the ground.

Moments before, as he waited before the door, Lucas had eased himself carefully out of the jacket, leaning the shotgun against the wall. He didn't know anything about firearms and wasn't even sure it was still loaded. The horrible wound in his side, courtesy of the man he was about to face, still leaked, his entire jean leg a horrible shade of red.

He slowly opened the door, half expecting a bullet to fly through and send him to Helen.

Nothing.

With as much force as he could muster, Lucas tossed the jacket over the threshold and into the tastefully decorated office, the desk sitting a sizeable distance from the door.

As the coat was mid-air, gunshots rang out from the left, bullets ripping through his most precious item of clothing.

Curtis had given away his position.

Before the final Drayton realised, Lucas stepped in on an unsteady foot and drove the back of the shotgun into Curtis's skull, the thick, wooden butt cracking him just above the eyelid.

Curtis tipped back, his feet sliding from under him as he collided with a bookshelf, knocking a few to the ground and following them swiftly. He cried out in pain, his gun falling to the floor amongst the chaos.

Lucas stumbled in, blood smearing the wall as he shuffled across after his adversary.

Curtis pushed the books away and crawled across the floor, whimpering.

"Please, Lucas. Don't do this."

Pathetic words from a pathetic man, and words that fell on deaf ears.

Lucas tried to raise the shotgun, but suddenly felt a surge of pain, a hand gripping him from the after-life and trying to pull him through.

The shotgun clattered to the floor.

He dropped to one knee.

He squeezed Helen's wedding band, his eyes closed as he pictured her. She was reaching out to him from her deathbed.

Curtis scrambled into the middle of the office, his eyes focused on the knife on his desk. He had never wanted to tarnish the blade with another man's blood, but he was desperate. He managed to get to his feet.

Lucas slowly picked up the gun that Curtis had dropped and took aim.

He pulled the trigger.

The bullet whizzed through the air and Lucas felt as if

he was watching it travel in slow motion, everything in the room appearing to blur out around it. The gun barrel shunted back into place in his hand and the bullet drilled a hole through Curtis's calf muscle.

Curtis collapsed forward, his outstretched arm a few inches from the edge of the desk. He howled in pain, the blood pouring from the back of his tailored trousers.

Lucas dropped his aim, his arm swinging loosely as he pushed himself up, his fist clenched around the wedding ring.

Each step brought him closer to Curtis. Closer to the end of it all.

Curtis had managed to pull himself to his knees, the pain burning his leg as he moaned for mercy.

"Please, Lucas."

Curtis looked up at the man he'd wronged, seeing the horrendous state of his face, the beatings he'd persevered through just to make these final steps. His clothes were heavy with blood, some of which was dripping from the rip in the side of his shirt and splattering delicate drops on the floor.

Lucas stopped a few feet from Curtis. The gun in his hand slowly rose.

Curtis looked at him, tears falling from his eyes. This man had taken everything from him as he'd promised: his brothers, his sister, and his strong grip on the city. Everything that Curtis had had was now gone.

There was no power anymore.

Curtis let the tears roll down his cheeks, weeping at the realisation of what he'd caused. He had raped a woman he hadn't cared about and had had her killed. For that, he had witnessed the swift and violent dismantling of his family. They had had bones shattered, body parts removed and they had all known it was because of him.

Because of his actions.

The barrel of the gun pointed at his head.

Curtis roared a mighty scream of emotional anguish and then looked up at Lucas. Their eyes met.

Both of them shed a tear.

Through the violent clattering of rain against the window, they heard the distant wailing of sirens.

The Drayton headquarters no longer held any fear for the Metropolitan Police. Curtis wiped a tear away and took a breath.

"Just fucking kill me."

Lucas's hand shook, pulling the trigger would send the bullet straight through Curtis's temple and it would all be over. He would have killed the man who had raped his wife.

But what about all the other women?

All the other families who'd been dismantled and torn apart by the fallen monster cowering before him. They wouldn't see this as their vengeance.

He shook his head clear and refocused his aim. His arm straightening, he pushed the gun closer to Curtis's skull.

The sirens grew louder.

"Just pull the fucking trigger!"

Lucas's finger stretched around the small, curved trigger.

A ghostly hand reached out, the delicate fingers wrapping themselves around Lucas's arm. Helen floated beside him, her soft touch tightening around his blood-spattered forearm. He felt her trying to pull his arm away.

Trying to get him to stop.

He knew it wasn't real. It was his projection of what he knew she would want. For him to stop. For him to put the gun down.

Lucas shrugged the arm off and pressed the gun against the weeping Curtis's forehead, the man a pathetic, frightened mess. A small stream of urine joined the blood oozing from his trouser leg, pooling around him.

He tried to pull the trigger.

The soft, wispy fingers rested themselves on Lucas's cheek, trying to turn his face and remove him from another murder.

He fought against it, another tear rolling down his cheek as he tried to ignore her. He tried to forget her voice telling him that he wasn't violent. That he was a good man.

She pulled with all her might, forcing Lucas to turn from Curtis and look at her.

Their eyes met.

She looked beautiful. It was the only time his memory had done her justice. Her angelic smile reached out and pressed down on Lucas's broken heart. Her blonde hair danced gently by the side of her face and for a moment, Lucas almost believed she had returned.

She slowly shook her head.

She didn't want another death in her name.

Not even Curtis.

With everything that had transpired, what did the man have left? The death of the entire family he'd held so dearly on his conscience. The police moments away from bursting through the door, ready to repay him for his years of tyranny.

The man had begged, cried and wet himself through fear.

He was nothing.

Lucas stared through his swollen eye at his wife, his fist still squeezing what was rightfully hers. Her soft, glowing hand ghosted forward and wrapped around his fist and he felt her touch encase his hand.

She moved in close to him, his body was shaking at the severity of his injuries.

Her piercing blue eyes searched his, she didn't need any words to tell him how much she had loved him.

He could feel her hand squeeze his tighter.

Then, with her other arm, she guided a spectral hand towards his face.

Sirens wailed loudly.

The rain lashed against the building.

Curtis wept softly.

Lucas heard none of it.

Her finger pressed the tip of his nose and pushed it upwards. He felt her touch.

He opened his eyes, allowing the tears to fall down as her face creased into a cute little scowl and she oinked at him.

He chuckled through his tears, remembering how often she would do it to him, how adorable she was when she did her impression.

He nodded his head.

There would not be another death in her name.

She slid her arms around his muscular, beaten body and pressed her head against his ever slowing heartbeat. He closed his eyes, feeling a closeness to her that he hadn't felt since she'd been taken from him.

He opened them a second later and she was gone.

The room was darker again, the radiance of his wife having momentarily illuminated everything around them. All there was now was Curtis, knelt down in a pool of blood and piss. He was still weeping, begging for Lucas to finish everything and not let the police take him. Lucas stepped in front of Curtis, the gun hanging in his hand.

Curtis, with blood trickling from the cut above his eye, tipped his head back to meet his gaze.

"Just fucking do it."

Lucas raised the gun.

Curtis closed his eyes.

He pulled the trigger.

Curtis screamed in agony, the gun not pointed at his head. The bullet burrowed its way through his crotch, ripping through his genitals. The pain grabbed and shook him with a violent rage, the blood pumping out from the wound where his manhood used to be.

It was the final thing Lucas wanted to take from him.

Curtis rolled around in anger, the blood and urine covering his back as he howled in agony. Lucas looked down at him.

It was over.

"Lucas. Don't go."

Curtis reached out a bloody hand as Lucas took his first step back towards the door, trying to grab at the cuff of his jeans. Lucas stepped back, looking down at Curtis with an emotionless stare.

Curtis vomited a little to the side, his once snarling face a pale definition of fear.

"Please, Lucas. Kill me. Just kill me."

Lucas looked at the window, the raindrops ricocheting off the glass panes and back into the sky. The sirens were nearly here.

They were welcome to Curtis if they could save him.

He looked down at the pitiful man clutching at him, begging him for the easy way out.

"I *have* killed you."

With that, Lucas stepped away, his feet dragging him across the floor and away from the desperate reach of Curtis, his other hand pressing down on the feminising wound between his legs. Lucas's steps splashed through the blood of a rapist.

As he got to the door, he dropped the gun and staggered a little, his moments fleeting.

He reached down with difficulty, clutching his leather

jacket as he returned upright. He slid it on, the leather accommodating a few bullet holes.

Curtis screamed after him as he took the steps one at a time, his bloody hand leaving a smeared print down the entire wall of the stairwell.

He glanced around the shop as he walked through, the three bodies all motionless, the blood still pooling from their respective bullet wounds. Starling lay motionless, his life, regrettably, had long since left.

Underneath the room, Tommy's body lay flat on the mats, his insides lying beside him.

The building was a chapel of death.

Lucas, leaning against the long counter decorated with the odd speck of blood, made his way to the back door of the shop. He fell into it, pushing it open and disregarding the alarm it set off. It was immediately drowned out by the sirens now racing up the high street.

Alone in the dark alley, the fresh rain fell over him as he shuffled further into the darkness and disappeared into an adjoining walkway.

The tactical team cut through the shutter in mere minutes, the red hot blade slicing through with minimum fuss. The rest of the team stood in covered positions, assault rifles at the ready and their bodies covered in kevlar. Sergeant Marshall gave directive hand gestures, ensuring his men were ready to breach the building.

Bailey and an army of officers stood further back, watching through the thunderous downpour behind the cover of their cars.

Nobody had attempted to infiltrate the Drayton building and everyone was prepared for an onslaught of gunfire.

There was none.

With the shutter removed, the first officer approached the glass door, immediately reporting the motionless bodies lying in a room almost entirely carpeted with blood.

They smashed through the large glass pane of a door and stepped in, sweeping the corners of the room and ready to unload a round of ammunition in a heartbeat.

The directive was to take Lucas Cole alive. Curtis too.

However there would be no second chances should they show aggression.

Marshall emerged into the room, directing a few of his men to the staircases on opposite sides, his men stepping through the puddles of blood and tactically entering their respective stairwells.

Marshall radioed out they needed paramedics and that one of the men was in uniform.

Bailey raced to the door as soon as it came through.

He stepped into the mess, his mouth ajar at the destruction and death decorating the room. He could see into the skull of one of the men, his body slumped forward behind him although he was sure he never felt a thing.

Then he saw him.

He looked away in anguish, not wanting to believe it was true.

His radio screamed for a paramedic, that there was a man alive upstairs bleeding profusely from a pelvic wound. The medical team raced through, ignoring the corpses on the ground floor and rushed upstairs to try and save the only survivor.

Another radio transmission came in, a report that a man of colossal stature had been killed downstairs. His entrails hanging from a sliced stomach. The entire police force, even those dealing with the gathering crowd in the freezing rain waited with bated breath.

They confirmed it wasn't Lucas. It was Tommy Drayton.

Bailey still couldn't bring himself to look, the guilt that not listening to the young man had led to this moment. What he was doing here, he would never know. Maybe he was trying to prove to Bailey that he was right all along. That going straight for the Draytons would bring everything to an end.

Bailey reached into his coat pocket, pulling out the police badge that Starling had furiously slapped into his chest a few nights ago. He turned and looked down at his corpse, a pale blood soaked hand covering the hole in his throat, trying to stop his life from escaping.

He shook his head as he squatted beside him, tucking the police badge into his pocket and letting him be carried out with some dignity.

Careful footsteps echoed down the stairs and Marshall emerged from the doorway, approaching Bailey with a look of defeat.

"No sign of Cole."

Bailey wasn't surprised, radioing to any available officers to search the surrounding area. More footsteps beat the wooden steps, as the two medics, with the help of a man in a bulletproof vest, carried a stretcher down. Adorning it, with a large bandage wrapped around his groin and a blood pack being held by another gun toting officer, was Curtis Drayton. His face was pale, lined with the streaks of tears.

The man looked pathetic, his eyes begging for mercy as the powerful Bailey approached the stretcher.

'Curtis Drayton. You are under arrest for the rape and murder of Helen Cole and the murder of Officer Oliver Starling.'

More pathetic tears fell from the man's once vicious eyes.

'Do I really need to say the rest to you?'

Bailey nodded to the paramedics, indicating for them to take him to the hospital. He wanted a few of his officers to tail them, knowing that Drayton was a priority that they needed to keep safe.

They carried him out, one of the most dangerous gang lords the city had ever known was now under arrest. He watched as they loaded him into the back of the ambulance, almost smiling at the man's tears.

He then pulled a small chair from the corner, not knowing that Starling had sat in it earlier that day, and sat down. He cast a careful eye over Starling's motionless body, wanting to sit with him until they could carry him out of the building like the hero he should be treated as.

He would still find Lucas.

But as far as Bailey could see, this whole war of vengeance was over.

Fletcher pulled up further down the high street, seeing the gathering crowds ahead and beyond that, blue lights sparkling in the night sky like a firework show. He clambered out, the rain smothering him within seconds as he slowly began to ease through the crowd of people. A sea of local residents and street urchins, hands in the air with mobile phones aimed at the commotion ahead of them.

He knew that if Bailey spotted him, he was confirming his suspicions. But as he squeezed past a few excitable teenagers, he didn't care. Lucas was either in custody or dead.

And he had to know.

As he got near to the front of the cordon line, he saw Officer Patriski, his first night of duty since he'd been attacked earlier in the week by the very man he was there to see. He approached the young officer, his handsome looks attracting the attention of a pretty, blonde woman huddled under an umbrella.

His radio cackled with Bailey's voice.

"Lucas Cole is not on the premises. I want all available units sweeping the vicinity and I want Brixton Station shut down."

Fletcher turned and rushed back through the crowd, ignoring the moans and insults as he pushed his way through.

After barging through a jungle of rain-soaked shoulders, he jumped back into his car. With swift ease, he skidded out of a three point turn and sped away from the crime scene.

The rain splashed against Lucas's face, washing away some of the blood clinging to it like sadistic war paint. His nose was cracked, his eye swollen and blood gently dripped from both.

His ribs shook loosely with each laboured step, his stab wound leaving a trail of blood from the metal gate on the wet concrete like a trail of breadcrumbs. He couldn't even remember how he'd got there, half recalling a discussion with a taxi driver.

He couldn't remember hobbling onto the next street down, the wailing sirens behind him surrounding the betting shop where he'd completed his vengeance. A cab stopped almost immediately, a helpful middle-aged driver with a beer belly and a thick, east London accent helping him into the back.

As he fell onto the seat, the driver wrapped his own coat around him, trying to help this man who had been savagely attacked. Once behind the wheel, he informed Lucas he was going to take him to the nearest hospital.

That was when he spoke, demanding the man take him to a specific location. The cabbie refused, but when Lucas lazily dropped a thick roll of fifty pound notes through the plastic partition, the man obliged.

Who was he to deny a man his final wish?

The journey cost Lucas over five thousand pounds, but he didn't even register it as an expense.

He took a few more steps, the well-maintained grass lawns empty of people and shrouded in darkness.

A white pavilion loomed to the right, pelted with rain drops but Lucas could barely see in front of him.

He shuffled another step.

He saw Alex smiling at him from across the dinner table after a cheeky comment to Dianne, who in turn lashed out with a playful slap.

Another step through the rain.

Helen waving goodbye to him from the train platform, the last time he'd seen her when she wasn't covered in blood.

He continued forward.

His mind began to flash, the various members of the Drayton family screaming in pain or begging for mercy. The blood, the pain and the death of the last few weeks laid out in a highlight reel of memories.

The next step was a struggle. His bloody soaked body shaking on legs close to giving up.

Life was leaving him more quickly now.

He took one more step.

It was Helen.

Not a memory.

But actually Helen.

He stepped into her arms, feeling the warmth she emitted as she embraced him. Her hand ran up his back, stroking his hair as she gently rocked with him. He couldn't feel the rain anymore, the drops falling next to him and casting his surroundings in wetness.

He felt dry.

The King Charles II statue watched them once again, the return of a love that had christened this spot all those years ago.

The pain in his side had subsided, his fingers clutching to the back of her dress, his head buried in her shoulder. He couldn't feel the broken ribs freely dancing in his chest, or the violent gash courtesy of Curtis Drayton's knife.

He clung to his wife.

The heartbreak subsided, the empty void of losing her vanishing in mere moments.

She held him tightly.

He brought his head up, his face a few inches away from hers. She gazed at him with deep blue eyes.

His face no longer wore the scars of battle, his handsome smile returned in all its glory. She ran her fingers across the side of his face and pulled him in.

They kissed, the rain falling around them.

He kissed her as hard as he could; he'd returned to his one true love and he would never lose her again.

He pressed a hand to her stomach, free of a stab wound and housing the child he couldn't wait to meet.

They let go of each other and he reached into his pocket, pulling the wedding ring he'd protected with such ferocity. She splayed her delicate fingers and he slid it on, returning the symbol of their love to its rightful place.

They turned together, clasping hands, as they walked on their own dry path through the downpour.

Together.

Fletcher locked his car and ran to the wet, rusted gate to Soho Square shaking violently in the wind. Despite his age, he managed to navigate it easier than before, dropping down within the grounds and jogging gently into the darkness. He remembered the pathway, the well-trimmed grass shimmering wetly in the light of the moon.

He spotted the pavilion, a white block in the distance.

He jogged further, the rain slamming against him until he neared the statue of King Charles II taking centre stage in the popular square.

As he arrived, he took one glance and then looked away with heartbreak.

His eyes began to water.

He slowly turned around and began to cry at what he saw.

Slumped against the base of the statue, soaked in blood, was the body of Lucas Cole. His broken face was soaked in bloody rainwater, which dripped into the puddle that had formed by his side.

He was not moving.

In his lifeless hand resting on his leg, was a modest gold ring that had once belonged to Helen.

Fletcher stood for a whole minute, his eyes locked on the body of a man who'd given everything for the woman he'd loved.

He wiped his eyes and exhaled a deep breath.

"Take care of him, Helen."

He hoped his words would find them somehow, carried on the whistling wind shooting through the park.

Fletcher took another look at the motionless body of Lucas Cole and nodded a silent goodbye.

The rain continued to fall on London.

AN EXTRACT FROM 'LIFE ON THE BEAT: MEMOIRS OF A THIRTY YEAR POLICE OFFICER.' BY PAUL FLETCHER.

This is the final entry to this memoir that relates to the Cole case. If that disappoints you, then I apologise profusely. If it was the reason you bought this book, then hopefully you got your money's worth. But I don't want to type more than I have to out of respect for what happened and to the people who suffered.

When they swept Lucas's house after Dianne had notified the police, a note was found that Lucas had written. I feel it is a fitting tribute to the man that I print it here:

To whoever finds this note,

I, Lucas Cole, am writing this as my final will and testament. I know what I have done will never be forgiven and I seek no forgiveness. I don't expect the world to understand my actions nor do I expect it to turn the other cheek and forget them either.

I know I will not be coming back. This journey will end and I will never return. I once told a policeman, Officer Fletcher was his name, that sometimes bad people need to see what bad truly is. I saw him at Helen's funeral and listened to his pathetic plea that I leave it to the police. I am glad that I have not seen him since due to their inability to bring the Draytons to the same level of justice that I have.

That is why my journey must continue and why I know I will never return from it.

So with that ahead of me, I wish to leave a few things to those who deserve them.

To my sister-in-law Kelly, I leave you this house. Helen was happy here and a number of those memories were with you. She loved you so much, as did I. You always made me feel welcome, like part of the family and I will always be truly grateful for that.

This home housed my family. I feel it is only right that you should have the keys. The jewellery box is on the bedside table.

Our savings, which Kelly will have access to, are to be given to Dianne Thornley. I know it will never bring Alex back, nor will it make right what has happened. An apology would seem pointless as how can I ask for forgiveness for depriving you of him? I loved your husband, he was the closest thing I ever had to a brother. Please accept the savings, if not for you but for your child. I never thought things would spiral this far out of control and if you hate me until your last day on this planet I will forgive you for it.

My apologies I leave to Graham and Patricia. I loved your daughter more than this world could ever imagine. She saved me from a world that I couldn't bear, pulling me out from the shadows and letting me live.

I promised her, and you both, on our wedding day that I would protect her and I failed. She is gone and I can only say I am sorry for not being the husband I should have been.

I know you will not condone what I have done. Nor will you want to see me again. But I truly am sorry.

And finally, to my darling wife, Helen. I leave you my love. You looked through the darkness of this world and saw a light in me that no one else ever tried to. You reached out and brought me to you and I have loved you for every minute of every day since we met. I know you would hate what I am doing in your name, but I am truly lost without you.

This is the 'me' that I am without you.

I miss you more than words will ever tell.

I leave you my love and I will be with you again one day.
I love you.
Lucas.

I will never condone the barbaric slaughter of the Draytons, but when I read that, I realised that it wasn't out of violent urges or a psychopathic rage that Lucas was retaliating.

It was simply out of grief.

Out of losing the love he relied upon.

It made me realise that there are things in this world worth fighting for, even when you are down to your final minutes. If you can find those things, hold them dear, for your life will forever be richer.

I stopped volunteering with the Metropolitan Police shortly after Lucas's death, Sergeant Robert Bailey dropping the investigation against me. We amicably shook hands and he wished me a wonderful retirement.

So far, it has been.

In the years since, I have reconnected with my daughters. Baby steps, but this past Christmas I was invited to dinner with them for the first time. I got to watch my granddaughter open the presents I bought for her and hold my new grandson while he slept.

These are moments that I would fight for.

That I would die for.

Last I heard, Dianne had given birth to a beautiful baby daughter who she named Alexandra Helen Thornley. A fitting tribute and I believe she is rapidly approaching her third birthday.

This will be the last mention of the name in this book.

Curtis Drayton.

I kept in touch with McCarthy but that has dropped off over the last year or so. The last update I had was that the man had been assaulted and beaten a number of times whilst in prison, one attack leaving him in a critical condition nursing stab wounds.

I don't condone violence. If anything, this whole experience taught us that it only begets more violence.

At the same time, it doesn't mean I need to feel pity for the man, *who I believe requested solitary confinement as he lives out his triple life sentence trapped in a prison of fear.*

Sometimes the mighty really do fall.

As this chapter draws to a close, I feel it only fitting that I write a small goodbye to Lucas and Helen. The violent nature of humanity has ensured it is a poorer place without the two of them. I can only hope that they have found each other again in whatever waits for us on the other side.

Until then, I will do my utmost to live my life and hold onto the things I hold dear.

Just like Lucas did. I will try to be like him.

A good man.

GET EXCLUSIVE ROBERT ENRIGHT MATERIAL

Hey there,

I really hope you enjoyed the book and hopefully, you will want to continue following Sam Pope's war on crime. If so, then why not sign up to my reader group? I send out regular updates, polls and special offers as well as some cool free stuff. Sound good?

Well, if you do sign up to the reader group I'll send you FREE copies of THE RIGHT REASON and RAINFALL, two thrilling Sam Pope prequel novellas. (RRP: 1.99)

You can get your FREE books by signing up at www.robertenright.co.uk

SAM POPE NOVELS

For more information about the Sam Pope series, please visit:

www.robertenright.co.uk

ABOUT THE AUTHOR

Robert lives in Buckinghamshire with his family, writing books and dreaming of getting a dog.

For more information:
www.robertenright.co.uk
robert@robertenright.co.uk

You can also connect with Robert on Social Media:

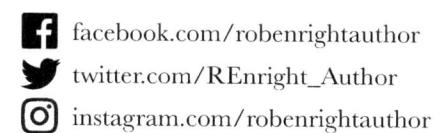

facebook.com/robenrightauthor
twitter.com/REnright_Author
instagram.com/robenrightauthor

COPYRIGHT © ROBERT ENRIGHT, 2018

All rights reserved. No part of this publication may be reproduced, stored in a retrieval system, or transmitted in any form or by any means, electronic, photocopying, mechanical, recording, or otherwise, without the prior permission of the copyright owner.

All characters in this book are fictitious and any resemblance to actual persons living or dead is purely coincidental.

Cover by The Cover Collection

Edited by Emma Mitchell

- *Previously published by Britain's Next Best Seller*

Printed in Great Britain
by Amazon

78957987R00277